PRAISE FOR SPINNER
BOOK 1 OF THE HEALER CHRONICLES

"Bowler…depicts his special needs kids not as victims, but as real heroes. Will both warm the heart and chill the spine."

— Kirkus Reviews

"Spinner incorporates elements of horror into a young adult read that is riveting and centered upon powerful protagonists that are well-drawn. The 'added value' in this story…lies in its…scenes that take the trappings of teen horror and turn them into something much more developed. Young adult to adult readers will find Spinner compelling and vivid."

—Midwest Book Review

"Bowler has created a tangible cast of characters who nearly leap off the page as they come to life in this highly suspenseful book…which is sure to keep readers enthralled clear through to its finale."

—Literary Classics

"Bowler offers some astute observations about teen life - capturing the doubt and insecurity of adolescence - and addresses important themes for maturing young adults, channeled through realistic character dynamics and camaraderie."

—Red City Review

"The book is littered with those A-ha moments that will arouse powerful emotions in readers. I loved Bowler's remarkable cast of characters, solid, convincing, and compelling enough to attract the sympathy of readers. I loved the humor. I loved the colorful and vivid descriptions that make readers feel like they were part of the intense drama, and I love the breathtaking action, the frenzy, and the race against time."

—Romuald Dzemo on Amazon

"Spinner is a paranormal story told from a special ed kid's perspective, which does make it somewhat unique. I live the SpEd mom life, and I love seeing disabled children portrayed as heroes rather than useless. I also work in adoption and enjoyed seeing that play a part in the story, as well."

—Ebienic on Amazon

"It's a story Stephen King would rightly be proud of."

— Lynne on Amazon

"OMG! It's Horror, Paranormal, Urban Fiction…and Scary Great! And I couldn't wait to finish this book… This is the first teen book I've chosen for a personal favorite! If you're willing to admit you read books for teens, then go for this one… Better yet, get it for a teen you know who loves horror at its finest, and a paranormal skill that I guarantee you will have never seen or read anywhere else."

—Glenda on Amazon

"There is danger, adventure and evil… real evil. The characters are fantastic, and the relationships intense. I couldn't put this book down."

— Author S.L. Dearing

THE HEALER CHRONICLES 2
SHIFTER

MICHAEL J. BOWLER

Shifter

PROLOGUE

AGE 12

H E HELD DEATH IN HIS hand. It was a small death, but it should work. They didn't know he had it. They didn't know the scope of his power. They kept his enclosure sealed so nothing could enter or leave, but that was because they worried about his voice getting out. They never thought about death getting in.

It had.

Now he just had to wait for Teacher.

AGE 7

His name was Andy. He knew that much, but he still didn't know any of *their* names, even after all the time he'd been there. They came and went. Some just stood and observed him. They took notes on clipboards and stared at him like he was an animal in a zoo. He'd learned about zoos from the books Teacher had given him.

Teacher had shorter hair than his and he always wondered how it got like that. It was a different color too. Brown. His own was dirty white. Teacher had brown eyes. Andy's were blue, and his hair trailed past his shoulders. It always got longer, not shorter. Since he hated Teacher, he didn't bother asking about the difference in their hair.

Teacher taught him words and gave him books with pictures. That's how he knew what a zoo looked like. Other books were all words. One was called a Dictionary. Many of the words were covered in black. Those were the ones he most wanted to learn, but he couldn't figure out how to see under the black.

Uncle taught him lessons in his dreams, though Andy didn't know whether Uncle existed or was just a figment of his imagination. Uncle had long gray hair, and his skin looked like wrinkled clothes. He said he was very old, but Andy had no concept of old. He knew what "age" meant, even though he didn't know his own. Teacher never told him.

Since Andy had no friends, he sometimes thought Uncle might be someone his lonely mind had conjured. Teacher taught him that there was no such thing as friendship or love. Andy wasn't so sure. Uncle made him believe Teacher was lying.

Then there was Doctor.

Doctor hurt him.

He despised Doctor.

Those were the only people he ever talked to.

AGE 12

He kept his fist closed. He felt Death wriggling against his skin and sensed it didn't have much time left. How did he know that? He wasn't sure. He just knew. He also knew Teacher would arrive in time. They tried to confuse him by not letting him see or hear anything except what they wanted him to know. He had been taught the concept of time but did not know how it worked. He'd seen Teacher wearing something around one wrist that indicated the time, but Teacher never explained the device.

It didn't matter. Andy sensed time anyway and always knew when Teacher or Doctor would come for him.

As though his thoughts were answered, the door to the chamber surrounding his glass cage opened and Teacher stepped inside.

AGE 7

He'd tried breaking the clear walls of his cage many times. Teacher always laughed and said the glass was bulletproof. Andy didn't know what that meant, but he did know hitting the walls with the furniture they'd given him didn't work. At first, the walls weren't soundproof because they didn't know what he could do. He didn't either, not until he'd begun talking more. He'd only known a few words when he arrived there, like "mama" and "dada," but Teacher insisted those words were no longer of value. Teacher taught him many words and phrases, and he learned rapidly.

Teacher said, "You have a quick mind," which sounded like it was a good thing, though Teacher never said so.

He knew the word "people" because Teacher said that's what they were called. "Human" was another word for people. He'd only ever talked with Teacher until Doctor came for him that first time. He didn't know how old he was then, but he knew how to say many things, and his white hair was longer than Doctor's short black hair.

Andy was taken to a place called "Lab." He saw many things he didn't recognize. Doctor only told him that the "equipment" was for tests, to learn what he could do.

"What do you think I can do?" Andy asked, for he honestly didn't know.

Doctor studied him a long moment, as though wondering if he was hiding something. "Your birth has been anticipated for millennia, Andy, but your power has still not materialized. We hope to speed up its arrival."

Andy was confused. He didn't know the word "millennia," but he did know what "power" meant. "What power?"

"That's what we need to discover. You're the key. Only through you can our plan come to fruition."

Andy knew about the "plan" from Teacher, though Teacher had never actually explained what it meant. He only knew it had something to do with destroying humans. Or was it humans destroying themselves? Teacher was always unclear on that point and refused to answer when Andy asked follow-up questions.

Doctor strapped him to a table so he couldn't move and then put little sticky pads on his head and his body. He wasn't even allowed to wear his clothes. He felt strange that first time, lying on that table with no clothes on, but, since his room was surrounded by glass and they watched him change his clothes all the time, he supposed it didn't matter much.

The equipment lit up and made sounds, and then terrible pain shot through Andy's body. His skin felt like his tongue had that time he'd tried gulping hot cocoa. He screamed again and again, begging Doctor to stop.

Doctor ignored him.

Andy had never experienced such agony. He wanted to tear off his skin it was so bad. He pleaded with Doctor to turn off the hurt as his body twisted and writhed against the restraints.

"Heal yourself, Andy!" That was all Doctor said.

Teacher stood nearby watching. Teacher kept coughing but tried hard not to. Andy had never been sick, but he understood what it meant. There was something inside of Teacher, a germ making Teacher's body weak, making Teacher cough. Even though Andy understood what "heal" meant, he didn't know how to heal his suffering or that of other people.

Finally, the agony became almost unbearable. Andy didn't know why he did this, but he looked at Teacher and muttered something.

Teacher stopped coughing and stared at him with wide eyes.

Andy began coughing. He glared at Doctor and spoke again.

Doctor coughed. And coughed. And coughed. Doctor staggered back, doubled over with fits of coughing.

The pain stopped when Doctor's hand left the equipment.

That's when they soundproofed his room. That's when they knew his voice was dangerous. And that's when he began to understand the power he wielded.

AGE 12

Teacher entered through the black door. Andy didn't know what else was on the other side of that door except Lab. He didn't feel the pain anymore when they hurt him, though he didn't tell this to Doctor or Teacher. He wanted them to think they controlled him, so he always acted like he was in agony, but he'd long ago trained his mind to ignore the hurt Doctor inflicted on him. Now they put the mask on him every time he was taken to Lab. The mask blocked his voice. It was removed once he was strapped down to the table.

In the Lab, Doctor and Teacher covered their ears with objects he didn't recognize. Then Doctor brought in the clipboard people and tried to force him into shifting germs from a sick person into someone who was well. He always refused to cooperate. Doctor used the machines to send pain throughout his body when he'd remain silent, and Andy cried tears that looked real. In his mind he sought ways to use his voice against Doctor or Teacher, but that opportunity hadn't yet arisen.

Until now.

Teacher stopped outside the glass wall. Andy stood beside his bed, fist clenched. Teacher reached out to flip a switch on the wall beside his glass cage. Now they could talk to each other.

"Hello, Andy. How are you today?"

Andy didn't answer. Every day was the same, and Teacher already knew the answer. He asked the question Uncle had suggested.

"What is the opposite of hate?"

Teacher looked surprised. "There is no opposite of hate. I taught you that."

"Everything has an opposite," Andy said. "You taught me that too."

Teacher shifted in place. Andy knew Teacher didn't like being challenged. "I taught you that *most* things have opposites. There is no opposite of hate."

"Then what is love?"

Teacher flinched and Andy forced himself not to smile.

"I thought I made it clear that love doesn't exist."

Andy had no intention of telling Teacher about Uncle and the dreams, so he just shrugged.

Teacher frowned. "Is this about the puppies again?"

Andy flinched this time. He'd tried to block out the puppies, but they still haunted his dreams.

"Did I love those puppies?" he asked, forcing himself to stay focused. The skittering movements within his fist lessened.

Teacher stared at him, as though wondering what he was doing. "No. You hated those puppies. Don't you remember?"

AGE 5

He was very small when Teacher put the first puppy into his cage. Andy had never seen anything like it. Teacher told him it was called "Puppy" and that it was an animal, which made it different from people. Andy tried to talk to Puppy. The animal just made little sounds and didn't answer back. Puppy rubbed up against him, licked his face and hands, and always wanted to lie next to him when he slept. Andy vaguely recalled feeling a similar tug in his heart before he'd come to this place, but his experience with Puppy was altogether different from that.

The animal had soft fur that Andy loved to stroke, and its eyes were big, and it had a tail that moved all the time and it made Andy feel… special. He only had vague memories of two people before coming here, but not many of the feelings associated with those people. Teacher and Doctor had never held him close the way he held Puppy, even when he was lonely and crying from despair.

Andy felt his heart beat with excitement and a sensation he couldn't describe. He only knew that Puppy made him feel…good. Every night he snuggled with Puppy in his bed. He felt safe. Each time, Puppy cuddled against him and seemed happy to be with him, Andy understood "love." He felt the reality of it.

Teacher kept saying there was only hate. Even when Andy tried to explain how Puppy made him feel, Teacher said those feelings weren't real. They were a false belief that made people weak, and he must not become weak.

Over time, Andy couldn't even fall asleep without Puppy beside him, and that was when Teacher did the unthinkable. One day when Andy was playing with Puppy—throwing a ball that Puppy retrieved and brought back to him—Teacher appeared outside his cage holding an object he didn't recognize.

"Hello, Andy."

Andy stopped throwing the ball. "Hello, Teacher. You're early for my lessons."

Teacher looked surprised that he was so keenly aware of time and said nothing for a long moment. Puppy danced around Andy's feet, making that happy sound it always made when playing. Puppy wanted Andy to throw the ball.

"How do you feel about Puppy?"

Andy considered a moment. "I love Puppy," he answered, knowing this wasn't the response Teacher wanted. "Puppy is my friend."

Teacher frowned. "I told you, Andy, love is a weakness. So is friendship. Both must be purged for you to be strong. You do not love Puppy. You hate Puppy."

Andy shook his head and tossed Puppy the ball. The small animal scurried after the ball as it bounced off Andy's bed and rolled under his desk. Puppy scooped the ball into its mouth and ran back, tail wagging.

Andy took the ball and gazed out at Teacher. "I do not hate Puppy. Puppy loves me."

"Put on your mask, Andy."

Andy recoiled. The mask was only used when he went to see Doctor. "Are you taking me to Doctor? It's not time for that."

Teacher looked impressed. "You seem to have gotten very good at telling time. Interesting. No, you aren't going to Doctor. I'm going to enter your cage. Put on the mask. Now."

Andy knew there would be more pain if he didn't obey, so he tossed the ball across the room and strode to his simple wooden desk. Puppy chased the ball as it bounced off one wall and rolled into his tiny bathroom. Andy picked up the dreaded mask. He hated it. It covered the lower half of his face and prevented him from talking.

More importantly, Teacher and Doctor could both send waves of agony through the mask into his head if he disobeyed or tried to speak. He knew if he didn't obey now, Teacher would fill his glass cage with something that put him to sleep. Then he'd awaken with the mask on anyway and be given a harsher punishment for his disobedience.

He slid the strap over his head and the heavy mask over his mouth. A little box called a remote dangled from a chain around Teacher's neck. Teacher pressed a button on the remote that locked the mask into place. Now Andy couldn't remove the mask no matter how hard he might try. Teacher pressed a button on the panel outside his cage and an invisible door slid open. Andy didn't move. When he used to try to escape, the mask shot terrible pain into his head and he collapsed onto the floor, writhing in agony. He'd learned that lesson well.

Teacher entered the cage and pressed a second button on the remote. The door slid shut and sealed itself.

Puppy jumped and raced around Andy's feet as Teacher stared at them with an unreadable expression.

"Step away from the desk, Andy."

Fear gripped Andy's heart. He used to feel afraid all the time. His whole body tightened, and his mind went numb. He'd adapted to the torment of the mask, so it no longer scared him. But now he sensed Teacher was going to do something new, something unknown.

He stepped back. Puppy raced around his feet.

Teacher squatted down and extended the hand that did not hold the object. "Here, puppy."

Puppy looked up at Andy a moment and, sensing that the ball wasn't going to be thrown, happily scampered to Teacher, ball in its mouth, tail wagging. Teacher's hand opened as though to take the ball. When Puppy skittered closer, Teacher grabbed it by the fur of its upper neck and pulled it in close. The ball dropped from its mouth and rolled languidly across the floor.

Andy froze, unable to speak or make a sound.

Teacher used the hand clutching the object to stroke Puppy's fur. Puppy liked being stroked. Teacher raised the object. The part in Teacher's hand was brown and looked like the leg of a tiny chair. The rest of the object was long and shiny and pointed.

"Love is your enemy, Andy. It makes you weak. There is no such thing as friendship. You do not love this puppy. You hate it. You want it dead."

Teacher plunged the object into Puppy's body. Puppy yelped. Blood splattered everywhere. Andy tried to gasp within the mask but couldn't. He rushed forward. Teacher touched the remote with one bloody finger. Pain coursed through Andy's face and head. He crumpled hard to the floor, rolling and twisting in agony.

As the burst of pain subsided, Andy watched through tear-filled eyes while Teacher stabbed at Puppy over and over again, spilling the animal's insides all over the smooth, shiny floor. Puppy had only given that one yelp and then lay still while Teacher speared it again and again. Andy understood that Puppy was dead, even though he'd never seen death before.

He sobbed.

Teacher stood and stared down at him. Andy couldn't pull his gaze from the bloody mess that had been Puppy. His friend. Something he loved that had loved him back. The smell made his stomach heave, and he felt the food he'd eaten struggling to rise up his throat. The mask kept his mouth clamped shut, so only a bitter, nasty taste reached his tongue. Puppy's dead eyes stared at him without seeing, and he sobbed all the more.

Teacher gave him a kick in the ribs. "You have cleaning supplies in your bathroom. Clean up this mess or live with the smell. Your choice."

Teacher turned and strode to the door. Andy heard it slide open and then close with a click. The mask loosened itself on his face and he absently slid it off, never removing his gaze from the dead body of his only friend.

That had been the first of many puppies. Every time was the same. He couldn't help himself. He was so lonely he always fell in love with each new puppy. And they always loved him back. They wanted him to love them. Teacher timed it differently. Sometimes Puppy was slaughtered within a few days, other times it took longer. It was always done in front of him, so he was forced to watch his friend suffer while Teacher gored the life from it. And always he was left alone to clean up the remains.

Finally, he couldn't take it anymore. He refused to play with the last puppy they gave him. He pushed it away whenever it brought him the ball. He shoved it away when it snuggled up against him. He refused to let it sleep in his bed. He yelled at it. He kicked out at it in anger, yet the animal still wanted to love him. It didn't give up and seemed confused by his hostility.

He woke up one day to find Teacher's knife on his desk. He'd long ago learned the name of the hated object that had murdered his friends. He stared at the brown handle and sharp blade. The puppy rubbed itself against his ankles, wanting to be his friend, wanting to be loved.

Andy knew what would happen if he gave into that love. It would be ripped from him. He'd feel that emptiness in the pit of his stomach. His heart would ache with anguish worse than anything he could imagine.

The knife beckoned.

Its blade gleamed beneath the overhead lights.

The puppy whimpered. It held the ball in its mouth. It pressed up against him, desperately seeking love, and Andy trembled with desire. His heart pounded and his breathing became ragged. He wanted to love that puppy. He *needed* to love it. Any moment now he would scoop the puppy into his arms, pull it tightly against his chest, and never let go. He'd love it and need it and then have it ripped from his heart like all the others. He'd cry for days on end and feel that empty place in his stomach, almost like he hadn't eaten for a really long time. He couldn't take that hurt again. He couldn't!

Snatching up the knife, he plunged it into the puppy over and over and over again. Blood splashed onto his hands and face. The puppy uttered a strangled yelp and went silent. Andy stabbed and stabbed and kept stabbing. He didn't even weep while doing it. He didn't feel anything. No sorrow. No emptiness. He didn't know this puppy. He'd never loved it. He'd never allowed it to love him. And now it was dead.

He looked up to find Teacher standing outside the cage. Teacher smiled.

After that, there were no more puppies. He'd learned his lesson, and passed the test.

AGE 12

"Yes, I learned the lesson of the puppies," Andy said evenly, fighting to mask his intense hatred of Teacher. "That doesn't mean love isn't real."

Teacher looked angry and confused. "It isn't."

The movements within Andy's fist ebbed.

"What about right and wrong? You taught me that those words have no meaning."

Teacher glowered even more. "They don't. Why are you questioning me?"

Because Uncle told me to, Andy thought, *in my dreams.*

"Repeat the lessons I have taught you," Teacher commanded.

Andy knew them all by heart. How could he not since he'd heard them for as long as he could remember?

"There is no right or wrong. There is only me and what I want. The only exception is if what I want goes against the Kalandrians. The Kalandrians are more important than me. The Kalandrians will fulfill the Plan and I am the key to that Plan. I must never use my voice against any Kalandrian. There is no such thing as love or friendship. Loyalty is a myth except loyalty to the Kalandrians. Humans are self-centered. Goodness is a weakness. Death is to be cherished. Darkness is stronger than light."

Teacher's face revealed pleasure at his recitation.

"Did I do good, Teacher?"

"Yes, Andy, you did good."

Andy hesitated and pretended to think deeply while the skittering in his fist grew weaker.

"Teacher, I have a question."

"Do not try to use your voice on me. You know the punishment."

Andy offered what he thought was an innocent smile. "This is a real question."

"Ask it."

Andy stepped closer to the glass wall. He knew the clipboard people were watching him through cameras positioned outside his cage, but he also knew just where to stand so those people couldn't see his every movement.

"You taught me that there is no right or wrong, correct?"

"Correct."

"You also taught me that killing is necessary."

"Correct. That was partially the lesson of the puppies. They had to be killed because they made you weak."

Andy tilted his head to regard Teacher. "If killing is necessary to keep me strong, then killing must be right."

Teacher looked surprised but maintained a calm demeanor. "There is no right or wrong."

"If killing someone helps me, it's the right thing to do, correct?"

The movements within his fist ceased.

Teacher looked annoyed. "What is your point, Andy?"

Andy smiled again.

Teacher finally noticed the closed fist. "Why is your hand closed? Open your fist at once!"

Andy's smile grew wider. "Killing *is* necessary, Teacher. I have thought of nothing else since the lesson of the puppies."

Teacher's face darkened with fear. "What are you talking about?"

Andy felt Death in his hand. It was a small Death, but it would do.

"Death, to me," he muttered. He felt it enter him, a kind of nothingness, almost like the moment between wakefulness and sleep when he felt himself slipping under and maybe never waking up. Death would take him into permanent darkness if he didn't shift it now.

Teacher took a fearful step back and reached for the button to sound-proof his cage.

Andy was faster. "Death, to Teacher."

He felt it leave his body like a wave of energy.

Teacher stiffened, finger inches from the "soundproof" button. Teacher's eyes bulged with stunned realization.

Andy grinned. "That's *your* lesson, Teacher." He opened his hand and revealed a dead fly on his palm. "You shouldn't have let this into my cage."

Teacher had left the door open longer than usual yesterday while delivering Andy's food. That's when the fly had entered.

Almost like a curtain dropping, Teacher's eyes lost their shiny life and then Teacher crumpled to the floor like a pile of old clothes.

Andy gazed at the dead fly in his hand and then at the dead Teacher outside his cage. They'd punish him for this, but they'd never know how he did it. Striding across the chamber to his tiny bathroom, he opened the toilet lid and, using his body as a shield to block out the clipboard people, dropped the fly into the water. He depressed the handle and watched his triumph whoosh out of sight to wherever this water went when it vanished down the hole.

He left the bathroom and lay down on his bed. He'd learned an important lesson today. He could shift Death. And that meant he had power they'd never even imagined. He wasn't sure he'd have another chance to employ it. The fly had been a fluke, after all. Still, if such an opportunity did arise, he'd shift Death again.

Into Doctor this time.

Andy smiled.

PRESENT DAY

CHAPTER ONE

YOU SURE SHE'S ALIVE?

ALEX AWOKE WITH A START, his body taut with fear. Sitting bolt upright in his wheelchair, he took in his surroundings at a glance, relaxing as he felt the limo bumping softly along beneath him. He observed the dirty, but peaceful face of Roy beside him, slumbering back against the soft leather of the limo's rear seat. Encircling Alex was the only family he'd ever known—one gang member, some special-ed kids, Roy's older brother, and Roy's dad.

He felt eyes boring into him and turned toward them. Andy was sitting up against the opposite seat, staring at him. Andy was Alex's mirror image, except that his hair—though an identical white blond—was much longer, trailing all the way down his back. Andy's stare held an intensity that made Alex shiver, but his face gave away nothing of his feelings.

Considering the dream Alex had just awoken from, he thought he understood why.

"You know what I just dreamed about, don't you?"

Andy's expression didn't shift, but he nodded.

Alex furrowed his brows in thought. "It was like…like I was watching a movie." He paused, shivering at the memory. "Was that all true, 'bout, you know, the puppies and stuff?"

Andy nodded again.

Alex shuddered, picturing his twin growing up in that glass room, having to suffer through daily tortures inflicted upon him by cruel, heartless adults.

"You really killed that puppy?"

Andy nodded a third time, still not displaying any emotion.

Can he feel anything, Alex wondered? After all he went through, maybe not. Andy had been truly mystified that Alex could love Roy and his other friends. What had he said about love? Oh yeah. "I never thought it was real."

And how did I dream all that, anyway?

"Our minds are, like, connected now, aren't they?" Alex asked his uncommunicative twin. "'Cause we mixed our power together?"

"I think so."

Andy's deep voice helped Alex relax a little. That silent nodding was making his skin crawl.

Do I sound like that?

As a fifteen-year-old, he probably had a somewhat deep voice, he realized, but never having heard himself on video, the flat, emotionless tone of Andy's voice gave him pause. He hesitated, recalling the scenes of Andy's life he'd somehow plucked from his brother's mind.

"Do we really have an uncle?"

Andy pushed his waterfall of white hair back over his shoulder and shrugged. "I might have made him up. I don't know." Andy met his gaze straight on, as though staring contests were a regular thing for him.

"Um," Alex began, uncertain how his brother might respond, "did you really, you know, kill that teacher guy?"

"Yes." The same flat tone, the same expressionless face.

He reminded Alex of one of those talking dummies in a horror flick he'd watched with Israel, all made of wood with creepy eyes and a straight mouth. Glancing across from him, he noted Israel's loopy expression as he snored like a pig, his head lolling on Java's solid shoulder. Bloodied and dirt-encrusted, both boys slept soundly from deep exhaustion. After all they'd gone through on his behalf, Alex understood their need for a few moments of peace.

He returned his gaze to Andy, who seemed unable to carry on a conversation except to ask and answer direct questions. Again, after the visions he'd experienced, Alex now understood that his brother might have to learn how to be around other people, especially kids his own age.

"Did it bother you to, you know, kill him?"

Andy looked a bit mystified. "Him?"

"Yeah, you know, the teacher."

"No. Teacher was cruel to me."

Alex took a moment to process that answer. Of course, it made sense for Andy to hate the man who'd tortured him his whole life.

But killing someone was wrong, wasn't it? Shouldn't we feel bad, even if we have to kill someone in self-defense?

His mouth felt dry, and he looked around for something to drink. He spotted a bunch of bottles and cans set securely on a special shelf behind Roy and eased his chair over to examine them. Mostly alcohol, but there were some water bottles, so he snagged one and twisted off the top, swigging gulp after gulp down his parched throat.

He felt eyes on him and realized Andy was staring again. He held up his near-empty bottle. "Water?"

Andy nodded, so Alex reached around behind Roy's lolling head to snag a second bottle, tossing it toward Andy. Even though the bottle was perfectly aimed for an easy catch, Andy didn't even raise his arms. The bottle struck his chest and dropped into his lap. Andy's blue eyes flashed with anger, the piercing cobalt color almost burning with fire.

"Why did you do that?" His hard tone unnerved Alex.

"You, uh, was supposed to, you know, catch it."

When Andy just stared at him with complete incomprehension, Alex tossed his own bottle into the air and caught it deftly with his right hand. Andy still didn't react, but the surge of anger in those pools of blue faded.

Alex furrowed his brow as he cradled his almost empty bottle. "Didn't no one ever teach you to play catch?"

Andy shook his head, his long blond hair swaying back and forth like dangling vines.

Alex began to understand that Andy hadn't experienced even the most basic childhood experiences.

And I thought I had it bad!

He offered a smile. "It's okay, bro. We's together now, so I'll help you learn all the stuff you missed. Long as it don't got much reading or math in it." He chuckled, but Andy's impassive expression told him that, once again, his brother didn't get the joke.

Well, Alex thought, *we have the rest of our lives to figure each other out. Long as we can stay free.*

He frowned at the last thought as he observed Andy twisting the cap off his bottle and swigging almost the entire contents in a loud, single gulp.

"Did you ever, you know, do the death thing to the doctor too?"

Andy shook his head again. "The others were careful after Teacher, and I never got another chance. I did get another teacher, though."

Alex leaned forward in his chair to listen with keen interest because an unsettling feeling had just come over him. "What did that one look like?"

"You have already seen Teacher. At the place where we saved Roy. Long yellow hair and a different shaped body from mine or yours."

Alex froze, his breathing on hold.

Ms. G!

"I know it looked like Teacher was dead, but that wasn't true," Andy went on conversationally, oblivious to the fear Alex felt squeezing his heart like a clenched fist, "I don't think this one can be killed like the other one. That's what Doctor told me, anyway."

Alex sat back in his chair, weak with renewed despair. He'd seen her shot when she tried to run away. He'd seen her fall. He'd thought his greatest enemy was finally gone.

"You sure she's alive?"

"She?" Andy tilted his head in confusion. "I don't know that word. If you mean Teacher, then yes, I'm sure."

Tight with renewed fear, Alex glanced at the others slumbering peacefully around him.

It wasn't over, after all.

CHAPTER TWO

THAT DEPENDS ON MR. SHAW

A S THEY EXITED THE FREEWAY onto Hawthorne Boulevard, Allison lounged in the back seat of the pickup truck, yearning to be home after her horrific abduction. The man hadn't hurt her, but he had threatened her life if she tried to escape. She'd never had a knife to her throat before and shuddered at the memory.

She'd fallen asleep almost the moment they'd left that old burned-out church where she'd been held prisoner. According to her dad, she'd been kidnapped to prevent him from interfering in the man's plans. But her dad had interfered anyway and helped Alex and his friends defeat…what, demons? That's what the priest told her when they were leaving, but she hadn't seen any of it for herself.

After Alex and the others drove off with Martin, her dad's friend and bodyguard, the priest—named Father Pat—and Allison's dad had collected a bunch of guns that had been left lying in the dirt and ashes. They wrapped them in a big cloth bag and stashed them in the back seat of the black F-250, where they now lay beneath her feet as the big but comfortable truck bounced along the heavily trafficked street.

Allison had tried not to look at the dead bodies, especially the kids her age, but it was hard. She hadn't known any of them, but she knew they were Alex's friends, and she felt sad for him. Only a few days earlier, she'd been near death herself from leukemia. Thanks to Alex, she was completely cured. Instinctively, she rubbed a hand over her smooth, bald head. The chemo had stolen her beautiful brown hair, but now that she was healed, it would grow back.

The man had kidnapped her because of Alex. Her dad explained that much. They'd been hoping to kidnap Alex too, but somehow Alex's friends had stopped them. Her dad explained some of it once they'd all gotten into the truck and left that place behind, and that's when Father Pat—a handsome, middle-aged man with wavy black hair and an inviting face—had told her about the demon-things, and about Alex having been written about thousands of years ago by people of various cultures around the world. She could tell her dad wasn't convinced about that part, but Father Pat said he had evidence to back up his claim. Allison was a "show me" kind of person, but she knew quite well about Alex's healing abilities, so maybe the rest was true too.

Her dad *had* seen demon-like things possessing Alex and assured her that they were very real, so she knew his professed skepticism was only skin deep. Father Pat explained how the government also wanted Alex and his twin brother, but he didn't know what for.

Allison couldn't begin to express her gratitude to Alex for giving her a second chance at life, and her dad felt the same way. He swore to her and Father Pat that no one would ever hurt Alex again.

And Russell Shaw always kept his word.

For the moment, though, he stared calmly out the side window as though what he'd seen the previous night was just another day at the office.

Father Pat attempted conversation with him about the bodies they'd left behind in their haste to vacate the scene, but he'd gotten no response thus far.

Shaw didn't even glance over at the priest, but after a long pause he said, "As I explained before we left, Padre, we had mere minutes to take what we could before one or both of those groups showed up to erase all trace of what had happened. It would not have been prudent to engage with either."

"But we should have taken those poor children with us, to return them to their families," Father Pat insisted once again, recalling for Allison the bloody images of two dead teens, a boy and a girl.

Shaw glanced back at Allison before responding. "And how would you explain to their parents how they died or how you happened to find the bodies?"

Father Pat grudgingly admitted he had no answer to either question. "But it just seems so wrong."

Her dad explained once again to the stubborn priest that all evidence of what had happened in that abandoned, burned-out hulk of a church had already been eradicated by whichever side arrived on the scene first, and that meant the parents of those teens would never know what had become of their children. They would go down as "missing persons" forever.

That part had seemed wrong to Allison, who imagined the pain her dad would have suffered if he'd never found her. She watched him raise one well-manicured hand to his ear, cell phone held securely within long, slender fingers.

"Checking in, Martin. Any sign of pursuit?"

She heard the muffled response. "Negative. We're about to enter the safe house. I'll get everyone settled in and secure the place."

"Roger that." Her dad ended the call with one finger and returned the phone to his front jacket pocket.

Father Pat, behind the wheel and keeping his eyes on the congested road ahead, asked, "What do you expect to happen next?"

Her dad turned from the window. He wore a weary expression, as though he bore a great yoke on his shoulders, looking much older than his fifty years. The lines on his face had deepened, the gray of his hair had grown more pronounced, and yet the set of his thin lips and the fire in his eyes displayed fierce determination.

"All of the incriminating evidence has been removed." His voice was deep and sonorous, easy to hear above road noise made by the large tires against rough pavement. "Once the kids are tucked away safely, I will make some calls, determine which Pentagon agency sent those soldiers. As for the apparent doomsday cult you described, my guess is the Vatican archives will have something. You have any connections there, Padre?"

"The Vatican? Are you kidding?"

"I never kid. My company installed their computerized archives and security system. You're more an expert on this Healer business than I am, so I'll get you access, and you do the research. Sound acceptable?"

"Just like that? You can get me access to the Vatican archives?"

Her dad offered for him what might pass as a smirk. "Technology rules the world, Padre."

Father Pat nodded. "Okay. Let me know who to contact, and I'm on it."

"No one will hurt that boy as long as I'm alive," Shaw went on, his voice tight as a guitar string and rock solid with conviction.

It made Allison feel good seeing him so determined to protect Alex, who was easily the most amazing boy she'd ever met. He even liked her favorite band, Hawthorne Heights. And he had miracle powers like a Marvel superhero. She smiled as she pictured his cute face with that thick, wavy blond hair almost always in front of his sparkling blue eyes.

Father Pat asked no more questions, turning onto North Prospect Ave into Palos Verdes Estates.

Allison sighed as a wave of fatigue overcame her.

Almost home.

***

The inside of what Martin called the "safe house" looked so different from the outside that Roy thought there must've been some kind of magic spell on the place. Seen from outside, it was a two-story, ramshackle building with peeling brown paint, weeds lining the chipped and broken front walkway, and shutters dangling from the upper story windows. A junker for sure, it looked almost as beat-up as that burned-out church where he'd…well, died, the night before.

Just recalling the moment he'd slipped away into darkness and then returned to find Alex's soft, milky-white face gazing down at him caused Roy to glance involuntarily at Andy, who sat at the kitchen table scarfing the scrambled eggs that Martin had cooked for them. Andy looked up at once and met Roy's gaze, holding it with those pools of deep blue that were the mirror image of Alex's. Unable to even guess what Andy might be thinking, Roy broke the intense eye contact and resumed shoveling food into his own eager mouth. He was starved!

In contrast to the way it looked outside, the inside of the house was tidy and filled with nice furniture, and the fridge and pantry were crammed with food. Martin had laughed at the reactions of the kids after they'd exited the limo inside the gigantic garage. The garage itself was bigger than any room in Roy's entire house, and well-stocked. Boxes of toilet paper, towels, canned food, bottled water. Everything was neatly piled against the clean, white walls. Whoever lived there could stay for months without needing to buy anything.

"Mr. Shaw owns all the acreage around here," Martin explained as everyone followed him along the back hallway. "He leaves the outside of the place looking like it needs a wrecking ball. That way, anyone who might spot it from the air will think it's abandoned. That's part of what makes it safe."

"What's the other part?" Roy's dad, Nathan, asked as they entered the high-ceilinged front hall, scanning it with interest. He was a middle-aged carpenter and all-around handyman, and as far as Roy was concerned, knew everything about construction.

Roy eyed Alex, who wheeled up alongside with Andy flanking him. Alex made eye contact and Roy felt more at ease, like he always did when Alex's amazing eyes met his.

Martin pulled a small remote from his pocket and pressed a button. Loud clanging and banging filled the entire house and Roy clamped both hands over his ears as huge sheets of metal slammed down over every door and window he could see.

"Oh, shit!" Izzy nearly jumped out of his skin as his gaze flew everywhere.

"That's crazy," Java muttered, and Carlos, the bald-headed, stocky gang member nodded his head in approval.

Alex pulled hands away from his ears and glanced around in awe at the sealed-up windows. Andy squirmed with discomfort as he stared fearfully at the barriers. Alex seemed to understand and nudged his twin.

"It's okay, bro. It's to protect us, not keep us locked in."

Andy studied him a long moment with squinting eyes and Roy knew something passed between them, but he couldn't tell what it was. He'd ask Alex later when he got a chance.

Jorge pulled one of the rumpled sheets of binder paper he never seemed to run out of from his pocket and held it out to Martin. On the paper was a large, red V.

"For victory."

Martin grinned and took the paper from Jorge. "You got that right, kid. Short of a missile strike, this place is pretty much invulnerable."

Izzy tossed off his loopy grin, and then his expression drooped. "You got food here? I'm hungry as hell."

Martin laughed. "Yeah. Follow me."

That was how they'd all ended up in the kitchen wolfing down the eggs, bacon, and potatoes Martin had whipped up faster than Roy would have thought possible. This guy could do everything, it seemed.

Martin was an older dude, maybe his dad's age, with short black hair and alert eyes, tall and rough, but he talked better than most of the guys Roy's dad worked with, like maybe he went to college. He had a white scar above his right eye that took away some of the brow and made him look pretty wicked, like maybe he got hit hard with a weapon that left its mark, deep and thick.

Roy felt someone staring at him and looked up, fork poised to shove a syrup-soaked pancake chunk into his mouth. It was Andy again. Alex's twin had already cleaned his plate and now stared at him from across the round kitchen table, those piercing cobalt eyes almost pinning him to the chair with their concentration. But as always with Andy, the blank facial expression gave away nothing behind the gaze.

Feeling unnerved, Roy offered a tiny smile before shoving the pancake into his mouth and glancing toward Alex, whose wheelchair rested beside him. Alex, too, was staring at him with raised eyebrows, shifting his gaze back and forth between him and Andy. Roy shrugged and Alex grinned. That perfect smile sent Roy's heartrate into overdrive, as always. But then, the splatters of dried blood in Alex's thick white hair—all that was left of their friend, Cuong—chilled him faster than a cold shower, and he lost what was left of his appetite.

Glancing around, he took in the dirt, the grime, the torn clothes, the bloodstains, the fatigue on the faces of his dad, brother, and circle of friends. They'd all gone through so much with him these past few days. He, himself, had never felt more dirty, both inside and out.

Dane, his tall, twenty-one-year-old brother whose rugged, handsome features Roy envied, was a man always itching for action, but at the moment he looked relaxed as he pushed his plate back and burped. Izzy howled with cackling laughter.

"Thanks for the chow, Martin," Dane said, winking at Roy before going on. "What happens now? How long we gotta stay here?"

Martin set down his fork. "That depends on Mr. Shaw."

"What does that mean?" Nathan studied him, and Roy wondered what his dad was thinking.

"Mr. Shaw will find out who's after you and take care of it."

"Sounds like a plan to me," Java said around a swig of orange juice, his torn sleeve showing a muscular, chocolate-colored upper arm and shoulder, both spattered with dried blood.

"Yeah," Izzy agreed. "Then we can go home."

Beneath his wavy brown hair, Dane eyed Martin with suspicion. "Just like that? Shaw'll take care of it?"

Martin nodded. "Mr. Shaw has contacts all over the world. And influence. He'll figure out what to do. In the meantime, we cool our heels here."

"Huh?" Roy had never heard that expression before.

Martin looked across the table at him and smiled. "That means we wait here until he contacts me."

Roy nodded.

Carlos shoved his empty plate away and turned to Jorge beside him. "Good stuff, eh, Quiet Man?"

He clapped Jorge on the shoulder, which Jorge—on the spectrum—normally hated, but not this time. He grinned and pointed at his own plate. He'd carved a V out of his last pancake and pushed the plate toward Carlos.

Carlos shook his head in amusement, glancing at Java on his other side. "This guy's a trip. I like him." He slid the V-shaped pancake onto his own plate and devoured it in two bites.

Jorge laughed. "This guy's a trip," he said to Roy, pointing at Carlos, who squinted at him with syrup dribbling down his chin before cracking up at Jorge's perfect imitation.

Roy was glad Carlos was fitting in so well, but right now he just wanted to clean up. "Uh, Mr. Martin?"

Martin raised his eyebrows questioningly.

"Do you maybe got any clothes we can wear and places to shower? We're all pretty nasty."

"Java smells worse than you, Roy," Izzy exclaimed, waving a hand in front of his face and grinning at Java beside him.

Java raised a meaty fist. "Keep talkin' mess, Izzy…," but he offered a tired smile all the same.

Martin grinned, looking amused by their interplay. "We have three showers and plenty of rooms so you guys can clean up and rest."

Roy sighed with relief.

****

Alex chose to share a room with Andy on the first floor because there was no elevator in the house to accommodate his wheelchair. Nathan would share a larger one upstairs with his sons, which left Izzy, Jorge, and Java in a third upstairs room that offered two sets of bunk beds.

The moment they entered their room, Andy lay down on one of the double beds without a word while Alex wheeled across the wine-colored carpet and entered the bathroom. It was large enough to accommodate his chair, but the shower was a standard variety, not the "walk-in" style he was used to. It did, fortunately, have a low barrier under the sliding door that wouldn't be hard for him to crawl over, and there was room enough for him to reach in and turn on the water before sliding out of his chair to the tiled floor.

He longed to feel that warm, soothing water washing away the blood and grime and, hopefully, some of the guilt. He felt weighted down, like someone was standing on his shoulders. Cuong was dead. Sweet, gentle Cuong. And Tami, the girl who'd ask him to homecoming, who'd been so nice to him and hoped to know him better. Both were gone and it was his fault. If he wasn't the Healer that Father Pat talked about, his friends would still be alive.

Filled with remorse, he wheeled back into the bedroom, noting wooden shutters covering the windows, a sliding door near the beds, a tall chest of drawers made of some kind of shiny, polished wood, and a little table beside each bed with a lamp on it. Andy lay in the same position, hands behind his head staring up at the ceiling as though seeing God himself.

"Uh, you wanna shower first, bro?"

There was a pause, as though Andy couldn't decide. "No."

Alex waited, but his brother said nothing more, so he wheeled to the chest of drawers and pulled them open one at a time. He found brand new underwear in different styles and sizes and chose size L boxers for himself, suspecting that the much slimmer Andy would need size M. He also pulled out a pair of black socks and plopped both into his lap. Wheeling to the closet door, he slid it aside and searched around for a light switch. Finding it on the wall above his head, he flipped it on.

The closet was huge, at least compared to any he'd ever known. Shirts and pants of every type and color hung from racks along each side and the path between was easily accessible to his chair. He glided forward atop thick, luxurious carpet, eyeing the clothing in wonder. There were more clothes in this closet than he'd ever owned in his life! Some shirts looked like they were for girls because of squiggly cuffs and collars, so he avoided those. His skinny jeans needed a good washing, and he didn't spot any pants that seemed similar, so he grabbed a pair of regular jeans from the lower rack that looked his size and then settled on a long-sleeve black pullover shirt that he had to yank down from above, causing the hanger to flip off the upper rack and land on the carpet near his wheels.

He guessed that Mr. Shaw never expected to have a handicapped kid staying at this place.

Reaching down, he snatched up the hanger and hooked it on the lower rack before wheeling himself backward into the bedroom because the closet wasn't wide enough for him to turn around. Andy lay exactly as Alex had left him, gazing at the ceiling like he was watching a movie.

"There's lots of clothes you can pick from, Andy," he offered, pointing behind him at the open closet door.

When Andy didn't even glance his way, Alex shrugged and wheeled across the carpet into the bathroom, closing the door behind him.

CHAPTER THREE

DEATH, TO ME!

ROY FELT AS THOUGH HE'D washed away death itself under the warm, soothing water, which sprayed out of a fancy-looking shower head in the most beautiful shower he'd ever stepped into. The tiles were a pattern of blue and white triangles, and cleaner than clean, like they'd never even gotten wet before. The shower fixtures were gold and gleamed so brightly he could see himself reflected back, and the glass shower door displayed a pattern of golden crowns.

The bathroom was as large as his bedroom back home and seemed to contain every kind of shampoo and deodorant imaginable. It was like shopping at the supermarket! And the towels? Softer than the velvet of his mother's favorite dress that she always wore for Christmas parties. Just picturing her in that shimmering red-and-green gown brought tears to Roy's eyes, especially after that bitch Ms. G had used his mother's image to try and trick him into ditching Alex. He didn't hate many people, but he was *so* glad Ms. G was dead.

Clean and dry, wearing fresh pants and a long-sleeve shirt he'd found in his bedroom closet, he joined his dad and Dane in the huge downstairs living room where everyone else had gathered in front of a colossal flat-screen TV that seemed to take up most of the wall to which it had been attached. His friends, all wearing fresh mismatched clothes, sat on sofas and stuffed armchairs gazing at some action movie on the screen, but most of them looked too tired to pay much attention. He suspected that they, like him, didn't feel safe in their rooms after all that had happened, so they'd gathered in the living room to keep each other company.

Only Alex and Andy were missing.

Sudden fear wrapped itself around his heart. Turning to hurry toward the back of the house where the twins would be staying, Roy almost gasped with relief as Alex rolled into the room, looking totally sick in his jeans and black pullover shirt that showed off his big arms. Andy trailed behind wearing cargo pants and a striped pullover shirt, damp blond hair dangling all the way down his back. Roy was about to say something when Andy's face twisted into one of shock. Roy spun around, but there was nothing except the television.

Andy moved catlike to the TV, eyes slits of suspicion. Roy exchanged a mystified glance with Alex, but his best friend didn't seem as surprised by his brother's behavior. Andy edged his way up to the wall and tried to see what might be behind the TV, but it was mounted so tightly there was no space available.

Izzy, who sat slumped over and watching the movie, grunted with annoyance when Andy moved in front of the screen to stare in wide-eyed wonder at the flickering images.

"Hey, man, you're blocking the screen," Izzy protested, leaning side to side to get a view of what Andy was blocking.

"'Sup, Andy?" Java said, his usually strong voice sounding thick with sleepiness. "Ain't you never seen a TV before?"

Andy turned to him. His face looked whiter than usual, and that was saying something since he looked like he hadn't seen the sun his whole life.

"How do people get inside this flat little thing?"

Java and Izzy exchanged a puzzled look, while Dane and Nathan did the same.

Alex rolled forward and stopped beside his brother.

"I can explain later, or I can tell 'em now 'bout you, Andy—about, you know, how you grew up."

"You can tell them," Andy replied, his gaze still fixated on the flickering screen.

"He grew up in, like, a glass box, or something," Alex explained to the startled group. "I saw it in a dream." He glanced at Andy, who was still mesmerized by the images on the flat screen, and then faced his gawking friends once more. "I don't know a lot yet, but they, like, tortured him and…I guess they didn't teach him much 'cept what they wanted him to know." He paused and glanced again at his astonished brother with a mix of sadness and embarrassment. "I don't think he even knows what girls are."

Everyone erupted with loud cries of incredulity.

"How the hell do he not know what girls are?" That was Java, suddenly perked up and full of energy.

"He never met any 'cept Ms. G," Alex explained, "and they never taught him about boys and girls, I don't think, because he don't even call her 'she,' just Teacher."

Izzy's mouth had dropped so low it almost dragged on the floor, and Roy couldn't help but smile despite hearing this crazy information about Andy.

Andy still gazed at them in stupefied wonder. "So, how do the people get inside here?" He pointed a long, slender finger at the screen.

"I'll tell 'im," Izzy announced, like he just got an A on a test at school.

Java stared at him with a "show me what you got" kind of look on his handsome face that displayed traces of dark hair sprouting on his upper lip.

Izzy uncurled himself from his chair and approached the expectant Andy. Roy noted Martin standing guard at the door and eyeing Izzy with amusement.

"Well, Andy, it's like this," Izzy began, pointing to the TV. "There's these cameras, see, that film people doing acting and shit, but it's all fake, especially the scary movies I like."

Andy furrowed his brows in confusion.

"Then," Izzy continued, "once everybody gets filmed, they put it out on the internet and we see it on TV."

"Internet?"

Uh oh, Roy thought as he stood twisting the snakebite piercing at the left side of his mouth, *here comes more questions.*

But Izzy didn't look fazed at all. "Yeah, man, the internet. It's got everything you want, well, 'cept real stuff cause it's only on your phone or computer."

"But what is it?"

Now Izzy looked uncertain, the confident grin fading. "Well, it's, um, you know…the internet."

Andy just stared at him a long moment before turning to Alex. "Does he always explain things this way?"

Alex giggled. "Yep."

Roy smiled, enjoying himself despite the horrors of the past few days.

"Good job, Crackhead," Java said to Izzy. "Now he understands perfect."

A cleared throat drew everyone's attention toward the door.

An amused Martin stood watching them, clearly fighting back a smile. "May I make a suggestion? Since the boy has been hidden away his whole life and knows very little, why not show him around this house and explain common objects to him. Didn't you see him in the kitchen earlier? I don't think he's ever seen a stove or refrigerator before."

Nathan added, "I agree with Martin. But try to keep what you say simple and if you don't know how to explain something, it's better not to. That work for you, Andy?"

Andy nodded.

"Dane, maybe you should go around with them, you know, to help," Nathan added.

Dane had been quiet most of the day, unusual for him. Roy had only gotten to really know his older half brother during the past week or so. He suspected Dane didn't talk much for fear of sounding dumb, because he was special ed like the rest of the boys.

"Sure, Pop," Dane agreed, giving Izzy a serious squint. "Who knows what this fool's gonna say."

Izzy offered a shrug and they set off.

Roy found teaching Andy to be fun—a good distraction from their immediate danger. What Alex and Martin said turned out to be true. Andy didn't know what anything was in a kitchen—he'd always had his food brought to him on trays and then taken away by "the clipboard people." He knew the basics of a bedroom and bathroom, but Roy was shocked to hear that he'd had no privacy in either one. All his walls were made of glass.

"I never took a shower before today without cameras watching me," Andy told them calmly, and Roy's face crumpled with sadness.

He felt greater empathy for Andy with each passing moment, and a thought hit him like a brick to the face.

Will Dad have to adopt him too?

Nathan had promised to adopt Alex after all this drama was over, but he hadn't known about Alex's twin. Would he be willing to take in both? Roy vowed to ask him first chance he got.

Fortunately, his dad gave him a clue later in the day that eased Roy's fear. Izzy started in on one of his rants about girls rejecting him all the time. Despite his lack of experience, he started giving Andy sketchy advice on how to pick up "females."

"Never tell females the truth, bro, and don't ever let 'em know how weird you are," he said in his usual mile-a-minute style. Without his meds, Izzy's ADHD was all over the map. "See, I never tell 'em I'm special ed 'cause they call me a dummy and shit like that, and then I cuss 'em out, and that don't ever end good, so never act like you don't know stuff."

"Uh, Izzy," Nathan began, and Alex looked relieved at the interruption, especially because Andy was actually listening to Izzy. "I'm planning to adopt Alex and so, I guess, that means Andy too, if he'll have me. So let me talk to him about, well, girl stuff and all that. I don't want you guys confusing him."

Izzy looked offended. "Who's confusing him?"

Java looked him in the eye. "You, fool, like always."

Izzy's thick eyebrows shot up in indignation, but then he shrugged.

After explaining almost everything in the two-story home to Andy—who absorbed the information like a sponge soaking up water—the entire group gathered back in the living room to watch more movies. Andy had stayed at Alex's side the entire day and now sat on a chair beside his brother, as though afraid his twin might disappear.

Roy found his gaze flitting to the identical boys more often than he wanted it to. Andy was every bit as beautiful as Alex, and Roy felt once again that emptiness in the pit of his stomach, that longing for all that Alex could never give him. And now he had to live with two Alex's, in a sense, and maybe even a rival for his best friend's attention.

Andy had clung so closely to his twin since they'd met at the church that Roy hadn't had any time alone with Alex. He fought down the pangs of jealousy. The brothers had only just met, he told himself, having not been together since they were babies. It was only natural they'd want to spend all their time together.

Don't be so selfish, Roy, he told himself. *Alex is your friend for life.*

How often had they proclaimed those words to each other? Too many to count.

As though reading his mind, Alex glanced over and smiled. The beauty in that smile, the love and commitment, melted Roy's fear like snow under a warm summer sun, and he sat back to enjoy another action flick.

***

It was dark and warm. Alex felt uneven ground beneath his wheels, but he couldn't get his bearings. Other than his wheels crunching against pebbled earth, he heard nothing. Where was he? He wasn't in the safe house anymore; he knew that much. The air felt stale, like it came from an air conditioning system that needed cleaning, but he didn't have the sense of being inside a house.

Where am I?

Pushing himself forward, he squinted in the blackness ahead for any signs of light, but there was none. He stopped and listened.

Footsteps!

But from what direction?

Heart hammering, he spun around in his wheelchair, searching the darkness for the approaching figure. He ceased all movement and listened, but the footsteps were gone.

What the hell?

Hands wrapped around his eyes from behind. "Guess who?"

He yelped and whirled about, backing away as the figure became visible. Where the light had come from, he didn't know, but the figure before him was one he'd never forget.

Ms. G!

She wore pants and some kind of jacket, and her long flowing hair seemed darker beneath the harsh lighting, but it was definitely her.

"You're dead!" he blurted as he wheeled back even more. "I seen you get shot."

She offered that twisted grin that made him once again think of an evil jack-o-lantern. "I'm not that easy to kill, Alex. I thought you knew that."

He recalled what Andy had said about her not being able to die. "Are you like a vampire or something?"

She tossed off that mocking laugh he hated, the one she used when she wanted him to feel stupid. "Of course not." She clucked her tongue, again making fun of him.

"What are you, then?" he persisted. "Why don't you leave me alone?"

She took a step closer.

He pushed his chair back, crashing it against a rocky wall behind him. His heart thundered with dread. He glanced around, searching for an escape route, but outside of the harsh pool of light engulfing them, he saw nothing.

"We cannot escape our destiny, Alex," she said in a smooth, silky voice, like she wanted to ask him out on a date. "Andy already belongs to me, and so will you, very soon. Together we'll fulfill the prophecy that began all those thousands of years ago. You can't stop me from finding you. Even now, in your dreams, I'm getting closer and closer."

Grinning, she lunged forward to grab him with long fingers that looked like claws.

Alex bolted upright in bed, shirt drenched in sweat, heart pounding with terror.

A dream!

That's all it was!

But it was so real...

He paused a moment to catch his breath. Looking past the night table beside his bed, he searched in the dark for Andy. The covers of his brother's bed were tossed back and twisted, as though Andy had had the same terrifying dream.

But his brother was gone.

Andy already belongs to me.

Ms. G's words came back like a slap to the face. He hadn't understood everything she'd said, but those words were crystal clear. He recalled his other dream about Andy growing up in that cage and the weird stuff they'd taught him. He hadn't understood that either, except something about a plan and that Andy had to stay loyal to them. Alex knew the word "loyal." That word defined Roy and his other friends, but what was all that about a "plan."?

He had to find Andy.

Throwing back his damp comforter, Alex slid from his bed into his wheelchair and pulled his feet up onto the footrest. His sweaty shirt clung to his torso and made him feel like blood was sticking to his skin, so he yanked it up over his head and tossed it to the floor. Rolling across the carpet, he slid open the closet door and wheeled inside. Not bothering with the light, he reached up and pulled down a long-sleeve shirt and slipped into it, not even caring about the color. Then he wheeled from the bedroom in search of his brother.

The house lay dark and quiet as he propelled himself down the side hall toward the living room. He paused to listen but heard nothing. Everyone had been so tired they knocked out early, leaving a heavy silence that unnerved Alex. He decided to try the kitchen, since Andy had seemed especially excited that he could open the fridge whenever he wanted to snag some food.

The kitchen light was on when he entered, but no one was there. Then he noticed the door to the backyard hanging open, and he pressed forward in that directions. As he neared the door, voices drifted in over the peaceful night air.

Andy and Martin.

Alex pushed through the door onto the back porch. A high metal fence circled the yard and vanished out of sight around the rest of the house. There was no wheelchair ramp, but he was used to that, so he just pushed forward to work up speed and flew off the single step onto the pavement below, his wheels breaking the silence with their impact.

"What was that?" Martin's voice asked, his voice tense.

"Alex," replied Andy with certainty.

"How do you know that?"

"Just do."

The voices came from around the side of the house. It was dark because no lights were turned on, but the night sky was littered with more stars than Alex had ever seen. He wheeled forward and rounded the corner to find Martin and Andy sitting on some chairs looking up at those stars. Martin eyed Alex, but Andy never turned his gaze away from the heavens, which looked like it had been sprinkled with flecks of gold dust. Alex understood Andy's fascination. It was an incredible sight.

"We're out in the countryside," Martin explained as Alex wheeled forward, his mouth hanging open in awe. "No city lights means you see more stars."

Alex nodded. "It's amazing."

"Yeah. I was telling Andy I got used to this kind of view in Afghanistan during my last tour of duty."

Alex must have looked as puzzled as he felt because Martin chuckled.

"I served in the military before going to work for Mr. Shaw," he explained. "Special forces."

"What's that?"

"We're more highly trained than regular troops," Martin went on, his voice not the least bit arrogant like Ms. G or other adults often sounded when Alex asked them a question. "That's one of the reasons Mr. Shaw hired me. I also have a degree in computer science and a minor in business."

Alex nodded. Degrees meant college. That meant Martin had to be smarter than him because no way could Alex ever handle college. He studied his silent brother, staring upward as though hypnotized.

"You okay, Andy?"

Without dropping his gaze in the slightest, Andy said, "You dreamed about Teacher too, didn't you?"

Alex flinched, his breath momentarily on hold. "Yeah."

Now it was Martin who looked confused. He shifted position on the chair and that's when Alex noticed the gun strapped to his belt. Martin studied them both in the dark, his face hidden in shadow. "What are you guys talking about?"

When Andy remained silent, Alex pulled his gaze from his brother's back and faced Martin. "A teacher we both had. She's part of the group that's trying to get me. She says she's gonna find me no matter where I go."

Martin's expression turned from grim to resolute. "I'll protect you." He patted the gun in its holster.

Alex eyed his brother once more. "She...she said you belong to her, Andy."

Alex thought he saw his brother recoil, but the moon wasn't completely full, so he couldn't be sure.

"I won't be in a cage ever again," Andy said quietly, his voice almost a whisper, as though talking to himself. "I told that to Teacher and I meant it."

Martin leaped to his feet, startling the boys.

Alex whirled to face him. "What?"

Martin threw a finger to his lips and reached down, pulling out the gun and pointing it over Alex's head.

Now Alex heard it. Movement. The sound of people trying hard to be quiet, but a slight crunch of gravel gave them away.

Martin waved the boys behind him and darted in front, gun aimed toward the house.

A red light rounded the corner and before Alex could even think of the red light that had killed Juan back at the church, Martin fired his weapon. One *pop*, muffled, like he had a heavy sock over the barrel. The red light spun crazily and then toppled to the grass.

Alex glanced at Andy with wide eyes. They'd been found!

After that, everything happened so fast Alex could barely process it. Another figure rounded the corner with a gun and fired. A tiny burst of light accompanied the *pop* of a gunshot, and then Martin grunted, collapsing to the lawn.

"Martin!" Andy dashed around Alex's chair and knelt by the unmoving form of their protector.

More figures rounded the corner of the house and bore down on them. Alex backed up, but suddenly Andy grasped his hand. Alex felt the rush of power surging through him—just as it had at the church when they'd brought Roy back to life—heavy floodwaters that meant their combined powers had been activated. He looked down at Andy, still kneeling beside Martin's body.

Andy whispered, "Death, to me!"

Alex stiffened, his vision growing dim, his mind filled with a gray nothingness that terrified him.

As though from miles away, he heard Andy hiss, "Death to them!"

The nothingness left him in a surging wave as Andy pointed at the men who'd attacked them. Alex looked over just in time to see three figures crumple to the grass in a heap.

What had just happened?

Andy leaped to his feet and grabbed Alex's wheelchair, pushing him away from the oncoming men with their guns, around to the front of the house toward the main door. A grunt from Andy stopped their forward momentum, and Alex spun his chair around to see his brother staggering.

"Andy!"

Andy toppled to the dead grass. Something pierced Alex's chest and he felt a sharp sting of pain, like getting a shot from the doctor. He glanced down and saw some kind of dart sticking out of him. His vision blurred. He heard running footsteps, but when he looked up, the only thing he made out was the indistinct outline of a cat sitting on the fence.

A cat?

His mind whirled, and he lost all sense of where he was and even of being in his own body. He swam through the suddenly heavy air.

Then everything went black.

CHAPTER FOUR

SOMEONE'S COMING!

ALLISON WOKE WITH A START. Had she been dreaming? She wasn't sure, but she *was* sure she'd heard her father's voice. She sat up in bed, the coverlet tumbling into her lap, and listened. Yes. It *was* her dad. His room was next to hers, but the voice was muffled enough that she couldn't make out the words.

She slipped out of bed and dropped to the plush carpet. Not bothering with a robe to cover her pajamas, she padded across her expansive bedroom to the door. Easing it open, she peered out into the dimly lit, lushly paneled hallway. None of the household staff were up. Why should they be? It was the middle of the night.

The burnished wood flooring felt cold against her bare feet as she darted to the door next to hers. It was closed, but she pressed her ear up against it and listened.

"…just you and the two men left? Did you find any blood in the house?"

Allison gasped. Blood? Somehow, she knew her dad was talking about Alex. She yanked open his door, trembling with fear.

Her dad sat on his bed, wearing his fancy brocaded silk robe and black velvet slippers with the gold crown insignia, cell phone to one ear, worry creasing his face. He looked over as she rushed inside but didn't seem surprised to see her. He held up a hand for silence and listened intently.

"All right. Get back here with the men. I'm going to contact my sources for any clues as to who took them."

He ended the call and eyed Allison with a grim expression. The worry lines around his eyes looked deeper, almost like they'd been carved with a knife, and there seemed to be even *more* gray peppering his short dark hair.

"It's Alex, isn't it?"

"Yes. Armed men attacked the safe house and took him along with the other kids. Nathan and his older son were knocked out by some kind of drug and left behind, along with Martin."

Allison felt her chest constrict with worry. "Does Martin know who took them?"

He shook his head. "The brief glimpse he had made him think military, so it might be the same group who brought Andy to that church."

"Our government?" Allison felt disgust well up within her.

He didn't look the least bit surprised at the idea. "There are some at the Pentagon who will use anyone or anything in the interest of national security, even children."

Allison knew she should be angry, but she'd overheard enough of her father's business dealings with the government over the years to know he spoke the truth.

"Go back to bed, Allison," he said. "I've got to do some research."

She knew better than to argue. "Just find him, Dad. Find all of them."

"I will."

She returned to her room. Knowing she could never sleep now, she sat on her bed and lay back against the heavy wooden headboard, thinking about Alex. He'd literally brought her back from the brink of death at the risk of his own life. What kind of boy would do that? Most people seemed to care only about themselves. He had to be all right. He had to be!

She snatched her phone off its charger on the night table and stuffed the buds into her ears, cranking her favorite Hawthorne Heights tunes. She felt closer to him this way. They had so much in common. Maybe it was because he was special ed and in a wheelchair, but he'd never once commented on her bald head like every other kid she knew.

She'd gotten so used to the look by now that she knew she'd feel funny once it grew back. *Will Alex like me with hair?*

As the music pounded in her ears, she realized that she cared what Alex thought about her. Never having cared what anyone thought, this was a new and almost frightening feeling. She liked Alex despite having spent only a short time with him—despite all the horror that had followed in his wake. And they shared a deep connection through his healing of her.

Unable to put this amazing boy and his strange power out of her mind, Allison lowered her head to the soft downy pillow and lost herself in the lyrics of "Put Me Back Together," a song they both loved.

***

Father Pat paced in his small living room at St. Joseph's rectory in Hawthorne, unable to sleep after all that had happened the past twenty-four hours. He'd witnessed the senseless killing of three innocent teenagers and the possession of another by creatures he'd always believed didn't exist. He'd been healed of a bullet wound by a boy prophesied thousands of years in the past. And he might yet be implicated in the murder of Alex's evil foster parent.

Then there was Russell Shaw, billionaire entrepreneur and technocrat. They'd put all their trust in this singular man simply because Alex had vouched for him. True, Alex was the best judge of character Father Pat had ever met, but a man like Shaw, who had the power to manipulate elected officials and accomplish who knew what else on the world stage, might be capable of fooling even Alex.

Father Pat replayed in his mind all that Shaw had said and done. He was a good judge of character in his own right, and as he considered Shaw's words and pondered the expressions on his face, he came to the conclusion that Alex's judgment was likely sound. In any case, he really had no choice in the trust arena because Shaw had already spirited the kids into hiding.

The man had been as good as his word, however, and put Father Pat in contact with an Italian cardinal named Leone who oversaw the Vatican archives. Shaw's word must carry much weight. On the strength of that alone, Leone had granted Father Pat access to almost any book or file, at least those involving doomsday cults, which was his area of research.

Cardinal Leone proved effusively chatty and shared an interest in that very subject. Once Father Pat explained that his search revolved around the Healer, the cardinal erupted with animated conversation on the topic.

Needless to say, Father Pat didn't mention that he knew the Healer personally, nor did he explain why he needed the information other than for scholarly research.

After directing him to the necessary section within the archives and showing him how to navigate the complexities of the computer catalogue system, the cardinal left Father Pat to his own devices. He'd only been working a few hours but had already taken numerous screen shots and copious notes on possible "end of the world" cults that might be related to the one he'd encountered. He even cross-referenced Native American mentions of the Healer, since Alex was one quarter Onondaga.

He logged back into the system to resume his search. He decided to focus on the boys' substitute teacher, Ms. Garrett, who had seemed to be in command during the failed attempt to possess Alex.

Most of these cults were led by self-styled demigods, like Jim Jones, who had charisma and an almost hypnotic hold over their followers, but no otherworldly power. They were just effective at controlling gullible people.

He contacted Cardinal Leone to ask an important question. The Cardinal appeared on his computer screen looking like he'd just rolled out of bed despite it being after eleven a.m. in Rome. The gray hair that remained on his balding head was ruffled and unkempt, and his wire-rimmed glasses looked askew, as though he'd fallen asleep with them on and rolled over several times. But he offered Father Pat a toothy grin and a hearty, accented, "Buongiorno, Father Patrick. Rather early in the day for you, is it not?"

"I couldn't sleep, so I wanted to continue my research."

The Cardinal smiled. "Care to tell me yet why you are so keen on the Healer? Have you knowledge I lack?"

Father Pat did not want to lie, and, in truth, Vatican involvement might prove useful in fighting this enemy. But for now, he chose to keep his knowledge of Alex a secret. He'd only just met this man, after all, and with the varied politics that twisted and writhed behind the scenes at the Vatican, he needed to know Leone much better before taking him into his full confidence.

"I do, Cardinal," he admitted, choosing his words with care, "But I cannot share what I know at present, not until I learn more."

The old man smiled. "Fair enough, my friend. How may I assist you now?"

"Are you aware of any cults at any time in history run by a woman, or at least with a woman prominent in the hierarchy?"

"There were some in the Twentieth Century, but those were not interested in facilitating Armageddon or even fomenting mass chaos. But I did find something that might interest you—a secret society called the Kalandrians."

Father Pat frowned. He'd never heard of them. "What did you find out?"

The Cardinal grinned, as he always did when imparting information he'd uncovered. "Well, the name is a variant on Calandria, a mythical bird with the power to heal."

Father Pat lurched upright, his fatigue gone.

"There are few references to them in any texts, which means they are either long gone or have been astonishingly good at concealing their presence in modern society. They fixated on the Healer prophecy and seemed intent on finding him whensoever such a person was born. I found no information that they sought to bring about the end of the world, but it's possible that was another of their aims."

Father Pat's mind raced with possibilities. Could this be the group that was stalking Alex?

He leaned in more closely. "Did you find any visuals, photos or drawings, of this group?"

Leone nodded. "A few of some apparent members. The images are dark, but I'll email them to you. The most recent photo was taken in…" He trailed off to consult something offscreen. "Two thousand. The earliest I found dated back to World War II."

"Please send whatever you have, Cardinal. And thank you!"

Leone peered at him from beneath his spectacles, his cluttered office at the Vatican surrounding his face like a picture frame. "I trust you will share with me what you know? When you're ready, of course."

Father Pat hesitated a split second before responding, "Of course, Your Excellency. I'm sure I'll need your expertise when the time comes."

The Cardinal nodded and Father Pat ended the video chat. He didn't have long to wait before his inbox lit up with new mail. With trembling fingers, he opened the message and clicked on the first attached image, the one from 2000.

The image was color and a side angle, as though someone snapped the picture surreptitiously. There were six people in the photo, all men except one woman, standing in front of what looked like rocks—or perhaps a rock wall? The woman was in the back, with only part of her face and hair showing, and the lighting was poor, like maybe it was dusk, but…

He zoomed in on the woman and tried to clean up the image as much as possible with the free image software on his computer. He was sure her hair was blonde, and she bore a distinct resemblance to… Yes! He would swear it was the same woman from the church, the one who'd been shot in the back!

He opened the second color photo, this one dated 1970. Again, it showed a group of men, though not the same people as in the previous image, gathered outside a large three-story house. They stood close around a woman as though trying to hide her face from the camera. He zoomed in on her. The hair was dark and short, but her features…

It was the same woman! And she looked exactly as she did thirty years later!

Fingers trembling, Father Pat opened the last photo and noted the date: 1940. This one was black and white and grainy, but he studied a small cluster of men wearing clothes and hats of the period standing together on a street. The buildings behind them looked European to him, small and tightly packed together. In the midst of the group, blonde once again, was the woman Alex called Ms. G, looking exactly as she did when Father Pat had seen her the previous night! She was speaking to a young man dressed in a Nazi SS uniform.

He expanded the photo and zoomed into the man's face. It was grainy, but a sharp nose was evident, as well as what looked like a large birthmark surrounding the left eye and covering part of the man's forehead and upper cheek.

Stunned, Father Pat sat back in his desk chair and rubbed a hand through his thick black hair. From 1940 to the present, that woman hadn't aged a day! If he hadn't seen the photos for himself, he wouldn't have believed it. Since he and Shaw had left the church shortly after Martin drove away with the others, they never knew which group had come to "clean up" after the incident. Did that cleanup crew find her dead body? Or maybe, had it vanished because, in addition to not aging, she couldn't be killed by conventional means?

The phone rang and Father Pat jumped two inches off his chair, heart soaring into overdrive. He stared at the cell phone on his desk as his ringtone blasted out once more. The name flashing on screen was "Shaw."

Hand trembling, he reached for the phone and opened the call, placing the device up against his ear. "Mr. Shaw." His body stiffened with fear as he listened to Shaw's report. "I thought you said they were safe." He paused and listened again. "Can you find out who took them?"

Shaw's calm assurance that he could did not assuage Father Pat's anxiety. If that woman had gotten them back...

"Listen, Shaw, I found out some information about the woman and her group. I can come right—"

Shaw insisted Father Pat should stay put until more was known about who the kidnappers were and where they'd taken the boys. "Just email what you found about the woman, and I'll put my people on it."

Father Pat reluctantly agreed but insisted on being informed the moment Shaw had any updates.

"Don't worry, Padre. I'll keep you in the loop. Now I have work to do. Good night."

The call ended before Father Pat could say another word. He set the phone down and took a deep breath. The boys had all been taken, but not the adults. Martin was driving back to Shaw's home with Nathan and Dane. Father Pat felt he should be there. They'd been a team long before Shaw entered the picture and he felt uneasy deferring the entire operation to a stranger.

Still, he told himself, there was nothing he could do for Alex and the others right then, but he could learn as much as possible about Ms. G and her Kalandrians. He turned back to the computer and resumed his research.

***

Alex woke with a start in semidarkness. "Andy! Roy!"

There was no answer. The bed beneath him felt hard and unfamiliar as he scanned his surroundings. A pool of light came from above, a bulb encased in metal attached to the wall like some kind of weird nightlight. What he could see of the small room confused his fuzzy brain. There was no furniture except the bed and a closed door just across from him, and a large photograph on the opposite wall.

Where was he?

I remember! Andy and me got shot by something… a dart!

He felt around his chest where he recalled the dart striking him, but there was nothing there. He still wore the clothes he'd been wearing before he'd gone outside to find Andy and Martin.

Martin!

He was shot! Was he dead? Alex struggled to clear his mind. He'd been drugged once before when Shaw's men kidnapped him off the street, and he felt much the same sensations now, light-headed, and fuzzy.

No. I remember Andy grabbing my hand and then the power.…

The men in black, the ones with the guns. They died! But not all of them, because he and Andy were drugged. What about Roy and the others?

His wheelchair sat beside the bed as though awaiting him, so he slid into it and adjusted the footrests beneath his bare feet. He sat a moment because he still felt a bit dizzy, and then wheeled over to the closed door across the room. He gripped the knob and turned.

Locked.

Afraid now, he turned to examine the rest of the room. There was another door set into the wall near the bed. He raced across the concrete floor and tried that knob.

Also locked.

Frustrated, he pounded on the metal door. "Is anyone there? I'm locked in!"

"Alex!"

Roy!

"Roy, I'm here. Are you okay?"

Alex heard someone slump up against the door and a loud sigh of relief.

"I was so afraid something…" Roy trailed off, his voice sounding strained, as though he'd been crying, or was about to start. "Yeah, yeah, we're good, 'cept Dad and Dane ain't here. They with you?"

Alex felt his chest tighten with fear. Where could they be?

"Alex?"

"Uh, no, they ain't here. You got Andy with you?"

There was a momentary pause. "Um, no. We figured he was with you."

Alex's heart sank. Where was his brother?

"Are you locked in, Alex?"

"Yeah. Any clue where we are?"

"No."

"Did you see much that happened?" Alex asked.

"No," Roy answered. "I heard a noise and when I woke up, I seen little red dots floating in the room. Then I got hit with something in the chest and…woke up here."

"Same for me, Alex," said another voice. Carlos. "I couldn't see nothin' till I woke in this tiny-ass room."

Then a very familiar voice boomed through the door. "Hey, Alex, you got any food in there? I'm hungry as hell."

Izzy.

Despite his anxiety, Alex smiled. The smile broadened when he heard Java pipe up in his usual disgruntled tone.

"Even if he did, fool, how's he gonna get it to you through a locked door?"

Izzy groaned. "Oh, yeah."

A key rattling in a lock drew Alex's gaze to the other door on the opposite side of his room. The knob was turning.

"Someone's coming," he said to his friends in the next room, and then wheeled rapidly forward to face whoever might enter.

CHAPTER FIVE

WHERE'S MY BROTHER?

THE DOOR SWUNG OPEN AND in stepped two men. One was definitely a soldier, judging by the blue uniform he wore. Alex had seen some like it in movies. The man had little wings pinned to his chest, and under that were a ton of colorful little patterns, like decorations. The man looked older than Nathan, though not as tall. But he was thicker in the chest, like maybe he hit the weights the way Java did. He was also mostly bald, except for a little hair around the sides that had some gray in it. He wore a serious expression on his face, almost like he was worried, but he didn't look threatening.

The other man, however, wore a smile that Alex knew was fake. It reminded him of the smiles his foster mother Jane used to flash at visiting social workers so they wouldn't figure out what a mean, cruel person she really was. This man was dressed in a gray suit and light-blue tie. He looked younger than the other man because his short, curly hair was a light brown color and his face seemed smoother, not as hard or lined. He displayed an underlying edge of excitement, like he could barely keep himself from jumping up and down with glee.

"Good morning, Alex," he said, his voice silver-tongued, almost like his jaw had been oiled. "I've searched for you since before you were even born."

That caught Alex by surprise. "Why?"

"Because you're the Healer, obviously."

Alex frowned, but the man's grin grew even larger.

"Forgive my rudeness," the man went on. "I'm Mr. Jones and this is the colonel. He's base commander, but I give the orders when it comes to you."

The guy in the uniform—the colonel—looked like he wanted to strangle Mr. Jones. But he kept his anger under control and nodded at Alex.

"Morning, son," the colonel said, his voice gruff, but tinged with compassion, something Alex did not sense from Jones.

Alex made a spur of the moment decision. He was done cowering to all these people who wanted to use him for whatever they desired no matter what he wanted or needed. He rolled forward aggressively, forcing the smirk off Jones's face as he took a step back.

"You work for Ms. G?" Alex didn't have to try for authority in his voice. It was already there.

"No, Alex," Jones replied, warier now than when he walked in. "I know who she is and a little about what she wants. My goal is to keep you from falling into her clutches."

Alex knew the man was telling the truth. It was in his tone and his eyes.

"Where's my brother?"

Jones clasped both hands behind his back and glanced at the colonel.

"I'd like to know the same thing," the colonel said, squinting at Jones with suspicion.

Jones eyed the colonel a long moment. "Very well, I'll show you."

He pulled a small remote control from his jacket pocket and aimed it at the wall to Alex's right.

Alex looked over, seeing only what he'd noticed before—a large photograph of military planes against a backdrop of the setting sun. He heard a click from the remote and then, to his astonishment, the photo shimmered and disappeared, revealing a window. Beyond the window was another room, nearly identical to the one he was in, except this one housed his twin brother!

Alex gasped and rolled toward the window. Andy sat on his bed, staring off into space, apparently deep in thought.

"Andy!"

"He can't hear you, Alex."

Alex whirled around to face Jones. "Why not?"

"That room is completely soundproof," Jones replied as though Alex should know this already. "His voice is, as you well know, dangerous."

"It is not!"

"What are you talking about, Dav—Jones?" The colonel faced Jones with an accusatory look on his face.

Alex wasn't so rattled that he didn't catch the change of name. So Mr. Jones wasn't Mr. Jones after all.

Jones studied Alex as though waiting for him to explain, but Alex didn't know what he was supposed to say, so he remained silent.

"I'm sure Alex can best tell you how your men died during the capture, Colonel," Jones said, his tone conversational. "The body cam footage doesn't quite capture it all."

"Those men were shot by Alex's bodyguard," the colonel announced with barely contained fury, "which was *your* fault for underestimating the situation."

"Negative," Jones replied, still poker-faced. "Only one man was shot by the bodyguard. The other three were killed by Alex's brother." He pointed at the window, where the oblivious Andy brooded in silence.

"That's not true!" But even as he blurted out an automatic defense of his twin, Alex's mind raced with images of the night before, which swam disturbingly into focus.

"What happened out there, Alex?"

Alex looked long and hard at the colonel. He felt the inherent decency within this man, not to mention devotion to the men he commanded. He owed the commander the truth.

"When the soldiers snuck up on us, Martin, that's the guy who was guarding us, well, he shot one of 'em. He didn't know what they were doing, and he was protecting me and Andy."

For some reason, he decided not to mention Mr. Shaw and that Martin worked for him. He wasn't sure why but sensed that information shouldn't be revealed just yet.

The colonel glanced at Jones, who stood like a wax statue. "Go on, Alex."

"One of the soldiers, maybe 'cause *he* told them to, I don't know," Alex went on, pointing at Jones, "shot Martin with a real bullet. Everything happened so fast, but I think...Martin was dead. Andy grabbed my hand and then..." He trailed off, afraid to continue, afraid to admit the truth.

"And then what?" The colonel focused fully on Alex now, ignoring Jones completely.

Alex gulped and forced calm into his voice. "And then Andy, uh, shifted Death, I think, from Martin to the other soldiers. I, uh, I guess he, uh, he must've got three of 'em."

Jones smiled, which filled Alex with disgust. Didn't the man care that four soldiers were dead because of him?

"He only did it to save Martin," Alex insisted, determined to defend his brother.

The colonel studied him a moment. "I don't understand, Alex."

"That's how it works for Andy," Alex explained. "He can take stuff inside, but he gots to shift it to somebody else or it could hurt him."

The colonel glowered at Jones, his anger simmering near the surface. "You knew the danger to my men and you went ahead anyway?"

"We had intel that the other group discovered the boys' location and were moving in. I was authorized by the Pentagon to capture the boys first, to make certain they didn't fall into enemy hands."

"You don't have to talk to the grieving families of those men like I do!"

"True, which is why I'm not base commander. And may I remind you, Colonel, that you're still commander *only* because I had your back after the Los Angeles fiasco three years ago."

The colonel looked slightly chastised, but still angry. "I can't forget because you bring it up every chance you get."

"We are the most unorthodox base in the US military, Colonel, and you know that better than I because you grew up here, working on your own failed experiment, I might add. Unlike you, I don't intend to fail."

Alex watched this exchange, liking the colonel more and Jones less with each passing second. He didn't know what they were talking about, but clearly Jones was in charge, which gave him an uneasy feeling in the pit of his stomach.

"You took us to protect us from…them?"

Mr. Jones nodded. "It's not our way to abduct U.S. citizens, but you and your friends are too important to allow the others to have you."

"What do you want from me?"

"Well, I'm hoping, while you're here, to study your powers."

"I won't do anything you want till I get what I want," Alex announced, wheeling closer to Jones to make his point.

Jones looked amused by his challenge and forced back a smirk. "And what is it you want?"

"My friends and me stay together, and my brother too."

Jones lost the smirk. "Your brother is—"

"I can control him," Alex asserted, not at all sure it was true, but he did his best to sound convincing. "He can only use his full power if I let him." He recalled what Andy had done by himself with only a fly but decided not to mention that.

Jones didn't look convinced. "I'm afraid I can't—"

"So it's true, Davalos. You *did* bring children here," came a harsh female voice from the open doorway.

Alex wheeled around to face the newcomer. She looked like maybe the colonel's age. But her wavy brown hair hung down to her shoulders and her hazel eyes had a young-looking sparkle. Unlike Jones in his business suit and the colonel in his uniform, she was dressed in casual pants and a pullover shirt. Only her face revealed her feelings, twisted as it was with fury.

Both the colonel and Jones looked surprised to see her.

"Amanda, what are you doing here?"

She strode up to the colonel and slipped one arm around his. "I don't know what you're up to, Davalos, but I'll wager the White House doesn't know you kidnapped these civilians."

Jones, who Alex now knew was really named Davalos, suddenly looked much less confident than a moment before. "Hello, Mrs. Walker. As always, it's a pleasure."

Alex heard the exact opposite in his voice, but thought it best not to speak at the moment. To his surprise, the woman marched forward and looked him over, as though checking for injuries.

"Are you all right, young man?"

"Uh, yes," Alex replied, not sure how he should respond.

"And your friends?"

"They sounded okay."

She offered a sympathetic smile. "Good. I'm having bunk beds moved into our house and you'll live there with the colonel and me while you're on this base."

Both the colonel and Davalos reacted with surprise, but Davalos spoke first, his tone angry. "Now just a moment, Mrs.—"

"Don't just a moment me, *Mister* Davalos," she snapped, cutting him off and causing the colonel to hide his smile. "You may have the ear of every single Pentagon official, but I'm friends with the vice-president and I'm under no military mandate to keep this knowledge to myself. You brought civilian teenagers onto a top-secret military base. Even if it's for their own protection, you haven't notified their parents, and none of this will go over well with the administration or the public. Those boys will stay in our home during their time here, and if we treat them well enough, they might not sue the government when they're released. Do I make myself clear?"

Davalos changed his expression so many times during her speech that Alex couldn't keep track. He went from angry to insulted to surprised to worried and finally to reprimanded, like a little kid who's being sent to bed without dinner.

"Of course, Mrs. Walker," he finally responded, his tone no longer smug, "you are absolutely right. I was in such a hurry to protect them from the others, I didn't think through the rest."

She gazed at him with squinty eyes. "I know you have something planned for them and I assure you *they* will keep me informed. Won't you, young man?"

Alex was caught off-guard being addressed directly. "Yes, ma'am," he said without hesitation. He liked this lady already and knew he could trust her.

She offered a genuine smile that put Alex at ease. "I'm going to get the house ready, and when you're finished with Mr. Davalos or Jones or whatever he chooses to call himself today, the colonel will bring you home."

No longer feeling like he was up against a wall, Alex smiled. "Thank you so much."

"My pleasure." She took the colonel's hand and gave it a small squeeze before marching from the room like a retreating tornado.

Davalos glared at the colonel, but Alex could tell the older man was amused by the incident. "Your wife was out of line, Colonel."

"I may be under orders to defer to you in these Healer matters," the colonel replied tightly, "but my wife is not. And she's correct. This base is no place for civilians, especially minors, even if it is for their protection. They'll stay with us, and they'll have no access to any part of this facility except when accompanied by you or I. Now, I suggest we get these boys some food, and then I will observe your 'tests.'"

Davalos looked like a bird that had its feathers ruffled up. "I do not need your supervision, colonel."

"Ordinarily not, when your subjects are legal adults who are participating of their own free will. Alex and Andy are neither. I am base commander. They are my responsibility."

Davalos knew he was beaten, for the moment, but Alex could tell he was up to something sketchy.

"You are correct, of course. Feed them and then bring them to the lab." Without another word, the haughty man strode from the room.

Alex eyed the colonel, who winked. At that point, Alex found himself grinning. "Thanks, Colonel Walker."

The colonel's face became serious again. "Don't thank me yet, Alex. If what Davalos said about your brother is true, he could pose a serious threat to national security. Then it becomes my problem, and I must deal with it."

Alex only had a vague idea of what "national security" really involved, but Andy *was* dangerous and unpredictable, and those things could be a big problem.

"Can I see my brother now?"

"Of course." Colonel Walker ushered Alex through the open door.

The corridor they entered was stark and painted an ugly shade of dark green. There were several doors on each side, all of which were closed, and overhead lights that bathed everything in a bright, but soft glow.

Colonel Walker led Alex to the door next to the one they'd come out of and detached a ring of keys from his belt. Sifting through them, he selected one and unlocked the door. As he swung the door outward, Alex nearly flinched with surprise. Andy stood on the other side, long hair streaming down each side of his face, staring at them like a psycho killer from one of Izzy's horror movies. The evil look on Andy's face was terrifying, but when Andy realized who it was, the expression vanished.

"Big brother," Andy said, his voice neutral like always. "I wasn't sure who it might be."

"Hello, Andy," said the colonel. "I'm Colonel Walker."

He extended a hand, but Andy merely looked at it, baffled.

"He, uh, he don't know much about being around other people," Alex explained, brushing his thick white bangs away from his face. "He been locked up in a box his whole life."

Colonel Walker flinched, trying not to look shocked. "I'm sorry that happened to you, Andy, but we will not keep you locked up here. You'll be staying at my house with Alex and the other boys."

Andy eyed Alex, awaiting confirmation that this was true.

Alex nodded. "The other guy is sketchy, but the colonel and his wife have our backs."

Andy seemed to accept this on face value and stepped past the colonel into the corridor. "What is this place?"

"It's a military base," the colonel explained. "You and the others were brought here to protect you from that woman and her group."

"You mean Teacher?"

Colonel Walker eyed Alex, who nodded.

"Yes."

Andy studied the colonel a long moment. "You want to experiment on Alex and me."

The colonel looked surprised. So did Alex. Since Andy's room was soundproof, how could he have known this?

"Actually, it's a man from the Pentagon who wants to run some tests on you boys. I think Alex is willing to cooperate, depending on the tests. Did I read that right back there, Alex?"

Andy turned to Alex again. "Is that true, Big Brother?"

Alex nodded. "He wants to test our power. I'm kinda curious what else you and me can do together." He eyed Colonel Walker. "If we don't wanna do something, can we say no, Colonel?"

"Absolutely. You are under no obligation to participate in any test on this base."

Andy nodded his agreement.

"I expect you're both hungry, so let's gather up your friends and head to the DFAC."

Alex raised his eyebrows quizzically.

The colonel smiled for the first time that day. "Dining facility."

***

Allison sat in her dad's expansive computer room listening to Martin's report of what had happened the previous night. Sitting in various chairs around the room were Nathan and Dane, both of whom Allison had met briefly at the burned-out church, and Father Pat, who had returned to make his own report.

At first, her dad told her she couldn't sit in on the meeting, but she'd insisted. "Alex is my friend, Dad, and I owe him more than anyone else does."

Her plea had won him over, but she knew it was only the first step. Allowing her to help find Alex was one thing; letting her help rescue him would be another.

"I know it sounds crazy, Mr. Shaw," Martin was saying as she tuned back into his recitation, "but I'm almost positive I was dead."

Nathan and Dane exchanged a look.

"Andy," Dane said, glancing around the room for confirmation.

"It must have been," Father Pat added, sounding as though he hadn't slept all night. "Like he did with Roy."

"Andy *and* Alex," Nathan interjected, his weathered face creased with worry.

Dane leaned forward abruptly. "But when they saved Roy, they did something, moved his death into that cop, which means…" He trailed off, considering the possibilities.

"Which means," Shaw spoke, his deep voice firm and clipped, "that at least one of the abductors was killed, in addition to the one Martin shot."

"That also means," Father Pat said, his voice rimmed with alarm, "that they now know what the boys can do."

"Yes," agreed Shaw. "Which makes this situation even more problematic."

"What do you mean?"

Shaw glanced at Father Pat but didn't answer directly. "Let's hear your report first, Padre. What did you learn?"

Father Pat rose heavily from a plush chair and slipped a flash drive from his pocket, handing it to Shaw. Allison leaned forward as her dad slid the drive into a USB slot on his desktop computer. Multiple monitors rested on either side of the machine, and more adorned the wall above it, making that side of the room look like the television department at Best Buy. Her dad was an inveterate multi-tasker and often worked on multiple programs simultaneously.

He opened the files on the drive. "Shall I put these photos on separate screens?"

Father Pat nodded. "That would be helpful, yes." He looked rumpled, his dark hair askew.

Allison saw several photos appear on different screens. Two looked recent, but one was quite old and grainy.

Father Pat described a group of people who seemed to go back a long way who wanted to bring about the end of the world, or at least create worldwide anarchy. Somehow, Alex and Andy were the key to their plans. The part that freaked Allison out the most was the woman in the photos. Everyone agreed it was the same woman, and yet the fact that she hadn't aged was impossible, wasn't it?

"I'm just a businessman and tech genius, Padre," Shaw said after the priest finished his recitation. "You're the supernatural guy. How could she stay the same?" He pointed at the photos on screen.

Father Pat shook his head. "I don't know. This is way out of my league. The cardinal I spoke with could offer no explanation either. One thing we do know – that woman is dangerous and, if she still lives, she must be kept away from Alex at all costs."

"On that, we're agreed," Shaw affirmed, shifting in his high-end leather desk chair.

Martin cleared his throat, and everyone looked at him. "Any clues yet, boss, on who has the kids?"

Shaw frowned. "I'm sure you're correct about the military snatching them, but my contacts at the Pentagon are more tight-lipped than ever, which means this goes to the highest levels of government."

"The government has my son?" Nathan sounded shocked.

"It would appear so," Shaw went on. "I don't know why they grabbed the other kids, except maybe as leverage to force Alex to help them."

"They'd do that?" Dane clenched and unclenched his fists, his jaw tightened with fury. "No better than the asshole cops who harassed me as a kid."

"Alex and Andy possess a tremendous power, especially their ability to manipulate death," Shaw explained, his tone matter of fact, like he was setting up a business deal. "Something like that would be of great value to our enemies. The only upside of where they are is that the others can't get to them."

"Are you sure?" Everyone looked at Father Pat, who continued. "These people, especially that woman, seem capable of anything. I'm not sure Alex is safe anywhere."

"The priest is right," Dane affirmed, his expression resolute. "I still got scars from them cat attacks." He absently fingered one scratch mark across his cheek that hadn't fully healed.

Shaw leaned back in his plush chair and pondered their words. "They must be at a base where tests can be performed. That eliminates many of our military sites. The Pentagon might have failed me, but my own paranoia won't."

"What does that mean?" asked Father Pat, exchanging a mystified look with Nathan.

"My company installed the security systems on most of our top-secret military sites per a lucrative Pentagon contract I negotiated several years ago."

"How will that help us find the boys?"

"Since I trust no one, I built into every system a backdoor that only I can access. I've never felt compelled to use it until now."

Martin's face lit up with understanding. "So you can spy on the spies?"

Shaw nodded. "Precisely. I've already begun scrolling through base camera systems searching for any sign of the boys. I can only see what the cameras see, but it should be enough to eventually find them. In the meantime, is there a chance we can zero in on that woman and her group, Padre?"

Father Pat shook his head. "They're like ghosts who seem to move around a lot. I took the liberty of going to her apartment, the one the boys visited, but it was vacated. The landlord said the woman left no forwarding address, and the name she gave the school was phony."

"You make a decent detective, Padre," Shaw said, looking impressed.

Martin and Allison nodded in agreement before Shaw continued, addressing the entire group. "I'm going to continue my scan of the various bases. Martin, you and the others use the secondary computer room to search for any clues to that woman. If we can shut her down, the primary threat will have been neutralized."

"Sure thing, Mr. Shaw."

Nathan stood and approached Shaw. "Those are my kids out there, Mr. Shaw. Whatever you find, I'm in."

Dane jumped up. "Me too!"

"And me, Dad." Allison stood and approached her father, figuring she needed to be bold while everyone else was present.

Shaw surveyed the group with care. "I have professionals who will do the heavy lifting, but once the boys are located, you'll all be included in deciding how to move forward."

It sounded vague, but Allison knew her dad, and that was the best answer they'd get at the moment. The others seemed satisfied too, and she watched as they followed Martin from the room.

When they were alone, she faced her somber-looking dad. "You think Alex is in danger, don't you?"

He studied her a long moment. "When did you become so grown up?"

She shrugged.

"To answer your question, yes, I think he *might* be in danger, depending on the type of tests they have planned for him."

Dread filled her stomach like lead. She grabbed her dad and pulled him into a hug.

CHAPTER SIX

WHAT DO YOU WANT ME TO SHIFT?

ROY HAD TO ADMIT THAT eating in the dining facility was kind of fun. Several soldiers drifted in and out—mostly young men who looked around Dane's age, but a couple of women too. For the most part, though, it was him and the others, with that colonel guy being the only adult. Alex assured them that the colonel was cool, and Roy had never had any reason to doubt Alex when it came to people. Maybe it was the spinning thing he had, but Alex could read people better than any of them could read a book.

They'd had to leave the building they slept in and head outside into blinding sun and the heat, which was strong for October. The boys had all gawked at rows of jet fighters and enormous helicopters. They were amazing to look at just from the outside, and Java seemed to soak up those aircraft like they were the prettiest girls he'd ever seen. Roy knew he longed to view the interior—especially the place where the pilots sat.

A pathway led to the next building over, which had lots of windows and double glass doors. Inside, the dining hall was brightly lit and had metal tables that reminded Roy of the spanking new cafeteria at Mark Twain High. Just the thought of high school and its "normalness" made him feel homesick, even for the most boring of classes.

They grabbed trays and slid them along a steel track while cooks behind the glass spooned scrambled eggs, bacon, sausage, pancakes—just about any breakfast food they could want—onto their trays. Even Izzy was slack jawed at the choices.

Having listened at the door, Roy and the others had heard everything that went down with Alex and the adults, and they were excited about meeting the woman who told off that Davalos creep. That seemed to amuse the colonel, and he assured them they'd meet her later in the day after the initial tests were completed.

"What about my dad and brother?" Roy demanded as he set his tray onto one of the tables across from the colonel.

"Yeah, and my parents," Izzy put in, his loud voice drawing the attention of the cooks.

"Can we let 'em know we's okay?" Java asked, fork in hand. "My mom'll be worried something fierce."

The colonel eyed the boys with compassion. "From what I read last night in Davalos's Healer report, as he called it, if your parents know your whereabouts, they will be in grave danger."

"Why can't we just get 'em a message that we's safe and we'll talk soon?" Java persisted.

Izzy and Jorge nodded, but not Carlos. Roy knew he was in foster care and might not have anyone to contact.

"The other group trying to get to Andy and Alex is brutal and relentless," the colonel went on, his voice somber. "If they figure out your parents have heard from you, they'll torture them. Likely kill them."

"Holy shit," Izzy mumbled, suddenly looking very pale.

"Davalos assures me he has people tracking down that group. Once we know they are no longer an immediate threat, we can get word to your families. Deal?"

He surveyed the boys. All of them nodded.

"But what about my dad and Dane?" Roy insisted, picturing them left behind and drugged when those evil people showed up. "Maybe they got captured and might get tortured."

"My men on site planted a couple of cameras on the walls surrounding the house before they retreated. Footage showed two older men and a younger one leaving the house an hour after the incident."

"Why weren't they brought here too?" Roy persisted, stressing over his missing family.

"The men I debriefed said that after several of them had been killed, they made the choice to retreat with just you boys. That was Davalos's order."

Roy nodded, but he didn't feel relieved.

"Roy, isn't it" the colonel asked.

Roy nodded.

"I'll do some digging, try to get intel on your family. That work for you?"

Roy nodded, feeling less tense for the first time since he'd awakened. "Thank you, Colonel."

"Least I can do. Now dig in before this food gets cold. You boys must be starved."

That part was true for Roy, and he started in on his scrambled eggs. The others all dug in, as well, and there was no more talking while they ate.

After everyone had eaten his fill, the colonel escorted them out of that building and all the way across the tarmac to single story building set off by itself at the very back of the base. The only good part of this long trek under the blinding sun was passing even closer to the jets and choppers, causing Java to hang back and stare.

"I'd love to fly one o' them," Java commented, gawking at a sleek, new fighter jet and practically drooling.

"No reason why you can't join up after high school, Java," the colonel told him, indicating the aircraft around him. "This base is one of the more isolated, but you could be stationed anywhere in the world. It's not a bad life."

Java's momentary excitement crumbled. "No way I could pass them tests, Colonel. Too much a dummy."

Colonel Walker frowned at Java's use of the word "dummy," but Roy understood his friend's point. To get in the military, you had to read good, and probably know math—stuff none of them were good at.

The colonel didn't seem deterred by what Java said. "Son, speaking from experience, there's nothing you can't do if you really want to."

Java squinted against the harsh sunlight at the taller man but didn't respond.

Beneath the sweltering sun, Roy wondered why their destination was so far away from the other buildings. Perspiration dribbling from his armpits, he trudged past the aircraft behind Alex and Andy, deciding it didn't really matter how far away it was. All that mattered was what tests Davalos planned to perform. That was what worried him.

Izzy's mouth ran a mile a minute pointing out everything he saw, which the others had obviously already seen. Still, with every jeep that cruised past—or even a soldier in uniform—Izzy would exclaim, "Oh, look at that!"

Java finally waved a fist and growled, "Shut up, Izzy, or you'll be lookin' at my fist in your face!"

Izzy flinched back a moment and then something caught his eye off to one side. "Hey, is that a rabbit over there?"

Roy thought he must be joking, but something did move fast as it vanished behind a storage bin of some kind. He put a hand to his forehead to shield his eyes from the sun and scanned the area. He'd thought the tail looked familiar…like…a cat's, maybe? Even under the extreme desert heat, he shivered at the thought.

Jorge strolled along in silence, ignoring everything like usual, but he stuck close to Carlos, which seemed to please the bigger boy. Roy had never much liked Carlos because he'd always mocked Alex for his disabilities, but since they'd had to join forces against Jane and Ms. G, he'd come to grudgingly accept the other boy as one of them. The kid was even good-looking, Roy had noted on more than one occasion, if only he didn't glower so much.

Roy scuttled forward to catch up with Alex. "You sure you're good with this?"

Alex glanced up at him as he continued pushing himself along. His wheels made *crunch* sounds against the crushed rock of the tarmac.

"Dunno. Depends on what they wanna test. Like I told Andy, I'm curious about what else we can do."

"I won't let that jerk mess with you." Roy put as much force into his declaration as he could, and Alex offered up his beautiful smile in return. Andy glanced a moment at him but said nothing. Roy ached to hug Alex or even just hold his hand, but he knew this wasn't the time or place.

Upon reaching the building, the colonel slipped an ID card from his jacket pocket. He pressed it flat against an electronic box located just above the knob on an otherwise unmarked door. Roy heard a loud *bbbeeeppp*, and then a small area at the top of the box flashed. The colonel pressed his thumbprint into a tiny glass window, and only then did the door pop open with a *click*.

Roy exchanged a look with Alex and knew they were thinking the same thing. *What goes on in this place that they try so hard to keep people out?*

The colonel pulled open the door and ushered them inside. To Roy's surprise, Andy brushed past to enter with Alex, shouldering him into the doorjamb. Roy grunted in surprise but decided not to say anything because they were all inside and the door had closed behind them with a second click. Roy glanced back past Jorge, who'd entered last, and saw the same electronic box on the inside of the door.

I guess we can't get in or out, he thought as he picked up the pace behind Alex and Andy. *That's not good.*

Cool air wafted all around him, and despite his worry over the locked door, Roy appreciated its cool comfort. He saw Izzy suck in deep breaths, while the others just looked contented with the change in temperature. The long hallway was empty and stark, the plain walls painted dirty white, with overhead fluorescent lights making the place look like the hospital where his dad had been less than two weeks before. It amazed Roy how much had happened in such a short time, how his world—how all of their worlds—had been so upended after the death of their teacher. Just thinking about his father brought another ache to his stomach.

His drifting thoughts were interrupted when the colonel did his ID/fingerprint thing a second time and pulled open another unmarked door. He ushered Alex and Andy through, and Roy darted in right after, worrying that somehow he'd be separated from his best friend. But the colonel allowed them all to enter, making no effort to keep anyone out.

"Holy shit!" That was Izzy, of course.

They stood inside a gigantic lab of some kind that resembled places Roy had only seen in superhero movies. There were more computers than he could probably count, not to mention tons of screens along the upper walls. Each one displayed information or a big circle with an eagle in front of a cloud, and wings that had a bunch of lightning bolts sticking out. He recognized most of the words surrounding the images: United States Air Force. He'd seen United States enough times at school and he knew that the Air Force were the guys who flew planes, which was why he'd seen so many out on the tarmac. All around him were tables and countertops laden with glass bottles filled with colored liquids and other equipment he couldn't hope to name. One entire wall was dominated by a massive machine with blinking lights and colorful buttons.

Three people approached them from across the vast facility. One was the man named Davalos, and the other two looked like doctors. One was a man, the other a woman, and both sported long white coats. The man had gray hair, large ears, and wore glasses and a serious expression. The woman, maybe a little younger than Roy's dad, looked seriously stressed out. Even her light brown hair was messed up, like she'd pulled it up and tied it off in a hurry and didn't care how it turned out. He had a sense that they'd been arguing, but he couldn't be sure.

Davalos scowled at seeing the group and reached out to slap Izzy's hand away from some electronic device sitting on a white countertop.

"The hell?" Izzy glowered at Davalos, drawing a smirk from Java.

"Colonel," the man said, his voice testy, "you were to only bring the twins."

"Alex insisted," the colonel replied calmly, clearly enjoying Davalos's annoyance. "Take it up with him."

Davalos glared a moment longer before turning to Alex. "This lab is top secret and filled with delicate instruments. It's not for outsiders."

Alex met his gaze straight on, not the least bit cowed by the man's threatening tone. "Then I guess it ain't for me, neither." He turned his chair around. "Come on, guys, we're outta here."

He began wheeling back the way they'd come when Davalos called out, "Wait!"

Alex turned back, staring at the man with hard, flinty eyes.

Davalos looked like he wanted to scream but kept himself under control. "Very well, but don't touch anything!" This last was directed at Izzy, who chuckled, but didn't attempt to disobey.

"May I introduce the doctors now, *Mr.* Davalos?" The colonel looked like he wanted to laugh, but he didn't.

Jaw clenched, Davalos nodded.

The two doctors stood gazing at the twins with keen interest.

"Alex, Andy, this is Doctor Avila." The colonel indicated the man, who was quite a bit shorter than the colonel and rail thin, like he hardly ever ate anything.

"How do you do, boys?" The man extended a hand to Alex and offered a smile Roy didn't like. It reminded him of the Grinch when he got the idea to steal Christmas. Alex shook his hand.

But when Avila stuck out his hand to Andy, the other boy just stared at it. Avila's smile faltered and he pulled his hand back.

"And this," the colonel went on, indicating the woman, "is Doctor Shepherd. She and I have worked together for many years."

She had an uncomfortable look on her face, as though she didn't approve of whatever they were going to do, but she forced that expression to vanish in favor of a smile much more genuine than Avila's. "Nice to meet you both."

She didn't extend her hand, obviously wary of Andy ignoring it.

Alex glanced at his brother, whose blue eyes gleamed with suspicion.

Unlike Davalos or Avila, Dr. Shepherd greeted Roy and the others too. Carlos grunted a sullen "Hello," typical for him, but the others were more polite, even Izzy. Roy stepped up to the doctors in such a confident way that Alex looked surprised.

"Alex is my best friend and…" Roy trailed off, noticing Alex eyeing in a way that made him almost blush. "He's the best guy ever, so you treat him right."

Davalos opened his mouth to offer what looked like an angry response, but Dr. Shepherd spoke first. "I assure you we will not hurt him. Or his brother."

Satisfied with her response, Roy folded up into himself after his burst of valor. He glanced over at Andy and found the other boy glaring at him something fierce.

"Chill, Andy," Alex warned, clearly not happy with his brother's behavior.

Andy looked away from Roy and made eye contact with Alex. Alex must've done something because Andy lost the fire in his eyes and his face relaxed.

I'll have to ask Alex about that later, Roy thought, as he turned his attention back to the doctors. It was time for the tests to begin.

Despite assurances from both Alex and Andy that taking blood or doing brain scans wouldn't show anything, the two doctors insisted anyway.

"Best to be thorough," Avila intoned, as though the boys knew nothing.

Roy and the other boys were placed in a corner of the lab, each given his own chair, and told to "stay put" by Davalos, but they quickly became bored. The physical tests seemed to drag on forever and Alex grew more and more fidgety. Andy was also reaching his limit. Fortunately, Java and Izzy made the experience almost fun.

"Izzy, you keep drummin' on that table and I'm gonna pound you."

"Are not."

"Am so, fool!"

Then Carlos got into the act. "I'll help you pound 'im, Java."

"Don't need no help with Izzy. He's a weak-ass fool."

"Am not," Izzy retorted. "I can lift as much as you."

"Too bad there ain't no gym at this place or I'd show you," Java snorted.

"You think you're all badass," Carlos tossed in, "but I can bench more 'n you."

Java cackled with laughter.

"Okay, guys, now you're driving *me* crazy," Roy jumped in, feeling irritated partly because he was worried about Alex. He'd watched the doctors attaching pads to Alex's head and chest and running machines that must be recording information. He knew none of it was dangerous; he just hated Alex being used like some kind of lab rat.

Davalos looked like a volcano about to erupt and drew the colonel off to one side. "Colonel, you need to do something about these boys."

The colonel glanced over at Alex, who was in the process of having a cat scan. Alex said, "If you do got a gym here, that's a good place for 'em."

The colonel approached the boys. "You boys want to go to the fitness center?"

Java jumped up from his chair like he'd been bit by fire ants. "Oh, hell yeah! I haven't hit the weights in a long-ass time."

Carlos also rose to his feet, flexing his thick chest a few times. "I'm in."

They looked at Izzy, still drumming endlessly on the countertop with his fingers, tongue hanging from his mouth like a slobbery dog.

"I guess. I can mess with Java just as easy there." He busted up, but Java merely growled.

Roy gazed across the lab at Alex. "I don' know…" He bit his lip, making the snakebite piercings at each corner of his mouth glint under the overhead lights.

"It's okay, Roy," Alex assured him from across the lab. "I'll be fine."

Roy was still worried, though he tried not to show it. "Okay."

"Sides," Alex added, with a smile, "You gotta keep them others in line."

Roy grinned and then followed as the colonel led them out of the lab and back down the hall.

***

Alex was surprised to see Colonel Walker return moments later, causing Davalos to eye him with curiosity.

"That was a quick trip. The fitness center is on the other side of the base."

"I had one of my men take them," Colonel Walker replied evenly, glancing at Alex lying on the table. "My place is here with the twins."

Davalos smiled. "Still don't trust me?"

Colonel Walker offered no expression that indicated his thoughts. "These boys are my responsibility, and since they're undergoing tests, I belong here."

Warmth filled Alex. He felt, deep down, that this man would do everything he could to protect him and Andy, which eased his mind considerably.

Finally, to Alex's intense relief, Dr. Avila said, "I think that's all the physical tests, unless you have any other thoughts, Dr. Shepherd?"

She picked up a chart from one of the white countertops and scanned it. "No, we've covered everything on my list."

Dr. Avila nodded and turned to the boys. Andy stood next to Alex, his posture stiff, his face set in a defiant scowl.

"I wasn't going to do any more anyway," Andy asserted, his deep voice firm as steel. "I had too much of this stuff from Doctor."

Alex noted the Band-Aid in the crook of his brother's arm, covering the spot where blood had been taken, eyeing the matching one on his own arm. Once again, he considered Andy's childhood with all the torture and cruel treatment and felt an upsurge of love and protectiveness for his twin.

"I'm done with these too," he said, sharing a look of solidarity with Andy.

Davalos, who had scrutinized the administration of every test with great care stepped forward. "I'm sorry you had to go through so much pain growing up, Andy, and you too, Alex, but that's not our goal here. We just want a complete picture of you boys before we ask you to demonstrate your, well, let's call them your abilities."

Andy didn't look mollified, and Alex didn't feel much better. Being poked and prodded and studied made him feel like a frog and he hated anything that made him feel even more different than he already was.

Colonel Walker placed a calming hand on Alex's shoulder. "Let's find out if the fitness center survived your friends and then we'll get some lunch."

***

As Alex learned once they all met up in the dining hall, even Roy had enjoyed the fitness center. Java and Carlos had competed for a while to see who could bench press and curl more weight, with Java ending up the winner. At that point, the two boys decided to teach Izzy, Jorge, and Roy how to lift and, according to Roy, everyone had fun. Java coached Izzy and Roy, while Carlos took Jorge under his wing and proved to be a very solid, patient teacher, which surprised Alex. The exercise had definitely been therapeutic for Izzy because he actually ate his lunch in the dining hall without popping up and down like a jack-in-the-box.

Maybe he needs more working out instead of the meds, Alex thought as they all devoured grilled cheese sandwiches and burgers.

"You okay?" Roy asked, interrupting his thoughts. "Those docs didn't try anything crazy while I was gone?"

"We're fine, aren't we, Andy?"

Andy paused in his eating to glower at Roy, which troubled Alex. Was his brother jealous that they were so close?

"Yeah," Andy grumbled. "Fine." He ripped off a bite of grilled cheese like a shark might tear into a tuna.

Roy raised his eyebrows at Alex, but Alex just shook his head. Best not to say anything more.

After lunch, the other boys were eager to return to the fitness center, which left Alex and Andy alone with Colonel Walker once again crossing the steaming tarmac toward the lab. It was even hotter than it had been in the morning and Alex felt as if the hot air cut right through his clothes. Beads of sweat broke out everywhere on his body.

How do these guys live out here?

"Remember, boys," Colonel Walker advised as he popped open the outside door with his thumbprint, "you're not obligated to do any tests you object to."

When they reentered the lab, Alex noted that Davalos sat off by himself studying two computer monitors side by side on a table. Dr. Shepherd approached the boys and offered a genuine smile that made her look pretty, despite the haphazard hair.

"How was lunch, boys?"

"It was good," Alex replied, "wasn't it, Andy?"

"I guess," Andy answered, his face expressionless and his voice monotone.

Once again, Alex wondered if his voice sounded like Andy's.

Colonel Walker planted himself in a rolling desk chair off to one side where he had a clear view of everything going in the lab.

Dr. Avila joined Dr. Shepherd. Both still wore the same white coats they had sported that morning, but Shepherd looked more relaxed than before, while Avila was all business.

"So," Avila began, "Detective Cole gave us some information about you, Alex." He paused a moment. "You remember him, right?"

"Of course, I do," Alex snapped, more rudely than he'd intended. It had only been a few days since the man who had initially deceived him had given up his life to save Roy. "You think I'm stupid?"

Avila's face fell and he realized his misstep. Andy grinned at Alex, but Alex just felt special ed like always, and he detested that feeling.

"I'm sorry, Alex. That was a foolish question. In any case, we know something about how you heal people, but we know very little about how Andy…what's the word you use, Andy?"

"Shift," Andy replied without inflection.

Avila nodded. "Yes. How Andy shifts. Tell me, Alex, have you ever healed anyone who was in a different room than you?"

Alex was caught off guard by the question. "No. How could I do that?"

To his credit, Avila did not act like it was a dumb question. "I mean someone on FaceTime or Zoom, something like that."

"No. They's always been right there with me."

Avila turned to Andy. "What about you, Andy?"

Andy paused a moment, as though he wouldn't answer. "They had me shift colds and stuff from one person to another. It worked in the same room, but when the sick person left and I couldn't see him, I couldn't do it."

"What about on a computer screen, like these up on the wall behind me? Did you ever try shifting while looking at someone on a screen like this?"

"Yes. It didn't work."

Alex spoke before he thought it through. "Maybe you and me could do it."

Andy cast him a withering look and Alex realized his blunder. These people didn't know how much more powerful the boys were together.

Avila glanced hungrily at Shepherd, like this was the knowledge he'd most sought. She looked dispassionate, clearly not as interested as her partner. Or else she was a really good actor.

"We'd like to try some experiments with each of you separately, and some with you working together," Avila went on, nodding at Shepherd.

She stepped to the long computer console that ran the entire length of the room and pressed some buttons. Images flickered to life on several of the monitors attached to the wall above her.

Each monitor showed a small, stark room with one person sitting in a wooden chair. A few of the people were sneezing or blowing their noses. The others just sat and looked bored. All of them were adults, maybe in their twenties or thirties. Alex wasn't good at guessing peoples' ages.

"These people have all volunteered for this experiment, just so you know," Davalos spoke from his spot in the corner. "For pay, of course."

Alex nodded, having wondered about that.

"So, Alex, let's start with you," Avila spoke, interrupting Alex's thoughts as he gazed at the three rooms that housed a sick person. As always upon seeing someone ill, his stomach clenched with empathy, and he longed to make them well.

"I'm going to engage the microphone on monitor number one," Avila went on, the excitement in his voice palpable. "Then I'll tell that individual to describe his symptoms. Now, he has no idea you're here and doesn't understand the purpose of the experiment. See if you can heal him, Alex. You willing to try?"

Alex nodded without hesitation, brushing his limp bangs away from his eyes. He was curious, himself. If this worked, it might explain something Ms. G. had told him, something about spinning people over the internet.

"I'm ready," he said, stealing himself for the discomfort to come.

Avila pointed at the monitor. "Notice that the man's current temperature is displayed on screen. The room has a built-in thermometer." The virtual thermometer in the upper corner of the screen showed 101 degrees. Avila flipped a switch on the console. "Room A, can you hear me?"

The young, dark-haired man on Monitor One finished blowing his nose with a loud snorting noise and looked up at the camera. His face was flushed and there were beads of sweat coating his forehead. "Yeah, doc, I hear you."

"Good. I want you to look at the camera and describe, in as much detail as you can, every symptom you're feeling right now. The more description, the better."

The man nodded. He'd obviously been briefed on this part earlier. "Well, I have a fever. My forehead is burning up, my whole head, really." He placed a hand to his forehead and quickly lowered it. "My entire body aches, like maybe I was thrown out of a moving car. I can hardly breathe through my nose because it feels like it's stuffed with cotton, and..."

The man continued speaking and Alex absorbed every word. And with every word came every symptom. He burned from within. He felt like he'd been beaten up. Every muscle hurt. Chills wracked his body. He fought against the germs, whatever they were, and exerted his power.

"Look at the temperature reading!" Avila's voice sounded far away, at first.

"Incredible." That was Dr. Shepherd.

"Exactly as Cole described," Davalos added, his voice giddy with excitement.

Alex tuned them out and used his power like a surgeon used a scalpel, cutting away the symptoms one by one. He felt his body cool, his muscles relax, the chills fade away. The headache disappeared last, leaving only a hollow spot in the pit of his stomach that told him the spin was over.

He opened his eyes and found Andy right before him, on his knees, looking concerned.

"Are you well, Big Brother?"

Alex smiled. "Perfect."

Andy sighed, pointing up at the monitor. Alex looked up and saw exactly what he expected. The temperature reading displayed "98.6" and the man was touching himself in astonishment.

"I'm not sick anymore," the man exclaimed, stunned. "No fever, no aches, not even a runny nose!" He looked directly into the camera, no longer flushed, no longer sweating. "I don't know what you did but thank you!"

Dr. Shepherd gazed at Alex with such wonder in her eyes that he blushed and looked down.

"Very impressive, Alex," Avila said, the admiration evident in his voice. "Astonishing, really." He paused a moment, thinking. "What's the most serious illness you've cured?"

Alex knew the answer but didn't quite recall the word. "Leu—something. It was cancer in the blood."

"Leukemia?"

"That's it. It's the hardest thing I done so far."

Avila looked almost as stunned as the man on the monitor, whose mic had been cut off by Shepherd. "I bet." He stared a moment longer at Alex before turning his gaze on Andy. "You're up, Andy."

Andy stood and faced him, mystified. "Up what?"

"It's just an expression. You're next."

Andy nodded, exchanging a quick look with Alex, who offered an encouraging smile. Andy didn't return it. He stepped forward and gazed hard at Avila, making the doctor squirm. "What do you want me to shift?"

Avila turned and flipped a different switch on the console. Another monitor sprang to life, this one housing a blonde-haired woman with boxes of tissue laid out on the counter before her. She snatched tissue after tissue, sneezing into them and tossing them into a wastebasket at her side.

Avila flipped yet another switch and the monitor next to that one came on. This room revealed a young man sitting in a chair, looking bored and quite healthy.

"The woman is sick, obviously," Avila began, "with the flu. You can see that her temperature is high."

Alex noted the temperature as 103.

"The man in the room next to her is, as you can also see, perfectly healthy. Temp 98.5, no symptoms. I'd like you to shift the germs from the woman into the man. Can you do it?"

Andy studied the monitors a moment. "If they were both in this room, yes."

"Try," Avila prodded. "Please."

Andy glanced again at Alex and looked as though he didn't want to disappoint him. Then he gazed up at the monitor displaying the sick woman. "You are not sick. The germs that make you sick are not in you anymore. All that hurts, all that ails you, all the germs that are in you are in me. Germs, to me! Now!"

He waited a moment, clearly expecting something to happen. Alex held his breath. But the woman continued sneezing and Andy didn't so much as cough. He turned to Alex, his handsome face twisted with frustration.

"I can't do it."

Alex extended his hand. "Maybe we can."

Andy stared at his hand but made no move to take it. "Why are you stronger than me?"

"Dunno. Maybe God wanted us to be together. I know *I* did the second I found out you were alive. I'm okay that we're stronger together. Why can't you be?"

Andy's back stiffened with pride. "Because I've always been alone."

"Me too. But I'm not no more. *We're* not."

Alex had no idea how he managed to say all that without messing up, but he realized in this moment that he needed Andy to accept him, to love him, if love was even possible for a boy like Andy after all he'd suffered. He suddenly recalled Thor and his brother, Loki, from one of those movies, and how Loki always felt weak compared to Thor. He didn't want Andy to feel like that.

"I'm not stronger than you, Andy. The things you can do are so wicked that I'm jealous."

Andy scrunched up his face. "Wicked?"

"It means awesome, amazing. You're awesome and amazing, Andy, but together we can be even more amazing. Don't you see?"

Andy stared long and hard at Alex's extended hand, and then made eye contact. The pride in those sparkling blue eyes began to fade. "Thank you, Big Brother. Let's show them what we can do."

Alex felt a sudden upsurge of love for his twin, and then, as Andy clasped his hand, an upwelling of power, like water pounding through a pipe. He didn't know what it felt like to glow, but that's how his insides seemed in that moment—hot and glowing, almost like lava from a volcano. Together they looked up at the sneezing woman and Andy whispered, "Germs, to me."

Instantly, the woman stopped sneezing. Her temperature dropped to 98.5 and she gaped in astonishment at the tissue in her hand that she no longer needed.

Alex felt his nose congested and his lungs so full he could barely breathe. Andy sneezed once and said, "Germs, to him." He focused his gaze on the healthy man in the second room and Alex felt the outpouring of whatever it was Andy had shifted when it gushed from his body as quickly as it had entered.

The man on the monitor suddenly doubled over with a powerful sneeze. His temperature reading shot up over one hundred and he began sneezing again and again, like machine gun fire, as he grasped frantically for the box of tissue on the floor beside him.

"Incredible!" Avila looked first in amazement at the sneezing man on screen and then stared open-mouthed at Alex and Andy.

Dr. Shepherd had gone pale, like she'd just seen a ghost, and kept scribbling data onto a clipboard.

Alex grinned at his brother. An ecstatic Andy returned it and they released hands.

Now Davalos was beside them, almost drooling with excitement. "Absolutely brilliant. There may be no limit to what you boys can do."

Alex and Andy exchanged a look, but Davalos didn't go on. What had he meant by that?

Davalos turned to Avila. "A private word, Doctor."

Avila tossed the boys another look of astonishment and followed Davalos to the far corner of the lab, where they spoke in such low tones that Alex couldn't make out what they were saying. He turned to Colonel Walker, who had wandered closer during the demonstration, and nodded in the direction of the two men, but the colonel just shrugged.

Why doesn't he want to know what they're talking about?

"Very impressive demonstration, boys" was all Colonel Walker said before eyeing Dr. Shepherd. "Is that all for today, Doctor?"

Pulling her wide-eyed gaze from the boys, she set down her clipboard. "That's all we had planned, yes. Now that we know this much, we'll arrange more challenging tests for tomorrow."

"I wanna heal that guy we made sick," Alex said, eyeing the sneezing man with concern.

"Of course," Dr, Shepherd said. She flipped a switch and spoke. "Room D, please look at the camera and describe all of your symptoms in as much detail as you can."

Between sneezes and blowing of his nose, the man described how he felt. Once again, Alex absorbed it all and then pushed it away. Within a couple of minutes, the spin was over. The man glowed with health and relief, while Alex felt good that he'd helped someone heal. He also felt pumped up and excited, especially because now he was working with his brother, and they could do astounding things together.

Dr. Shepherd looked at the healthy man on screen in wonder. "It's incredible." She turned to Alex and Andy. "You willing to try some other tests tomorrow?"

"Long as we don't hurt anyone," Alex assured her, "I'm down. What about you, Andy?"

Andy's eyebrows shot up. "Down?"

Alex chuckled. "It's another way to say yes."

"Oh. You say strange things, Big Brother."

"It's called slang, Andy," Colonel Walker said. "You'll catch on quickly, I'm sure. So, can we count on your cooperation tomorrow?"

Andy nodded.

The only thing that worried Alex was when Davalos and Avila ended their secret conversation to say goodbye, and they were both smiling. It was a mysterious smile that Alex didn't like.

Not one bit.

CHAPTER SEVEN

DO YOU THINK THEY'RE ON TO ME?

ROY ENJOYED DINNER AT THE colonel's house that night, even though he could barely lift fork to mouth because every muscle in his body ached from the intense workout Java put him through in the fitness center. Java had promised "to make a man out of you," whatever that meant. Roy shuddered with fear that his friend had discovered his secret, but if the other boy did know, he never said so. He just wanted to make Roy strong like him, and to show off his smarts in the one area he was good at.

Unfortunately, Carlos was the same way. The two boys, both muscular and strong, competed to see who could push the others harder. As a result, Izzy sat slumped at the table, eating his food with slow deliberation and not even mumbling, let alone his usual mile-a-minute yammering. Jorge, who had clearly enjoyed being Carlos's sidekick, hadn't drawn a single red V—a compulsive habit based on an old TV show—since they finished their workout, so Roy knew he was tired too.

If this is what getting healthy means, somebody goofed, he thought as he shoveled another mouthful of Amanda's amazing spaghetti into his mouth. And yes, she'd insisted they call her Amanda and not Mrs. Walker. The house had two floors, like his own back in Hawthorne, with one bedroom downstairs and two upstairs. It was new and clean, not old and messy like his.

From the moment the colonel ushered the boys inside, Amanda had swept them up into a cocoon of mothering that warmed Roy's heart in a way he thought he'd forgotten. Deep down, he still yearned for his long dead mom, and it wasn't often he experienced the sensations that had been so commonplace when she was alive. Amanda had shown them to their rooms and presented an array of clothing they could wear. Sure, it was all Air Force stuff—some uniform pieces and some she'd described as "Off-duty attire,"—and much of the stuff didn't fit just right. But when Roy donned the camo pants and blue polo displaying Air Force wings, he felt important somehow, even though he hadn't accomplished anything. All the boys wore mixtures of uniform and off-duty garments while Amanda put their own clothes into the washer.

The colonel spoke little about the tests done that afternoon except to say they were successful. Roy pumped Alex for details while they were changing clothes, but Andy was also in the room and all Roy could get out of them was that they could heal and shift using people who weren't in the same room with them. Roy found that interesting, but what disturbed him, and continued to trouble him as he washed his spaghetti down with a glass of water, was how different Alex and Andy seemed—not as individuals, but as brothers. They appeared closer, somehow, more joined at the hip, more like…like Alex had once been with *him*.

Andy still wasn't sociable and didn't speak but a few words throughout the meal, but it was the looks he exchanged with Alex, and the ones Alex shot back at him, that showed Roy so much more than could've been said with words. He didn't want to be jealous, and he hated himself even for thinking that way, and yet his love for Alex, his intense need for the other boy kept intruding. He knew Alex could never love him the way he wanted, but Roy still craved the closeness they'd always shared. Would Alex transfer that closeness to Andy and leave *him* behind?

His thoughts were interrupted by the sensation of being watched. He glanced across the table and found Andy staring at him with deep curiosity. The boy's eyes bore into him so deeply that Roy blushed and looked down at his food. That was another problem he must confront. Andy was every bit as beautiful as Alex, maybe even more so with his long blond hair—a feature he loved in other boys—and Roy was drawn to Andy in ways that made him squirm with discomfort.

Was it possible Andy was gay? He hadn't even known what girls were until they told him at the safe house. Could twins be different like that? Andy was too distant—too unplugged into his feelings to be someone Roy could love, but that was right now. In the future, who knew what might develop?

He forced these uncomfortable thoughts aside to focus on Amanda, who was doing most of the talking since the boys were wiped out from their long day.

"—so happy to have kids in the house," she was saying, her voice strong yet bubbly. "This being such a top-secret base and all, we never get visitors. Feel free to watch TV after dinner, if you want. We also have some board games."

"Any video games?" That was Izzy, his tongue hanging from his mouth.

She smiled. "Sorry, no, Israel. The Colonel gave those up some years back."

Izzy's face lit up. "You was a gamer?"

The colonel offered a wan smile. "In my youth, prior to taking command of this base. I was a PS2 man back then."

"Wicked." That was Alex, who made eye contact with Roy and grinned.

Roy returned the grin, recalling their many afternoons glued to his system at home, battling each other and feeling pure contentment. He missed those days....

"Aww, man," Izzy groaned at the colonel. "PS2 is so old school."

The colonel and Amanda both laughed.

After dinner, they all gathered in the small but tidy living room. A flat screen TV was mounted to the wall above a stereo cabinet housing a Blu-ray player and surround system. Roy didn't know the size of the screen, but it looked maybe four feet across. They watched *The Avengers* movie, but the only ones with much energy to focus were Java and Carlos. Roy winced with pain every time he moved his arms or picked anything up, and he saw the others were feeling just as bad. The worst part was, Java and Carlos promised to hit them even harder the next day! Roy didn't think his body could handle any more.

His eyes drifted from the scene in the movie where the Avenger guys and Nick Fury were arguing with each other about what was right and wrong, to where Andy sat on the floor beside Alex's wheelchair, resting his head up against it. He wanted to be with the twins in the lab tomorrow. He knew it was selfish, but he didn't want them getting any closer to each other without him being part of it too. Hopefully Alex would allow him to be there.

By the time the movie ended, even Java said he needed to "knock out," so he, Carlos, Izzy, and Jorge trudged up the carpeted stairs to the second floor. Amanda had brought in two sets of bunk beds for the spare bedroom upstairs and two sets for the first-floor bedroom at the back of the house. That room would house Alex, Andy, and Roy. Amanda was one of the nicest people Roy had ever met. But also, from what Alex had told Roy, she was super tough and not to be messed with. Roy had no plans to do so.

Changing for bed proved awkward because they had no pajamas to wear, and Andy seemed immune to the presence of others as he pulled off all his clothes and tossed them on the floor. Fortunately, he left his boxers on, but Roy couldn't help but stare at the other boy's slim, pale torso and long legs. Andy didn't have much of a six-pack, but the lines were there, waiting for a workout to make them more prominent, and his pure white skin was proof he'd never been outside since he'd been stolen as a toddler.

Andy didn't notice Roy's gawking expression, but Alex did. Roy felt eyes on him and turned to find his best friend gazing at him from the lower bunk he'd slid into. Blushing, Roy decided to keep his own clothes on and climbed up the ladder to the bed above Alex. Andy eyed them both a moment before padding barefoot to the other set of beds and sliding into the bottom bunk.

Still embarrassed, Roy realized that the lights were on.

"I'll get the lights," he announced and clambered down the ladder. Forcing himself not to look at Andy, he hurried to the switch next to the door and flicked it down, filling the room with darkness. Then he moved back to his bed. As he started up the ladder, he heard Alex's voice, soft and reassuring.

"It's okay, Roy."

Burning again with shame, he scrambled into his bed and pulled the comforter up and over him. He brooded beneath the darkness, thinking of the twins and wondering if he had a future with either one of them.

***

Allison grew weary of playing online video games. Her mind could not shut out Alex and what might be happening to him. Their three guests—Father Pat, Nathan, and Dane—were in her dad's office, probably still pacing like they'd been when she left an hour ago. Father Pat and her dad had concluded that the presence of that substitute teacher in the group photos meant they were, for certain, the ones who had held Alex's brother for so long and who so desperately sought control of both boys.

It was after eleven o'clock, but she doubted any of them would get much sleep that night, not while her dad searched through his security camera software for any sign of the boys. She stood up from her desk and stretched, unconsciously rubbing her bald head and actually feeling the faintest bit of stubble. She had wigs to wear, but they were itchy, and she would only wear one if she went out somewhere. Right now, the only place she wanted to go was downstairs to her father's office.

As expected, she found the men pacing, while her dad and Martin scoured image after image. It was painstaking work, she knew, because ShawTech had installed security cameras on almost every U.S. military base in the world.

Allison padded across the vast office and sat beside her father in a luxurious, soft leather desk chair. "Nothing yet?"

He shook his head, but his eyes remained focused on the monitor before him.

She studied the screen. Images flashed past almost as rapidly as in a video game, some showing the interiors of military bases, others the exteriors. She saw men and women in uniform engaged in various tasks or just relaxing in the mess hall or exercising in the fitness centers. Soldiers repaired planes and jeeps. They engaged in target practice and weapons drills. Nowhere did she see anything that looked remotely like a wheelchair—or even kids in general.

"Uh, boss," Martin broke the silence. "I got something."

Heart suddenly hammering, Allison almost jumped from her chair as her dad whipped his head around to examine Martin's monitor.

"Which base?"

"Groom Lake," Martin replied, rolling his chair aside so Shaw could move in for a closer look.

Allison stood behind her dad, flanked by Nathan and Dane, who were looking over her shoulders at the monitor.

"I scoured this base," Shaw mumbled. "First place I looked."

"Yeah, but remember they didn't allow any cameras inside, only around the perimeter."

"True." Shaw leaned in and squinted at the screen.

Allison gripped that back of his chair and leaned in as close as she dared, focusing on the monitor. She saw a large tarmac under bright sunlight. There were helicopters visible, as well as parts of hangars and other large buildings. Her dad tapped a few keys and suddenly a group of people appeared in one corner of the screen heading for a sizable building set apart from all the others. He tapped more keys, zooming in on them. She gasped. It was a group of boys following a young soldier and an older man who looked high in rank, based on the bars she saw on his uniform. And beside the older man was a shaggy-haired blond boy in a wheelchair.

Dane exclaimed, "There's Alex!"

Shaw studied the screen, ignoring Dane's outburst. "Good work, Martin."

Shaw sat back and ran fingers over his beard stubble. The fact that he hadn't shaved since their return told Allison how stressed he felt.

"That place is the most secure base in the country," Martin offered, studying Shaw with care. "Any idea how we get in?"

Shaw leaned away from the monitor and considered the matter. "Even my contacts can't get me in that front door."

"Then we go in the back." That was Dane again, his face etched with determination.

Shaw glanced over at him. "Son, this base is beyond classified. You may have heard it referred to as Area 51."

The blank expression on Dane's face proved he had not.

"The alien place?" That was Nathan this time.

Dane swung around to face him. "You heard of this place before, Pop?"

"Only from TV. Roy and me watched some stuff about aliens before." He faced Shaw, looking a bit sheepish. "They, uh, really got alien bodies there?"

"No," replied Shaw. "The alien angle is just a cover."

"What *do* they have there, Dad?" Allison waited expectantly as her father considered how best to answer.

"No one knows for certain. Bioengineering is the primary suspicion, especially after what happened three years ago."

"What happened then?" Dane again. He looked pumped up and ready for action.

Again, Shaw paused before answering. "Let's just say that a bio-engineered weapon did considerable damage in downtown LA. On the plus side, it did take out a human trafficking ring in the process. Word I got was this weapon came from Groom Lake."

Allison could tell that neither Dane nor Nathan understood much of what her dad said, and she suspected they might having learning disabilities like Alex. She decided to help them out. "Do you mean they try to, like, mix animals with humans or something?"

"Perhaps. Other than that one unplanned incident, we have no intel on what they're doing."

Now Dane seemed to catch on. "What the hell do they want with Alex?"

"I suspect," Shaw went on with surprising patience, "they want to test the twins to determine the extent of their power. We saw a glimpse of what the boys can do—as you well know, Nathan, seeing as how they brought your other son back to life."

Nathan nodded, his weathered face looking grim at the remembrance.

"Well, boss," Martin interjected. "Any thoughts on how to breach their security?"

Before Shaw could reply, Dane jumped in again. "I'm going with you. They got my brother, and I'm gonna help get him out."

"Me too, Mr. Shaw," Nathan added. "We been through too much together to sit this one out."

Allison expected her dad to immediately object, but he didn't. He sat and stared at the monitor again, at the frozen image of Alex.

The silence in the room seemed thick as fog.

"Ordinarily, I'd say no one could go but Martin and a few hand-picked men—"

Dane flinched. "But—"

"—however," Shaw continued, "a military operation would be ineffective against the military. We need a more creative approach." He paused another moment, and then his eyes lit up with an idea. He swiveled the chair around and faced Allison. "Remember that play you performed in last semester?"

Allison was mystified. That was the last thing she expected him to say. "Yeah, so?"

"You're a gifted actress."

She blushed, despite the seriousness of the moment. "Thanks, Dad. But what—"

He took her hand in his, cutting her off. "Are you ready for the role of a lifetime?"

She tilted her head, eyebrows furrowed in confusion.

***

Alex woke with a start. Had he been dreaming? He didn't know. What time was it anyway? The room was bathed in darkness. He heard Roy's even breathing above him and Andy's from the bed up against the far wall.

He sat up and listened. He heard voices coming from down the hall. One was unmistakably Colonel Walker. But the other was…a kid? He couldn't tell whether it was a boy or girl because whoever it was spoke quietly. Consumed with curiosity, Alex threw back his comforter and slid off the bed into his wheelchair. Moving with caution to not wake the others, he rolled toward the door. Fortunately, he had left all his clothes on so there was no need to waste time getting dressed.

As he eased out into the hallway, he saw light up ahead, a dim light, coming from around the corner in the living room. The voices grew louder as his wheels inched their way along the thick carpet.

A boy! The other voice was a boy.

How was that possible? Hadn't Colonel Walker and Amanda told them they were the only kids on this base?

Alex stopped halfway down the hall and listened, not fully understanding what he heard.

The boy was saying, "—couldn't hear everything they said when they went over to the corner. They were too far from my hiding place." It was a young voice, Alex noted, not deep like his or Andy's, so probably younger than him.

"Yes, I noticed they picked that spot as far from the air conditioning duct as possible."

"Do you think they're onto me?"

"With Davalos, who knows? He's the most paranoid individual I know."

Alex recalled Davalos taking Avila off to that corner of the lab so they could talk in private. But who was this boy?

"Colonel," the boy said, his young voice tinged with hope. "Can't I please meet these boys? I'm bored with only grownups."

"William, you know you're not like other kids."

The boy sighed, and it sounded heavy with sadness. "Of course, I know that, sir. I get reminded every day, especially by Davalos!" The anger in his voice was palpable. "I apologize, sir. You're my commanding officer. I have no right to speak to you in that way."

Commanding officer? This kid was a soldier?

"No offense taken, William," Colonel Walker assured him in that easy tone he always employed. "But ever since the Los Angeles incident, I've had to do everything in my power to make sure they didn't destroy you."

The boy gasped in shock. "Is that true? You never told me."

"I didn't want to hurt you any more than you already were."

"Do they still…?"

"No." Colonel Walker sounded positive. "The joint chiefs have seen your progress over the past three years. You *will* get a mission one day."

"One day." The boy sounded as glum as Alex had ever heard any child.

Suddenly, Alex felt a hand on his shoulder and spun around. Roy clamped a hand over his mouth to keep him from calling out and Alex relaxed upon seeing his best friend.

"What's going on?" Roy mouthed.

Alex shrugged and pointed to the light at the end of the hall.

"Please, Colonel," the boy's voice pleaded. "I really want to meet Alex."

Alex flinched and listened more intently.

"Why him, in particular?"

There was a pause. "I think it's the way he cured those people. And he has a kind face. Maybe he…?"

"Maybe he what?"

"Maybe he can, you know, help me feel better about, well, being me."

There was a long moment of silence. Alex glanced at Roy, pressed up against him, breathing on hold.

"Perhaps you're right, William," Colonel Walker finally said. "As you pointed out, Davalos might already suspect you're spying on him. So let's bring you out in the open. That way, you won't miss anything."

"Really?"

The excitement in the boy's voice touched Alex's heart. There was so much need in that voice, desperation almost.

"Really. We still don't have access to Davalos's secret lab, which doesn't concern me too much. That's between him and the Pentagon. I'm only concerned with Alex and Andy and whether or not Davalos plans to include them in his secret experiments."

"What do you want me to do?"

"Report to the lab at 08:00 tomorrow. As we always do, I'll arrange with Dr. Shepherd to introduce you as her nephew who's helping out as a lab assistant. She can assign you some menial tasks that will allow you to focus on the tests Alex and Andy are subjected to. I'll tell Davalos I authorized your presence. He won't let on who you really are."

"But he'll know I'm there to spy on him."

"Of course he will. But you're an outstanding actor. No one else will suspect that. Now, it's my intention to never let either of those boys out of my sight. But if by some chance Davalos gets either or both away from me, you track them and report back at once."

"Yes, sir." The boy sounded more energized and filled with purpose. "This sounds like a real mission."

"It is, William. You are to protect those boys no matter what happens to me, understand?"

"Yes, sir."

"Good. Now return to your quarters. I'll see you at 08:00."

"Yes, Colonel."

Alex couldn't see what was happening at the end of the hallway, but he spotted a shadow move in the light and had a feeling it was the boy saluting.

"Colonel?"

"Yes?"

"Thank you."

"You're welcome."

Alex heard quiet footsteps against the squeaky floorboards of the entry hall and then silence. A moment later, the light went off, plunging the hallway into near total darkness. He waited until he was sure he heard the colonel climb the stairs to the second floor before facing Roy in the gloom.

Roy's pallid face floated so close to his they might have kissed. Recalling the one time they did kiss filled Alex with peace, not embarrassment.

"Any idea what that all meant?" Roy's whisper was filled with uncertainty.

"Not much," Alex whispered back, trying to recall the conversation as best he could. "But I get that Colonel Walker don't like that Davalos guy any more 'n I do. I guess I'll find out more tomorrow when I meet that kid. He sounded younger than us. What's he doing here?"

The conversation stalled as Alex considered the possibilities of a child soldier on this base.

"Alex, can you please ask the colonel if I can go with you tomorrow?"

Alex searched for Roy's eyes in the blackness. He detected fear in his voice. "Why?"

"Why? Alex, I'm your best friend, man. I get scared shitless they might hurt you."

"And I'm scared they might hurt *you*."

"Huh?"

"What if I don't wanna do some test Davalos gots in mind for me? He might use you to force me."

A moment of heavy stillness descended on them. Obviously, Roy hadn't considered this possibility.

"The colonel won't let that happen."

"He might not be able to stop it if them guys above him, them joint chiefs or whoever they are, order him to allow it," Alex whispered, the very thought of Roy being tortured or worse ripping into his gut like a knife. "Please, stay with the other guys. I don't wanna hafta worry about you."

Alex held his breath through another long pause, hoping Roy would agree. After what seemed like forever, Roy sighed.

"Okay, Alex, if that's what you want." His voice sounded sad, like he felt he was losing something important to him.

Alex noted the tone, but his mind had already moved on to other matters. "Thanks, man. Let's go back to bed."

Roy turned and led the way back to their room.

CHAPTER EIGHT

I'M GOING TO SHIFT IT INTO YOU

ALEX COULD HARDLY LOOK AT Roy the next morning during breakfast for fear of giving away what they'd overheard the night before. Colonel Walker had left early, Amanda told them, but would return to escort them all to where they would spend the morning. Alex knew where the colonel had gone, to the lab to meet that boy and Dr. Shepherd.

Amanda served delicious pancakes flavored with cherry extract, lots of syrup and whipped cream, and strawberries on the side. She bubbled over with joy at having the boys to cook for and encouraged them to "eat hearty, especially if you're going back to the fitness center."

Java grinned. "Hell, yeah."

Carlos raised a large fist and they bumped. Their mutual love of weight lifting and showing off their muscles had bonded them in ways that surprised Alex, but Izzy and Roy groaned at the prospect of more exercise. Jorge, on the other hand, looked happier than Alex could ever recall seeing him. Jorge was an only child, so maybe that's why Carlos paying attention to him meant so much.

Whatever the reason, Jorge grinned and repeated, "Hell, yeah!"

Carlos laughed and did the fist bump with the excited boy.

Well, I'm glad they're having fun, Alex thought, as he pushed back his plate and forced down a burp.

Roy had said his entire body burned with pain when he'd risen from bed that morning and, even after taking a warm shower, commented to Alex, "Now I know what it's like to get run down by a big-ass truck."

Alex smiled, though his mind was on the lab and the mysterious boy he would meet, a boy younger than himself who acted like a soldier. It didn't make any sense.

Andy didn't converse with anyone, which was typical, but his gaze flicked continuously between Alex and Roy, as though he was wondering about them. Could he know that they'd snuck out to listen in on the colonel the night before? Had he even heard some of it himself? Alex didn't know how he could find out, so he decided not to bring it up at all.

"Thank you, Amanda, for the amazing food," Alex gushed, offering the lady a huge smile. "It was sick."

She chuckled and reached for his plate. "Hopefully, it won't *make* you sick."

All the boys laughed at that and carried their plates to the sink. Surprising Alex, Andy offered to help wash the dishes. Amanda was delighted. His offer prompted Alex to join in and then the others too. Alex observed Andy handing clean plates to Amanda, who passed them around to the boys to be dried. Andy wasn't smiling, exactly, but Alex felt his contentment, as though this was the happiest he'd been since they'd met.

Once the dishes were cleaned and dried, they all set off to brush their teeth. Amanda had found new toothbrushes for each of them and some toothpaste. Alex had to admit it felt kind of nice to have a mother-figure fussing over him, especially after living with Jane and his other terrible foster parents over the years. He felt secure in a way he couldn't remember feeling since he was four.

***

Allison understood her part well. She would use the hours during the drive to Nevada to think about her "character" and rehearse what she would say. She had to be convincing, her father had emphasized that over and over. If she wasn't, the entire plan would fail, and it was a pretty sketchy plan to begin with, Shaw had admitted to the team. But it was the best he could come up with and, even if they all were arrested afterward, they would at least have verified the safety of the kidnapped boys, or lack thereof. And, Shaw pointed out to the group, he had the best lawyers that money could buy.

They gathered in his study, reviewing the plan one more time before departure. Allison sat twirling around her finger strands of the long-haired wig she would wear to play her part.

The base was less than a five-hour drive, and they couldn't arrive until well after dark if the plan were to have any chance of success. All the men were dressed in black, including black beanies, making them look like a group of ninjas. Father Pat fidgeted, clearly nervous, but Nathan and Dane seemed gung-ho to leave, like they snuck into top-secret military bases all the time. Martin and two of her dad's bodyguards would accompany them on the mission.

Shaw had been vague about what they would actually do once they gained entry to the base. He admitted smuggling the boys out was a long shot, but thought it possible that a diversion might keep the base personnel occupied while they made their escape. Allison's job, as her dad had made crystal clear, was to pinpoint the location of the boys and signal him—assuming, of course, that she gained access to the base.

He was just finishing his final review. "Any questions?"

No one spoke or raised a hand.

"Last chance to change your mind." That was directed at Father Pat, Nathan, and Dane.

"Hell no," Dane spat, holding his black face mask in a tight fist. "I'm gettin' my little brother back."

Nathan and Father Pat exchanged a look of nervous agreement.

"We're all in, Mr. Shaw," Nathan said, his voice firm with conviction.

"What if she gets there first, you know, the boys' teacher?" Father Pat's voice sounded a bit shaky.

Shaw fixed his gaze on the priest. "We cross that bridge when we come to it. The vehicles are being loaded as we speak. We depart at four." He turned to face Allison, reaching out and placing both hands on her shoulders. The look of concern in his alert brown eyes touched her deeply.

"I'll be fine, Dad," she assured him. "They're not gonna shoot a girl my age."

"No, they won't. Let's just hope they believe you."

Allison smirked, filled with confidence and bravado. "I'm gonna win an Oscar, Dad."

He chuckled and pulled her into a hug.

***

Colonel Walker returned at nine, according to the digital clock in the kitchen, and Alex was itching to go. Not because he longed for the tests he'd have to do, but he desperately sought answers to the mysteries he was uncovering. Andy greeted the colonel politely but said nothing more. Roy tossed Alex a pleading glance as Java was pumping them up for "another hard-ass workout," but Alex shook his head. He felt safer with Roy out of the lab building.

The same young soldier from the previous day had accompanied the colonel and led the other boys out of the house in the direction of the fitness center. Then, guided by Colonel Walker, Alex and Andy headed out across the tarmac toward that distant unmarked building. The sun was high in the sky, and the outside temperature was already warm. After the others were out of earshot, Colonel Walker faced the twins.

"Ready, boys?"

Andy glanced at Alex, taking his cues from him. Alex nodded.

"You know, you don't have to do any of these tests. I'll back you up on that."

Alex squinted up at him beneath the bright sunlight. "How much do you know about the Healer, Colonel?"

Colonel Walker looked surprised by the question. "I read Davalos's report. The consensus among most religious traditions, especially Christianity, is that the Healer will be a positive force, helping people stay in touch with their better selves."

'Ms. G said she could make me and Andy spin the whole world on the internet and make them bad."

The colonel frowned. "Well, she's dead, so far as we know."

"Our mom said me and Andy have Indian blood from her dad's side." He glanced at Andy for confirmation, but his brother just shrugged.

"Uncle never told me that in my dreams," Andy said.

"Anyway," Alex went on, "they said a long time ago that the Healer would be a Great Peacemaker or a Great Destroyer. I been called a dummy my whole life, but I know what those words mean."

"It might be just a legend, Alex," Colonel Walker said, studying him.

"Maybe, but I don't wanna destroy anything or hurt anyone. I know

Mr. Davalos and Dr. Avila are hiding something, but you're not and Dr. Shepherd isn't either. I wanna do these tests, Colonel, because I need to know everything I can do, and what me and Andy can do together. That's the only way I can control what I am. Do you understand?"

Colonel Walker offered him a warm smile and placed one hand on his shoulder. "Perfectly. And I have to say you're one of the smartest kids I've ever met."

Alex couldn't help but smile at that. He turned to Andy, who had remained silent during most of the conversation. "Do you understand, Andy?"

"Yes. I also want to know what we can do."

When he said nothing more, Alex said to the colonel, "Can we go now?"

"Of course." He suddenly seemed to recall something. "By the way, you'll meet someone new today. I misspoke when I told you there were no other kids on base. Dr. Shepherd has an orphaned nephew living with her. He's thirteen and will be assisting her in the lab from now on. Are you comfortable with that?"

Alex eyed Andy, studying his face for signs he already knew about the boy, but his brother offered no clue whatsoever. Knowing Andy would go along with whatever he decided, Alex faced Colonel Walker. "I think it's cool, having a new kid to hang out with."

"Good."

As Alex pressed his way across the vast tarmac, he scanned the sparseness of the desert surrounding the base. He noticed cameras posted at intervals atop the chain-link fence running along the edges of the base. The cameras appeared to rotate almost all the way around, but mainly pointed outward at the empty landscape, not inward at the base buildings. He wondered what other experiments were being done here besides those involving him and Andy.

Some of the airmen working on planes or helicopters stopped to observe the small procession working its way toward the rear of the base. Alex figured they weren't used to seeing kids on the base, or maybe they'd just never seen a kid in a wheelchair. He got those kinds of looks *all* the time.

The lab appeared exactly the same as it had yesterday, except only Dr.

Shepherd and the boy were present. Alex decided Colonel Walker must've planned it this way so he could introduce the younger boy before Avila and Davalos arrived.

The boy could barely contain his excitement upon seeing them, bouncing slightly on his heels, but clearly trying hard to not show any emotion on his face. The colonel had said he was thirteen and he was shorter than Andy, but wider in the shoulders, more like Java, like maybe he worked out a lot. What struck Alex was the blond hair and blue eyes, which made him look like he could be his and Andy's younger brother. The white-blond hair was somewhere between the twins in length, but long enough to be tied back into a short ponytail. His features were soft, with no angles at all, no doubt due to his age. He wore a white lab coat over a blue Air Force tee shirt, sweat pants, and Converse sneakers. He bounded forward to meet them.

"Boys," Colonel Walker said, "this is William. William, meet Alex and Andy."

William stuck out his hand with great eagerness. Alex shook at once, but Andy responded more slowly, scrutinizing the other boy's face. He finally shook, commenting, "You look like us."

William grinned, having obviously noticed the same thing. "We could almost be brothers."

Andy frowned at that, but Alex heard the intense need in William's voice. There was pain beneath those words, so he offered the best smile he could manage. "Good to meet you, William."

Dr. Shepherd approached and offered a congenial smile. "Did Colonel Walker take good care of you boys?"

Alex nodded. "Amanda gave us so much food I almost couldn't eat it all."

"Just what teenage boys need." She looked pleased to see them. But her smile faltered a moment later when in walked Davalos and Dr. Avila. They were talking about something but stopped abruptly upon spotting William standing with the twins.

Colonel Walker was obviously prepared. "Good morning Mr. Davalos, Dr. Avila. As you can see, I've authorized William to assist with these tests. I felt it would help with his socialization and might put the twins more at ease, having another adolescent present. I trust you don't have any objection."

Alex plainly saw the anger on Davalos's hard face. The man was practically gritting his teeth, clearly caught off-guard. He *wanted* to object, but he didn't want to say anything in front of the kids.

"Whatever you think best, Colonel, of course. It's your base."

Avila didn't look quite as perturbed as Davalos, but it was obvious he would've preferred William not be present.

Just who *was* William, anyway? Alex determined to find that out first chance he got.

William looked eager to talk to them, but Dr. Shepherd sent him off to one side of the lab to work on a lone computer. Having overheard the late-night conversation, Alex already knew William was there to spy, not work. The boy complied at once, like he was used to taking orders.

The two doctors put Alex and Andy through tasks similar to those they did the day before. Alex cured several people, gasping for breath with the third one, who'd suffered a punctured lung. Then Andy joined him to shift several ailments, a severe case of the flu being the worst, from a person on one screen to someone on another. The doctors and Davalos seemed stunned by the positive results, which confused Alex because it was exactly the same tests they'd successfully completed yesterday. Alex insisted on healing those he made sick, which the doctors encouraged.

Finally, after healing the most recent person they'd made sick, Alex spoke up. "I don't wanna be rude, but we showed you this stuff yesterday. Aren't we gonna do nothing new?"

Andy nodded his agreement, looking both bored and frustrated with the morning so far. Alex felt eyes fixed on him and glanced over to find William staring, clearly awaiting an answer from the adults.

"You're not doing the same tests as yesterday, Alex," Avila said, the excitement in his voice raising it to a fever pitch. He pointed at the monitors. "Yesterday, the people you worked on were all within this complex, but not today." He pointed to the first two people Alex and Andy had been tested on. "These two are in a military van two miles from here."

Alex gasped. Two miles? That sounded far. He glanced at Andy, who actually displayed surprise on his soft, pale face.

"The next two you worked on," Avila continued, pointing at two more monitors, "are in a city one hundred miles from here."

Alex's jaw dropped open in astonishment. Even Andy gasped with surprise.

"These last two are in the city of Los Angeles," Avila said, pointing and grinning. "That's two-hundred sixty miles away."

Colonel Walker had left his perch by now and approached, clearly captivated by the results. "Very impressive, Doctors. Your idea Davalos?"

Davalos stood off to one side, eyeing the proceedings with glee. "Indeed it was, and we have one more test scheduled for this morning."

This time, Dr. Shepherd piped up. "Our goal is to find out just how far the boys can reach with their…power. Our theory is that as long as they can see the target individual, there may be no limit in terms of distance."

"That's why our next test," Avila said, eyes glittering with elation, "involves an astronaut aboard the International Space Station."

The colonel's mouth dropped open in stunned disbelief and Alex had never seen him look so astonished.

Avila went on, "One of the astronauts has developed a fever. Down here, that's not a problem, but up there in space it can be serious."

Alex didn't know a lot about space. "Where in space?"

"You've heard of the International Space Station?"

Alex shrugged, not sure if he'd heard about it or not.

Fortunately, Colonel Walker came to his rescue. "No reason you should have, Alex. It's a giant laboratory orbiting the earth. Astronauts conduct experiments up there to see how those experiments test out in space, as opposed to down here, because there's no air or gravity in space."

"Oh. Thanks for explaining." He eyed Andy, whose expression didn't give away whether he'd already known this or not.

"As I was saying," Avila continued, sounding cross that he'd been interrupted, "a fever up there can be devastating, so we've been given permission by NASA to try and help the man. This time, we'd like Andy to shift the cold from the man into Alex, and then Alex, you purge yourself."

"Purge?" Alex knew that was a movie title, but…

"Spin it away, as you say," Avila clarified, his lined face glowing with anticipation.

Colonel Walker looked concerned. "Why not have Alex simply pull the cold from the astronaut directly?"

"At the moment, he's sleeping," Avila said, though the tone of his voice sounded odd to Alex, as though this wasn't entirely the truth. "We felt it would be better for Andy to talk the virus out of him as quickly as possible before it can escalate to something more serious."

The colonel studied him with guarded suspicion and then turned to Alex and Andy. "How do you boys feel about this? Andy, have you ever shifted something into Alex?"

Andy shook his head. "I never thought about that."

"Alex, what are your thoughts?"

Alex considered the situation. He wanted to help that man up in space. He always wanted to help people. "If it's just a fever, it should be easy."

"What if it's not?" Andy looked grave. "I'll be sick too, right, since we're combined?"

Alex saw the worry on his face, even through his usual mask of indifference. "I guess, but I'm willing to try if you are."

Andy paused a moment and then stared at Davalos, his cobalt eyes penetrating in their intensity. "If Alex can't spin whatever it is, I'm going to shift it into you. Agreed?"

Davalos flinched but maintained his composure. Colonel Walker looked pleased with this arrangement. Davalos glanced at Avila, though the doctor offered no opinion. Neither did Dr. Shepherd, who stood and awaited his answer.

Davalos made momentary eye contact with Andy. "Agreed." Then he looked away, as though Andy's gaze was too strong for him.

There was no movement for a long moment, and Alex felt like time had stopped. He glanced over at William and found the other boy watching the proceedings with avid interest while also typing on his computer keyboard.

Dr. Shepherd stepped up to Dr. Avila. "Are you ready, Doctor?"

"Yes." Avila strode to the bank of computer keyboards and tapped some keys. A moment later, two of the monitors sprang to life. On one was an older military guy with lots of stars and bars on his shirt, sitting in an office. The wall behind him was hung with pictures showing him shaking hands with people Alex figured were important.

The other guy was younger and had black hair. He wore a white shirt with the sleeves rolled up and a blue tie. Lots of people moved around behind him, and lights blinked and flashed on pieces of equipment. The younger guy looked stressed out. Alex could practically feel his unease through the glass of the monitor. The military guy looked as indifferent as Andy.

Davalos stepped forward and flipped a switch. "General, the boys have agreed to the attempt."

The General said, "Excellent. I defer you to Mr. Hastings over at Houston Space Center."

The other man looked so relieved Alex thought he might faint. He leaned in closer to the camera and said, "Thank you, Mr. Davalos, and I want to thank the two boys." His voice sounded breathless, like he'd just come in from running. His fear filled Alex's stomach with dread.

Davalos waved them over. Andy led the way, and Alex wheeled after him. They stopped before the monitor and looked up at the man's tight, anxious face.

"Do you boys understand the situation?"

When Andy didn't respond, Alex said, "Yes, sir."

"Good. The astronaut, Lt. Kirby, is isolated in his room to prevent contamination. There is a camera in each of the sleeping quarters. What do you need me to do?"

Andy gazed up at the monitor. "I need to see the man."

This simple answer seemed to surprise Mr. Hastings, but he merely nodded. He looked off camera and pointed. A moment later, his face was replaced by that of a sleeping man. The man looked like he was in some kind of zipped-up sleeping bag that wrapped around his head so only his face was visible, but not his eyes because he wore a black mask over them.

"Can you get closer to his face?" Andy placed both hands on the console and leaned in toward the monitor.

The image on screen began to zoom in from showing the man's body to just his face.

"Stop there," Andy said, and the zoom ceased.

Alex could now plainly see beads of sweat on the sleeping man's fore-head and felt his sickness.

Andy grasped Alex's hand and the power swelled within his mind and body. Andy stared long and hard at the image of the sleeping Lt. Kirby. "Germs, to me."

Instantly, Alex felt himself aflame with hot, searing fire in his head as weakness assailed every muscle in his body. His vision blurred and he heard, "Germs, to Alex."

Now the heat became so intense, Alex felt like he would turn to ashes. His lungs, especially, felt like they were a raging inferno. What germ had that man caught? Alex fought to control it, to master the virus pulsing through him. He shuddered with chills and focused on containing the bug in his belly.

Andy leaned in to him. "Big Brother, can you control it?"

Alex didn't respond. He couldn't break his concentration. He'd never felt anything like this kind of illness before. Had the man caught some-thing in space that no one down here ever had? He trembled and shook, the fire in his head and lungs raging out of control.

"Big Brother!"

"Alex, can you hear me?" That was Colonel Walker, sounding wor-ried.

Another voice intruded, a boy's voice. "Fight, Alex. You can do this." William was by his side.

Alex pushed and squeezed the germ within him, his mind's eye crush-ing it into a little ball and preparing to eject it from his body. Little by little, he made it smaller and smaller, his fever diminishing. He heard Andy's voice again, shrill, and afraid.

"I'm shifting it now."

Alex muttered, "No, Andy. I…I got this."

And then he did have it. He had control. Squeezing with his mind, he crushed the germ into such tiny particles he knew it could no longer be seen by any device on earth. He demolished it and sent the remnants into nothingness, never to return.

Alex sighed and opened his eyes. He saw Andy, William, and Colo-nel Walker right in front of him. His body felt like Roy's must have after

Java's workout, like he'd been pounded by the Hulk. His forehead dripped with sweat.

Realizing he had slumped to one side in his chair, he righted himself. "That was a…tough one."

William patted him awkwardly on one shoulder. "I knew you could do it."

Alex was touched that this boy he'd only just met had been so concerned. "Thanks, William." He glanced at Andy, who had resumed his poker face and now stared at him with intense curiosity.

"Was that fever as bad as it felt to me?"

Alex offered a wan smile. "Worse."

That made Andy grin, slightly, and the brothers released their hold on each other.

Davalos approached, looking quite pleased with himself. "You boys trust me now?"

Alex exchanged a quick glance with Colonel Walker, before shrugging.

The colonel faced Davalos. "What was *really* wrong with Lt. Kirby?"

"A space contagion he picked up outside the station. Nothing we've ever seen before."

The colonel's face flushed red with anger. "And you were willing to risk—"

"It was my call, Colonel."

Everyone gazed up at the monitors again. It was the general who had spoken.

"I gave the order when Mr. Davalos assured me there would be no danger to the boys."

"With all due respect, General Lewis, he didn't know that." Colonel Walker looked like he wanted to strangle Davalos.

"Nonetheless, Colonel, the mission appears to have succeeded. Mr. Hastings, what's the report from ISS?"

Hastings had returned to the other screen and was listening in on something over his headset that no one in the lab could hear. His tense expression melted into a grin.

"He's all right now. Temperature normal, no symptoms whatsoever."

His eyes filled with deep admiration. "You boys are a miracle. On behalf of everyone here at NASA, I can't thank you enough!"

The boys said nothing, so Davalos spoke up. "We're glad the operation was a success, Mr. Hastings. Let me know if we can be of further assistance."

"Will do, Mr. Davalos. And thank you, General Lewis."

He signed off and his screen went blank.

General Lewis said, "I want a full report, Mr. Davalos. I need to brief the rest of the Joint Chiefs."

"Absolutely, General," Davalos replied, his tone no longer haughty, but more like a servant. "Within the hour."

The general paused a moment, staring intently into the camera. "Thank you, Alex and Andy. You have the gratitude of the United States government." With that, he was gone, and his screen went blank.

Colonel Walker ignored the preening Davalos and faced the boys. "I'm proud of you both, especially you, Alex. That looked painful."

Alex reddened at the compliment but managed a smile. "A little."

"You were really brave," William said, his young voice filled with admiration.

Andy glowered and Alex realized he was feeling left out, like he hadn't done anything, so he grabbed his brother's arm and said, "Couldn't've done it without my bro."

Andy nodded his thanks and now William frowned, making Alex wonder what he'd said wrong.

"Well," Colonel Walker began, eyeing the doctors and Davalos, "what's next?"

The two men exchanged a look that made Alex uneasy. Despite the good deed he and Andy had just accomplished, he still didn't trust these two men. He glanced at Dr. Shepherd and noticed her fidgeting, as though she already knew what was "next."

Davalos stepped forward, shooing William away like he was an annoying mosquito. Alex grew angry, but he maintained control. William stepped back, and Dr. Shepherd told him to resume his duties. With great reluctance, the boy shuffled his way back to his corner. Davalos didn't give him a second look.

"Now that we know you can shift and spin, to use your words, across any distance on earth, we're most interested in how you… well, shift Death."

Colonel Walker gave a slight exhalation of surprise and Alex figured he was thinking about his men. "Davalos, I don't think—"

"Colonel, these orders come from the highest levels of government. We need to explore this arena."

The colonel's posture stiffened. "Only if the boys agree to your test."

"You blaming us for those guys that killed Martin?" That was Andy, and his tone was threatening as he glowered at Davalos.

Davalos took a slight step back. "No, Andy. My men were never supposed to harm anyone. They reported that when your friend Martin fired a real gun, they responded in kind per their training. It was a mistake."

Andy stared at him. "I don't believe in mistakes. People have always hurt me on purpose."

Alex felt he'd better intervene. "Andy, I known lotta bad people, but there be good ones too, who just, you know, make bad mistakes, I guess. He ain't lying about that."

Andy made eye contact with him, Alex surmised, to determine if he was telling the truth, and then offered a stiff nod, seemingly satisfied. He turned back to Davalos. "What do you wanna know?"

"The man who told us where to find you the first time, when you were still in your glass cage, said you made your teacher die, but they couldn't determine how you did it."

Andy smirked, looking happier than Alex had ever seen him. "A fly got into my cage. I shifted its death into Teacher."

All the adults looked surprised, but Alex already knew this, having "seen" it in his dream.

"That's it? A fly to kill a man?" Avila looked fascinated, while Shepherd pulled a face of displeasure.

Andy nodded. "I think Death is a small thing that can kill much bigger things."

"What about…" Davalos glanced at the attentively listening Colonel Walker. "The men the other night?"

Andy squinted in a dangerous way, but his voice remained calm. "When I join with Alex, I can do bigger shifts, like we're doing here." He offered a devilish grin. "Shall I try it out on you?"

Davalos lost his eager look. So did Avila, who took a step back, making Andy laugh.

"Andy, that's not funny." Alex glowered at him, but his brother merely shrugged, amused by his joke.

"No, Andy," Davalos began, clearing his throat, "you'll not try it out on us. But I do want to try some experiments in this arena."

Now the colonel looked concerned. "How do you propose we do that, Mr. Davalos? We can't go around killing people."

"No, but small animals are fair game, are they not?"

Alex recoiled. "I don't wanna kill animals. They didn't do nothing to me."

Davalos frowned. "Really, Alex, a few small—"

"No!" Alex hadn't meant to blurt it out like that, but he was serious. He didn't want to kill anything, even though he knew Andy didn't mind at all. In fact, Alex suspected that Andy kind of liked shifting Death.

"You know the agreement, Davalos," Colonel Walker said, sounding pleased. "Only tests both boys agree to."

Davalos looked annoyed, but he nodded. "We'll break for now and consider other ways to test that power," he said, glancing at Avila, who nodded, but also looked irritated.

Alex realized that Dr. Shepherd was no longer there and glanced around the lab. He found her in the far corner with William. They were talking quietly, making certain not to be overheard. Alex wondered what they were talking about.

"Well, boys," Colonel Walker said, "let's join your friends in the fitness center."

Andy furrowed his brows in confusion, but Alex liked that idea. He wanted—no needed—Roy's calming presence.

As they left the lab, Alex felt William staring at him and paused beside the boy and Dr. Shepherd. He *really* wanted to know more about this kid and what he was up to.

"Hope I see you at lunch, William. We can hang out then."

William grinned, obviously happy with that idea, making Alex feel bad for wanting to try and get information out of the boy. He returned the smile, following the colonel and Andy out the secure exit.

CHAPTER NINE

DEATH TO IT!

R OY FELT THAT IF HE lifted one more dumbbell, he'd collapse onto the hard rubber floor and never get up again. On the plus side, he'd never seen Java and Carlos so happy, and so united in a single cause—to kill the others while pretending to get them in shape.

The fitness center was huge, with a flat ceiling and lots of windows up high that made everything bright and shiny. It was much bigger than the tiny weight room he'd seen at Mark Twain High. His eyes nearly fell out of his head at all the machines and weights. There were many machines for running—and even some with moving stairs to climb. There were machines for every body part, not to mention bench presses and racks of shiny metal dumbbells.

Not being a work-out nut like Java, he'd never paid much attention to stuff like this, and now that Java had been making him do what felt like every single machine at least three times over the past two days, Roy never wanted to see another weight again!

That morning his muscles had felt so stiff he couldn't move without sharp, stabbing pain slicing through his body, but now they felt like jelly. Izzy felt the same way, but Jorge had practically glued himself to Carlos the moment they'd entered the place and still looked full of energy, despite following Carlos's brutal routine.

What made the whole experience especially negative for Roy was the absence of Alex. He so badly wanted to know what was going on with his best friend that he'd become absent-minded. Twice he forgot to clamp a ten-pound weight to the end of the curl bar and watched it slide off as he tried to lift it, once barely missing Java's foot as it bounced on the rubber floor.

"Shit, Roy, keep your head in the game."

Roy was too sweaty and drained to argue, so he just grunted and replaced the fallen weight. They'd been at it for almost two hours, and his shirt was plastered to his body with perspiration by the time the outside door opened and Alex entered, followed by Andy and the colonel.

Alex grinned as he rolled over the rubber floor between the machines to where Roy stood facing stacks of various sized metal plates. Andy trailed behind, long hair swishing back and forth like a horse's tail, gawking in wonder at everything around him.

"You're looking buffer already, Roy," Alex said, flexing one arm. "Those guns are bigger than mine."

Roy groaned but smiled anyway. "These water pistols are too tired to even move."

Alex laughed and Roy realized how much he missed that laugh. It had been way too long.

"This place is sick," Alex exclaimed, his eyes roving about the expansive room, taking in all the equipment. "Check it out, Andy."

Andy looked impressed. "What is it all for?"

Java stepped up to him and clapped a meaty hand to his shoulder. "To get buff, my man. And that's what I'm gonna do for you."

Andy tossed off a mystified look that made Roy smile. "Buff? What's that?"

Java rolled up his sleeves and flexed his impressive arm muscles. "This is buff. Feel these guns."

Andy eyed Alex, who looked amused. "Go ahead. He's like a rock."

Andy reached up and squeezed one of Java's upper arms, his expression shifting to one of shock. "Wow. It *is* like a rock." He lifted his own arm and flexed, feeling it with his other hand. "Mine feels like cotton."

Java laughed. "I can fix that real fast. Maybe you can even beat Alex at arm wrestling someday."

Andy tilted his head in confusion.

"I'll explain later, bro," Alex replied. "Let's work out." He looked up at the colonel, who seemed amused at their antics. "You gonna work out with us, Colonel?"

"I never miss a workout if I can help it," he replied, slipping off his jacket and hanging it on a nearby machine. "Let's do this."

Izzy, slumped over a bench like a sack of old potatoes, groaned in pain and glanced at Jorge, who sat beside him leaning up against a chest machine, grinning with delight. "Again?"

Carlos, looking swoll in his tight tee shirt, stepped over and dragged Izzy to his feet. "We're just starting, fool."

Jorge laughed and followed them to the dumbbell racks.

Roy had to admit, working out with Alex was much more fun than with Java. Alex didn't push him, but he did dare him to match what he could do. Since Andy took every one of Alex's dares, Roy felt he had to as well. The three of them ended up enjoying the experience, even though Roy knew he'd regret his showing off come morning.

The colonel taught Java and Carlos how to improve their bench press technique and impressed both boys with his strength. Izzy and Jorge had finally clambered onto some bicycles, which they pedaled like old ladies who could barely walk.

Roy didn't care, just so long as he had Alex. He didn't even ask what happened in the lab or why the boys finished so early. He figured he'd do that later, maybe during lunch. Andy wanted to feel Alex's arm muscle, and when he squeezed, proclaimed it harder than Java's. But then he surprised Roy by asking to feel his biceps. Embarrassed, Roy flexed his skinny arm, and Andy squeezed it. For some reason, the way Andy looked at him as he squeezed the muscle sent Roy's body temperature soaring and his heart pounding.

Andy nodded in approval, his blue eyes gleaming. "Alex's is bigger, but yours is hard too."

Roy squirmed and felt color rise to his cheeks. Andy took his hand away, and Roy wished he'd put it back. He knew his face was redder than a tomato, and while Andy may not have noticed his reaction, Alex sure did. But rather than looking angry or disgusted he just smiled with understanding.

Roy was proud to see that Alex could curl heavier dumbbells than all the other boys, even though Java could bench press the most. Alex had no trouble slipping out of his chair and onto the seats for most of the machines, and they both enjoyed helping Andy, who seemed fascinated by the whole process of exercise and willingly tried everything the others did. The time flew by until the colonel announced it was time for lunch.

By then, the excitement of having Alex and Andy back had waned, and Roy's exhaustion hit him like a slap to the face. He was starved!

***

The moment Alex and the others entered Colonel Walker's house, Amanda wrinkled her nose and playfully glowered at their sweaty appearance.

"To your rooms to change, boys," she ordered with a grin. "Your own clothes have been washed and dried. Feel free to use those or the Air Force garb I gave you."

Alex returned the grin, while Izzy groaned and looked at the stairs in dismay.

"I'll die going up there."

Full of energy, Java clapped him on the back with a huge grin. "I can carry ya, if ya want, Izzy."

Izzy made such a face that even Andy laughed. "No way, fool."

He stumbled toward the stairs, but Jorge, who seemed to have much more energy, handed Izzy a paper with his usual red V scrawled all over it.

"For victory," Jorge offered, breaking into a smile, and then he sprinted up the stairs with ease.

"That's my boy," Carlos exclaimed, and raced up after him.

Izzy grunted and held the paper, but he didn't otherwise speak as he tromped up the stairs. Java tossed Alex a grin before following.

Alex glanced around the entry hall. "Is William here?"

"Yes, he's in the kitchen," Amanda answered, exchanging a look with Colonel Walker, who so far had remained silent.

"Go on and change, boys," the colonel said. "You'll see him when we eat."

Alex nodded and wheeled himself down the hallway towards the back bedroom. Roy and Andy followed. Alex noticed for the first time that there were no family photos on the walls, just nature art and one big picture in a heavy wood frame that looked like Colonel Walker and Amanda when they got married. Both were younger, and the colonel had more hair, while Amanda wore a fancy white dress and something in her hair. Entering the room, he wondered why they'd never had kids, since they seemed to like them so much.

As Alex stripped off his shirt, Andy did the same, eying Alex's thicker arms and shoulders with admiration. "You're a lot…what was that word…oh yeah, buffer than me, Big Brother."

Alex shrugged. "Been only usin' my arms my whole life. You'll catch up."

He glanced over at Roy, who stood stock still staring at both of them like he couldn't look away, his mouth slightly open.

"Are you all right, Roy?" Andy took a few steps closer.

Roy snapped out of his momentary trance and nodded. "Uh, yeah. I'll change in the bathroom."

He snatched his clothes off of Alex's bed and disappeared behind the bathroom door, closing it with a click.

Alex found Andy staring at him. "I'll explain someday."

Andy stared hard at the closed bathroom door, like he somehow already understood.

***

The moment Alex wheeled into the dining room with Andy and Roy, William was at his side and insisted on sitting next to him. Alex saw that Roy wanted that spot, but he whispered, "This way I can talk to him."

Roy nodded, but still looked irked until Andy, who sat to Alex's left, offered him the next seat over. Roy lost his annoyed look and sat down. Colonel Walker sat at one end of the rectangular table and Amanda at the other. As at every meal, she beamed with joy at having such a full house. The boys spread out on both sides and stared at all the food in amazement. She'd made fresh pizza and bread, salad, lemonade, and a cake for dessert.

"Why a cake, ma'am?" Carlos asked, his deep voice very polite. "Is it somebody's birthday?"

She offered that warm smile Alex loved. "It must be close to somebody's birthday here, isn't it?"

Roy looked up from the slice of pizza on his plate. "Alex had a birthday couple weeks back."

Alex looked embarrassed and then noticed Andy frown. "And Andy," he said, clapping his brother on the back. "Let's celebrate for him since I bet them people never did."

Andy wore a trace of sadness on his face. "I didn't even know how old I was till you told me."

Amanda gasped in shock and exchanged a look with her husband.

Colonel Walker held up his glass of lemonade. "To Andy," he offered.

At first the boys didn't understand even when Amanda lifted her glass, but then Alex raised his and tapped Andy's beside him, and the others figured out what to do. When Alex tapped William's glass, he noted a sad wistfulness in the boy's eyes.

"You're a good brother, Alex," the younger boy said, his monotone voice tinged with woe. "I wish I had one."

"Do you got any sisters?"

"Nobody," the boy replied, taking a sip of his lemonade.

"'Cept your aunty," Alex offered, hoping to sound cheerful.

He barely reacted to that. "Yeah." He looked down at his food and mumbled, "I never had a birthday either."

Alex almost choked on his pizza and eyed the younger boy in horror. "Why not?"

He leaned closer and whispered, "It's top secret."

Alex furrowed his brows in confusion. How could a birthday be top secret?

William focused on eating, so Alex worked on his own pizza. It was steaming hot, with thick cheese and greasy slices of pepperoni dotting the surface. He was hungry after that workout, so the lack of conversation didn't bother him. But William had seemed so excited about sitting next to him that his silence gave Alex the feeling he didn't have much practice talking with other kids. How long had he lived on this base, anyway?

Given what he'd overheard the night before, William must be a spy for Colonel Walker, but why have a kid do a job like that? It sounded dangerous, especially if Davalos, who seemed to be the main target of the spying, was up to something really bad.

"So, how long you lived here?"

William stopped midchew. "Uh, since I was..." He paused as though he couldn't remember. "Thirteen." He swallowed and washed it down with a swig of lemonade.

Alex was confused because Colonel Walker had told them in the lab that William was thirteen. "I thought you were thirteen now. That's what the colonel said."

"Uh, yeah," William said, then quickly pulled a face, like he shouldn't have said that.

"So you just got here, you mean?"

William recovered himself quickly, returning to the stark expression he usually wore. "Sorry. I'm not used to being around kids. I've been here for a few years, but I'm thirteen now."

Alex nodded, his mind turning over and over with doubt. That last part sounded like something he planned to say. When he had spoken before, that sounded more real.

Alex tried to think of something else to say, but this time, William asked him a question. "Do you like healing people? It looks painful."

"It is," Alex replied, considering this question that no one had ever asked him. "When I feel sickness or sadness in someone, I need to spin 'em. I don't know why, but I got to make 'em feel better."

William met his gaze straight on, and Alex saw the pain he had previously detected in the boy's voice.

"You're sad, aren't you?"

Caught off guard, William looked down at his empty plate. "Sometimes, I guess. I get…lonely. I guess I want a sibling, maybe a big brother like you, but it's not gonna happen."

"Why not?"

"It just isn't." William reached out and snagged another piece of pizza, shoving it into his mouth as though that might ease his pain.

Alex felt hollow as he absorbed the emptiness within this younger boy. "I can be your big brother, if you want."

William looked over so fast Alex thought his head might snap off. "Yeah?"

"Yeah. I been an orphan most of my life. Them guys here, 'specially Roy, they been my family since I first met 'em. I only just found Andy, but there's always room for more. That's what a family is, right?"

William stared at him, open-mouthed, his pale blue eyes wide with wonder. Then his vibrant expression sagged. "But I can never leave this base."

"Why not?"

"Just can't."

"Then we can talk on FaceTime or something," Alex said, meaning every word. "Just cause we can't be together much don't mean we can't be family."

William smiled, and Alex felt the sadness he'd been spinning from the boy drain away, leaving behind the peace that always filled him after a successful spin.

He finally noticed what the others were talking about and turned to listen. Izzy and Roy were recounting all that had happened to them since Ms. Ashley, their former teacher, had been murdered. The adults listened with keen interest, and horror. Alex was called upon to share what he knew, and, in some odd way, it felt good to tell someone everything that had happened to them. Having it out in the open made it not quite so terrifying.

Even Andy shared some of his past, mainly because Amanda was so interested. Most of what Alex heard, he already knew, so he just listened.

When silence finally fell across the table like a heavy blanket, Amanda said, "You boys have been through hell, there's no mistaking that." She looked across at her husband, who sat in deep contemplation. "You won't let Davalos put them through more, will you, Bryan?"

"I don't plan to, but I'm not in the loop on what the Joint Chiefs have in mind."

Alex blurted out his question before giving it any thought. "Do you trust Mr. Davalos, Colonel?"

Colonel Walker studied him a long moment and Alex feared he'd said something wrong.

"Not entirely," the colonel finally answered. "Don't get me wrong, Davalos loves this country and will do anything to protect it. But he's just paranoid enough to be dangerous."

Alex exchanged a look with Roy. He saw the other boy's face twisted with confusion.

Obviously, Colonel Walker noticed because he added, "What I mean is, he sees threats that might not be legitimate, and if he takes action against them, he could cause real trouble."

Alex thought he understood. "Do you know what he really wants us for?"

The colonel shook his head. "I know he's got something bigger planned than what we've seen, but as I've said, it's up to you to draw the line."

"What if Mr. Davalos wants to force them?" Roy asked, casting a fearful look at Alex and Andy.

Colonel Walker fell silent, and Alex knew he'd been thinking the same thing, probably ever since they'd arrived at the base. "I don't know what his bosses—well, they're my bosses too—have in mind. Let's hope it doesn't come to that."

His words did not soothe Alex's troubled heart, nor Roy's based on the frightened look he wore.

An uncomfortable silence fell upon them all, until Izzy broke it. "Can we have that cake now? I'm still hungry."

That broke up the somber moment. Izzy could always be counted on to take nothing seriously.

Alex and Andy shared the first piece of cake while everyone sang "Happy Birthday."

Alex looked his brother straight in the eye. "Happy Birthday, bro."

Andy's face softened and his vibrant eyes danced with emotion, like he might even cry. "To you too, Big Brother."

***

After lunch, the boys stayed at the house to watch TV, or in Izzy's case, "crash my ass out to sleep." That left Alex following Colonel Walker, William, and Andy back across the long, hot tarmac to the lab building. The heat wasn't as bad as Hawthorne during the summer, but he still felt sweat trickling down his face and arms as he wheeled himself along, and the air just above the black ground shimmered.

The quiet of the base got to him most of all, especially at night. Hawthorne was a busy place and so was school, so back before all this craziness happened, his life had been nothing but noise. Even his body felt different, but not necessarily bad.

When they entered the lab, they found Davalos, Avila, and Shepherd clustered around what looked like a small fish tank. Colonel Walker marched up to them, the boys in tow.

"So, Mr. Davalos, have you come up with a test that Alex can agree to?"

Davalos smiled and stepped away from the tank. Alex cringed at the sight of cockroaches—big ones—scuttling around on the dirt littering the bottom of the tank. He heard a slight gasp and turned to find William staring at the tank in horror.

"Does it bother you, *William,* to know we'll sacrifice some of your friends?"

The way Davalos said William's name confused Alex, as did William's expression and reaction.

"Uh, no, sir."

"Good." Davalos faced Alex. "I presume you have no love for roaches?"

Disgusted at the sight of the slimy, crawling bugs with the huge antennae and smooth wings folded against their backs, Alex shook his head. Andy, he noticed, seemed amused by his disgusted expression.

He's probably never found 'em in his bed, Alex thought with a shudder of revulsion.

"Excellent." Davalos waved a hand to the doctors to begin.

Dr. Shepherd eyed William a long moment before walking over to the large console and pressing some buttons. One of the monitors popped on and Alex flinched again. It was a closeup of a cockroach, even nastier looking than the ones in the tank. He looked away and focused on Avila.

"This test is simple," the doctor began, pointing to the tank. "We'll remove one of these roaches and inject it with insecticide. When it's almost dead, Andy can hold it in his hand. Then, when it dies, he will shift death into the roach on the screen. Is that the procedure, Andy?"

Andy nodded, back to his sullen self. The moments of softness Alex had seen at the house had vanished.

Doctor Avila tried to hold Andy's firm gaze but was unable to. With a nervous titter, he looked away and reached for a box of latex gloves on the counter beside the tank. He stretched a pair over his hands and reached into the tank, grabbing one of the skittery roaches and lifting it out.

To Alex's horror, the roach slipped out of the doctor's hands and fell into *his* lap. He lurched back in his chair and was about to swat the slimy thing off him when something incredible happened – the roach stopped moving. It looked up at him as though trying to communicate. He was so shocked that it took a moment to realize the roach wasn't "looking" at him, but at William standing just behind him.

William stepped around his wheelchair and stared at the roach. It didn't budge, like it was listening to him, except William wasn't speaking, and roaches had no ears, did they? Avila seemed to understand, though, because he laid his gloved hand palm up onto Alex's knee, and the roach walked right onto it as though following orders. When he lifted his hand, it did nothing, didn't even move or try to escape.

The hell?

Dr. Shepherd handed Avila a tiny syringe with some yellow-colored liquid in it. He pointed the needle at the roach, which remained perfectly still, like it knew it was supposed to get a shot. The needle pierced the outer shell of the roach and Avila squeezed the yellow liquid into it.

Alex heard a slight groan and glanced over at William, who looked guilty, like he'd betrayed a friend.

What was going on here?

The roach began thrashing about, extending its wings and trying to fly, but unable to do much except flop over onto its back in the doctor's gloved hand. As its legs twitched, he extended his hand to Andy, who held out his own and received the dying bug like it was a piece of candy. He closed his hand, but gently so as to not crush the roach. Then he took Alex's hand with his other.

Alex felt the now familiar cascading rush of power course through him and gazed straight at his brother. Andy smiled, but it was a twisted smile that chilled Alex to his core.

Andy *did* like playing with Death!

It only took a moment before Andy whispered, "Death to me."

As before, Alex felt the gray blanket of nothingness descend upon him, but only for a split-second.

"Death to it."

Alex looked up at the monitor as the nothingness rushed out of him like a river and saw the giant roach, perfectly healthy, suddenly twitch and flop over onto its back. It was dead.

Andy released his hand and smirked. Alex didn't return it. Even using bugs, shifting Death creeped him out, and he hated that Andy so enjoyed the experience.

Davalos was rubbing his hands together with glee, while both doctors looked stunned.

Colonel Walker stepped to Davalos's side and indicated the monitor. "I take it there's something about this you haven't mentioned?"

Elated, Davalos pointed at the dead roach on the monitor. "That roach, my dear Colonel, is at one of our bases in Germany."

The colonel's face twitched with shock, and he eyed the boys in wonder. "Impressive," was all he said, but Alex heard the tone of concern underlying that one word.

"You know what this means, don't you, Colonel?" Davalos looked happier and more energized than Alex had yet seen him.

"Why don't you tell me?"

Alex stared at both men, finally hoping to understand what Davalos really wanted from him and Andy.

Davalos looked giddy. "Nothing less than the end of war on this planet."

Alex's mouth dropped open and he turned to Andy, but his brother didn't seem to understand.

The end of war?

CHAPTER TEN

IT'S NOT DEAD YET

OLONEL WALKER LOOKED TROUBLED BUT kept his composure. "Explain."

Now Davalos faltered. "In front of them?" He waved a hand at the three boys.

"If it involves the twins, they have more right to know than anyone."

"Very well." Davalos turned to include Alex and Andy in his line of sight as he began speaking, his voice almost trembling with exhilaration. "America has many enemies in the world, and while we're not at war right now, that could easily change on a dime. Countries like North Korea, China, Russia, and Iran, to name four, would like nothing better than to destroy this country."

Alex felt a chill settle over him. He recalled Ms. Ashley teaching them about war. There were a lot of them in history, he knew, even if the details hadn't stuck with him, and they were all bloody and terrible.

"Let's say we go to war with an enemy," Davalos went on, gesticulating with his hands as he spoke. "Now, depending on the reason behind the war, the primary culprits are always the leaders of the country and the leaders of the military—not the civilian population, though they are always the most damaged by any armed conflict. An army doesn't fight without a commander. Colonel Walker knows that better than any of us in this room. Am I right, Colonel?"

"You are," the colonel confirmed, arms folded across his chest. "Go on."

Alex had a sense Colonel Walker already knew what Davalos was going to say.

"If we take out the commanders, we stop the war before it begins."

Now William spoke, surprising Alex because he'd almost forgotten the boy was right behind him. "A new commander would be appointed. It's happened throughout history."

Davalos eyed him, not with annoyance, but agreement. "Exactly. Unless the leader of that country knew that any commander he appointed would be killed before he could begin, killed in a way that's both inexplicable and unstoppable."

"You want these boys to commit assassinations?" Colonel Walker sounded angry.

"That means kill people, right?" Alex was horrified.

"Yes," the Colonel said, facing him, eyes squinting with disgust.

"We're only talking about bad people, Alex," Davalos went on, squatting down before Alex's wheelchair and making eye contact. "Evil people. If you boys had been alive in the 1930s, for example, you could've stopped Adolf Hitler and saved millions. You could've stopped dictators like Stalin and Mao and saved over a hundred million innocent lives. Even taking out Osama Bin Ladin before he could launch his 9/11 attack against us would've saved thousands."

Davalos was so excited that Alex couldn't have interrupted him if he tried, but in truth, the only names he recognized were Hitler and Bin Ladin. He knew they were evil.

Now Andy spoke up, his voice calm as always. "You want us to send Death into them."

Davalos looked up at him. "Exactly."

"But, I don't wanna kill people," Alex said, forcing his thoughts into words. "I only wanna help them."

Davalos fixed his gaze on to Alex again, his eyes dancing with elation. "And you would be, Alex. You two could save more lives than anyone in history."

"By killing," Alex said, his voice barely a whisper. "How is that good?"

"Because some people need to be killed so others may live," Davalos answered. "We can't always lock them up, Alex, not if we can't get to them. But with you boys working hand in hand with us, we could stop them for good."

Alex looked up at Colonel Walker, who no longer looked angry, but rather, thoughtful.

"He's telling you the truth, Alex. There are people who are truly evil. If they could be easily eliminated, lives would be saved. Many lives. But it would have to be your decision, because I can foresee major problems for you and Andy."

Davalos leaped to his feet. "What problems?"

The colonel eyed him appraisingly. "At first, your plan will work perfectly. Our enemies won't know what hit them. But what if they learn about the boys? They'll stop at nothing to capture or kill them. These boys will have to be protected for the rest of their lives. You're asking them to forever give up their freedom of movement."

Davalos lost the gleam in his eyes and Alex realized the man hadn't considered what Colonel Walker just suggested.

Before he could reply, Andy's voice filled the room, strong and deep. "No."

Alex turned to him and sensed that everyone else had, too.

"I'll never be in a cage again."

Davalos glared daggers at the colonel before addressing Andy. "It won't be like that, Andy. We'll make certain no one finds out about you. Your lives will be your own. If we happen to need you, and it would only be in the event of an extreme emergency, we'd determine a secret way of contacting you. At this point, we're just talking possibilities. Such choices would have to be weighed by many people and approved by the president, so it's not something in the near future. Just an idea right now."

Andy considered for a moment and then turned to Alex. "What do you think, Big Brother?"

Alex didn't have an answer. Killing was against who he was at his core. He was the Healer, after all, ordained by God—according to Father Pat—to help people, not hurt them. He wished the priest was there now to help him sort out his conflicting thoughts.

"I don't know." He couldn't think of another response.

Davalos nodded. "There's a small example happening right now of what I'm talking about."

He strode to the console and pressed a couple of buttons. Another monitor sprang to life, this one showing the letters CNN in the lower corner. Alex recognized it as the news, though he had seldom spent any time watching it. He couldn't read some of the other words at the bottom of the screen, but the camera seemed to be pointed at a large stone building. It was in a city somewhere because Alex saw other tall buildings to either side and the street in front had tons of unmoving police cars with cops crouched behind them, guns aimed at the building.

"What's all this, Davalos?" That was Colonel Walker, striding forward and studying the monitor.

"A hostage situation in New York City," Davalos answered calmly, glancing at Alex, and making quick eye contact before continuing. "There's a perp in there with a semiautomatic rifle threatening to kill thirty men, women, and children."

The colonel frowned and exchanged a quick look with Dr. Shepherd. She nodded, as if to say, "This is legit."

"What does he want, money?"

Davalos shook his head. "No. He just wants to kill people."

"Then why hasn't he done it?"

"He's waiting for the media to send in a live feed so he can commit murder on camera," Davalos replied, his tone filled with disgust. "The police are stymied. The guy already killed the security guard, so he means business."

Colonel Walker rubbed his chin absently and turned to Alex, regarding him and Andy, but also William. "If only William…" he muttered.

"He's here, not there," Davalos retorted, anger now obvious in his voice. "The only hope those people have is right in this room." He focused on Alex and Andy so intently that Alex felt his face redden.

The entire situation terrified Alex as he stared up at the screen where an Asian lady with a microphone in one hand was talking into the camera, though the sound was muted.

"Why don't we just watch for a while," Davalos suggested.

He pressed a button. The silence of the lab was broken by the voice of the news lady on screen.

"—police chief and the mayor are conferring with the FBI on how best to handle this volatile situation. CNN is prepared to allow our cameraman into the bank, but only if there is a plan in place to defuse the situation and save the hostages."

She continued talking while the camera showed that police were positioned at various spots along the street, aiming handguns and rifles at the bank windows. The camera zoomed in on the largest window, and Alex gasped. A woman inside sat crouched on the floor, arms draped over two young children. Alex couldn't tell how old the kids were, but maybe young enough to not even be in school yet. His stomach lurched, and he felt like his lunch was about to come up.

As the news continued, William stepped up to Colonel Walker and whispered something into his ear. The colonel nodded.

William approached Alex. "Can I talk to you in private, Alex?"

Davalos whirled and opened his mouth, but Colonel Walker raised a hand to silence him. "It's all right, Alex."

Flummoxed by what a thirteen-year-old could say at a time like this, Alex wheeled himself to the far corner of the lab, and William followed. Once they were well apart from the others, William squatted down in front of him, his face twisted with shame.

"What's wrong?" Alex asked, feeling the remorse wafting off the other boy like heat.

"I…I know what it's like to kill, Alex," William said, so quietly Alex had to lean in closer. "A few years ago, when I didn't know as much as I do now, I killed some people in Los Angeles."

Alex sucked in a sharp breath of surprise. "You…killed…"

William nodded. "One of them was a good man, a police officer. I killed him because he hurt me, but he was just scared when he did that."

"Oh." Alex couldn't think what else to say except, "How did you…?"

"That doesn't matter right now. The others I killed, Alex, they were bad people, especially the man in charge, a Mr. Alvarez. They kidnapped children and sold them as slaves."

Alex felt his blood run cold. "What?"

William nodded, looking grave. "Little children, Alex, younger than me. I captured Mr. Alvarez, and I could have given him to the police but…"

Alex had by now tuned out everything around him. "You killed him anyway?"

William nodded again. "I don't like Mr. Davalos, and he doesn't like me. But he's right about one thing. Sometimes bad people have to be killed to protect good people."

Alex understood, suddenly hearing the newscaster's voice in the background. "—have to decide soon because the gunman has threatened to open fire at three-thirty, less than twenty minutes from now."

Alex locked eyes with William. He saw sincerity and, unconsciously, he began spinning the remorse from the younger boy over the death of that cop. William's emotions were too strong to ignore.

"You think I should help kill that man on TV, don't you?"

William nodded a third time, understanding of the difficult choice Alex had to make clear on his young face.

Alex bit his lip as the pain he absorbed from William ripped through him. Then he turned and wheeled back to the others. They all stood in silence staring at him, awaiting his decision. He avoided Colonel Walker's eyes and stopped in front of his brother.

"You okay with this, Andy?" Andy nodded, so Alex turned his wheelchair to face Davalos. "We need to see the guy's face."

Davalos sagged slightly, as though with relief. "I have a line to the mayor. I will tell him to allow the CNN cameraman into the bank, that we have a plan to take out the gunman. The cameraman will be told to aim the camera squarely at the gunman. The second he does, you get him."

"What will we use for Death?" Alex shivered at the thought of using another human being.

Davalos eyed Andy. "Won't a cockroach work?"

Andy nodded again and Davalos fixed intense brown eyes upon Alex. "Well, Alex? Is it a go?" When Alex hesitated, he added, "When you see the people you saved streaming unharmed out of that bank, you won't have a second's regret."

Alex nodded this time, and Davalos waved a hand to Avila. As the doctor reached into the tank for another cockroach, Davalos grabbed a phone and lifted the receiver, pressing a button and holding the handset to his ear.

"Mr. Mayor, we're a go at our end. No, sir, I can't give you specifics. You've checked on my identity by now, I'm sure. This project is top secret. We only aim to help the people in that bank. Yes, sir. The moment the cameraman focuses on the gunman, this standoff will end. Yes, sir, I'll keep this line open. We're watching live, but I need to know how many seconds delay is involved with this broadcast. We have to time this to the exact second." He listened a moment. "Excellent. We'll wait until CNN sends that link." He pressed another button and set down the receiver. "CNN will send us their direct link to the camera entering the bank. That way, there will be not the slightest delay." A beep sounded and he glanced at the screens. On a separate one, next to the television feed, a link popped up in blue. Davalos clicked on it, and an image appeared of the street right in front of the bank entrance. "We're in." He faced Dr, Avila. "This must be timed exactly. How long will it take for the roach to fully expire?"

Avila considered only a moment. "Just like before, a few seconds."

"Then you must inject it right when the cameraman enters the bank," Davalos instructed. "Since we don't know exactly where the perp is standing, it might take a few additional seconds to focus on him. Andy, how soon after the roach expires can you shift Death?"

"It has to be right away," Andy replied, like he was answering a math problem instead of talking about the lives of thirty people. "Death is small, remember, and it goes away fast."

Davalos considered a moment. He turned to the monitor. On the street near the front entrance to the bank, a man with a large camera on his shoulder walked toward he entrance, police on either side of him. On the monitor next to it was what the cameraman was filming, the entrance to the bank inching closer as he walked.

"Okay, he's about to go in. Have a second roach ready, doctor, just in case." He turned to William. "William can help with that."

William placed his hand inside the tank. A roach crawled onto it and just sat there, like a pet hamster. He lifted out his hand and stood next to Dr. Avila, who held the other roach between thumb and forefinger. It didn't struggle either. The tip of the needle rested against its shell as Avila dutifully awaited Davalos's command.

"Remember boys," Davalos said, his voice tight with concern, "focus on this monitor." He pointed to the monitor showing the camera-view-only, muted the sound, and turned off the one with the newsfeed.

Alex had his hand poised to clasp Andy's as he watched the unfolding drama on screen. Two police officers eased open the doors, and the camera image moved forward slowly. He figured the guy holding it was walking into the bank.

As the interior came into view, Alex gasped. People huddled against the walls or lay sprawled on the brown carpet, including more than a few children! He saw a girl who looked his age, but she had two younger brothers crying and holding on to her for dear life. Everyone was whimpering or crying or gripping tightly to the people they loved, and Alex's stomach did nauseous flips at the pain he felt emanating from that screen.

"You there, with the camera!"

The camera swung wildly, trying to find the source of the voice.

"Be ready," Davalos murmured.

Alex's fingertips brushed against Andy's, but his eyes remained fixed to the unfolding action on screen. The camera found the man with the gun. It looked like a weapon out of some action movie, big and long and terrifying. The man aimed it straight at the camera and Alex flinched back, eliciting a slight chuckle from Andy. Alex glanced up at him and saw his brother eyeing him with amusement.

How can he laugh at a time like this?

"You with the camera, come closer!"

Alex returned his gaze to the screen. The camera moved in slowly toward the man with the gun. The camera wobbled a little, like maybe the guy holding it was frightened.

"Almost there," said Davalos, his gaze riveted to the screen.

The gunman seemed to move closer to the camera, even though it was the other way around. Davalos raised one hand, prepared to signal the doctor. Just then someone, a man, it looked like, rushed at the gunman from behind. The gunman spun around. The camera wobbled as the guy holding it probably stumbled back. The gun went off in a loud *rat tat tat* and the other man cried out in pain, toppling off to the side, out of camera range. The gunman spun around the room, aiming his weapon wildly.

"Nobody else try anything!"

Then he whirled back to face the camera and aimed his rifle. "Don't you do anything but film or you go next!" He let go of one hand to brush back straggly long hair that had drifted in front of his face. "Why am I killing these people? Cause they're part of the capitalist machine that crushes guys like me. Why should they have more money than me? Huh? Why?"

The guy holding the camera tried to focus on the gunman's face, but the man kept looking off to the side at the terrified people who huddled as far from him as they could get. The man turned back and looked directly into the camera.

"Now!" hissed Davalos, dropping his hand in a slashing motion.

Avila injected the roach. It shook and wriggled and flipped onto its back. He handed it to Andy.

"Shift!" Davalos spun around to Andy, his face a mask of urgency.

"It's not dead yet," Andy replied as calmly as if he was presenting a school report.

Davalos whirled back to face the screen.

The gunman's leering face filled the monitor. "It begins."

He'd begun to turn his head away when Alex felt Andy clasp his hand.

"Death to me," Andy whispered.

As before, Alex felt the rush of power, the gray blanket of nothingness filling his mind and body. His vision of the gunman blurred. Was he still on camera?

Alex heard, as though from miles away, "Death to him!"

The grayness vanished, and his vision cleared. The image on the monitor came into focus. It was the gunman raising his rifle at the crowd of screaming people. They were begging for their lives. The gunman laughed, then stiffened like the roach had done. His face went slack. The gun slipped from his hands. The hostages flung themselves to the floor. The gunman collapsed out of camera range.

The image shook, like the guy with the camera stumbled again, but Alex plainly saw the gunman lying on the brown carpet, the rifle by his side. Then everything became crazy. Cops rushed past the camera to the gunman's body. Others hurried to the hostages, helping people to their feet and hustling them past the wobbling camera.

Shirt soaked with sweat, Alex released his breath and made eye contact with Davalos, who glowed with triumph. Then Alex turned to Andy, who released his hand and smiled, looking calm as could be. Was his brother really so empty that something like this didn't bother him?

Davalos picked up the phone receiver again, pressing a button. "Mr. Mayor? Yes. Your people have confirmed it? Excellent. No, I cannot give you more details. We're happy to have helped save those hostages."

He hung up the phone and glanced again at Alex, who was sure his line about saving the hostages had been meant for him, not the guy on the phone. "How are you feeling about this now, Alex?"

Alex wasn't sure. He'd been so uptight and scared that he hadn't yet processed his thoughts.

Then Andy spoke up. "I thought it was fun. When can we do it again?"

Davalos offered a smile of camaraderie, like they were on the same team that had just scored a winning touchdown. "Whenever there's a need."

Alex turned away from them both, still managing his feelings about having committed murder. Yes, that man was evil and about to kill all those people. But that didn't make killing him easy to swallow. He found William suddenly in front of him, looking directly into his eyes. In William's pale pools of blue, Alex saw understanding. Yes, William knew how he felt.

A hand fell on his shoulder, and he pulled his gaze away from William. It was Colonel Walker. "Come, Alex. I'll take you back to the house. We're finished for today."

Alex nodded, still unable to speak because he didn't know what to say.

"I want to stay and talk to Mr. Davalos," Andy said, shoving his long hair back over his shoulders as he so often did.

Shocked, Alex faced his brother. "About what?"

"How we can use our power more," Andy answered, tossing Davalos a look of support.

Davalos stepped forward as Colonel Walker opened his mouth to speak. "I assure you, Colonel, I'll bring him back to the house post-haste."

The colonel studied him a long moment, glancing at Andy several times as he did. "All right, Andy. You can stay. I'll be back for you in thirty minutes."

Davalos shook his head in mock dismay. "Still don't trust me, Colonel?"

Colonel Walker eyed him a moment before focusing on Andy. "Thirty minutes, Andy."

Without awaiting a response, he turned and strode through the gleaming lab toward the exit. Feeling as though he was losing Andy so soon after finding him, Alex made brief eye contact with his smirking brother before reluctantly following William and the colonel.

CHAPTER ELEVEN

HE MADE ME PROMISE NOT TO TELL

T HE SUN BEAT DOWN ON Alex like a hammer as he wheeled across the steaming tarmac, adding to his troubled mood. Colonel Walker walked on one side of him and William on the other.

"You know, Alex, what Davalos said about you helping to end wars—that was just an idea, not approved by anyone," the colonel said. "He's thinking ahead, that's all, throwing out a possibility."

Alex nodded. "What do you think? I kinda got the feeling you liked the idea."

Colonel Walker stopped and the boys stopped with him. "War is hell, Alex. I've never approved of movies or video games that try to glorify war or make it look fun. It's brutal and ugly, but it's been a staple of human history since the beginning."

"Why do most wars start?" Alex asked, one hand on his forehead to shade his eyes from the sun.

Colonel Walker considered that a moment. "I'd say, self-absorption, mostly. We all have a kind of 'selfish gene' that makes us do things that hurt others, and we need to control that part of our nature or else it will lead to negative consequences, usually for innocent people. The self-absorbed, especially in politics or the military, often seek power for its own sake and they'll do anything to hold on to that power once they get it. Some wars have been fought over land or ideology, like against the Nazi's or international communism." He paused a moment. "Hearing Davalos's idea, I can't help thinking about all the lives that would've been saved if someone had been able to take out Hitler, Mao, Stalin, and so many other dictators in the last century alone."

"So you do like the idea?" Alex understood the colonel's thinking, and it made sense, but it was still killing.

Colonel Walker looked thoughtful. "I like the idea of saving lives."

Alex nodded. He liked that part of the plan too. They fell silent and continued across the hot tarmac for a few minutes while Alex thought about his brother.

"Why do you think Andy wanted to stay with Mr. Davalos?"

The colonel looked down at him, squinting against the sunlight. "I don't know. You know him better than I do."

Alex considered that. "I only just met him. His whole life was pretty shitty, though. Oh, sorry, Colonel. Didn't mean to cuss."

"Not to worry," Colonel Walker assured him, waving the apology away with one of his large hands. "I had the feeling he enjoyed shifting Death. What did you think?"

Alex shivered, despite the battering heat. "I think so too." He paused to consider. "Maybe it's like how I do crazy-ass stunts in my chair at the skatepark back in Hawthorne."

"The thrill gene, you mean?"

Alex furrowed his brow and eyed the man as they neared the house. "What's that?"

"It's something in some people that makes them want to take extreme chances," the colonel explained. "Perhaps Andy likes the thrill of bringing himself—and you, I might add—to the verge of death before shifting it."

Alex pondered that. William had been silent the entire way, so Alex looked at him. "Do you have the thrill gene, William?"

William exchanged a quick glance with Colonel Walker before offering a tight smile. "Oh, yeah."

***

Per the colonel's instructions, Dr. Shepherd did not plan to let Andy out of her sight. When Davalos left the lab with the boy, Shepherd excused herself to use the facilities, leaving Avila alone.

Rather than head to the right toward the unisex restrooms, she turned left down the stark, dingy hallway, following the sounds of echoing footsteps. Because this base was so old and hadn't been renovated except in the technical areas, it was easy for her to follow the retreating steps. To make certain her own footsteps were not detected, she slipped off her loafers and carried them in her left hand.

She heard Davalos speaking and Andy replying, but she was too far back to make out what they were saying. William would have been better for this job, but Davalos already suspected the boy of spying, so Colonel Walker had recruited her as a supplement. After all that had happened with William over the years, she was determined not to let the twins be used in a similar fashion.

She expected Davalos to head in the direction of his own lab, the one where he'd taken over her Weapon Development Project and put the slimy Avila in charge. She was happy to be out of that project, considering the grief the original version had caused to so many people, but she also knew Davalos's take on the idea was far more questionable. And Avila, unlike herself and Victor, who'd headed up the old program, had no scruples. That frightened her. Davalos surprised her, however, by heading in the opposite direction toward…the morgue?

Why the hell would he bring the boy there?

Soldiers who died in training exercises, which almost never happened, were kept in the morgue until arrangements could be made with their families. It was kept cold enough to preserve the bodies and they never remained on base for more than a day or two. Four soldiers had been killed the night the twins were captured, and their remains hadn't been moved because the operation was so top secret, the Pentagon had not yet released an "official" version of how the "accident" occurred.

She froze where her corridor intersected another when she heard Davalos say, "In here, Andy," accompanied by the grinding of a heavy door being pulled open.

She listened, but there were no other sounds, meaning Davalos had not closed the door. She eased herself around the corner and saw it - the faded metal door to the morgue standing wide open. Beyond the door, overhead fluorescent lights cast the room in a faint, bluish glow. She scuttled along the wall and darted behind the open door, not certain where in the room Davalos and Andy might be. She'd only been there once, when her father had been killed.

No! Don't even go there! It was Dad's choice, like Victor said.

Just the thought of Victor pulled her heart tight in her chest. She'd squandered the opportunity to be with him when he was alive, and all she had left of him now was William. And *he'd* been so brainwashed three years before that he'd killed her father because her father had ordered him to—just to prove a point to Pentagon officials. Her dad had been obsessed with the Weapon project, and now she saw the same behaviors in Avila, who'd been her dad's assistant. Victor—the love of her life—had been the only one to see William as truly human at his core, capable of making good choices if taught properly. He'd be ecstatic if he could see the progress in the boy, how civilized he'd become, how smart and clever. Over the years, Dr. Shepherd had come to feel true affection for the child, maybe even love.

Clearing her mind of such thoughts, she gripped the edge of the door and eased her head around to peek into the room. It was stark, made of dull metal to keep it cool, with rows of large cold-storage units at the far side. Davalos and Andy stood before them, backs to Shepherd. She went rigid and observed their exchange.

"Have you ever shifted Life, Andy?"

"Life? I don't know what you mean." The boy sounded mystified but intrigued.

"I mean shifting Life from a living creature into a dead one, bringing it alive," Davalos replied dispassionately.

Dr. Shepherd shivered at the thought.

"No, I never tried that. Even Teacher and Doctor never asked me to do that."

There was a long pause between them.

"Would you like to try?"

The eagerness in Davalos's voice was not lost on Shepherd. What was he up to, anyway?

"Yes." Andy's normally deep voice rose an octave, maybe from anticipation.

"I thought you might."

Dr. Shepherd leaned out a bit farther as Davalos slipped something from his pocket—a small plastic box. Then he pulled open the door of one storage unit and slid out the tray. Andy stepped aside to give it room and glanced in her direction. She yanked her head back, her breathing on hold.

"Something wrong, Andy?"

There was a pause. She listened for footsteps, but none seemed to be approaching.

"No."

"Good. Now, this is one of the men who died the night you were captured."

"You mean that I killed, don't you?"

"Well, yes, I suppose, if we're to be accurate." Even Davalos sounded perturbed by Andy's callousness.

Shivering with revulsion that a boy could be so devoid of compassion, she peered once more around the edge of the door. The tray was all the way out now, the corpse covered with a protective blanket. Andy gazed down at the dead body in wonder, not distaste as Dr. Shepherd would've thought, and awaited his instructions.

Davalos pulled back the blanket, revealing the pallid face of a dark-haired young man, no older than twenty-one, if Shepherd recollected the ages of the deceased correctly. Davalos pulled the sheet back farther, revealing the slim, naked torso. She could barely make out ragged edges of skin in the upper chest, likely where the bullet had entered.

Davalos rested the blanket across the man's waist and set his little box atop it.

"Now, I want you to shift the life from that roach into this man," Davalos explained.

"All right."

No hesitation, Dr, Shepherd thought, *just eagerness.*

Davalos blocked her view as he shifted position, but she presumed he'd opened the box to reveal the cockroach because Andy said, "Life, to me." Then, "Life force, come into me." A pause. "It's not working."

"Relax, Andy," Davalos urged. "This is something new. Focus on what you want from this creature."

There was another pause. She heard Andy sigh heavily, like he was refocusing his energies. "Life, come into me. Now!"

There was a moment of silence.

"It worked! The roach is dead." Davalos sounded like a kid with a new game system.

"It feels weird," Andy said, his voice otherworldly, "like there's something else living inside of me."

"Shift it, quickly!"

"Life, to him."

Andy flinched, like he'd issued a tiny sneeze and then, to Shepherd's utter horror, the body on the table twitched.

"It worked!" Davalos hissed, over the moon with elation.

The man on the tray jerkily sat up. The pallid face, devoid of blood, looked blank and expressionless. But the eyes shifted in their sockets, taking in Andy and Davalos without comprehension, like there was nothing behind those eyes except an animating life force.

A zombie!

She couldn't believe her eyes! What kind of sick game was Davalos playing at, anyway?

"Can you hear me?" Davalos gazed with intensity at the young man's face, but there was no reply, not even a flicker in those wide, staring eyes to indicate he'd heard. "Do you know who you are?" Still nothing.

Andy studied the resuscitated man as though this was something he witnessed every day. His voice, when he spoke, sounded clinical, like solving a math problem.

"I think maybe Life isn't like Death," he said.

"What do you mean?"

"Only a small Death will kill anything," Andy explained thoughtfully, as though working out the explanation in his mind. "But maybe Life is bigger than Death and such a small thing, like that bug, isn't enough to bring something this big back."

Some*thing*, Shepherd noted, not some*one*.

"You think you need a human to revive a human?" In a matter-of-fact tone, Davalos was talking about killing one person to revive another.

There was a pause. "Yes." Another pause. "But I know I can't do it alone."

"You need Alex, you mean?"

"Unfortunately, yes." The tone of distaste was palpable. "But I won't always need him."

"What do you mean?"

"Nothing. Look, he's getting weaker."

Shepherd edged out further to watch the revived soldier's eyes flutter. He slowly lay back down on the tray, convulsed a couple of times, then ceased all movement. Davalos leaned in and lifted the man's eyelids.

"He's dead. I think you're right. That roach was too small. No matter. I just wanted to know if you could do it. The project I have in mind already has the necessary participants."

"Are you going to tell me about it?"

"Not yet. Soon."

He slid the rack back into the storage unit and closed the heavy door. It locked with a click.

"We'll let this be our secret, eh, Andy?"

"If that's what you want," the boy replied and started to turn.

Dr. Shepherd ducked back behind the door.

"Let's get you back to the lab. The colonel will be there shortly."

Dr. Shepherd hurried back down the corridor as fast as she could, her bare feet making only the tiniest *slap, slap, slap* sounds against the hard floor. Once she'd rounded the far corner, she raced back to the lab, remembering to replace her shoes before entering.

Avila was examining some blood samples when she entered. He glanced up and nodded before returning his eye to the microscope. Still shaking from her experience, she eased her way to her usual station and sat on the stool, pretending to organize her notes on the counter before her.

Moments later, Davalos entered with Andy in tow. They said nothing, but as they strode past her station, Andy fixed his gaze on her, his eyes dancing with mirth. He knew she'd been listening outside the morgue! She was sure of it.

Before she could even think about what he might do, Colonel Walker entered the lab and caught her eye. She nodded ever so slightly, but he pretended not to have seen. Instead, he marched on past to where Andy and Davalos were staring at the blood samples Avila had projected up onto one of his screens.

"Ready to go, Andy?"

"Yes, Colonel."

"Good night, Mr. Davalos," the colonel said, and then with one hand guided Andy back toward the exit.

"Good night, Colonel," Davalos replied, his face neutral.

Shepherd studied him a moment until he caught her staring, then she turned back to her work, hoping she hadn't aroused his suspicions.

***

When Andy brushed off his questions, Alex waited until his brother joined the others in the living room, where they were watching another of those Avengers movies, before facing Colonel Walker.

"What happened?"

The colonel shrugged. "He wouldn't tell me. Just said Davalos showed him some of the lab animals he has in the back."

"Do you believe him?"

"No, but I'm sure Davalos swore him to secrecy. I'll find out, Alex, don't worry."

Except Alex couldn't help but worry. Even though he felt some measure of success that he'd helped save lives, he was filled with guilt over the New York incident. After all, despite the outcome, it had been murder, hadn't it? And Andy's casual reaction to it all troubled Alex at a level deep in his soul. But then he thought back on what he knew of Andy's childhood. After having been forced to slice and dice puppies, he was amazed Andy could feel much of anything except anger.

The moment Alex had entered the house with Colonel Walker, Roy had practically suffocated him with questions, but Alex had held him off. He needed time to process all that had happened. He promised to fill Roy in later, after everyone had gone to bed.

Roy had studied his face so intently that Alex squirmed, but he knew Roy was just worried about him. As always, such care on the part of his best friend warmed Alex's heart and drove away some of the distress he'd been feeling.

Amanda had spent the day with the other boys, teaching them how to play poker and then taking all their money—they'd been using toothpicks rather than cash. She'd become like a mother to them in such a short time that it was remarkable. Alex had even mentioned to Carlos over breakfast that morning, "Why can't all foster parents be like Amanda, huh?"

Carlos had grinned around a mouthful of grapefruit. "I know, right?"

Since it was almost six, Amanda had excused herself to the kitchen to work on dinner.

"I have a special surprise for you boys," she hinted as she swept past Alex. Then, as though an afterthought, she returned and bent down to his ear. "Don't worry, Alex," she whispered softly, her breath tickling his earlobe. "Davalos won't get away with whatever he's up to. I'll see to that."

Then she was gone, vanishing into the kitchen through a door that swung back and forth on double hinges. Oddly enough, Andy announced to Alex, "I'm going to help Amanda with dinner," and then followed her into the kitchen.

Andy stayed in the kitchen until dinner and then sat between Jorge and Izzy for the first time, rather than next to Alex. This troubled Alex, and when he looked at Roy, sitting on his right, he saw his own surprise mirrored in his friend's face. But the spare ribs with potatoes were so tasty and the chattering of the other boys so infectious, that Alex began to loosen up.

William had taken the seat on Alex's left, and even though he didn't say much, it comforted Alex to have him there. He still didn't understand how and why William had come to kill those people three years before, but he now understood the underlying sadness he felt seeping out of the boy.

Having had a rest from the weightlifting, Izzy's motormouth was back in gear, rambling on about everything from which Avenger had the goofiest costume to why spare ribs should be called spare ribs.

"Are they like spare tires?" he asked, cackling at his own joke, which brought a smile to Alex's face.

After dinner, all the boys helped Amanda do the dishes, with Andy the most eager. Alex was speechless at the sight of Izzy and Carlos tripping over themselves to see who could help her first. She just laughed and happily accepted their assistance. Roy piled plates onto Alex's lap, and he wheeled them over to Jorge, who handed them one by one to Java, who slipped them into the soapy water that filled the sink.

In no time at all, the table was cleared, and there was nothing more for Alex or Roy to do. Andy had already left without a word, and that made Alex curious. Then, amid the splashing of water and good-natured ribbing, punctuated by Amanda's contagious laugh, Alex noticed that

William and Colonel Walker had also disappeared. He nudged Roy and then wheeled out of the kitchen.

Roy followed him toward the rear of the house, to an open door leading into the backyard. He heard muffled voices. One was female.

"Shssh," Alex whispered, rolling cautiously closer, Roy practically breathing down his neck.

Dr. Shepherd's voice grew clearer, and Alex stopped to listen, Roy pressed in close to his face.

"—and he said the roach didn't have enough life to keep the dead man alive for long, that he'd need another human for that. And I think he's jealous of Alex."

Someone sighed. The colonel. "What the hell is Davalos planning?"

"I don't know," she answered. "It was inhuman, Bryan, what they did to that airman."

"I'm sorry you had to see it, Liz, but now we know a lot more than we did before." There was a pause. "William, have you seen anything in his other lab that looks like it could be something dead that was brought back to life?"

"No, sir. Just his variations on…me, you know, my…cousins." The grief in his voice cut straight into Alex's heart. "I feel sorry for Francis."

"I do too, William," Dr. Shepherd said, her voice filled with more compassion than Alex had heard in all his encounters with the woman doctor.

"I wish I could help him," Colonel Walker replied, "but orders, as you know, must be followed. The Pentagon has high hopes for those… variations. They should have had more confidence in you, William. You're the best we have. The Pentagon just doesn't know it yet. Both of you, keep me informed of any new developments."

There was a long pause, and Alex thought maybe they had finished.

"Is it time to show Alex my cousins?" That was William. "Tell him the truth?"

Another pause.

"Yes, I think so," replied Colonel Walker. "With Davalos making his move on Andy, we don't dare wait. You're sure Alex will be able to control them?"

"Yes, Colonel. They do whatever I say and when they meet Alex, they will know he is good."

"Tonight, then."

"Yes, sir."

"I'll be awake, if you need me."

A chair creaked and Alex figured William had stood up.

"And William."

"Yes, Colonel?"

"I'm proud of you, son."

There was such a long pause that Alex thought William had gone away. Then, in a voice that sounded breathy, William muttered, "Thank you, sir."

Deciding the talk was over, Alex feared they would reenter the house, so he shooed Roy back down the hallway and they headed to their room. Once inside with the door closed, they were about to discuss what they'd heard when Andy stepped out of the bathroom. He was naked, his damp hair tumbling all the way down his back and his pale body glistening with tiny water droplets.

Roy gasped, his mouth open with shock and obvious attraction.

"Hello Big Brother," Andy said, as though walking into a room naked and finding two people there was a regular experience. From what Andy had told them at the safe house, it was. "I just took a shower."

Alex knew he had to say something. "Uh, yeah, looks like."

Andy strode to the top drawer of the bureau where he was keeping his clothes and pulled out some boxers, slipping them up and over his butt as though the others weren't even there.

Alex looked at Roy. His best friend's mouth hung open and his face had flamed bright red, his glazed eyes fixed on Andy's bare back as he pulled out some sweatpants and slipped them on. He turned to face them, holding an Air Force tee, clearly amused by the reaction he had provoked in the other two. He eyed Roy with curiosity.

"Is something wrong, Roy?"

Like a light switch turning off, Roy seemed to snap out of his daze and look away, down at the floor, at Alex, anywhere but at Andy.

"Yeah, sorry, man. You just surprised me, being buck-ass naked and all."

Alex couldn't help but smile at that and even Andy grinned.

"I keep forgetting," Andy said, "that out here I need to put my clothes on before I come out of the bathroom. Is that right, Big Brother?"

Alex nodded, giving the embarrassed Roy a playful nudge. Roy met his gaze and then they burst out laughing. Even Andy joined in. Alex hadn't realized how much he'd needed to laugh.

Roy looked considerably more relaxed once Andy donned his tee and stretched out onto his bed. When Roy abruptly excused himself and entered the bathroom, Alex figured he'd have a few minutes to question Andy. He wheeled over to his brother's bed.

"Sure you can't tell me why Mr. Davalos wanted you to stay? We're brothers, Andy. Shouldn't have no secrets from each other."

Andy sat up and eyed the bathroom door a moment. "He made me promise not to tell, but I will if you tell me about Roy. Why does he always stare at me like that, like he's…hungry?"

Alex was caught off-guard by the question. "Oh, well, that's kinda his business, bro. You gotta ask him. You can ask with me here, if you want. He don't mind."

Andy nodded, his eyes fixed again on the closed bathroom door, his face taking on a faraway look that puzzled Alex. Then he said, "Davalos wants us to learn how to shift Life."

Completely baffled, Alex could only grunt, "Huh?"

Gaze still fixed on the door, as though willing Roy to exit, Andy went on in his monotone voice. "Like we shift Death. He wanted to know if we could shift Life from one thing to another."

"What did you tell 'im?"

"I said we could."

Alex mulled this over in his mind. Shifting Death meant taking it from something that died. But shifting Life…how would that work? Then it hit him over the head like a load of falling books.

"He wants us to kill someone to bring someone else alive?"

Andy shrugged, still fixated on the bathroom door. "He didn't say."

Alex felt his stomach roiling with fear. It was one thing to kill bugs to save someone's life, but he would never murder a person just to…to what? Bring back somebody who died? What about the soul? Father Pat had taught him about the soul. Without it, weren't we just, like, zombies?

The bathroom door popped open, and Roy emerged, giving his pants a final adjustment. Since there had been no flush of the toilet, Alex felt sure he knew what Roy had been doing, but his mind was whirling with Andy's news.

"What's up, Alex?" Roy sounded worried. "You look like you just saw that spooky-ass cat again."

Before he could answer, Andy asked, "Roy, how come you stare at me so much?"

Caught off-guard, Roy flushed deep red and glanced away.

Alex shoved aside his fears and wheeled over to him, placing a hand on his arm. "I'll help if you wanna tell 'im."

Roy looked ready to faint. "What if he tells them others? Izzy'll freak."

Alex faced his curious brother. "This really is just Roy's business, Andy. So you can't tell the others. K?"

Andy nodded, his deep blue eyes fixed on Roy without wavering. He brushed his wet hair off his face and Roy issued a slight groan.

Alex looked over to see his friend sitting down on the bottom bunk bed, struggling to collect his thoughts.

"Well, um," Roy mumbled, "remember at the safe house how the guys was telling you about girls and stuff?"

Andy nodded, his face the picture of innocent curiosity.

"Well, see, most boys like girls, you know, to kiss and hug and…well, other stuff too." Roy cast a pleading look Alex's way.

"See, Andy," Alex took up the explanation, "Roy don't like girls like most boys do. He likes other boys. See?"

Andy tilted his head in consideration of what both boys had said. "He loves them, you mean, like he loves you?"

Roy flinched. "You told him how I…?"

Alex shook his head. "No, he…well, we can, I don' know, like, see in each other's heads sometimes. I dunno know how, but I dreamed about some of his childhood, and he saw…." Now it was his turn to blush.

Andy faced Roy. "I saw you press your lips to his. It's a powerful memory for him."

Alex didn't think Roy's face could get any redder, but it did. He looked like a fire truck. "Yeah, well, um…yeah. I kissed him. But see, he likes girls, so…"

The room fell into a heavy silence as Roy eyed Alex, and Alex eyed Andy.

Finally, Andy spoke. "I think I understand. So when you look at me, you see my brother."

"Yes," Roy blurted, and then looked mortified at Andy's unhappy expression. "I mean, no, that's only part of it. I mean, you're drop-dead beautiful, just like him, but you're also yourself too, and—" He stopped abruptly, clearly not having planned to say so much.

"I'm beautiful?" Andy looked pleased. "Nobody ever called me that before."

Roy nodded and Alex knew his best friend needed to end this conversation now, so he said, "Anyway, Andy, that's why he stares at you sometimes, but it's no big deal. Roy is the bestest friend I ever had, and he can be one for you too, if you let him."

Andy looked lost in thought again. "Thank you for explaining," he said, and then lay back on his bed, signaling the end of the conversation.

Alex exchanged a look with Roy and shrugged. They may never fully understand Andy. Besides, he knew Roy wanted to discuss what they'd overheard in the backyard, but Alex didn't feel comfortable discussing it right then. He wasn't sure why and that troubled him. Did he still not fully trust his brother? It hurt him like a punch to the gut to admit that no, he didn't.

CHAPTER TWELVE

WHAT'S HE UP TO, YOU THINK?

ALLISON SAT IN THE BACK seat of the unmarked, beat-up old van with Martin as her driver, awaiting their cue to enter the restricted zone. Her dad trusted him more than anyone else to keep her safe. The two men were more than employer and employee. They were friends, with Martin often taking part in her father's business deals and political wheelings and dealings. Allison had grown up having Martin around, and she'd always seen him as an uncle. He was strong and rugged and very handsome, which had become more apparent to her as she grew older. Even that scar above his left eye gave him a mysterious, movie-star quality that she liked.

Earlier, the team her dad had assembled had parked their vehicles south of a dry lakebed. They planned to wait there until after dark before going any closer to the restricted area around the base, so they took the opportunity to eat and stretch their legs. And to review final instructions one more time.

Mostly for me, Allison noted wryly.

But then, that made sense. Her part was the most crucial.

Allison had never been anywhere so desolate. As far as she could see in every direction there was only desert with low shrubs and low hills, but no life. It seemed like they'd waited there for hours—even after dark. Her dad had explained to the group that they had to wait until activity on the base quieted down for the night. He would first need to gain control of the perimeter cameras so he could display video loops, which he'd already uploaded to the server. If, for some reason, Allison wasn't admitted onto the base despite her "desperate plight," her dad and the others could still attempt to breach base security and find the boys on their own.

But Allison had no doubts about her acting prowess. Those men would be begging to help her. Of course, with her loss of memory, they couldn't immediately contact any family, but that was part of the plan. The only possible snag was how Alex, and his friends, might react when they saw her. That could blow the whole plan sky high. The others might not recognize her with the long, brown-haired wig and her face smudged with dirt and grime, but Alex wouldn't be fooled. She'd have to do her best to find out where they were being held, but not let them see her.

Piece of cake.

Maybe.

It was almost time to move out. Martin glanced back from the driver's seat, smiling. "Nervous, Allison?"

"Me, never." She chuckled.

"That's my girl."

She lifted the hand mirror and checked her appearance. The long wig looked disheveled, as though she'd been slapped around or been on the run, and she'd drawn a few fake scratches with a theatrical makeup pen to add to the smudges of dirt on her cheeks and chin. She set down the mirror and checked her clothes. Yes, torn in the right places, as though she'd been roughly grabbed and held down.

Perfect.

***

Roy woke with a start. He'd been dreaming about…he felt his face burn hot. Andy. About kissing Andy. Their kiss was intense, deeper and more meaningful than the one kiss he'd shared with Alex that time they were both drunk. Moonlight streamed through the window drapes and bathed his face in its soft glow, confusing him and making him think it might be morning already.

Then he realized what had awakened him. Voices. Poking his head over the side of the bed, he looked down to find William whispering to Alex. Then Alex slid out of the lower bunk into his wheelchair.

Roy didn't wait. He swung his lanky legs up and over the railing and skittered down the ladder as quietly as he could. William put a finger to his lips.

Roy leaned into Alex and whispered, "What's up?"

"William wants me to come with him."

"Can I come too?"

Alex eyed William in the shadowy darkness. "It's okay with me."

William nodded, glancing back over his shoulder at the slumbering form of Andy, barely a raised lump in the darkness. The even breathing assured Roy that Andy was sound asleep. He blushed again thinking of his dream, but quickly brushed it aside. William tiptoed to the open door and ushered them through. Alex wheeled out first, and Roy followed. William eased the door closed behind him and then led the way down the dark, silent hallway.

Outside, the air was warm, and the full moon overhead illuminated the empty base like a floodlight, making the safety lights on the tops and sides of buildings almost unnecessary.

"What's going on?" Roy whispered, though no one was in sight as far as he could see. The planes and helicopters looked creepy in the moonlight, like giant insects poised to attack anything that moved.

"William wants to show me something," was all Alex whispered back.

Roy followed, content to be with Alex—like always.

***

Java couldn't sleep. It wasn't that his body needed exercise, though he often had trouble sleeping if he'd been unable to work out. This time his mind raced with too many worries. He loved the fitness center and he loved showing off his strength to Izzy and the others, but he couldn't help thinking of his parents back home. He wished he could contact them, but he understood why he wasn't able to. The last thing he wanted was to put them in danger.

Sure, his dad didn't understand why Java was special ed and had always thought he was just lazy, but Java missed him anyway, and he especially longed to hug his mom, who'd always stood up for him against the "laziness" charge. She was the one who'd been to every IEP meeting at school since he was a little kid—his dad would never take time off work. But all that didn't matter, did it? They were his parents and he loved them. What were they thinking right now? They must be freaked out with worry. The others were thinking about the people at home too.

They'd talked about it in the gym. Even Carlos worried about his grams, who was the only family he had except a brother in prison.

And what about all these tests the base doctors were doing on Alex and Andy? How long would that take, and where would they go afterward? All these thoughts raced through his brain and kept sleep at bay.

Loud snoring made him look over the railing at the bed below where Izzy, obviously not so troubled, slumbered noisily. Java eyed the other set of bunk beds across the room where Carlos and Jorge slept quietly, then sighed and threw off his covers. So much light filled the room, even through the thick drapes, that he knew he wouldn't get back to sleep any time soon. Sitting up, he slid over to the ladder and eased his bare feet onto the smooth wood, descending to the floor without making a sound. He gazed a moment at Izzy snoring away like an old car engine and shook his head. Yeah, Izzy drove him crazy, but that fool was honestly his best friend. He'd known Izzy before he'd met any of the others. They went all the way back to first grade, and Izzy hadn't changed much except that he'd gotten bigger and louder.

Wandering to the window, Java pulled back the drapes. The full moon hovering over the base almost blinded him. Its intense, weirdly yellow light made the planes and helicopters—and even the large buildings—look unsettling.

Movement caught his eye below, and he directed his gaze toward the front of the house. Three figures rounded the corner from the direction of the front door, one of them in a wheelchair. Java gasped. What the hell? It was Roy and that kid William with Alex. They were obviously sneaking out for something. Java was tired of being kept in the dark. This time, he'd be in on the action. He let the drapes fall back into place and went to rouse the others.

***

William said nothing, merely led Alex and Roy alongside the buildings so they'd be out of sight of any sentries patrolling the base. Roy recognized the building with that lab inside, but that wasn't where William was headed. He skirted around behind that building and headed for a much larger structure with a curved roof that looked like the gym at Mark Twain High. There was a well-lit entrance, but William avoided that and led them along the side of the building toward the back.

Roy had never seen anyone so quiet as William. Despite wearing sneakers, he made not a sound, while Roy kept hearing his own shoes squeaking and Alex's wheels crunching along the pebbly tarmac with every rotation. But William? Silent as a cat! Weird.

Darting around the side toward the rear of the curved structure, the younger boy stopped at a door made of solid metal. Roy knew how to arc weld and solder, so he recognized solid construction when he saw it. This was a door meant to keep intruders out.

William surveyed the base, sweeping his eyes over everything within their line of sight. The glimmering moonlight made it quite clear they hadn't been followed because the base and the rear fence were visible. Apparently satisfied, he turned back to the door. It had an electronic lock on it, like the one at the lab building. Roy was good at picking locks, but the old-fashioned kind. He wondered how William planned to pick this one.

The younger boy reached into his pocket and slipped out what looked like an ID badge, similar to what the doctors wore. Then he pulled out a small plastic sandwich bag and opened it. Inside was a piece of Scotch tape with markings on it.

Alex whispered, "What are you doing?"

"This is one of Mr. Davalos's fingerprints I copied off the lab door, and this is a Level Four security pass. The pass alone won't get me in, but…just watch."

He held the ID card up to the little box. There was a beep, and a blue light scanned the card. A small glowing light changed from red to green, but the one next to it continued to glow bright red. William pressed the tape with the fingerprint on it up against a glass spot shaped like a finger. Roy heard another beep and the second light changed from red to green. The door popped open.

"Sick," Alex muttered.

William cast him a confused look, eyebrows raised, as he returned the items to his pocket.

"It means awesome," Alex explained, drawing a child-like smile out of the younger boy that Roy found endearing.

William pulled open the door and ushered them in, searching the area one last time. Apparently satisfied, he filed in after Roy and closed the door.

It locked with a *click*.

***

Java had quickly tugged a shirt over his thick torso before waking the others, but he didn't have time to change his pajama pants. Izzy almost screamed when Java touched him. Fortunately, thanks to the bright moonlight streaming through the drapes, before any sound came out, he recognized who had awakened him. Once everyone was up, he urged them to hurry or they would lose the others, so the boys slipped on shoes without socks and tip-toed down the stairs. Spotting the kitchen light spilling into the front hall, Java heard muffled conversation between the colonel and Amanda. Figuring this was their only chance, he waved the others down, and they crept out the front door and into the night.

Alex, Roy, and the other kid were nowhere in sight.

Carlos sidled up to him. "Where'd they go?"

"Dunno." Java started out across the silent but well-lit tarmac, the others following.

"Java, I'm tired," Izzy whined. "An' I'm still hurting from all that weight lifting you made me do."

"Quiet, Izzy!" Java hissed, pointing across the base toward the far buildings.

In the distance, three figures could be seen beneath the light of the full moon. One was in a wheelchair.

"Come on," Java urged and sprinted as quietly as he could in that direction.

They dashed past the empty jets to the far building where he'd spotted their friends, but the three boys were already gone when they got there. Deciding they might have entered one of the hangars through a back door, Java waved the others forward and was grateful when Izzy didn't complain. That's one thing Java loved about Jorge—he never complained.

They reached the rear of the lab building where the testing on Alex and Andy had been conducted, but silence reigned, and no one was in sight. Frustrated, yet not wanting to give up, Java was about to continue searching when he spotted a lone figure skulking along the next building over.

It was Andy!

What was he doing out here by himself?

Java waited until Andy rounded the edge of a huge hangar with a curved roof that looked like the gym at school.

Carlos leaned in. "What's he up to, you think?"

Java eyed him in the gloom. Carlo's bald head gleamed in the moonlight, his face tight with anticipation.

"Let's find out."

With Java leading the way, they all trotted off in the same direction as Andy.

***

Allison stumbled over the rough desert terrain, running with frantic abandon toward the only place within many miles, the military base directly ahead. She kept looking back over her shoulder, but the van, which she'd jumped out of as planned, was no longer in sight. By now the base must've seen her on their cameras, so she pressed on even harder, despite the pain in her knees from when she struck the hard desert floor.

Even though it was night, the full moon hovering lazily in the sky provided more than enough illumination, so she didn't trip over every rock or dried piece of shrubbery. She panted heavily like she'd seen dogs do after a long run, her breaths coming in frightened gasps. Her tangled hair stuck to the dampness of her face like it was glued. She didn't know how far the security cameras on the base could zoom, so she had to be convincing.

The base loomed closer. She'd seen some No Trespassing signs farther out in the desert and stumbled past even more of them as her faltering pace brought her closer to the large, rolling, chain-link gate and the guardhouse just in front of it. She could make out another sign reading, "No Photography Beyond This Point," but she didn't have her phone so that wouldn't be a problem. Hoping she looked close to collapse from exhaustion and hunger, she staggered on, grateful when the door to the guardhouse opened and a man in uniform stepped onto the unpaved road.

He held a walkie-talkie to the side of his head, but she couldn't make out his words. Then he reached back into the guardhouse with the walkie-talkie, apparently to set it down. He began sprinting toward her, and she plowed forward to meet him.

***

Colonel Walker sat fully clothed in his kitchen beside Amanda, who'd insisted she wait up with him until Alex returned from his visit to the Weapon Lab. He needed to be ready to head over there if something went wrong, but for now the two of them sat in a companionable silence sipping coffee, Amanda's small hand resting atop his larger one.

"Don't worry, honey," she said quietly. "We won't let anyone else hurt those boys."

He nodded, pulled from his thoughts to regard her with love. "I was thinking again how much William has changed. He's so human now that no one could tell the difference. I hope Alex takes the truth well. Having his approval is more important to William than I would've imagined."

She smiled, stretching her laugh lines in all directions. "Alex will be fine. He's seen too much pain in his life to want to hurt anyone else. You know that better than I."

Before he could respond, his phone vibrated. Slipping it off the clip on his belt, he held it to his ear. "This is Colonel Walker." He listened, stunned by what he was hearing. "A girl? Out in the desert? She said she escaped from her abductor?"

Amanda gasped, leaning in to listen, her soft features creased with concern.

"No sign of anyone out there?" He listened again. "What did the cameras record?" He paused and then, "Send that footage to my phone. I'll be right over."

He ended the call, but held the phone out, waiting. "You heard?" He glanced at Amanda.

"Most of it. What would a girl being doing this far out?"

He frowned. "Good question, but she appears to be unharmed, physically."

A message with a video share popped up on his screen. He opened the file as Amanda scooted her chair to his side so she could watch.

The moon illuminated the desert with great clarity, but the moving object was far distant and only vaguely resembled a vehicle. A van, maybe. The colonel noted the shape, while its white coloring helped set it apart from the darkness surrounding it.

Something dropped from the rear of the van and felt to the desert floor, where it lay unmoving. Whoever was driving didn't seem to notice, as the vehicle continued on, leaving a dust trail in its wake.

When the vehicle was no longer in sight, something moved and then a figure arose against the night. Nothing of its size or features could be distinguished. It paused a long moment and then began an erratic course toward the camera, weaving and stumbling.

The video ended, and Colonel Walker set down his phone.

"My God," Amanda whispered. "That poor thing."

He considered the matter. It looked legitimate, but he'd been harboring secrets longer than most people had been alive and he couldn't take any chances that this might be some kind of setup. It could just be another UFO nut desperate to impress her friends by getting onto the base, or it could be something much more sinister, especially after what Davalos had told him about the group of zealots hunting Alex.

"I'll go up and talk to her. If I need you, I'll call."

***

Dane had known guys from high school who went into the military, and he'd envied them at the time. Unfortunately, he'd been too stupid to score a grade worth shit on that test they make you take. And then there was his idiot mother, thinking he'd go to college and become a doctor! Hell, he'd barely passed his high school special-ed classes!

Now, dressed like a ninja and crawling along a rough desert floor in the dead of night, Dane finally had a taste of the excitement his buddies so often talked about. The outer base fence was still quite a ways ahead. He glanced back at his dad and the priest, almost invisible in their pitch-black attire. If it wasn't for the bright-ass full moon, they'd be like ghosts out there.

At the front of their group, Shaw, Martin, and two other guys who looked like they could take down a grizzly bear paused, while Shaw fiddled with his tablet. Dane didn't know much about that stuff, but he wasn't so dumb that he didn't understand the plan. Shaw had recorded a loop of the empty desert and, if all went well, he would hack into the base system and replace the live feed with that loop, all the while making it seem like the camera was still live. He'd even snagged some footage of the trap door area that was their target so the base soldiers watching those cameras would never see anything but empty desert. As Roy would say, it was a wicked plan. Dane still didn't fully trust Shaw, but he liked how the guy thought.

He was also stoked that his dad had a big role to play. When Shaw told Martin he needed a locksmith, Nathan had announced that he used to work as one. Intrigued, Shaw had set him to work picking a complex lock system that matched what they'd be facing at the base. It had taken his dad two hours to crack it the first time, one hour the second, and fifteen minutes on his third attempt. Shaw was satisfied.

Now Dane waited, something he'd never been good at as a boy or a man. He liked activity. He yearned to be doing something every minute. All this sneaking around wasn't his thing, but he knew it was the only way to get to Roy, the most kickass little brother a guy could hope for. Every time he recalled how his mother had kept them apart growing up and poisoned his heart against his dad, he wanted to punch every wall he encountered—a bad habit from his youth that had broken more than a few knuckles over the years.

If nothing else, all this crazy-ass drama about Alex that they'd been dragged into had forced Dane to slow down and learn some patience. That explained how he'd come to be lying flat on his stomach, gloved hands pressed into the hard desert earth, awaiting the signal from Shaw to proceed. Once his daughter gained entry, Shaw would raise one hand. That was the cue to move forward, slowly and with extreme silence. The cameras were taken care of, but it was possible, Shaw had warned them, that the base commander had installed sound detectors too. With absolute stillness pressing in on him from all sides, Dane understood the need for stealth.

He squinted at the lights of the base up ahead. He sucked at distances because he sucked at math, but he figured they were maybe ten or fifteen minutes away at crawling speed. He'd never imagined as a custodial worker for Mark Twain High School that he'd be attempting to sneak into a top-secret military base. But then, he'd never imagined his brother's best friend would have crazy-ass powers that everybody in the world seemed to want.

He spotted a hand raised into the air, the lights of the base in the distance making it look like a shadow puppet.

Time to move in.

CHAPTER THIRTEEN

I'M...AN EXPERIMENT

ALEX FOLLOWED WILLIAM DOWN A dark corridor, Roy inching his way along behind. He honestly couldn't see anything except William's blond hair since the boy was wearing a black pullover shirt and black sweatpants. William had no trouble finding his way, though. It was weird how easily the kid could see in this darkness. Alex pressed forward, his wheels squeaking against the shiny wood floor, sounding like little mice.

Closed doors on either side ignited Alex's curiosity, but William made no move toward any of them. He continued down the corridor—toward whatever lay at the end, Alex guessed. He glanced back at Roy just to reassure himself that his friend was still there, and relaxed when Roy's pale face floated out of the gloom a few feet back.

William finally stopped in front of double doors that, as well as Alex could make out, seemed to have a locking system similar to the outside door. William fumbled in his pocket and Alex presumed he would use the same method he used before. When he heard the first beep followed swiftly by the second, he knew he'd guessed right. William stepped back and pulled open one of the doors with ease.

Alex eyed him in the darkness, but could make out nothing of his facial expression, so he wheeled himself through the door and heard Roy scuttle in behind him. The door closed with a click, and Alex looked around.

Small lights along the upper walls near the ceiling revealed that he was in another lab, much larger and taller than the one in which he and Andy were being tested. Much of the wall to his left was taken up by what looked like gigantic fish tanks filled with a strange blueish liquid, each easily big enough to house a large shark. There was also a huge glass room taking up most of the far corner. Alex could make out furniture inside, including a bed, and he shivered, thinking of the glass room Andy had grown up in.

Turning to William, he whispered, "What is this place?"

William met his gaze in the murk. "This is where I was born."

Roy gasped. "The hell?"

William shifted his piercing eyes to Roy and then back to Alex. "I'm not like you, Alex, or you, Roy. I'm…an experiment."

A cold fear washed through Alex, chilling him to his core. "I don't get it."

"Me either," echoed Roy, his voice trembling.

William strode toward the nearest fish tank and gazed in at the weird-looking liquid. "I grew up in here until I was thirteen years old and that's when they woke me up. That was four years ago, but I'm still thirteen. They told me I won't get any older."

Alex gagged, absorbing the pain William's voice radiated. He'd never felt so much despair in his life. William's tone was informational, but the underlying hurt almost suffocated Alex, and he wanted to just pull the kid into a hug and never let go.

"Dr. Shepherd helped make me," William went on, his boyish voice sober and serious, "along with other doctors who are dead now. Colonel Walker was in charge of the project until I went, as he tells me, a bit off the rails in Los Angeles three years ago."

He paused, and Alex exchanged a horrified glance with Roy. His friend's open mouth and scrunched eyebrows revealed that Roy was confused too.

William obviously comprehended their puzzlement because he said, "I know it's hard to understand, but I was made in this lab. It's called genetic engineering. Also something called transgenics, which I don't fully understand. I'm mostly human, but I have animal DNA spliced in that gives me certain abilities."

Abilities. Alex knew that word. He'd focus on that. "What abilities?"

"I can control those roaches, like you saw in the lab. I can also communicate with other animals, get them to do what I want, even understand what they're trying to tell me at times. I'm strong. Stronger than any man alive. And I have a hard layer under my skin to repel bullets."

He said these things as if it was ordinary stuff, talking to animals and bugs and being super strong. Alex was completely bewildered, but his innate power assured him that William spoke the truth. There was too much agony surrounding his confession for it to be even a tiny bit false. The biggest question he could think of was, "Why? Why would they do this?"

William sighed, and the hurt within that simple sound stabbed Alex through the heart.

"To create an unstoppable weapon to be used in war, a weapon no one would ever suspect. That's my real name – Weapon. I chose to call myself William because my friend thought it was a cool name."

"I gotta sit down." That was Roy, who pulled over a rolling chair and plopped into it, gazing at William in horror. "It's crazy! It's like one of Izzy's crazy-ass horror movies!"

That was exactly what Alex had been thinking. It *was* a horror movie, except it was real. "He's telling the truth, Roy, though I don't got a clue how it happened."

Roy looked like he might be sick. "Uh," he began, clearing his throat, "what happened in LA?"

"I killed a police officer," William replied. His voice sounded casual, but Alex heard the remorse.

"Holy shit!"

"He shot me, and I reacted without thinking," William explained, "because that was my training. I've since learned that people can make poor choices, especially when they're scared, and that's what that man did."

There was a long moment of silence as Alex digested this information. He eyed Roy and noted his friend staring at William with distrust.

"He feels bad about it, Roy. I can tell."

Roy faced him a moment, then asked William, "What did you mean by unstoppable?"

"I can't be killed, as far as we know. Or hurt." He stepped closer to Alex and flexed his arm. The tight sleeve bulged at the upper arm. "Feel that."

Nervous, Alex reached up and squeezed the muscle. It felt like solid metal. His eyes bulged. "It's like a rock. Harder even."

William lowered his arm and faced Roy. "Punch me, Roy, here." He pointed to his midsection.

Roy looked startled by the request. "I'm no fighter, man."

"I just want you to understand. Do it. Hard as you can."

Roy eyed Alex, who shrugged. Then he stood and faced William, noting how much taller he was than the younger boy, well over a foot.

"You sure?"

William nodded. "Hard as you can."

With extreme reluctance, Roy clenched his fist and pulled back his right arm. William pointed to his midsection again, and Roy punched with all the force he could muster, making contact with the younger boy and—

"Shit!"

William stood as though nothing had happened. Roy hadn't even moved him an inch!

Roy gaped in astonishment, shaking his injured hand to relieve the pain. "You're like a wall! Alex, he's…it's crazy!"

Alex had watched the display with a mixture of fear and astonishment. He extended his arm and tapped his fist against William's abs a few times, feeling the hardness Roy described. Unbelievable!

He studied the younger boy a moment. "How could you, you know, grow up in this…?" He pointed to the tank. "Everybody gots to have a mom."

William shook his head. "No. Doctors can make babies in labs like this."

Alex's mouth dropped open in horror. This was *worse* than Izzy's monster movies!

William glanced down, as though afraid to look Alex in the eye, even in such dim lighting. "That's why I needed a big brother, Alex. My only family is…"

He trailed off and Alex squinted at him. "You have family? I thought…"

William raised his eyes and fixed his gaze on Alex. "I was the first. They called me a prototype. After Los Angeles, the government wanted to destroy me, but Colonel Walker stopped them. He convinced them to let him work with me. They agreed, mostly because they spent so much money to create me, but they took the Weapon project away from the colonel and gave it to Davalos. He decided to do something…different.”

“Uh, William?” Roy began, the tremor in his voice more pronounced. “If that tank you be standing near is where you was born, what are the other ones for?”

“I'll show you,” William intoned soberly, “but please don't freak out.”

“Okay,” Alex replied, because Roy was silent. Alex made eye contact with his best friend and felt Roy's fear pour into him like a flood.

William led the way past the large tanks. Almost like he was sleep-walking, Alex followed, Roy at his side, flexing and unflexing his right hand, looking like he was about to enter Hell itself.

***

“—and I was so scared he might come back that I just lay there in the desert for a while till I couldn't hear the van anymore. Then I ran here as fast as I could.”

Colonel Walker had listened intently as the girl—who'd described being hit on the head when she was kidnapped and couldn't remember her name—finished her breathless and tearful explanation, sobbing into tissue after tissue as she described her abduction and eventual escape.

He stood before her, flanked by several of his airmen, including one female named Peters who'd taken the lead in helping the girl the moment she'd entered the base. Her story sounded convincing—on the surface—except the amnesia part. It was a stale movie trope that almost never materialized in real life. The colonel had been in the secrecy business all his life. He could smell a ruse a mile away, and this girl's story didn't gel for him.

He rubbed his chin, considering her recitation. “And you have no idea why you were taken?”

“I think I was living on the streets,” Allison said, choking back sobs, “because I remember him saying he'd help me, but…” She blew her nose into a crumpled wad of tissues and looked up at him. “I think he wanted to sell me for…” She trailed off, tears welling in her eyes.

“Try not to cry, you're safe now,” he said, feeling an upsurge of sympathy for whatever she might have gone through. He turned to the female. "Airman Peters, take her to the infirmary and have the medics give her a full exam. Then we'll decide what to do."

The teen girl gushed with relief. "Oh, thank you, Colonel, thank you for not sending me back out there."

"We would never do that. You'll be safe here."

Peters, a feisty young pilot, helped the girl to her feet and received a grateful smile in return. She placed one arm around the girl and guided her from the room.

Sergeant Stern waited until the door closed behind them before asking, "Do you believe her, sir?"

"I'm not sure her story adds up," Walker replied. "Assuming she was being kidnapped, why drive her all the way out here? It's not enroute to anywhere."

"I agree, Colonel," Stern replied. He was in his midthirties, a master sergeant and the colonel's right-hand man for the past five years, an indispensable aide. "But what reason could she have for being here?"

Walker considered a moment. This base was always popular with the fringe crowd because of the UFO propaganda put out by the government to disguise their real activities. He considered once again that she might be there on a dare from her nerd friends.

"She could be an advance scout looking for aliens."

Stern, typically stoic and dead serious, offered what could pass, for him, as a smile.

"Watch her, Sergeant, you and Peters. Don't let her out of your sight."

"Yes, Sir." Stern saluted and strode from the room, leaving Colonel Walker feeling a deep sense of unease.

***

Java led the others quietly along the side of a large building without windows, but with small overhead lights placed high up near the roof. With the full moon still lighting up the base like it was daytime, those tiny-ass lights barely registered. The only thing the moon didn't show him was where the hell Andy had gone!

His swirling blond hair had vanished around the side of this building, but when Java and the others followed, he'd disappeared. They stopped and looked at the other buildings surrounding them, but there was no sign of Andy. Figuring he must've ducked into one of these structures, Java waved the others forward.

Just as he neared the corner, a hand grabbed his shoulder. He whirled, fist clenched.

"Shit, Java, it's me!"

"The hell're you sneakin' up on me for, Izzy?"

"I heard something," Izzy hissed, pointing to an area between the building they'd huddled up against and another one a short distance away.

Java looked where Izzy was pointing. He saw nothing but empty tarmac and another plain building without windows directly across from them. He thought some of these buildings might be hangars, but he wasn't sure.

Carlos crept up to them and Java said, "Crackhead says he heard something. Did you?"

Carlos shook his head, eyes squinting as he surveyed their surroundings.

Jorge joined them and pointed in the same direction as Izzy.

Java stared but saw nothing. This place creeped him out and he wasn't afraid to admit it. Not as much as that graveyard where'd they'd been attacked by all them cats, but close.

"Show me," he whispered to Izzy and Jorge.

The two boys exchanged a look. Jorge looked calm, as always, but Izzy seemed spooked, like he'd freak any moment. Jorge padded away from the wall, his slippers making tiny *slap-slap* sounds against the ground. Java nudged Izzy. Izzy's face was twisted with fear, and he stayed rooted to the spot.

"Fool," Java hissed, "we're on an army base. What's to hurt us here?"

"Air Force, fool," whispered Carlos.

Java shot him a look that would kill. "Whatever." To Izzy, "Show me where the sound came from."

Trembling, Izzy crept silently after Jorge, looking side to side even though it was obvious no one could sneak up on them out in the open. Jorge had stopped in the empty space between the two buildings and stood staring down at the sandy tarmac.

A metal trapdoor, heavy looking, lay flush with the ground, covered in a slight dusting of sand that had recently been disturbed. Java could tell because much of the sand had slid to one end and lay pooled together.

"He's right," Izzy whispered, staring at the door in fear. "I still hear it, like somebody climbing down a ladder."

Java eyed Carlos, who just shrugged.

"Must be his ADHD," Carlos whispered. "I heard kids like that see and hear more better than us."

Java nodded. He knew that already. Izzy had proven it on more than one occasion. Java bent to examine the metal door. There was a large ring to lift it, and beside that, completely embedded in the metal, was some kind of electronic box covered with numbers.

Carlos squatted beside him to study it. "Looks like you need some kinda code to get in."

Java nodded. "Maybe this be where Andy went."

"How would he know the code?"

"Dunno. Maybe from working in that lab with Alex."

Carlos seemed to accept that explanation and they both stood. Izzy looked ready to bolt, while Jorge was calmly taking in the conversation.

"I say we hide and watch this trapdoor," Java suggested, "see if somebody goes in or out."

"Hell no!" Izzy's eyes were wide with indignation. "We're going back, Java!"

Java eyed Carlos and Jorge.

"I'll stay," Carlos whispered. "How 'bout you, Jorge?"

Jorge smiled, which for him meant "yes."

"You can go back, Izzy," Java said, "but we's staying."

Izzy looked horrified, like Java had asked him to walk over broken glass barefooted. "Are you crazy? I might get attacked or killed or something!"

Java sighed. "Then I guess you be staying with us."

He turned and walked toward the rear of the building where a large brown storage container rested against the wall. Carlos and Jorge followed without hesitation. Izzy cursed under his breath and loped after them.

***

Alex relaxed—a little—and so did Roy, once William had led them past those creepy fish tanks with the thick, swirling bits of color that looked like seaweed, through a door at the rear of the lab, and out into another dark corridor that seemed to stretch on forever. At the far end appeared to be double metal doors large enough to let an elephant pass through.

Roy slogged along beside him, and Alex felt his best friend's terror and confusion. He wasn't sure which emotion was dominant after all they'd just learned. He did a quick spin on Roy as they moved toward those giant doors, pulling the fear and uncertainty from his friend.

Roy looked over at him so suddenly that Alex stopped a moment to stare.

"You just spinned me, didn't you?"

Alex nodded, forcing the last bits of Roy's fear out of himself.

Roy offered a grateful smile, placing one hand on Alex's shoulder. "Thanks, man. After all that, I was scared shitless."

William had stopped a few feet ahead and turned to face them. "You guys coming?"

"Yeah," Roy replied, his voice filled with steady calmness.

He ushered Alex forward and then followed, his footsteps echoing throughout the vast chamber.

Shadows covered Alex like a hoodie and his mind drifted back to that night in the cemetery when they'd dug up his parents' graves. That was the night his whole world view had shifted, never to return to where it had once been. He felt, deep in his soul, that tonight would be another of those nights. What William already confessed had changed him, and now he was about to see something else that he'd never be able to forget.

William's silent steps unnerved him, though now he sort-of understood how the other boy could accomplish something seemingly impossible. He'd been made that way. With parts of animals. DNA or something.

William stopped at the massive double doors and now Alex could make out for certain that they were made of solid metal.

To keep something out or in?

Resting his sweating hands in his lap, he waited for William to open the doors. The younger boy stepped in front of another electronic panel and pressed several buttons, a code, Alex guessed. There was a low beep. Then William used the thumbprint trick once more and there was a second, higher pitched beep. But then he pulled a plastic card from his pocket and slid it through a slot, like he'd seen people do with credit cards. With a slight buzz sound, one of the doors popped open.

William showed Alex the card. "I got this from Dr. Shepherd because she wanted me to make friends with…the others."

Alex nodded. Just what were these others?

To accommodate the swinging door, Alex wheeled himself back, bumping into Roy, who grunted in pain.

"Sorry, man."

Roy leaned on the wheelchair and rubbed his left foot. "I'm good."

By now, William had the enormous door swung wide and ushered them inside. Alex saw nothing ahead except more blackness. At the far end of this cavernous room, there was a small window set high up in one corner near the ceiling. Moonlight streamed through it and Alex could just make out what looked like bars. Was that a cage? Wait! Something moved! It looked hairy and small.

Then Alex became aware of movement on both sides of him, scuttling and shifting movements, as though something was stirring in the darkness. Then he heard a growl, followed by a snuffle, and heavy breathing coming from all around him.

Feeling unease creep into his heart, he wheeled forward; Roy pressed up against him, nervous and skittish. Alex heard the flick of a light switch. With a gradualness that further added to the menacing surroundings, six pools of light began to appear along the upper walls on both sides. The pools grew brighter, but stayed soft and pale, like whatever was in this chamber didn't like bright lights.

Cages materialized out of the gloom. Big cages, like he'd seen at the zoo. The scuffling of feet grew louder. No, not feet, he realized. Paws. And claws. The lights increased, the growling and chittering grew louder. The cages became visible, and so did their occupants.

Alex gasped, and Roy screamed.

CHAPTER FOURTEEN
YOU CAN COME OR NOT

DANE CROUCHED LOW, SHAW AND his men on their knees around him, watching Nathan manipulate his pick tools, working his way through the complicated tumblers within the heavy-duty padlock. The circular trap door resting on the surface of the desert blended in so well that Dane would never have found it on his own. They'd had to sweep away a thick layer of sand to uncover it, but Shaw had known just where to look. He'd learned about it when he supervised the positioning of cameras at this base. He had, in fact, suggested that one of the perimeter cameras be fixed on this specific spot, since it might allow unauthorized entry into the base. Right now, whoever was watching the cameras inside would be seeing the hidden trapdoor covered with dirt and untouched, thanks to the repeating video loop Shaw had uploaded.

Dane glanced at his watch—digital, since he'd never figured out the other kind. His dad had been working for ten minutes. He eyed Shaw's men, who focused their attention on the base, making certain no one happened to spot them through the tall chain-link fencing. Perimeter guards could prove to be a problem the longer they lingered out in the open. If they were spotted, the whole gig was over, since none of them had any weapons. But, so far, the place had been crazy-quiet. In fact, the whole damned desert was too quiet, nothing like Dane's noisy apartment complex back in Hawthorne.

A low sigh of satisfaction made him swivel his head back toward his dad. Grinning, Nathan slipped the heavy shaft from the lock and slid the padlock out of the thick rings through which it had been fastened. Shaw motioned Martin over.

The tall man crawled to the trapdoor and tugged at the ring. The thick metal door shifted, loosening dirt wedged in between it and the base buried in the earth. He pulled harder and the door rose up into the air.

Shaw had explained that underground bomb shelters like this had been built in the 1950s and 1960s to protect personnel and equipment against possible nuclear attack—not to mention atomic bomb testing in the desert.

Martin eased the trap door flat against the desert floor. They waited in silence, listening for sounds that would indicate anyone below might have heard something. When nothing moved, either from below or in the direction of the base, Shaw waved Martin forward. Swift as a ninja, Martin was through the hole and clambering down a metal ladder attached to the wall. Shaw signaled Dane, and he eagerly followed.

***

Java's legs felt so cramped he didn't think he'd ever loosen them up. Izzy kept spinning in circles like some kind of ballet dancer and it was getting on his nerves. Carlos's too, he could tell. Jorge just drew imaginary V's all over the storage container with his finger and looked happy as could be.

Carlos leaned in and whispered, "Java, this ain't going nowhere. I'm for headin' back to the house."

Java sulked. He didn't want to give up just when he thought they might be on to something big. He didn't know how long they'd already waited, but there was no sign of Andy or anyone else, for that matter. This place was deader than dead.

"Okay," he agreed, his voice thick with failure, a taste he hated more than being called a dummy. He stood and stretched out his quads and hamstrings the way he used to when he played football back in the day. "Let's go. C'mon, Izzy."

Izzy ignored him, spinning around with a distracted expression on his face, like he was on some other planet. Java reached out to grab his shoulder. Izzy stopped and glared at him. "What?"

"We're going back, fool."

Izzy's eyes widened with joy. "About time, fool. I hate it out here."

With Carlos in the lead this time, they rounded the huge storage container and started to walk past the weird trap door when suddenly, without warning, it popped open, and Andy stuck his head out. The boys froze, but it was too late. They'd been spotted.

"Hi, guys," Andy offered, like there was nothing strange about him being in some kind of bomb shelter.

Java stepped forward, the others flanking him. "We been lookin' for you." He noticed that Andy was dressed in regular clothes, while they were all wearing at least pajama pants. Hadn't Andy gone to bed at all?

"I found this really amazing underground hideout," Andy replied, brushing long strands of blond hair off his face. "Come on down and check it out."

"No way," blurted Izzy.

Java turned to him in annoyance. "Why not?"

"Cause it's dark down there," Izzy replied smugly. "It's underground, right?"

Java was ready to punch him.

"There's lights down here, Israel," Andy said. "I'm going to explore some more. You can come or not."

He dropped below their line of sight and Java heard feet clanking on metal as Andy descended. Java and Carlos exchanged a look.

"I'm in," said Carlos.

Java eyed the silent Jorge. "You, Jorge?"

Jorge nodded. "I'm in," repeating Carlos's words and sounding weirdly like him.

Izzy shook his head.

"Okay, Izzy, you go back to the house," whispered Java. "We'll see you later."

He turned and lowered one leg into the hole, his foot finding the first ladder rung. Planting his other foot beside the first, he began his descent.

"Hell no, I ain't staying here," hissed Izzy, flicking his gaze this way and that, shivering.

"Good," whispered Carlos. "You go next."

He pushed Izzy in front of him.

Java's head was still visible just below. "Hurry up, fool!"

Izzy lowered his foot into the hole.

***

Colonel Walker stood beside Sergeant Stern inside the monitor room studying the images that flashed across multiple screens—images from each of the perimeter cameras encircling the base.

"This camera captured the van far out in the distance," Stern said, pointing at a screen at the right of the console.

"Play me that footage," Walker told the young airman monitoring the live camera feeds.

The airman, midtwenties, close-cropped brown hair, deftly punched some buttons on the console that looked as though it belonged inside a fighter jet. Walker had overseen the installation of this setup personally. Russell Shaw had been in attendance to make certain the job was done correctly. These cameras had extreme magnification and zoom capabilities because Walker, not to mention the brass at the Pentagon, sought to head off any potential intruders while they were still miles out in the desert.

"Here it is, sir," the airman said, his voice crisp as a new dollar bill.

Walker studied the screen. The night-vision image clearly showed a van far out in the desert barreling along at a high rate of speed, similar to the footage he'd seen on his phone, only much clearer. The van appeared to be heading past the base, but its movements were erratic, like the driver was drunk or high. Or perhaps he was pretending his van was an ATV and could handle sharp, extreme shifts in direction? The driver seemed to suddenly lose control and the van skidded into a spin, kicking up a cloud of dust that momentarily hid the vehicle from view.

When the dust cleared, the van had straightened out and continued its erratic course past the base. But as it pulled away, something stirred on the desert floor. It looked like it could be a prairie dog, at first, until it rose higher and began staggering in the direction of the base.

It was the girl.

"Pause," Walker said to the airman, who obeyed. The image froze on the dark figure, still a small speck in the distance. "There's been no movement at any of the other perimeter cameras?"

"No, sir. They've been exactly the same ever since my shift began."

Walker studied screen after screen. Each displayed a different sector of the desert landscape, almost like the base was the sun and these cameras were its rays.

"What are you looking for, Colonel?" Stern asked, studying the screens alongside him.

"Something doesn't add up, Sergeant. This base isn't on the way to anywhere. If the girl was abducted, why would the kidnapper risk being caught on camera by getting so close to the perimeter?"

"Perhaps the driver is high, Colonel," Stern replied evenly. "You saw how he was driving."

Walker nodded, his eyebrows furrowed with concentration. "But it almost seemed as though his bad driving was intentional."

"For what purpose?"

"That's the question, isn't it, Sergeant?"

Stern returned to examining the various desert scenes laid out before them.

Walker had noticed something odd on one of these screens. Which one…? He focused on the western perimeter, specifically at the image of the carefully hidden trapdoor entrance to the underground radiation shelter. Most of the men and women on base didn't even know it was there—only senior officers like himself and Stern, and Davalos because he'd been given control of the underground. What was it about this image that troubled him?

Wait a minute…

"Zoom in on camera five," he ordered the airman, who complied at once with deft movements of his fingers.

The image became larger and then, with the press of a few buttons, the airman cleared up its appearance. It showed a tiny desert shrew, sitting atop the hidden trap door. Walker stared at it. The creature didn't move. In fact, it hadn't moved the entire time he'd been examining these different camera angles.

"How long has that shrew been there?"

The airman gazed at the camera a moment before facing the colonel. "Since I came on duty. I noticed it right away. Strange that it's still there, sir."

Walker stood to his full height and rubbed his chin. Something was wrong. He felt it. "Sergeant Stern, send some men around to every perimeter camera, starting with this one. I want to know if that shrew is there now and if anything looks amiss. Call me with anything out of the ordinary. I'm going to take our guest to my house for the time being."

"Yes, sir." Stern saluted and strode off toward the exit.

Walker faced the monitor, fixing his gaze once more on that shrew. It had not moved, which meant someone had fed a loop into the system.

And that girl was in on it.

CHAPTER FIFTEEN

WHAT THE HELL ARE THESE THINGS FOR?

ALEX'S MOUTH HUNG OPEN IN astonishment. It was like a zoo for monsters! And yet, there were familiar aspects to each of these… things, aspects that reminded him of real animals he'd seen at the zoo or on TV.

"This is my… family," William said so quietly Alex almost missed it.

"Your *family*?" That came from Roy.

Alex glanced over his shoulder to find Roy gawking like a fish, his eyes the size of eggs as he stared at the creatures surrounding them. "What *are* these things?"

William took several steps toward the first cage on the right side of the chamber. Alex noted that each cage had thick metal bars that reached from the floor to ceiling, clearly constructed to contain really big, strong animals. And the creature in front of him sure fit that bill.

It looked something like a massive brown bear, but the fur seemed weird, like there was something underneath it, something hard and shiny that the hair grew out of. Its nose was longer than any bear he'd ever seen, and its eyes were large, with lids sticking out and up and over, as though covering the eyes to protect them? The strangeness of the creature made Alex shudder, like he had with the roaches.

"This is Bear," William explained, as though introducing him. "He's made up of many animals, like we all are, but mainly a grizzly bear with enhanced armadillo plating and bone deposits under the skin to protect vital organs from bullets. Oh, and he possesses the bite of a crocodile."

Roy glanced nervously at Alex, then back at the creature. "Huh?"

William faced the cage and extended his hand. "Stand, Bear."

"Bear" raised itself on its back legs and Alex gasped. It was taller than anything he'd ever seen, almost like him and Roy put together, it's head nearly brushing the ceiling of its cage.

"Come here, Alex," William said quietly. "I want him to know you."

"Uh…why?" Alex gripped his wheel handles hard, heart pounding. He didn't want to get any closer.

William studied him a moment. "I want them to protect you, no matter what. That's what the colonel wants too."

Alex hesitated, glancing at Roy for support. But Roy looked just as confused.

"Protect me from what?" Alex couldn't pull his gaze from the oddly distorted creature before him. He almost felt sorry for it.

"From anyone and anything that might try to harm you," William explained. "They obey me, Alex. I'm one of them, remember?"

Alex felt the truth in William's voice and knew, as well as he knew anything, that William could be trusted. He wheeled himself up to the cage. The bear-thing towered over him, and Alex realized it could crush him with one swipe of its paw, which was as big as his head.

"Bear," William said in a soft voice, "this is my brother, Alex. You will never harm him. You will protect him always." Then he made sounds like grumbling or maybe growling, and the creature growled back like it understood. "Alex, put out your hand."

"What?" Alex wasn't prepared for that.

"Your hand, so he can sniff you," William said, as though talking about a cute little puppy. "Once he's done that, he will never forget you."

Alex felt Roy grip his shoulder and it gave him strength. Arm trembling, he extended his hand and stretched out his fingers, inching them between two of the thick gray bars.

Bear bent down, his wet, cool nose brushing Alex's fingertips. Rather than feel revulsion, Alex sensed innate gentleness in this massive animal.

"Can I pet him?"

Roy gasped in horror, but William nodded.

Alex pushed his arm farther into the cage and lightly brushed his fingertips along the animal's muzzle. Bear bent down so Alex could caress the top of its immense head. The fur was soft and fuzzy, but the skin underneath felt like metal.

"He likes you, Alex," William said, breaking the silence, "as I knew he would."

With reluctance, Alex withdrew his hand and gazed up at the colossal beast in wonder. "Didn't you say something about a crocodile?"

William nodded and waved a hand at Bear. The creature rose to his full height and William gave a single, short growl. Before Alex could react, Bear opened his jaws to reveal huge, razor-sharp teeth, but it still looked like a regular bear to him. But then, without warning, the jaws opened wider, and a gigantic snout shot out like it was on a spring mechanism.

Roy cried out and stumbled back, grabbing Alex's chair for support. It was the snout of a crocodile extending outward from inside the mouth of the bear! The croc jaws spread apart, revealing even more wet, jagged teeth. This thing could chomp off someone's head with a single bite!

Roy gaped in horror as the creature somehow retracted the croc's mouth down its throat, so it looked like a giant, oddly proportioned bear once again.

He turned to William, aghast. "What the hell are these things for?"

"I told you," William replied, though his voice contained no mockery, "they are weapons, like me. Davalos has been trying to convince a general at the Pentagon to use them to stop riots and looting around the country, but I don't know if that will happen. Mainly they're intended for use in a ground war, a preinvasion force."

Roy turned to Alex, who well understood his friend's feelings. His hands still trembled from that crocodile mouth with those spiky teeth snapping so close to him. And yet…Bear seemed gentle, not dangerous.

"Let me show you the others," William said, stepping past Alex to the next cage. Reluctantly, Alex wheeled over to look inside, the flabbergasted Roy at his side.

Within was something like a huge wolf, but, as with the bear, the fur poked out of what appeared to be armor plating that shimmered and undulated as the animal strode toward the bars to nuzzle William's out-stretched hand.

"We call this one Dog, even though he's mixed with wolf and hyena and, like Bear, has the same enhanced armadillo armor and bone deposits under the fur to repel bullets. This is the one most likely to be used to stop rioting or looting, assuming the Pentagon allows that."

Roy gazed in at the wolf-dog in amazement. "Are they trained to, you know, only *kill* people?"

"No, they can also subdue them," William explained, so calmly that Alex shivered. "Davalos put computer chips into their brains, and he has a device that controls how vicious they get."

Alex suddenly had a thought. "Do you have a chip like that inside you?"

William shook his head. "That's why Davalos thinks I'm a failure, because I can think on my own and make choices."

"I like your way better," Alex said, offering a tight smile for William's benefit.

"So do I." He spoke to the wolf-dog, first in English and then with odd sounds that were part bark, part growl, part mewl. The creature seemed to understand and stuck his pointed snout through the bars. "You can pet him now. He knows to protect you."

Alex reached out with less fear this time, even though he could see rows of gigantic teeth as the wolf-dog panted lazily. The fur felt like cotton, but the skin underneath was rough like an iguana he'd touched one time, and it sent a surge of distaste throughout his body. But he sensed this animal, like Bear, would never hurt him, so he ignored the skin-crawling sensation and stroked its head and neck.

William indicated they should move on, so Alex pulled back his hand. "Thank you, Dog, for protecting me," he said.

Dog gave out a tiny bark that wasn't at all scary.

The next cage, however, contained a colossal cat that sported both stripes and spots. It was orange and black in color, with a head bigger than Alex's upper body and teeth as long as his hand. The glassy eyes glinted red in the dim lighting, and they fixed on Alex with such intensity that he rolled back a few feet. Roy, his breathing raspy, hovered behind Alex's chair and gave no indication he would go closer.

Alex stared long and hard at the animal's fur. It looked odd, not soft, but rather like was made out of tiny little spikes.

"This is Kitty," William said, by way of an introduction.

"Kitty? You shittin' me?" Roy stepped forward to offer Alex a look of horror, but Alex just shrugged. With all he'd already seen and heard that night, "Kitty" was as good a name as any.

"What is, uh, Kitty, you know, made of?" Alex wasn't sure he wanted to know about those tiny spikes.

"Mostly a tiger and a jaguar because they are fierce predators and will attack humans," William explained. "But did you notice the little spikes that make up his fur?"

"Uh, huh," Alex replied, his gaze riveted to that strange orange and black fur.

"Those are like tiny porcupine quills. When he's in attack mode, they stick out. They're so close together that he's almost bullet proof, and they're also poisonous."

"You mean like a rattlesnake or something?" Roy asked, studying the animal with more interest now.

"More deadly. These have cone snail venom in them and there's virtually no antidote."

"What's anti…what you said?" Roy glanced at Alex, but Alex didn't know either.

"There's no way to stop the poison. The person will be dead in a few minutes."

"If they don't get ripped apart first," Roy commented, pointing at the animal's massive feet. The claws were as long as his middle finger.

William went through the same process with Kitty as he had with the others and Alex knew that, once again, he'd made a lifelong friend that would protect him against any threat. Alex didn't want to pet Kitty for fear of the poison, but William assured him that it only came out when the spikes were sticking up. The flat, prickly fur felt strange against his hand, even rougher than the hard, scaly fur of the other two, and Alex was only too happy to pull his hand out of the cage. He thanked Kitty, not even considering it weird anymore to be thanking monstrous, unnatural animals, and then they moved back to the cage across from Bear.

Standing on all fours, this creature was taller than Alex was when seated in his wheelchair, and it was the weirdest looking one yet. It had the head of a lion—including the fat, fluffy mane—a body similar to Bear's, gigantic wings folded against its body, and thick, wavy horns spread out across the top of its head. It was brown in color, except the wings were black.

"What's this one?" Alex asked, unable to take his eyes off the terrifying creature. It focused its yellow eyes on him, making Alex shiver because it reminded him of that vicious cat Ms. G had under her control.

"This is Griffin," William replied, stroking the hair around the head. "I didn't know what it meant, but it's named after some animal from Greek mythology."

"I heard that word before," Roy said, though he looked like he'd forgotten its meaning.

"Griffin has the head of a lion, the body of a grizzly bear, the horns of a cape buffalo, and the wings of a giant condor. He can attack from the ground or the sky, even pick people up and throw them. He can be vicious, but to me he's always been friendly. Pet him, Alex. The mane is very soft."

Before reaching his hand through the bars and stroking the thick, lush fur, Alex glanced at Roy, who tossed him a "better you than me" look. The fur felt wonderful, so silky and smooth, that Alex began to relax for the first time that night.

"Feel it, Roy," he said, smiling. "It's amazing!"

Roy grimaced, glancing at William.

"Go ahead," the younger boy said. "Griffin likes being petted."

Looking like he was heading for the electric chair, Roy stepped up to the cage and eased one trembling hand between the bars. When Griffin made no move to chomp it off, he let his fingers drop into the abundant fur of the creature's mane. The broad smile creeping across Roy's face was all Alex needed to see.

"Sick, isn't it?"

Roy nodded, still smiling with joy.

William explained to Griffin about protecting Alex, punctuating his English with some mewls and growls, and the huge animal seemed to immediately understand, fixing those glassy yellow eyes upon Alex. It opened its mouth, extending a thick red tongue that slurped Alex's hand. The sensation was wet and slobbery, but Alex didn't mind.

"You're a nice boy, aren't you, Griffin?" Alex grinned at William, who grinned back.

Roy pulled his hand out of the cage. "That was *so* cool." Still smiling, he moved on to the next cage over and let out such a shriek of horror that Alex spun his chair around.

What he saw chilled his blood and sent his heart racing all over again. It was the biggest freaking scorpion he'd ever seen, like seriously, bigger than him and his wheelchair combined and longer than Roy was tall!

"I'm not petting that one," he announced, his voice breathy and weak. "I hate bugs."

William flinched slightly, but Alex barely noticed, so repulsed was he by the repellent scorpion. The stinger curved up and over its back, but the shell looked different than scorpions he remembered seeing on TV. It was dark gray and rough looking, with big indents everywhere, and it had long feeler-type things sticking out of its head and maybe…. Oh, hell, no! Wings? The horrible thing could fly?

"This is mainly a Deathstalker scorpion, mixed with ironclad beetle to make it's shell almost impossible to penetrate, and it has the wings of a roach so it can fly. The venom is deadly to humans."

"You can talk to that?" Roy blurted, grimacing with revulsion as the scorpion shifted position and stretched out its shiny, plastic-like brown wings.

"I told you, I have many kinds of animals within me. Like with the roaches, I only need my mind to communicate with him. Watch."

William stared at the thing, and Alex saw with disgust that it returned the stare. It made a kind of hissing sound that reminded Alex of an air pump he'd once used on his wheelchair tires. The scorpion bounced up and down slightly, like it was…happy? Alex didn't care if this thing would protect him or not. No way in hell would he get near it!

Fortunately, he didn't have to. William stopped his silent staring and turned to him. "Stalker says he will protect you, if the need arises."

"I'm…that's…uh, great." Alex tried for a smile, but he knew it must look like he was in pain. "Um, what's in the last cage, the one with the window over it?" He *really* wanted to get away from the monster in front of him.

William's face shifted from one of tour guide to saddened friend. "He's the closest thing I have to a genetic brother."

Alex had heard the word "genetic" before and thought it might be about having the same blood, like him and Andy. He wheeled along after William, with Roy—still speechless at the sight of the scorpion—hurrying after.

They stopped before the last occupied cage and Alex gasped. "It's…" He couldn't bring himself to say it.

"Oh, my God," Roy blurted, his tone filled with wonder and terror. "Is that a…a werewolf?"

"Yes," William replied, like being related to a werewolf was commonplace.

The werewolf wasn't very tall. In fact, it looked shorter than William as it stood gripping the bars of its cage with hairy hands that had fingernails long enough to scratch somebody's face right off. It was wearing a long-sleeved shirt and short pants, the hairy legs bending somewhat at the knees and forming into elongated wolfish feet with pads on the bottom and long claws extending out from its toes.

It had a wolfish face covered in hair, with pointed ears and sharp, protruding fangs that poked out from the lower jaw and rested against the upper lip in a perpetual snarl. The nose was only slightly longer than a human one, but black at the end like that of a dog.

But the eyes…they pierced Alex's very soul and nearly brought him to tears. To most people, they probably looked cold, and menacing, but Alex felt the pain behind them, the human suffering within this creature that hated itself for what it had become.

"You feel his pain, don't you?" William said, resting a hand on Alex's shoulder.

Alex nodded, feeling a strong urge to weep for this poor young creature. How did he know it was young? The size, maybe, but mostly the soul. It felt like that of a boy.

"He's only a kid, isn't he?"

"Yes," William said, his voice laced with sadness. "Only twelve."

"The hell?" Roy sounded horrified and outraged, like he'd get any time someone was bullied. "Who did this to a kid? That's evil!"

William faced them, clearly needing to avoid the plaintiff gaze of the panting, young werewolf. "Davalos calls him Wolfboy, but I gave him a human name, Francis. Amanda once told me about a man named Francis of Assisi who loved and cared for animals, even wolves, so I thought it was a good name."

Alex couldn't pry his eyes away from those of Wolfboy. "Why would Davalos make a kid suffer like this?"

"Francis was his first experiment after he took over the Weapon project. Dr. Avila figured out how to speed up the growth process for something that was mostly human, and Davalos liked the idea of a werewolf who could be lethal but could also just subdue enemies. His claws secrete some kind of venom that knocks people out, like what's in Dog's fur back there."

He pointed back at the wolf-dog that was gazing through the bars of its cage at them, or maybe at Francis. Alex couldn't tell.

"But why a twelve-year-old?" Roy asked, his voice sounding strained, like he was in pain, himself.

"Davalos got bored waiting for him to grow to adulthood," William explained, "so he had him born at twelve. The chip in his brain can trigger the transformation at any time, so Davalos figured no one would suspect a boy his age was up to anything until he attacked. That was the idea with me too, by the way."

"But a werewolf?" Alex still couldn't imagine doing that to a kid. His stomach roiled with anger.

"Davalos thought it was funny," William spat in disgust. "I heard him laughing about how Francis was his tribute to some old horror movie he liked as a boy. But the generals who gave him the money weren't amused and demanded he come up with something they could use in battle. That's how the others were born, and Davalos hates Francis because the Pentagon didn't like him."

Alex now thought he understood why the window was open over the young boy's head. "That's why he leaves the window open, isn't it, so Francis gotta keep suffering when the moon is full?"

William nodded. "Even though Davalos was supposed to control the change, for some reason he can't all the time. But the moon can, so Davalos likes to punish Francis for the chip not working right, like it's his fault. See, when Francis isn't in direct moonlight, he's himself, but the change is painful. I'll show you."

He strode to a darkened wall and flicked his hand down. Alex couldn't see what he did, but he heard a *click* and then some kind of screen slid over the window, covering it, and blocking out the light.

Wolfboy lurched and dropped to the floor, writhing around, unable to control his spasming body, whimpering and growling in agony. Alex felt his misery and did his best to spin some of it away. It seemed to work because Wolfboy stopped his thrashing and lay still.

Roy gasped, and Alex watched in amazement as the hair began sinking into the skin. First his hands looked human and then his feet. He was barefoot and Alex stared at the small feet of a young boy before focusing his attention on the face.

Wolfboy's entire head seemed to shrink in on itself as the thick fur slid beneath the light-brown skin, revealing a floppy mass of curly black hair atop a soft, thin face with a small mouth and piercing hazel eyes that retained a wolf-like quality, yet brimmed with misery.

The deep compassion within him kept Alex spinning until he pulled as much of the despondency as he could from the young boy. He knew he'd succeeded because he felt like he wanted to die, and Francis smiled up at him from the floor. It was a beautiful smile as only a child can manage.

"I don't know what you do to me, but I thank you," he said, his voice high and boyish, like he could be one of those choirboy singers Roy used to like.

"Welcome," Alex muttered, purging the despair he'd soaked into himself. This is what the boy lived with every day!

William stepped over and took Francis's hand through the bars, giving it a slight squeeze before helping him stand. "I taught Francis to talk and how to act after Davalos gave up on him," he said with a smile at the younger boy. "Davalos doesn't know I sneak in here at night. I'm a very good spy. Francis, this is my big brother, Alex, and his friend, Roy."

Francis eyed them with curiosity. "I thought I was your brother?"

"You are, but I needed a *big* brother, and Alex said he would be mine," William explained, clearly hoping to not hurt the youngster's feelings.

Francis nodded, studying Alex and Roy with immense curiosity. "You are real humans? Not like us?"

Alex flinched. "You're real too, Francis." He considered how to explain what he'd felt from both boys, Francis, *and* William. "Father Pat—he's this friend of mine and real smart—says humans have a soul that animals don't have, something that comes from God."

Francis tilted his head, a confused look on his face.

"I heard about God from a girl in Los Angeles," William commented, "and also from Amanda. But we're not real humans."

"Yeah, you are," Alex insisted. "That's what I'm trying to say. I spinned both of you and—"

The look on Francis's face became even more puzzled.

"That means I can see inside of you, and both you guys gots a real soul. I felt it, and I spinned a lot of people, so I know."

The eyes of young Francis became round circles of astonishment. "I'm human?"

Alex nodded, glancing at William, who seemed to have the same trouble processing this information.

"Me too?" William's blond eyebrows rose into his bangs.

"Yeah." Alex experienced so much relief flooding into him from the two boys that he almost felt giddy.

William did something that shocked Alex. He leaned down and pulled him into a hug. "Thank you so much for telling me, Alex. I was so afraid I was, well, some kind of monster."

He released Alex and stood, wiping a tear from one eye, and grinning at Francis.

"You and me are family, Francis, but if you want a big brother, I bet Roy would be good. He's pretty, what's that word you use, Alex…oh, yeah, sick."

Now Francis looked even more mystified, and Roy gasped out loud, staring at the boys in shock.

Alex smiled at the stunned look on his best friend's face. "No, Francis, Roy would be awesome. How 'bout it, Roy? You want a little brother?"

Roy looked dumbfounded. His mouth dropped open and, even in the dim light, Alex saw his face flush red with embarrassment. "Me?"

"There ain't nobody better," Alex assured Francis, drawing a joyful smile from the handsome young boy.

Francis studied Roy as though sizing him up. "But Mr. Davalos willn't never let me out."

"It's *won't*," William corrected him, "and Dr. Shepherd and Colonel Walker are working on that."

Francis blushed, making him and Roy look a lot alike, even down to the dark bushy hair. "Thanks, William. And thank *you*, Roy."

Roy smiled for the first time and reached in to ruffle the youngster's shaggy hair. "No prob, Little Brother."

William suddenly cocked his head to one side.

Alex studied him a moment. "What's up?"

"I hear something…" William stepped away from the cage and listened more intently. "Do you hear it, Francis?"

Francis scrunched up his young face and focused. "Yes. Voices."

"I don't hear nothing," Alex said, listening as hard as he could. "Do you, Roy?"

Happy to be out of the limelight, Roy shook his head. "No."

William dropped to his knees and placed one ear against the concrete floor outside Francis's cage. Alex exchanged a look with Roy, wondering what was going on.

"There's people down there," William murmured, his face twisted with concentration. Then he lifted his head. "One of them is your friend, Israel. He's very loud."

"The hell?" Roy looked from William to Alex.

"How could Izzy be down there?" Alex asked, his heart beginning to race once more.

William listened again and then frowned as he raised his head and made eye contact with Alex. "Your brother is with him. So are your other friends."

Alex felt a chill envelope him. "What's down there?"

William stood and gazed at him soberly. "Underground tunnels and chambers. Old bomb shelters from the Cold War when America worried about attacks from the Soviet Union and China. Colonel Walker told me about them, but he can't go down there anymore because the Pentagon gave them to Davalos. The colonel thinks Davalos and Avila are doing other experiments they don't want him to know about."

Alex only understood about half of the explanation but did get that there were tunnels underneath them and that Colonel Walker wasn't allowed in them.

"How could Izzy and the others get down there?" Roy looked as baffled as Alex felt.

William furrowed his slim eyebrows. "I don't know. I can't even get down there and I've been able to sneak into every other place on this base."

Francis reached out of his cage and pointed at the far wall, opposite to the door where they'd entered. "There be's a way through that wall. I seen Davalos go through a hidden door. He thought I'm dumb, but I seen the code he punches in."

"Where's the box?" William asked, moving toward the wall with smooth, catlike strides.

"In the corner," Francis answered, pointing to a dark space on the left side of the chamber.

Alex wheeled himself in that direction, and Roy trotted along after. William was running his fingers along the corner where the back and side walls met just behind the cage that housed Francis.

William's eyesight must be incredible, Alex realized, because the younger boy said, "Found it. What's the code, Francis?"

Francis rattled off a complicated series of numbers that Alex couldn't hope to remember.

As William punched the numbers into some kind of keypad Alex couldn't see, each punch made a slightly different beep, like the sounds were the code, not the actual numbers.

"Are you not glad you teached me about numbers, William?" Francis asked, gripping the bars of his cage and eying William with a kind of hero worship in his eyes.

"Yes," William replied, punching his index finger onto something Alex still couldn't see. It blended in too well with the dark brown of the walls.

The beeps stopped and a moment later, a door that hadn't been visible before separated itself from the back wall and eased open a few inches.

If someone didn't know the code, there was no way they could find that door, Alex thought.

But then he focused on what might be on the other side, and what his brother was doing in the underground.

William pulled open the door. Dim overhead lights revealed a chamber beyond. The only thing visible within that chamber was a round piece of metal sticking up from the floor. It looked like a manhole cover. Alex and Roy followed William inside.

CHAPTER SIXTEEN

IT'S TIME FOR OUR GREATEST TEST YET

WHEN COLONEL WALKER BROUGHT THE girl to his house, Amanda swept her into a cocoon of motherly affection and doted on her, delighted to have a new houseguest. Walker thought it best not to share his suspicions with his wife until they could be alone, and with an ever-expanding houseful of kids, that alone-time might be difficult to achieve.

Amanda immediately hustled the girl into the kitchen for some food, while Colonel Walker decided to check on Alex. William should have brought him back by now. He strode past the living room and down the back hall, treading softly on the carpet in case the boys were asleep.

He stopped at the closed door and listened for any movement on the other side. Hearing nothing, he turned the knob and eased open the door. The first bed he saw across the room was Andy's. It was empty, moonlight bathing the rumpled bedcovers in a soft, white brightness. With more haste, he stuck his head farther into the room and looked over at the bunk beds that should have housed Alex and Roy. The bottom bed was empty, the covers in disarray. Stepping toward the two beds, he scanned the upper bunk. Empty.

A feeling of unease crept over him. William was only supposed to take Alex. If this room was empty, maybe the other boys upstairs were...

He hurried from the room and closed the door. Whatever was going on, he didn't want to alarm Amanda. He returned to the entry hall and trotted up the stairs. He kept his movements stealthy in case the other boys were still in their room, but he had a feeling he knew what he'd find. Striding past the master bedroom and bathroom, he came to the guest room door. It was closed and there were no sounds from the other side. He eased it open. In the light of the full moon coming through the drapes, he clearly saw the far set of bunk beds were both empty, though they had been slept in. Stepping all the way inside, he discovered the other beds empty too.

Where could they have gone? William would not have taken them with him. He had his orders and he always followed orders. No, the others must've heard them leaving and decided to follow. Would William have let them into the Weapon Lab? Doubtful. So where could they have ended up?

He decided to wait until his men reported in on the perimeter before sending them out to search for the boys. They were kids, after all, and might just be wandering around exploring. He did his own share of that as a boy when his father was base commander. His dad had passed away before Weapon was born, and Colonel Walker wondered what he would think of the project now.

Weapon, or William as he preferred to be called, had surprised them all with his adaptability and innate humanity, which had overwritten much of the genetic programming that had gone into his creation. Walker was too pragmatic to wonder what it might feel like to *be* William, but one thing he did know was what he told him earlier that evening. He was proud of the boy and had no problem saying so, unlike his own father who'd never once expressed pride in him.

Walker glanced at his watch. Stern should be reporting in any moment.

***

Java had to admit these underground tunnels were way cool. Izzy kept whining about monsters lurking in all the dark corners, but Java could tell he was happy to be exploring and not working out. Carlos wanted to open every door, but they were all locked, which annoyed him. Jorge just wandered around looking at everything with wide eyes and a goofy grin.

Andy had told them these tunnels were built to withstand atomic bomb blasts. Java sort-of remembered learning about atom bombs with Ms. Ashley and he could picture that mushroom shaped cloud they made, but he didn't understand the radiation part Andy talked about. Davalos had supposedly told Andy all this stuff about radiation causing cancer.

All Java knew was that the metal walls, the old-school ceiling lightbulbs, and the many tunnels rife for exploration were the best thing about being stuck on this base—except the weight room, of course.

Andy seemed to be leading them somewhere because he didn't want to stop and open doors or go down side tunnels that snaked off to who knew where. He kept looking at a phone in his hand, or something like a phone. Whatever it was, he was using it to find his way through the tunnels. Java was curious where Andy was taking them, so he didn't mind not checking out every side tunnel they saw.

Andy turned a corner just ahead, and Java trotted after him, causing Izzy to blurt, "Wait up, Java!" Java didn't, but Izzy and the others soon caught up. Andy stood in front of double doors with some kind of fancy lock box next to the knob. Andy pocketed the phone-thing and knocked on the door. Java had never seen Andy so excited. He was bouncing on his heels. What was this place, anyway?

The door opened and that Davalos guy stood there. His smile dropped like a rock when he saw Java and the others and he quickly stepped into the tunnel, closing the door behind him.

"Andy, you were supposed to come alone." He sounded pissed but tried not to show it.

"They followed me," Andy explained, eyeing the others a moment. Then he leaned in to Davalos and whispered, "Please. They can do strong stuff in the fitness center and I'm weak. I really want them to see me be strong at something."

Java pretended he hadn't heard, but he knew that feeling better than most kids. They all did. Being special ed, everyone thought they were dumb and useless, even a lot of the teachers. That's why Java had gotten into weight lifting, because being strong made him feel better about himself. Yes, he felt a kinship with Andy he never had before.

Java figured Davalos would say no because he seemed like a hard-ass guy who didn't like kids. But the man's annoyed expression softened, like he was remembering being a kid himself.

"I understand, Andy," he said, placing a hand on the eager boy's shoulder. "I was always the odd kid out myself." He gazed intently, looking them over one at a time. Izzy practically had his tongue hanging out with anticipation, but Davalos settled his gaze on Java, checking out his size, his muscularity. "Yes, I could never compete with the jock-types either."

Java flinched because, even though he could beat down every jock at school, they still made fun of him for being a dummy, and that was something all the weight lifting in the world couldn't change. He figured the kid version of Davalos must've been picked on too, except he couldn't fight back.

"Now," Davalos went on, "what you will all see here is top secret. I will allow you inside because Andy asked, and because no one would believe you anyway, should you decide to tell them what you witness here. But do not touch anything, understood?"

Izzy nodded frantically while Java exchanged a look with Carlos, who shrugged. Java faced Davalos. "We're good with that."

Davalos pulled open one of the doors. "Then come in."

***

Dane's body was taut as a wire stretched to the snapping point. They had made it into the underground tunnels, and one of Shaw's guys had closed the trap door. Shaw wasn't worried that anyone inside the base would notice that it was now visible—because of the looping video he'd uploaded to that camera—but he didn't want to take any chances of it being spotted by a perimeter patrol.

The metal walls and the ceilings with their glowing white light bulbs gave Dane the creeps, mainly because he was out of his element and had no idea what to expect. He'd never been underground in his life, and these tunnels unnerved him.

So far, they'd met no resistance; it didn't seem like anyone was down there. The empty halls reminded him of a mirror maze he'd gone through as a kid, except there were no mirrors, just endless tunnels winding and snaking into and out of themselves. He knew some of them went under the desert outside the base, but he figured that, by now, they had passed beneath the fence and were under the base itself.

They'd been wandering around for what seemed like forever when Dane heard voices. As a group—led by Martin—they scuttled closer to where this particular tunnel branched off into an identical one. Martin held a long metal coil in his hand that he bent and slipped around the corner. Shaw tapped the tablet he carried, and images appeared on the screen. Dane stifled a gasp. A man stood at the end of the next tunnel with a group of boys. One was Java. Those big shoulders and arms were unmistakable. One of the other boys had long white hair. Andy!

Shaw zoomed in on the group and their images became crystal clear on the screen. Yes! Andy, Java, the gangster kid, and the quiet one. But where was Roy? And Alex? Shaw listened through wireless earbuds, so Dane couldn't hear what was being said, but he saw the boys follow the man somewhere out of sight from this angle.

Shaw looked up at them, but mostly focused on Martin as he spoke in low tones. "Mark Davalos. I suspected as much."

Martin whispered back, "What do you think he's up to with the kids?"

"Who is this Davalos?" Father Pat asked, "and why wasn't Alex with them?"

"And Roy," Nathan added, glancing at Dane with concern.

"Obviously, we don't have those answers," Shaw replied soberly. "As to Davalos, he means well, but his ideas on national security have always been…unusual." He paused and glanced upward at what looked like an air conditioning grill set into the wall just below the ceiling.

The grill wasn't very big, and it reminded Dane of the air-circulating system at Mark Twain High. On more than one occasion, he'd had to remove one of those grills and crawl into the metal ducts to clear a blockage or repair a hole—not because he wanted to, but because he was lean enough to fit through the opening. The school district didn't want to pay extra for a legit air-con guy.

Dane's thoughts were interrupted when he noticed Shaw staring intently at him. "What?"

"I need a man up in the ventilation system and you're the only one who looks like he could fit."

Odd, thought, Dane. *Like he read my mind.*

"Whadda I gotta do?"

Shaw took the metal coil from Martin and handed it to Dane. "I need this camera placed at the grill looking into that room Davalos went into. I'll give you an earpiece and direct your way. You game?"

"Yep. Crawled through these things at my job before."

Shaw nodded. "Martin, remove the grill."

Martin reached into a pouch on his belt and slipped out a screwdriver, standing on his tiptoes to reach the grill, attacking the four screws holding it in place.

Shaw eyed the door directly across the tunnel and signaled one of his other men. "Miguel, find us a room to hide."

The guy named Miguel, big and beefy and bald, strode silently to the door and tried the knob. It turned with ease, and he swung open the door. By now, Martin had the grill off and cradled it in his hands. Shaw handed Dane a small earpiece that looked like an Air Pod. Dane slipped it into his ear, where it fit snugly. Shaw spoke into the mic tacked to his lapel, "Testing, testing."

Dane nodded and Shaw waved him forward. Dane exchanged a quick look with Nathan before joining Martin, who set down the grill and made a stirrup with his hands. Dane placed one foot into the stirrup, and Martin easily hefted him up to the opening. The interior was the usual slippery metal, but Dane's long arms easily reached far enough inside to pull himself along, and with Martin pushing from below, he slid all the way in.

That was the easy part, he knew. He heard Shaw in his ear. "I'll direct you from this store room down here."

"Roger that," Dane said quietly, feeling important for the first time in his life. He'd failed to protect Roy back at that church, but there was no way he'd fail him now. Or Alex. The duct ran straight along the wall to his right and his left. He already knew the room Davalos went into had to be on his right, so he began inching in that direction, enjoying the cool air encircling him. The metal bent and creaked at times, so he did his best to pull with his hands and push with his shoes. Within a few moments, Shaw's voice popped into his ear, and he listened to his instructions.

***

Alex gazed at the round manhole cover, sizing it up to determine if his wheelchair might fit, at least when folded up. He decided it would.

William studied the blinking electronic gadget attached to the cover and frowned. "It doesn't appear to be in lock mode." He wrapped his fingers around the handle next to the box and tugged. The round lid opened with ease. Even though it looked like solid metal, the younger boy lifted it to the full-upright position like it was made of cardboard.

Alex saw light shining up from below. William knelt and looked into the hole, then turned back to Alex with concern. "There is a metal ladder along the wall." He stood and studied the wheelchair. "I have never seen one of these before and you're the only person I've ever met who has one. What is it?"

Alex was honestly surprised William hadn't mentioned his chair before this. He'd noticed the younger boy staring at it, but he supposed Colonel Walker might have told William not to ask. "I was born with a weird kind of spina bifida, so I can't walk. This chair is kinda like my legs."

William considered this answer. "It sounds like your brain is not talking to your legs. Dr. Shepherd has taught me a lot about the human body and how it works."

"Yeah, my spinal cord don't talk right with my brain," Alex agreed, impressed by how much the younger boy knew about, well, everything.

William pointed down at the opening in the floor. "Do you need me to carry you down the ladder?"

Roy gasped, and Alex knew it was because his friend feared he might go off on William for insulting him. But he knew the question was asked out of innocence.

"No worries, Little Brother, I can climb anything," Alex assured William with a wink. "I just need you guys to get my chair down."

Roy eyed William a moment. "I got that. Done it tons of times."

William nodded and stepped aside so Alex could roll closer to the opening. He stopped and secured his brakes. He craned his neck and saw the ladder William mentioned. He lifted his sneakers off the foot rests and set them on the floor and then, with the ease of lifelong practice, he slid down onto the floor like a snake. Roy lifted the chair and set it aside.

Alex lay on his stomach and pushed backwards into the hole, lowering his feet over the edge. Alex held fast to the lip of the opening until he could lower one hand far enough to grip the first rung of the ladder. He pulled his torso over and then swung his other hand out to grab the same rung.

He looked up and saw Roy biting his lip, but William eyed him with admiration. He lowered himself down the ladder rung by rung with ease, his powerful shoulders and hands making the descent a breeze. In seconds, his feet bumped the floor and he lowered himself the rest of the way onto hard concrete. He rolled over several times to put distance between himself and the ladder, to make room for the others.

Soft, echoing clangs accompanied Roy's feet as they clambered down moments later. He didn't have the chair and Alex raised his eyebrows questioningly.

"I couldn't hold it straight up over my head," Roy admitted sheepishly, "even with all Java's workouts." He chuckled. "William's got it."

Alex nodded as William's sneakered feet descended and dropped to the floor like a cat. The other boy held Alex's chair above his head with one arm as though it weighed nothing. The chair was light, Alex knew, but not that light. William brought over the chair, still above his head, and set it down with ease.

"Thanks, man." Alex offered a smile and pulled himself up into the chair with the same effortlessness he'd used getting out. Setting his feet into place, he released the brakes and scanned their surroundings.

A tunnel made of metal walls and ceiling extended in both directions. Dim overhead lamps cast weird pools of light at intervals as far as he could see, but there wasn't a sound. This place was so quiet it made him feel on edge.

He eyed William. "Now what?"

"Now we find out what Davalos is hiding down here." William glanced up and down the tunnel in both directions, and then pointed to his right. "Let's try this way."

William started down the tunnel, and Alex wheeled up to Roy. "You good?"

"No, but I don't got much choice, do I?" He was spinning one of his snakebite lip piercings with his tongue.

"I don't think we got to worry with William protecting us." Alex whispered even though there wasn't anyone around. "I bet he got some serious moves."

That drew a smile from Roy, and they hurried after William.

The only sound came from Alex's wheels against the concrete as they made their way forward, moving into and out of shadows as they passed beneath the lights. Cool air drifted from grills set in the walls high up near the ceiling and spaced at regular intervals. After the warm, muggy night air of the desert, the coolness felt refreshing.

The tunnel came to an end and veered to the right. William strode forward with confidence, but Alex could tell the boy's senses were on high alert. He kept tilting his head and listening, while his gaze seemed to roam everywhere at once. He arrived at an unmarked metal door with another of those electronic boxes stuck to it. Alex and Roy hurried forward as William repeated his trick with the ID card and fingerprint. With a tiny beep, the door popped open.

William pulled it open and glanced at the boys. "Stay behind me."

William stepped inside the dark room and Alex wheeled in after, with Roy practically in his lap. Despite his attempt at bravado, Alex knew his friend was really scared. If he was honest, he'd admit that he was too.

The room was pitch black, but William had no trouble moving about the darkness with ease. Alex needed time for his eyes to adjust and stayed put so he wouldn't bump into anything while he waited. Roy stuck to him like glue. He glanced up at his best friend, but Roy's features were too shadowed to make out any details. Alex felt his friend's fear, however. It was palpable and not too different from his own.

Gradually, his eyes made out the size of the room. It was huge but seemed empty in the center. He could make out large, tall containers lining the walls all around him. At first, he thought they had square corners. He wheeled himself forward inch by inch, heart thundering in his chest, and noticed that the top of each container was rounded and seemed to be made of glass. But the glass was fogged up from the inside, like it was super cold within. The room itself was cool, but not that cold. He also noted a thick cable snaking out from the side of each container and plugged into the wall.

What's in these things?

William stepped closer to the nearest container. It towered over him. Whatever was inside was as at least as tall as the doorway they'd used to enter. William waved Roy over, Alex figured because Roy was tall enough to at least reach up to the glass.

"Can you wipe off that glass, Roy?" William eyed him expectantly.

Roy glanced at Alex, fear chiseled into his face as though he was made of stone.

"Go ahead," Alex urged, his voice barely a hiss in the overpowering silence.

Roy stood on his tiptoes to reach up, and even then, he just was just barely able to swipe his right hand across the glass, back and forth as though cleaning the windshield of his truck, clearing a space large enough to see what was inside.

Alex clapped a hand over his mouth to stifle a scream.

There was a man in there! A big man, if his feet were at the bottom of the container. Now that his eyes had adjusted to the gloom, Alex looked around at the other containers. Each of them housed a…body! A human body! The glass had not fogged up on all of them and Alex noted that they all contained men; really big men, just like the first one. They were different races too, some blond, some dark, some Asian, some with red hair. The bottom part of each case was made of metal, so only the heads and shoulders of the men were visible, but they all had wide, thick torsos and looked like they could do a serious beat down on Captain America and Thor at the same time!

"What is this place?" Roy whispered, finally able to speak, his voice raspy with fear.

William stared at the bodies, his face devoid of expression.

"William?" Alex wheeled closer to him. "Do you know?"

After a long moment, William exhaled. "It looks like Davalos is trying to make more of…well, me, except adult versions."

Alex gasped, his pounding heart sending blood rushing to his ears. He looked around at the bodies again. There was something different… Then he had it! "There ain't no water in these cases, like in the ones you showed us up top."

"No," William replied, stepping up to the case nearest him. It housed a thick, well-built black guy. "It took thirteen years for me to be born in that tank upstairs, so unless Davalos found a way to speed up the process, he's been working on these for much longer."

"But you said you was alive while you were, you know, growing," Roy said, his voice as brittle as a cracker. "These guys don't look, well, alive."

"They aren't breathing," William agreed, placing one ear against the cannister. "I'd hear it if they were."

Alex stared at the man's face, trying to spin any sensation from him. "I don't think they ever been alive. I can't feel, well, you know, a soul."

William studied him. "Like you felt in me?"

Alex nodded. "You got one, for sure. But these guys…" He made eye contact with William, but he couldn't think how to finish.

"Maybe Davalos figured out some way to make the bodies so he could bring them to life later," William offered, almost more to himself than the others. "I must inform the colonel of this immediately."

"You won't inform the colonel of anything," said a voice from behind them.

Alex spun his chair around and gasped. Davalos stood in the doorway, smirking with glee, his hand resting atop Andy's shoulder.

"Hello, Big Brother," Andy said, his deep voice tinged with excitement. "It's time for our greatest test yet."

CHAPTER SEVENTEEN

WE GOTTA KILL HIM

ALLISON KNEW SHE HAD TO play her role of terrorized kidnap victim to the hilt, but she was also supposed to find out where the boys were being held, and that part was tricky. The colonel's wife—"Please, call me Amanda"—had been so sweet and attentive that Allison felt guilty for the charade. She knew her dad and the others had to have entered the base by now, but she had no way of contacting them. Her father had placed a tiny tracking device behind her ear, and when she found Alex and the others, she was supposed to tap it so the team would know where on the base to find both her and the boys. But so far, there'd been no sign of them.

She was lying on the living room couch with a blanket over her, Amanda hovering with warm milk and fresh cookies, asking if she needed this or that. While feigning exhaustion and shock, she tried to scope out the house and maybe glean some info from Amanda. The colonel, looking anxious, had remained for a while until he got a call on his cell and retreated to the kitchen a few minutes earlier.

"Do you and the colonel have any kids, Amanda?" She hoped mentioning kids might help bring up the subject of the boys.

Amanda offered a sad smile that touched Allison to the heart. "No, I couldn't have any, and we never got around to adopting, especially living on this base like we have for so long. It's no place for children."

"It is pretty bleak here," Allison admitted, then decided to try another tack. "Do any of the soldiers here have kids? Since I don't know how long I'll be here, it'd be cool to have someone my age. Maybe it would help my memory."

Amanda glanced over her shoulder, but the colonel's muffled voice still came from down the hall. "I shouldn't say this, but we do have other kids staying with us at the moment. They're all asleep right now; that's why I'm being so quiet. You'll meet them in the morning."

Her eyes widened in surprise. She'd expected the boys to be locked up somewhere, not staying in this house like they were visiting relatives. What was going on here anyway? At least now she knew where they were. Pretending to stretch, she reached behind her right ear as though to scratch it and tapped with her index finger the tiny tab attached there.

"That'll be cool," she said, stifling a major yawn that popped her ears as she finished her stretch.

Amanda reached out to place a comforting hand on her shoulder. "You're exhausted, dear. Sleep now. You're safe. We'll figure out the rest in the morning."

Allison smiled, and she wasn't acting this time. Amanda would make such an awesome mom. "Thanks, Amanda. You're amazing."

Amanda chuckled and rose from her chair. "Sleep well."

Allison smiled and pretended to drift off to sleep. She heard Amanda leave the living room.

After a few moments of silence, Amanda's voice drifted in from the entry hall. "Something wrong?"

"Someone hacked into our perimeter cameras, as I suspected," the colonel replied, his voice tight with concern. "There's been a breach. The underground."

"Oh, no!"

The colonel lowered his voice, but Allison heard, "Watch her like a hawk. My gut tells me she's involved."

"She seems like such a nice girl." Amanda sounded so devastated that Allison squirmed with discomfort.

"I'm getting some men and going down there now. Davalos isn't answering my calls. And the boys have all snuck out."

Amanda gasped, and Allison froze with fear. She'd just told her dad Alex and the others were here. Where could they have gone?

"I sent Alex out with William to meet his cousins, and the others must've followed. If any of them return here, tell them to wait for me."

"All right, honey. Be careful." She sounded afraid.

"I will."

Allison heard footsteps hurrying across the entry hall, and then the front door opened and closed. Fearing that Amanda—now suspicious of her—would come back, she closed her eyes and pretended to sleep.

***

Colonel Walker met up with Sergeant Stern near the Weapon Project building, right beside the trap door leading into the underground tunnels.

Stern arrived with ten armed men and saluted. "Do you want me to accompany you, Colonel?"

"No, Sergeant. I need you up here. Keep men all along the perimeter in case there are others out there in the desert. Station men at every entrance to the underground. Unless you hear directly from me, no one below may exit to the surface."

"Yes, sir. What about the girl?"

"Station men at my house. If, as I suspect, she was a ruse to distract us and allow them time to enter, she could be a useful bargaining chip, if the need arises. We'll be on radio silence until you hear from me, but if you need to contact me, send a text."

"Yes, Colonel. Good luck." Stern saluted again.

Walker waved the men to follow and squatted down to the electronic keypad on the trapdoor. After he punched in his secure code, the red light changed to green. He gripped the handle and tugged. It lifted with ease, making him certain it had already been used that night.

***

"Did you really think I wouldn't eventually learn of your late-night visits to my creations?" Davalos smirked at William, but the boy remained impassive. "I knew for certain when I heard Wolfboy practicing how to speak, something I never taught him."

Alex was more interested in what his brother was doing down there.

"Andy, why are you here?"

His twin looked pumped up, the way Java looked when he lifted a big-ass amount of weight, like he was proud of himself. But for what?

"I know something we can do, Big Brother, that you don't. And it's incredible."

Alex frowned. "What is it?"

"You'll see."

William hadn't taken his eyes off Davalos, and the man, looking like he was headed out to dinner in his suit and tie, kept his gaze fixed on the boy.

"In answer to your question, *William*, the only one of my creations I started before being given official authorization was the afore mentioned Wolfboy."

William flinched but said nothing.

"Unfortunately, it was taking too long to develop, and I wasn't sure if it would be worthwhile to finish, so I stopped. Simple as that. It hasn't been destroyed yet because the Pentagon might still have a use for it."

"*It* is a he," William asserted, gritting his teeth, but keeping his anger in check. "He is a boy, like me, with feelings, and a soul."

Davalos's eyebrows shot up and he chuckled. "A soul? You're part cockroach. What kind of *boy* is that?"

Alex couldn't take any more. "Why do you hate him so much? He's just a kid."

Davalos faced Alex, the smirk fading. "He was a mistake and I told that to the Joint Chiefs. If we're going to create artificial creatures to defend this country, they must not have the ability to choose. Otherwise, they could choose to disobey, like he does." He tossed a glare at William.

"That what these things are, robots?" Alex pointed around him at the cannisters.

"Not at all," Davalos said, his tone laced with pride. "These were not grown in those tanks upstairs. These were created using a machine, to use a simple term."

"What kind of machine?" Roy blurted, glancing at Alex with furrowed brows.

"Have you ever seen a 3-D printer?" Davalos glanced around at all of them, but only William nodded. "It's a machine that will create a physical object out of a specialized plastic, once someone programs into the machine the shape and dimensions of that object."

Alex still didn't get it and he saw that Roy didn't either. But that didn't matter. "So these guys came out of a machine?"

"Indeed they did," Davalos replied smugly. "A machine I had a hand in designing, I might add, though Dr. Avila was its creator. We input the DNA from whatever creatures we deem necessary, mostly human, of course, add in the necessary organic ingredients to generate skin, bones, muscles, design the size, shape, and color, and presto, a body is created over a period of three months, give, or take. It's the only machine of its kind in the world and so top secret even the president doesn't know of its existence. There's just one problem we haven't been able to solve."

Before Alex could ask what it was, William said, "How to bring them to life."

Davalos eyed him in annoyance but nodded. "Yes. We've tried everything we could think of, even resorting to lightning. It would seem that God has a patent on the whole "life" gig and stubbornly hordes that secret."

Alex was still confused, but William seemed to see the bigger picture.

"That's why you need Alex and Andy." William didn't phrase it as a question, just a statement of fact.

Again, Davalos looked annoyed that William was one step ahead. "Yes." He faced Alex and his expression became sober. "I know everything about the Healer prophecy. I've researched it from every religious tradition. Humans cannot create life, but I believe God has given you, Alex, in conjunction with your twin, the power to shift Life from one being to another."

Alex's mouth dropped open in horror and he turned to Andy, standing there calm as could be. "You knew about this?"

Andy nodded. "I already did it by myself, with a bug, but I need you to shift a bigger life." He frowned a moment, but then his face brightened once more with excitement. "This is our chance, Alex, to show your friends what we can do. To show the world."

Alex opened his mouth to protest, but Davalos held up a hand and said, "Let me show you how it will work, Alex. I can't force you, but I think once you know everything, you'll go along."

Alex closed his mouth, biting back the "No, I won't" that hung at the edge of his lips.

Can they talk me into it?

He'd know soon enough.

"Follow me," Davalos said and ushered them out of the chilly storage room.

***

Colonel Walker led his men through the winding tunnels, gun drawn, ready for anything. Having not been down there for over three years—since the Pentagon gave Davalos sole control of the area—he didn't know what he might encounter. Davalos, at least, didn't have soldiers at his beck and call, only the bioengineers employed by the Pentagon. Shepherd had been asked to consult on some details of whatever secret project Davalos had embarked on, but she was given too little information to understand the nature of these experiments. All Walker knew was that Davalos wanted to curry favor with the Joint Chiefs by creating a weapon that surpassed William in every way.

That was the part that frightened him.

His men tried every door they encountered, but most were locked and there was no sign, nor sound, of anyone. Walker knew the largest chamber to be at the west end of the base. Had there been a nuclear emergency in the fifties or sixties, key government officials would've been housed in that section, so it was the most developed. If Davalos had set up any sort of laboratory, it would be there. Walker led his men in that direction.

***

Father Pat huddled in the dark storage room alongside Nathan peering at Shaw's tablet. Dane was in position and the image on screen looked down on a large laboratory dominated by a humongous machine and many computer stations. Shaw had just informed them he'd gotten Allison's signal about the boys. But then Dane moved the mini camera around according to Shaw's instructions and Father Pat flinched when, seated together in one corner, the boys came into view. There were two soldiers standing with them, but it didn't appear the kids were being held against their will.

Shaw said nothing, but it was obvious he was confused, especially since Allison's signal had originated on the other side of the base. Father

Pat leaned in and studied the image. Only four of the boys were there. Alex, Andy, and Roy were missing. What could that mean? He knew Shaw would be thinking the same thing, so he thought it best not to say anything until they could determine what might be happening.

The camera view changed again, panning across the lab toward the other side. Father Pat saw what appeared to be an enormous operating table, replete with surgical instruments on a small rolling table next to it, but that wasn't what startled him. What startled him was the apparent size of the sheet-covered body lying atop that table. He assumed whoever it was must be dead because the sheet covered its face, but the height had to be over seven feet! And the sheet rose high enough off the table to indicate someone thick in the torso, probably very muscular, which led him to suspect it was a man, not a woman.

What on earth were the boys doing in a lab with a dead body? And why did they look bored, rather than frightened?

Double doors directly behind the two soldiers opened. The soldiers glanced back and then parted to allow a man to enter. Father Pat had never seen him before, but the man was impeccably dressed in a gray business suit with a navy-blue tie. His dark hair was slicked back, and he seemed excited, based on his bouncy step and the eager look on his face.

"Davalos," Shaw muttered, his tone laced with disgust.

"Who is Davalos, exactly?" Father Pat whispered.

"He's high up in the Pentagon and paranoid about national security. He clearly wants the twins for their power. Maybe now, we'll find out *how* he wants to use them."

Father Pat returned his gaze to the tablet. Davalos had stopped just inside the lab and extended his arm to someone in the outside tunnel who could not be seen. Then Father Pat gasped as Andy stepped into the room, followed by Alex and Roy.

Nathan sucked in a sharp breath and leaned closer. "Thank God, Roy is okay."

Father Pat offered him a reassuring smile and turned back to the tablet screen. What was going on in there? As Davalos began to speak, Father Pat leaned in closely to listen.

***

Alex wheeled past Davalos and gaped at the expansive lab surrounding him. Considering that it was underground, it was huge, but not as filled with computers like the other one up top. This one looked like the rooms he'd seen on TV that were used for operations and other medical stuff like that. But one entire wall was made up of a machine unlike anything he'd ever seen, even on TV. It had tons of brightly lit buttons and switches and a large opening at one end that looked like a bigger version of that MRI machine Dr. Avila had put him into upstairs. He had a sick feeling in the pit of his stomach that this was the machine Davalos had mentioned, the one that created all those dead men back in the storage room.

Before he could look around anymore, he heard, "Where you been, Alex? I'm bored as shit!" And then Izzy was by his side, bouncing up and down like a rubber ball, the others gathered behind him.

Alex grinned, never so happy to see his friends. Whatever happened now, at least he wouldn't be alone.

"You chill, Alex?" Java eyed him with concern.

Alex nodded. "How'd you guys get here?"

Carlos raised a thick arm and pointed at Andy. "Your bro brung us."

Alex glanced back at Andy, who shrugged.

Davalos stepped between them and swept an arm around Alex's shoulder, indicating the lab with his other hand. "Let's get down to business, shall we?"

Alex looked up at him and sensed the need for speed. Why? Then it hit him. "Colonel Walker doesn't know about this, does he?"

Davalos maintained his calm expression, but Alex felt the discomfort squirming inside him. "He will, once we're finished. It will be a surprise."

Alex met his gaze. "Okay. What's we supposed to do?"

Davalos started across the room, darting in between tables with glass jars, microscopes, and bottles of colored liquids, toward a long table with something lying on top, covered with a sheet. Alex, Andy, and William followed, but one of the soldiers blocked Izzy and the others.

"Hey, why can't we go?" Izzy looked annoyed and Java was scowling when Alex turned to observe the confrontation.

Davalos stopped and looked back. "You boys can see perfectly well from there," he told Izzy and Java. "For safety reasons, you need to stay put." He glared at William.

Knowing what Davalos was about to say, Alex announced, "William stays with me."

Davalos looked like he might protest, but Alex squinted at him something fierce, and Davalos backed down.

Izzy huffed and folded his arms across his chest, but Java clapped a hand on his shoulder and drew him back to where Jorge stood beside Carlos, watching the proceedings with wide eyes.

"Don't think you wanna see that up close, anyways, Izzy," Java said quietly.

Roy, casting Alex a pleading gaze, reluctantly joined them.

Davalos continued toward the table. Only when he drew closer did Alex realize what shape the sheet looked like. He stopped pushing himself forward and stared in horror. "You got a dead body under that?"

Davalos turned to face him, looking proud and eager. "Not dead, Alex. This man has never lived."

Alex flashed back to the storage room and what William told him about the bodies in there. "You made him, like them others in that room?"

"Not I," Davalos admitted, as Dr. Avila appeared from an adjoining room and approached them wearing his usual white smock and smug expression. "Dr. Avila is the genius behind this technology."

Avila offered a self-satisfied smile, clearly pleased with his accomplishments. "Yes, I developed the technology. Dr. Shepherd provided some knowledge on genetic engineering and my team of bioengineers helped create the man you see here, and all those others, I might add."

Avila pulled the sheet and it slid to the floor, revealing a huge man wearing a dark blue uniform that was similar, Alex noted, to the ones worn by the airmen on base, but a little fancier, like the guy wearing it thought he was better than all the others. Even with the long sleeve shirt on, Alex could tell the man's upper body was thick around the chest, and one upper arm looked almost as big as William's head!

"You want us to bring this guy to life?" Alex gazed at Davalos in amazement. Sure, he'd known this was the plan back in that store room, but now, seeing this huge guy up close, knowing that the man could crush one of their heads with his bare hands, now it didn't seem like a good idea at all. It suddenly occurred to him to ask, "How do you know you can control this guy, you know, so he don't go around killing everybody?"

Davalos smiled. That arrogance really irked Alex. "I used the same technology as with the animal hybrids upstairs. There are computer chips within his brain, grown organically as he developed, that will allow me complete control over his actions. Unlike the colonel's mistake"—he tossed a nasty look at William—"this one won't be able to make choices. Only follow orders."

"And what if those orders are immoral?"

Davalos whirled around to face the open double doors, his expression turning to one of anger. Colonel Walker stood in the entrance pointing a gun at them. A group of armed airmen stood behind him. The airmen guarding Java and the others spun on the newcomers, aiming their guns as though to shoot.

"Stand down," ordered the colonel, and the men instantly lowered their weapons. Colonel Walker replaced his gun into a holster on his belt and strode forward.

Davalos's face grew hot with rage. "You have no business down here, Colonel."

The colonel nodded at Alex but faced the taller Davalos. "Intruders have gotten into these tunnels, Davalos. They must be found." He turned to his men huddled near the door. "Two of you remain. The rest, continue to fan out. Search every room. If the door is locked, shoot it open. We must find the intruders."

The men saluted and disappeared through the doorway into the tunnels.

Davalos looked stunned. "Intruders? How?"

"They hacked into the perimeter cameras, looped a repeating feed through the ones guarding the desert entrance. They also sent in a girl to distract us."

"A girl? Seriously, Colonel?" Davalos looked suspicious, like he thought the colonel was lying.

"She claimed to have gotten away from a kidnapper in the desert. Her story didn't add up, so I checked the camera system."

Davalos paled and finally looked worried. "You said those camera were unhackable."

"That's what Shaw told me when he installed them."

Alex gasped so loudly that both men turned to him.

"Something wrong, Alex?" Colonel Walker studied him with concern.

"No, it's…uh, well," he stammered. "It's just that, is it Mr. Shaw from ShawTech?"

Both men looked surprised, and Davalos blurted, "You know him?"

Alex nodded, deciding this was the moment to tell them the truth. "It was his house you took us from."

Mr. Davalos's face became white as a sheet, like all the color had drained from his face. "And it was his man who was shot?"

Alex nodded.

Colonel Walker glared at Davalos. "What happened to your intel when you moved in for the grab? How did you not know this already?"

Davalos glanced at Alex and then settled on Andy. "We didn't have any intel except that the other group was moving in. But we did have a tracking device planted on Andy, in case we lost him at the church."

Now Andy looked surprised. "You mean something to find me wherever I go??"

Davalos lost his superior composure. "You lost consciousness from all the smoke when we rescued you from that woman and her group. I had one of my men attach a tiny tracking device behind your right ear. It's so tiny, you wouldn't even notice it in the shower."

Andy reached up and felt around behind his ear, sliding his index finger back and forth. "I don't…" His finger stopped moving. "It's under my skin!" He shot such a murderous glare at Davalos that the man stepped away in fear.

"It was for your protection, Andy, so if they recaptured you, we'd know where to look."

Colonel Walker's face was impassive, like maybe he didn't completely disapprove of this method.

Alex reached out and placed a hand on Andy's arm. "It's okay, bro. He'll take it out." He looked up at Davalos. "Especially if he wants my help."

Davalos looked surprised for a moment, then nodded. "Of course. After we—"

"Now," Alex said, arms folded across his chest in defiance.

"You tell him, Alex" came Izzy's shrill words from the other side of the lab.

Davalos knew he had no choice, so he waved Avila over. "Remove it."

Avila nodded and retrieved some instruments from one of the rolling tables. One looked like a sharp knife and the other like tweezers. "It might sting a bit," he said.

Andy glared. "I don't care. Get it out."

Alex watched as Avila moved behind Andy and pushed his long blond hair away from his ear.

Colonel Walker placed a hand on Alex's shoulder, drawing his attention away from Andy. "Do you think Shaw would try to rescue you?"

"Yes. I bet Roy's dad and brother are with him too. They're good people, Colonel. Probably thought you guys were hurting us."

The colonel nodded. "That makes sense."

A hiss of pain from Andy drew Alex's attention, and he spun around to see Avila applying a tiny Band-aid to the back of Andy's ear. Then he held up a minuscule piece of metal in the tweezers for everyone to see. "It's done." He exchanged a look with Davalos that Alex didn't understand, but it didn't matter.

"You okay, bro?"

Andy nodded, still smoldering, but not looking ready to explode, at least.

Davalos turned to Alex. "Do you think Shaw would be armed?"

"How should I know? Martin's probably with him, and that guy can shoot, I know that much."

"Hopefully, my men will round them up without anyone getting hurt," the colonel said, his tone noncommittal. "Breaking into a military base is a serious crime, despite their good intentions. A man as powerful as Shaw knows that." He offered Alex a tight smile. "You must mean a lot to him."

Alex blushed, feeling his face grow hot. Other than his friends and Nathan, he wasn't accustomed to people caring about him. But Mr. Shaw really *did* care, didn't he?

***

Father Pat saw Shaw flinch upon hearing the colonel's words and understood that all his suspicions about the tech mogul were unfounded. The man really did care about Alex, likely because Alex saved his daughter's life, but maybe also because Alex was, well, Alex. Who wouldn't want a son like him?

Martin stepped forward and leaned down toward Shaw. "What should we do?"

"Nothing, Martin. Walker is a good man with a stellar reputation. Salt of the earth, as they used to say. When they find us, we surrender. Our primary concern was the safety of the boys. We know they're all right and under the colonel's protection. For now, I'm more interested in this unorthodox experiment. We might need to protect them from that."

***

Colonel Walker stared at the body on the table, but Alex couldn't tell whether he was impressed or appalled. "This is your idea of a supersoldier, Davalos?"

Now back to his favorite topic, Davalos shrugged off his discomfort and stood haughtily beside the colonel. "This man makes your child over there look like a Model T compared to a high-end Tesla."

Colonel Walker glanced at William, who gazed back at him impassively. Either he didn't understand the insult, or he didn't care. Alex hadn't understood it either, but he did know his friend was being dissed, and anger swelled within him.

"As I entered, Davalos, I heard you say that your new and improved model, here, cannot make choices," the colonel said, shifting his gaze from the nonliving man to Mr. Davalos.

"That's correct," Davalos replied, smiling. "No chance of him disobeying orders like Weapon over there."

Colonel Walker didn't react to the insult. "I repeat the question I asked as I entered. What if the orders are immoral or illegal? Your creation will carry them out without question. Since William has learned how to make choices, he will think about the repercussions and do the right thing in the end. At first, I thought his ability to think and choose was a net negative, and it was something we sought to avoid. Now I know he's exactly what this country needs—a supersoldier with a moral compass."

Davalos sneered. "Spare me the bleeding-heart rhetoric, Colonel. You simply went soft on the boy, thought of him as the son your barren wife couldn't give you."

Colonel Walker's face clouded with fury, and Alex thought he might haul off and punch out Davalos, but the clenched fist quickly relaxed. "One more mention of my wife, Davalos, and Pentagon or no Pentagon, I'll beat you down like there's no tomorrow."

The smirk vanished from Davalos's face, and he took a nervous step back. "I, uh, I apologize, Colonel. That was out of line. My only point is that we need supersoldiers who will do the dirty work that has to be done and won't fret over it afterward."

Colonel Walker studied the large man once more. "How many of the Joint Chiefs are on board with this approach?"

"Most of them. Sometimes it's necessary to fight barbarity with barbarity, fire with fire," Davalos insisted. "You know me, Colonel. We may not always agree, but I love this country and will do whatever it takes to protect it."

"Which brings up the age-old argument," Colonel Walker said, eyeing him with a raised eyebrow. "If we engage in the same barbarity as our enemies, how can we be a positive example for the world?"

"I only care about national security."

"And I care about the soul of America," the colonel responded. "William represents that soul. He can be ruthless, if need be, but he's also capable of extreme compassion. Look how he's cared for those poor creatures upstairs. They follow your orders because of the chips you implanted, but they do what he wants out of love and loyalty."

Davalos grunted with disgust. "Love and loyalty are fickle. Computer chips are absolute."

Colonel Walker sighed and turned to Alex and Andy. "My guess is he wants you boys to bring this man to life. Is that right?"

"Yes, sir," Alex replied, nibbling on his lower lip. He hadn't understood everything the two men were arguing about, but he did get the part about this huge man being unable to make choices, and that didn't sound good to him.

"He hasn't told us how," Andy added, turning to face Davalos with a questioning look on his face.

Davalos brightened. "This is the part I think Alex will like. I know how he hates seeing anyone suffer."

From across the room, Izzy called out, "I seen every Frankenstein movie, you guys, and they don't never end good!"

Davalos's turned and tossed such a vicious glare at Izzy that the boy sat back down in his chair, looking chastised.

"I'm just trying to help."

Davalos sneered. "Your opinion has been noted, young man."

He turned back and nodded to Avila, who strode to the door from which he had entered and vanished inside the room.

Alex tossed Izzy a thumbs up and then focused on the door through which Avila disappeared.

There were some awkward moments of silence. Alex studied Andy, who looked more excited than ever, and wondered why doing this was so important to him. Andy hadn't seemed the least bit happy that he helped save all those people in that bank building, so why this?

As he waited, Alex realized how uptight he felt, so he tried to relax by thinking of Shaw and Nathan being close by, how they'd come all this way to save him. And that reminded him what Colonel Walker said about a girl. Could it be Allison? He wouldn't be surprised. He suspected she would be down for just about anything, no matter how dangerous.

The door opened and a wheelchair emerged, followed by Avila pushing it. A man sat in the chair, bundled up in thick clothing with a blanket over his legs. He was the oldest man Alex had ever seen. His face looked like wrinkled papier-mâché, his wispy white hair barely covered half his head, and his arms looked like broom handles. The hands were so shriveled that Alex knew at once he didn't have the strength to push his own chair. Avila wheeled the man forward and stopped in front of Davalos and Colonel Walker.

Davalos squatted down before the shrunken old man. "Are you ready, Mr. Jäger?"

The old man lifted his head so slowly Alex almost screamed with frustration. Who was this guy, anyway? Finally, the man muttered, "Yes, Mark." His voice was so raspy it sounded like sandpaper on wood.

There was a large brownish mark that covered half the man's face and, coupled with the wrinkles, made his face look like it was about to fall off.

Colonel Walker stepped forward. "Who is this civilian, Davalos, and why is he on this base without my authorization?"

Davalos eyed the colonel with cool dispassion. "His name is Kurt Jäger and he's here under the authorization of General Lewis of the Joint Chiefs."

Colonel Walker's face fell, but he maintained his composure. "Very well. Why is he here?"

"It's his life force the twins will shift into my creation," Avila replied, as though it were the most obvious answer in the world.

Alex's mouth dropped open. He glanced at Andy, who smiled and nodded with great eagerness.

"But that means…" Alex almost couldn't say it. "We gotta…kill him."

"Yes, Alex," said Davalos, "that's exactly what it means.

CHAPTER EIGHTEEN

THERE'S NOTHING WE CAN'T DO, BROTHER

FATHER PAT GASPED. THIS MAN wanted Alex to commit murder in the name of…what, national security? Science? The very thought was monstrous! Bringing some inhuman creature to life like this *was* a Frankenstein movie, just like Israel said! Why, the thing would not even have a soul!

Father Pat considered himself an open-minded priest, more so than many of his superiors appreciated, but bringing a body to life without a soul or even a unique spirit terrified him. Would it be just a robot made of flesh?

And who was this old man willing to sacrifice his life for such an experiment? He leaned closer to the screen and studied the man's face, as best he could make it out. There was something oddly familiar…

"Shaw," he whispered, "can you zoom in on that man's face?" He pointed at the elderly man in the wheelchair.

"Why?"

"Please, just do it."

Shaw pinched and spread the tablet image, pushing Alex and the others out of the frame so only the elderly man filled the screen. The tablet produced excellent resolution and the man's beaked nose became plainly visible. Father Pat held his breath as the man slowly lifted his head to look at Alex.

The man had a birthmark covering the left side of his face!

"Shaw, do you have those photos I sent you from the Vatican archives?"

Shaw eyed him with raised eyebrows. "Yes, but Padre—"

"Pull up the one from 1940!"

Shaw hesitated a moment, but then shrank the live video feed to a small corner of the screen and opened a folder on the desktop. Within was all the information Father Pat had sent him. Shaw tapped on one of the photos labeled "1940" and it filled the screen.

"Now zoom in on the young man she's talking to, the one in the SS uniform."

Shaw complied. The face became larger and larger. Shaw had already used his software enhancement programs to clean up these photos, so the man's face was more clearly defined than when Father Pat had first seen it. Now it was Shaw who gave a slight exhalation of surprise.

"It's the same man." Shaw pointed to the birthmark on the face of the man in the photo. It was in exactly the same place as on the elderly man speaking to Alex.

Father Pat felt a lump of fear fill his stomach. "What does it mean?"

Shaw expanded the video feed to full screen. "That's a very good question, Padre."

***

Alex's mouth hung open in horror. "No way I'm gonna kill nobody!"

Davalos squatted down to face Alex, his expression unexpectedly sympathetic. "I'm not asking you to do that. Please, just hear what Mr. Jäger has to say."

Alex glanced from Davalos to the old man, who struggled once more to lift his head high enough to make eye contact.

"Alex." The raspy voice came out sounding like wind through dead branches. "I'm old and sick. One hundred and two, to be exact."

Now that the man had spoken, Alex heard the sick in his voice and spinned him. Something bad had taken over his body, something that was killing him from the inside. Cancer, maybe.

"I know," he said. "You're dying."

The old man's surprisingly alert eyes widened in surprise. "Pancreatic cancer. It's already metastasized, and I have little time left. That's why I volunteered for this experiment, because I... I want to go on living."

Alex felt this man's searing pain—and his intense desire to extend his life. But there was something else, almost like a false note in a song, that made him shiver. He focused on what he wanted to say. "I can take all the sick from you."

The old man forced himself to look over at Davalos, who remained in a squat.

Davalos nodded. "He can do that."

The old man with the odd name faced Alex once more. He was so frail that Alex could practically hear his bones creak as he shifted position. "That's not…what I…want…Alex. Look at me. This body…is useless. Can you…fix that?"

Alex thought about it for a long moment. Could he take oldness out of people like he did sickness? He was certain he couldn't. "No, sir."

"Then please, boy, please shift my life-force into him." He pointed a thin, bony finger at the figure on the table.

Something wasn't right here. Alex felt it, but he couldn't define it. This man wasn't telling him everything.

Suddenly, Andy was there, right in his face. "Can I talk to you, Big Brother? Alone?"

Alex glanced at Davalos, who nodded. "You guys can go into that office." He pointed at the open door from where Avila had wheeled the old man. "It's private."

Alex nodded and grabbed his wheel handles, pushing himself away from the old man, away from the dead guy on the table, away from Davalos. Suddenly, he wanted to be away from all of it. Andy was right behind him and allowed Alex to pass through the door first.

He found himself in some kind of office. There was a desk with a computer screen on top and several filing cabinets, but no decorations or pictures on the wall. He guessed no one spent much time in there. Andy closed the door and faced him. Where normally, Andy maintained a neutral expression, now he displayed a deep longing that Alex felt with great intensity.

"You were going to say no, weren't you?"

Alex's eyebrows shot up. "How'd you know?"

"We're connected, remember? Alex, please do this with me."

Alex squirmed. The force of emotion pouring out of Andy hit him like a baseball bat, and yet that troubling feeling remained. "Andy, something's not right with that old guy. I can feel stuff like that."

"I know. I felt it through you," Andy replied, dropping to a squat before him. "Alex, look at me." He rolled up one sleeve and flexed. If Alex wanted to be a bully, he'd say Andy's arm looked like a stick.

"So?"

Andy dropped his sleeve and grabbed both wheels of the chair, gazing with deep passion into Alex's eyes. "Ever since I've been with you guys, I've felt like I'm the weakest boy in the world. Those others, especially Java and Carlos, bragging about their muscles, and Israel about how handsome he is. And you, you're like all powerful. Without you, I can't do much of anything. I really need to prove I can be strong too, Alex."

"But, well, you did. You saved all those people at that bank."

"But your friends didn't see that," Andy went on, the urgency intensifying. "I want to prove to them that I'm not weak. I don't know why, but it's important to me."

Alex didn't need to spin him to understand. Andy was a boy who'd never been around other kids his entire life. His pride hurt because he felt less than the others, less even, than his own brother.

"You don't care that the old man will die because of us?"

Andy shrugged. "It's what he wants, right? I mean, he's already dying. Alex, you said so yourself. Don't you want to know if we can do this? We're talking about shifting Life, the biggest kind of Life there is, from one human to another. If we can do that, no one will ever mess with us again!"

Andy's voice rose in pitch and his face lit up with a level of exhilaration that frightened Alex.

"We will not use our power to hurt good people, Andy. William learned that lesson the hard way."

Andy studied him so deeply that Alex squirmed. "Sometimes I think you wish he was your brother instead of me."

Alex's mouth dropped open in shock. "Course, I don't! But he's a good kid who needs a family. Why can't he be part of ours?"

Andy lost the accusatory expression. "I'm sorry. I guess that's being jealous, what I'm feeling?"

"Yeah," Alex replied. "It's okay."

"You don't need to worry about me hurting people. I can't do anything big without you anyway, you know that. Please, Alex?"

Alex pondered what would be the best choice. Like William, he understood that choices have consequences. He still believed the old man was hiding something. But then, they didn't even know if this would work. And if it did, weren't they just shifting the guy's life force from one body to the other, not his brain? When he came to life, would the artificial man know anything the old man knew? Alex had no way of knowing.

He studied Andy's eager expression. No, not eager. Needy. Andy may have been in a cage all his life, but he was still a teen boy whose pride had been bruised and he needed to prove himself.

"Okay, bro," he said, making his choice before he even knew he had. "Let's do it."

Andy grinned so broadly that Alex was caught off-guard by how beautiful his brother looked, especially with the long white hair framing his soft, delicate features.

No wonder Roy likes him, Alex thought.

And then Andy did something he never had before—he pulled Alex into a hug. "Thanks, Big Brother."

***

Dane needed to scratch his ass, but the air duct was so tight he'd make a loud noise if he budged even an inch. He also wished he could leave the tiny camera in the grill and head back to the others, but Shaw kept telling him to move it this direction or that and he feared someone would spot it if Dane left the camera in one of the grill holes.

Dane could hear everything happening below but understood almost none of it. The only thing he cared about was that Roy and Alex were unhurt. He'd figured out that the guy in the business suit wanted Alex and Andy to bring the dead body to life, but how they could do that he hadn't a clue. But he *was* ready to kick out this grill and drop into that room if anything went wrong and the boys were in danger. He didn't even care about the soldiers with their guns. No one would hurt his little brother. No one!

Through the speaker in his left ear, he heard Shaw whisper, "They're coming back. Keep the camera on the twins."

Dane shifted the camera in his hand toward the door through which the boys had vanished. It was open now and Alex was wheeling back toward the guy in the suit, his brother strutting proudly beside him. The brother wore a shit-eating grin that troubled Dane, but there was nothing he could do but see how everything played out.

***

Alex wheeled himself across the lab, working his way between tables laden with glass tubes and bottles, Andy bouncing along beside him. He'd never seen his brother this animated, and he noticed the self-satisfied look he offered Java and Carlos in the opposite corner. Alex met Roy's intense gaze from across the lab. His best friend's brows were furrowed with concern and Alex felt waves of anxiety even from this distance. Roy shook his head, and Alex got the message. Roy didn't want him to do this. Deep inside, Alex agreed with him. It all felt wrong, but he'd promised Andy, so he stifled his protesting conscience and stopped his chair before Davalos and Avila.

"Okay, I'll do it."

Davalos grinned broadly like a little kid in an ice cream store.

Alex glanced at the old man in the other wheelchair. He noted it was more of a medical chair, designed for temporary use and for someone else to push it. He eyed the old man's gnarled, twisted hands and shuddered.

Will that be me someday, too old and frail to even push my own chair?

Davalos studied Andy. "How shall we proceed?"

Andy shrugged like it was no big deal. "When I shifted Death out of Roy, I talked it out because that was my first time. Guess I'll try the same thing with Life." He turned to Alex. "Ready, Big Brother?"

Alex wasn't, but he nodded anyway.

Davalos squatted down in front of the old man. "Are you ready, Mr. Jäger?"

"Yes."

The man's voice sounded weaker than just a few minutes prior, and Alex sensed he didn't have much time left.

"We don't know what will happen," Davalos went on soberly. "If it will work at all, or whether or not you'll have your memories if it does."

"Just begin."

Davalos wheeled the man's chair over beside the unmoving form on the long table. Andy and Alex followed. Alex realized his hands were trembling as he gripped his wheel handles and he squeezed extra hard to control the vibrations. He stopped before the table and considered once more the sheer size and weight of the body. If this thing went out of control like Izzy said…he didn't even want to think about it!

Forcing himself to remain calm, he looked at the lifeless face for the first time. The man seemed as though he was asleep, rather than never having lived. And he resembled an action movie star with his short brown hair, square jaw, small nose and ears, and thin lips. Except for his size, he looked rather ordinary to Alex, which he supposed was what Davalos had wanted.

He felt someone nudge his shoulder and pulled his gaze away from the man to find Andy by his side.

"Are you ready, Big Brother?"

Alex gulped and nodded. His mouth felt dry as dust and he wished he had some water. Andy held up a hand. Alex paused a moment to get the shaking under control. Then he lifted his arm and grasped Andy's hand.

The rushing floodwaters engulfed him, starting in his belly and spreading outward to every inch of his body. He focused on Andy, rather than the old man or the body. He didn't want to see what happened to either of them.

"Mr. Jäger," Andy began, his voice calm and steady, "your life isn't yours anymore. It belongs to me. Let it go. Let it enter me."

Alex felt nothing, unlike when they'd shifted Death. This wasn't working.

Andy must've sensed it too because his voice rose an octave. "Life-force inside Mr. Jäger, come into me." He paused, as though thinking. "Whatever is in him that keeps him alive come into me. Now!" Another pause, but nothing happened. "I command you! Life, to me!"

Alex jolted in his chair, feeling like he'd been struck by lightning. His entire body felt warm, no, hot, like a fever raged through every bit of him. His muscles became strong, stronger than ever before and his brain burned with more power than he'd experienced at any time in his life, more than even when he'd spun the leukemia from Allison. Only this power didn't make him weak like that one had; it energized him so much he felt like Superman, like there was nothing he couldn't do!

Andy turned away from the old man and faced the younger one on the table. Andy appeared to be limned with power, almost blindingly bright, but Alex thought that must be his imagination because his eyes didn't hurt to look at him.

"Life, to him!" Andy raised his other arm and pointed at the dormant young man.

Alex felt the rushing of floodwaters again, only this time it was going in the opposite direction, leaving his body. The heat, the jolting power, all surged out of him in a massive wave that left him gasping for air, his vision blurred. He slumped in his chair, but Andy gripped his hand harder and pulled him back up.

"Look, Big Brother, look what we have done!"

Alex lifted his head and allowed his vision to clear. Avila was leaning over the man on the table with one of those doctor gadgets they always used. It was pressed to the man's thick chest, and Avila was listening through the earphones. He looked up at Davalos and grinned so broadly Alex thought the smile would rip his face open.

"He's alive, Davalos, alive!"

"Yes!" Davalos exclaimed, clapping the doctor on the back as Avila stood and lifted the supersoldier's eyelids with his fingers. He was about to shine a light into one of the eyes when he lurched back in surprise. The man on the table opened his eyes and looked around, seemingly confused.

Andy released Alex's hand, but before he did, he leaned in to Alex's ear and gushed, "There's nothing we can't do, brother!"

Alex grimaced at the clamminess of his hand and rubbed it against his sweatpants like it held dangerous germs, gazing at Andy in horror. His brother was looking back at the other boys with a huge smirk on his face. Alex turned his chair and noted the fear on Izzy's face, the horror on Roy's. The others seemed astonished, which he supposed was what so pleased Andy.

"He's dead," Avila said tonelessly, and Alex spun back around. The doctor was rising after using his listening gadget on the old man's heart. Alex stared at this man whose life he had just taken. The body looked even more shrunken than before, but Alex knew the pain was gone, and the pain had been extreme. Maybe he hadn't done such a bad thing after all. He eyed the now-alive man on the table who stared at Davalos and

Avila. Colonel Walker strode forward for a closer look, William trailing after.

William stopped beside Alex and placed a hand on his shoulder. Still shuddering from the experience, Alex welcomed the gesture, but couldn't take his eyes off the man he'd brought to life.

Colonel Walker eyed him with a look of wonder on his craggy face, and Alex felt his face redden. He hated being under a microscope, no matter who was looking.

"Help me sit him up," Avila said to Davalos, and the two men moved to opposite sides of the table. Each grabbed one massive arm, needing both hands to reach around the bulging muscles, and urged the man upward by tugging gently.

"Sit up," Davalos said, his tone firm, like he was giving orders.

The big man looked muddled, at first, or maybe his muscles were stiff from never having been used, but it took him a long moment of staring wide-eyed at Avila and Davalos before he seemed to understand.

The table groaned beneath his bulk as the man slowly let himself be hefted upward. Avila and Davalos strained under the weight and Alex saw beads of sweat break out on both their foreheads. How much did that guy weigh, anyway?

Finally, after several long moments, the man was sitting upright.

"Colonel," Davalos hissed, his breathing already strained, "if you will, pull his legs over the side of the table so he can sit on his own."

The colonel observed him a moment before stepping around the table and gripping the booted feet and sliding them toward the edge. Once the feet were over, he pushed the knees to one side.

Finally, the legs hung over the side of the table, dangling from bent knees, and the other two hefted the man's upper body to a seated position. The man used his large hands to grip the edge of the table and remain upright. He looked even more impressive this way, chest bulging, arms thick as tree branches, almost like he was Captain America and Superman combined.

"Well, Colonel," Davalos said, gasping slightly, his chest heaving from the exertion, "what do you think now?"

Colonel Walker displayed no discernable emotion. Alex figured this was a military trick in case he ever got captured by the enemy. "That depends on how fast he learns and obeys. We went through that period with"—he glanced at William, still standing beside Alex's chair—"well, with our own project."

Davalos eyed William with contempt. "Yes, and sadly, yours is already obsolete."

"We'll see about that," the colonel replied, his tone noncommittal. He studied Alex and Andy. "You boys all right?"

"Yes," Alex replied at once, because there didn't seem to be any weird after effects of the spin and shift, despite its magnitude.

Andy flexed his skinny arms and laughed. "All powerful, Colonel."

Colonel Walker frowned and so did Alex. He didn't like what he felt from his brother, and for the first time was glad their roles weren't reversed. If Andy had been the Healer and wielded the lion's share of the power, what might he do with it? As Alex studied Andy's gloating, smug expression, he shivered at the possibilities.

Instead, he looked up at William to see if the nasty comment from Davalos had hurt his feelings. William seemed unaffected, on the surface, but Alex felt the hurt inside him as their eyes met. Anger burned within Alex for the crummy way this kid was always treated, and he wanted more than anything to do something positive for him.

William seemed to understand. He leaned down and whispered into Alex's ear, "Bigger isn't better. He'll see."

He offered a little smile to go with the comment and Alex returned it, his body finally relaxing. As the doctor shined his little flashlight into the big man's eyes, Alex found his gaze wandering to Mr. Davalos, who had gripped the back of the old man's wheelchair and was steering it toward the open door of the office. Alex caught a quick glimpse of the shrunken face and sagging body one last time before Davalos's back blocked it, the wheels making a *crunch, crunch* sound as the wheelchair moved closer to the office.

That old man had been suffering excessive pain. Had Alex spun him, he would've felt even worse than he had from Allison's leukemia and the man would still have been a hundred years old and weak. He'd helped take that man's life, yes, but on the other hand, he'd also helped the man to live again. And he'd ended all that suffering. Maybe Andy wasn't wrong to feel elated about what they'd done.

He studied his brother, who was eagerly waving the other boys over from across the room. Maybe that was the reason Andy was so gleeful.

He'd wanted to show off his power and he'd succeeded. As a special-ed kid who'd been made fun of his entire school life, Alex understood that desperate need for validation. He'd found it at the skate park and even more strongly through Roy and his other friends. Now he hoped that Andy would find that the value of friendship was the best form of validation, not showing off stuff you could do.

As Avila continued his examination of the silent, cooperative man, Roy and the others hurried between tables and chairs to join Alex and Andy.

Roy's handsome face was creased with worry, and he leaned down to whisper, "You okay?"

Alex nodded. "Yeah."

"What did you guys think?" Andy asked the boys, with obvious eagerness in his voice and wide, expectant eyes.

"Amazing," said Carlos, staring at the newborn man in awe. "He looks bigger than The Rock from them movies."

"I wonder what that dude can bench press," Java muttered. "Look at them guns. Bigger than Izzy's mouth."

Alex couldn't help but laugh as Izzy's gaping expression of awe turned to one of annoyance and he punched Java hard on the shoulder.

Java grinned. "That's the best you got, fool?"

Izzy pouted. "I still say that monster gonna go bad. I seen all the movies."

"Yeah, yeah." Java rumpled Izzy's mop of back hair and turned to Alex. "That power you got be somethin' else, Alex."

Alex nodded but caught the hurt look on Andy's face and quickly said, "Yeah, but it's Andy who done the shifting."

The boys all faced Andy a moment, who wore a hopeful look on his face.

"Pretty trippy, Andy," Carlos said, "that power you got. Could you and Alex do that to anybody?"

"Yeah, we can, right, Big Brother?"

Alex considered a moment. If they could do it once, they could do it again. Based on past experience, the process would get easier every time. Assuming there were enough of these bodies available, lots of dying people could easily live again. How crazy was that?

"Yeah, bro, we can."

That drew a smile from Andy, but it was only partial. Alex knew his brother had hoped for more praise from the other boys, hoped they would marvel at his strength, even though it was a different kind of strength than they possessed. But Alex knew his friends weren't dissing Andy. It was just, to them, strength meant physical, like in the weight room or on the football field.

Mr. Davalos had returned by now, the office door behind him closed, and frowned when he saw all the boys so close to his creation. "I told you boys to wait over there."

Andy stuck out his chest. "I told them they could come."

Davalos eyed him a moment but seemed reluctant to argue.

Before he could respond, Colonel Walker stepped away from his scrutiny of the super soldier and approached. "Davalos, I assume you can control this man?"

Davalos turned from the boys and resumed his self-satisfied expression. "Of course. My voice, as well as the voices of every member of the Joint Chiefs has been programmed into the chip in his brain. He will follow our orders."

The colonel frowned. "And what about me? I'm base commander. Should something happen to you, someone needs to control him."

"What could possibly happen to me?"

Colonel Walker didn't answer, but Alex noted the troubled look on his face, like he knew of something bad that could happen, or maybe was already happening.

Davalos stepped around the colonel and returned to Avila's side. The doctor was using one of those rubber hammers and hitting the knees of the man. The guy's left leg bounced up a little and settled back down.

Avila looked up at Davalos with a grin. "Reflexes are good, Mark. He seems to be in excellent health. The cryogenic freeze preserved his body tissues exactly as planned."

Davalos stepped closer and looked directly into the man's face. "Can you hear me?"

The big guy pulled his gaze from Avila and fixed it upon Davalos.

"I'll take that as a yes," Davalos said, his voice rising with excitement. "Do you know who you are?"

The creature just stared at him without blinking.

"He might not have any of Jäger's memories, Mark," Avila said. "We don't know what transferring a lifeforce means."

Davalos nodded, but he didn't take his eyes off the newborn's face.

"Climb off the table and stand before me." He stepped back to give the tall man some space. Avila did the same.

Colonel Walker stood with Alex and the others watching the unfolding events with keen interest. But for the first time, Alex noted his right hand hung close to his belt, right next to…his gun. The gun handle poked out of a small holster and the colonel looked ready to grab for it. But even if something did go wrong, like Izzy suggested, from what Alex had been told about this supersoldier, bullets probably wouldn't hurt him.

The man shifted his ponderous weight and slid forward on the table, which creaked, breaking the eerie silence. Alex exchanged a look of trepidation with Roy.

Almost like a baby figuring out how to take its first steps, the seven-foot-tall man touched the floor with one foot and then the other. Davalos reached out a hand and grasped one of his larger ones, tugging gently. The big man rose to his full height, dwarfing Davalos and Avila, and then wobbled, looking like he might topple over. The two men darted to each side and clasped hard to the thick arms, steadying the swaying supersoldier. Alex was certain Davalos, or Avila would be crushed if the big guy fell on either of them.

The wobbling man quickly gained control of his legs, which looked as thick as small tree trunks, and stood up straight. Davalos and Avila took several steps back and the taller man looked down at them with a questioning look in his eyes. Alex was pretty sure he didn't have any of the old man's memories, which meant the lifeforce and the soul were different. Whenever he saw Father Pat again, he'd make sure to ask him about this.

"I am your commanding officer," Davalos said, his tone serious, his voice focused. "You will obey my orders without question. Do you understand?"

The quizzical look on the man's face became more pronounced and he opened his mouth. He looked like he wanted to speak but didn't quite know how. He grunted.

"That's right," Davalos urged. "Talk to me. My name is Mr. Davalos."

Alex felt his breath freeze in his chest as the huge man lifted his arms toward Davalos, but not to grab him; more like he was gesturing, the way teachers sometimes did while talking in front of the class. The man's mouth struggled to form sounds. Alex so wanted to spin him, but the man had to speak first.

"Mmmiissterr," rolled haltingly from the man's mouth, drawing a gigantic grin from Davalos. "Missterr Daavaaloss."

Davalos looked ready to leap into the air with delight. He exchanged a grin with an equally excited Avila before casting a smug look of triumph at Colonel Walker.

Alex eyed the colonel, whose hand still hovered just above his gun, looking like one of those guys in old western movies.

Davalos took four steps back and said, "Come to me."

The supersoldier looked down at Davalos's legs, then at his own, which looked almost two times larger. He haltingly lifted his right leg and moved it forward, planting his booted foot firmly on the ground. He swayed a bit but kept his balance. Then he stepped forward with the left foot. It only took him two steps to cover the distance, until he once again towered over the shorter Davalos. Avila grinned and hurried to a large wooden chair with no arms. He slid it out into an open area.

"Have him practice sitting," he told Davalos.

Davalos walked to the chair. The creature turned and watched his movements. Davalos stood in front of the chair facing the man.

"Sit." He sat in the chair. "Stand." He stood once more. "Now you."

Davalos stepped aside and waved the guy over with a sweep of his arm. The big man lumbered forward, each step smoother as he got the feel of his new body. He stopped and stared at the chair as though it was the most interesting thing ever.

"Sit," repeated Davalos, his tone firm and commanding. This was an order and Alex sensed he wanted the guy to know that.

The super soldier turned his head and studied Davalos for a long moment. Then he turned his body around with slow, jerky movements, until he was facing Alex and the others. Alex stared into his eyes, struggling to spin anything from him, but picked up nothing. The man lowered himself into the chair, and then sat against the back of it in exactly the same posture Davalos had assumed.

He learns fast, Alex thought, realizing that maybe Izzy was wrong after all.

That was before a cat trotted into the lab and jumped onto the man's lap.

CHAPTER NINETEEN

JUST WHAT IS YOUR PLAN?

Father Pat stared at Shaw's tablet, his mouth agape with horror at what the twins had been able to do as much as at the inhuman monster to whom they'd given life. The ability to steal life itself from one person and pass it on to another was staggering. He couldn't fathom why God would give humans such power, but perhaps this was why it was split between the two boys.

Father Pat had full confidence that Alex would never allow his gifts to be exploited. Not willingly, at least. But Andy? He was the big question mark. His attitude and facial expressions revealed a boy drunk with power, and such boys always proved dangerous in the end.

As the creature on screen finally uttered Davalos's name, Father Pat leaned closer to Shaw. "We need to get the boys out of there."

Shaw glanced up at him, his expression hidden in shadow. "And how do you propose we do that?"

Father Pat paused, flustered because he had no idea. It was just a feeling gnawing away at his insides, a feeling that everyone in that room was in mortal danger.

"At this point, all we can do is watch this scenario play out. The colonel's men are searching for us as we speak. It's only a matter of time till we're discovered."

"Yes, but the soul of that Nazi is inside the creature," Father Pat reminded him, fighting to keep the edge out of his voice.

"I'm well aware of that fact, Padre," Shaw continued, clearly losing patience. "Whatever the boys did to bring that thing to life doesn't appear to have transferred the Nazi's consciousness. That can only be for the good, wouldn't you agree?"

Father Pat nodded. He knew he must sound foolish, but that anxiety in the pit his stomach roiled like an abscess. He focused once more on the tablet. The creature was seated in a chair and…he leaned closer. A large, long-haired cat had just leaped into the monster's lap!

***

Alex's fearful reaction to the sudden appearance of a cat was mirrored in his friends. Izzy blurted, "Oh, shit!" and stepped behind Java who, for all his bravado, stiffened and looked ready to flee at a moment's notice. Andy remained calm, but he hadn't had the experiences with cats that they had suffered through, especially that horrific night at the graveyard. Alex shivered and gripped his wheel handles, ready to bolt.

Davalos reacted with surprise as the thick, furry feline leaped into the huge man's lap and just sat there, staring up at the man's face and flicking its tail side to side, but Avila looked like he'd expected it to show up, which aroused Alex's suspicions.

Colonel Walker stepped closer to Davalos. "Is this one of your lab animals, Dr. Avila?"

The doctor shook his head. "I found him wandering the base and brought him down here because he proved to be good company when I was alone."

The colonel frowned. "How could a stray cat get onto this base? We're in the middle of nowhere."

Davalos, eyes still fixed on the cat in his creation's lap said, "It stowed away in one of the transport vehicles the night your men brought in the boys."

Alex flinched, his mind whirling with an elusive memory. A cat.… He studied the animal, struggling to remember…

"Why wasn't I informed of this earlier?" Colonel Walker was clearly annoyed.

Davalos glanced over. "It's just a cat, Colonel. What harm could it do?"

Alex wondered the same thing, except there was something about this particular cat that troubled him. Something about the night they were knocked out and brought to this place…

"Look, Mr. Davalos," Avila exclaimed, pointing at the artificial man.

The man had tilted his head downward and was gazing at the cat. That part made sense. The weird part, and what drew Alex out of his thoughts, was that the cat stared right back! They were making direct eye contact, almost like it was a staring contest, which Alex had only ever seen one cat do before, the one that belonged to Ms. G!

The colonel frowned. "Isn't that odd behavior for a cat, Doctor?"

"Not necessarily," Avila replied, his tone cagey. "Animals often stare at things they find interesting, just as we do."

The supersoldier's eyes seemed to flicker and his face twitched, like the cat was controlling or hypnotizing him. That's when Alex remembered where he'd seen this animal before. It had been on the fence the night he was captured! He'd seen it just before he was knocked out from the dart in his chest!

He'd already opened his mouth to warn the colonel when the big man spoke. "I am Kurt Jäger."

Avila beamed, like he'd expected this, but Colonel Walker and Davalos stared in amazement.

"It worked," Andy muttered, excitement in his voice.

Alex wanted to ask what he meant, but he was distracted when the cat jumped down from the man's lap and scampered off toward the open door into the corridor.

And then he knew!

"Colonel," Alex barked. "She's here! Somewhere!"

The colonel whirled to face him. "Who's here, Alex?"

"Ms. G!"

Roy gasped, while Izzy expelled a breathy, "Oh, shit, where?"

Colonel Walker turned to Davalos. "You told me that woman died in the shootout at the church."

Davalos squirmed, his face paling. "That's what our man reported at the time. But when the cleanup team arrived, there was…no sign of her body, only the others. We just…assumed her people got there first and took it."

Alex whirled on Andy. "Tell them what you told me about her."

Andy looked uncomfortable and glanced around as though he thought she might be lurking somewhere in the lab.

"I don't think you can kill her," he told the two men solemnly. "She has supernatural powers."

Davalos scowled. "You might have told us this before, kid."

"You didn't ask."

Alex registered fear in the look his brother tossed his way, and he knew Andy was thinking about that glass cage he grew up in.

Colonel Walker slipped a small walkie-talkie off his belt. "I'll have Stern lock down the base, even though she likely entered with the team that breached these tunnels." He turned to the soldiers guarding the open door. "You men, join the search team. These tunnels aren't that extensive. Find the intruders."

The two men did not move or even respond to the direct order because at that moment, someone stepped between them into the lab, holding the large furry cat in her arms.

Alex groaned.

"Holy shit!" cried Izzy, his voice trembling with fear.

***

Dane practically jumped out of his skin when he saw her! That evil bitch who'd tried to kidnap Alex was dead! He'd seen her collapse, riddled with bullets. How the hell could she be down there now?

He so desperately wanted to contact Shaw and his dad, but knew he'd be overheard if he did, and then he'd be no use to Roy or the other kids. He shifted his body to relieve the stiffness, preparing himself in case he needed to bust out the grill and drop down there to help. It was about eight feet to the floor, but he thought he could make it safely. Whether he could or couldn't, if Roy or Alex was threatened, he was going for it.

***

"Holy Mother of God," whispered Father Pat as he gazed into the face of Ms. G on Shaw's tablet. Her long blonde hair tumbled around her shoulders, and she was dressed all in black like a cat burglar. At the church, he'd been certain they'd seen the last of her, but after what he'd learned in the Vatican archives, he now understood that destroying her would not be so simple. And here she was, back to claim the boys who'd slipped through her fingers.

"Before you say anything, Padre, I'm one step ahead." Shaw turned to Martin, standing beside him. "Martin, take George and Miguel and search these tunnels for weapons. Disarm soldiers, if you have to, just don't hurt them, even if they do work for her."

"What do you mean, Shaw?" Father Pat gaped at him.

"Those airmen down there didn't flinch when she walked in because they expected her. I suspect at least some of the others who came down here with Walker are turncoats too. Since we're not sure who's friend and who's foe, I want to be careful. But we need to be armed. This situation just got personal."

"Yes, Mr. Shaw," Martin said, his deep voice unusually quiet. "Let's go, guys."

He cracked open the door and peered out. Then he darted into the tunnel and the other two followed, easing the door closed behind them.

Shaw gave Father Pat a scrutinizing look. "This may be the moment you decide whether or not to fight, Padre. There will be a gun for you."

Without awaiting an answer, he returned his full attention to the tablet screen.

Father Pat stared at the smirking woman stroking the cat. Could he fire a gun at another human being? He'd soon find out.

***

Roy's mouth hung open as Colonel Walker pulled his gun and pointed it over the heads of the boys straight at Ms. G. Alex and Andy had been right. She didn't die back at that church! Behind him, Roy heard Izzy keening like a wounded animal, while Java cursed under his breath.

Four airmen appeared in the tunnel and flanked Ms. G as she ambled into the lab, smiling, and caressing the purring cat like she hadn't a care in the world. Her smirking expression irked Roy and his fear was partially replaced by fury.

"Hello, boys," she purred. "How are my favorite students doing? I do hope these men are taking good care of you."

"How did you get in here?" Colonel Walker's voice boomed through the room and Roy glanced in his direction. The gun was up and ready, pointed at Ms. G with a steady hand.

Ms. G faced the base commander. "You must be Colonel Walker," she cooed, her long, slender fingers weaving their way through the cat's thick fur. "I've heard a lot about you."

"From whom?"

She smiled. "Why, from your men, of course. At least, those who are loyal to me, like these six." She waved a casual hand toward the four airmen behind her and the two who'd already been present. All of them had their guns drawn and aimed at the colonel. Roy noticed that none of them were young guys, like right out of high school. They all looked at least twenty-five or thirty, but he was bad at guessing people's ages.

Colonel Walker winced, then glanced at the airmen. "You men will all be court-martialed."

"Yes, sir," the Latino one replied. He looked about thirty, handsome, but solemn. "That's better than being dead, which is what will happen if we betray her."

Ms. G's grin widened. "You see, Colonel, I know how to control my troops."

The colonel gave no indication what he felt about her comment, but he did lower his gun and slip it back into his holster. "What do you want here?"

She sauntered past the boys toward the chair where the newly revived man still sat. The big guy looked different, Roy noticed, and nudged Alex.

"Look at his face," he whispered. "His eyes."

Alex nodded, studying the big man, maybe spinning him, but Roy couldn't be sure.

"He's not the same," Alex said, focused on the man with concentration. "He's different from when we brung him to life."

Ms. G. tossed him a phony smile of congratulations. "Of course, the Healer would notice the change. Have you also figured it out, Andy?"

Andy stared at her a moment and then focused on the man. "He's Jäger now."

"Indeed, he is," Ms. G. responded, her voice edged with triumph. "Under the Third Reich, he was a young, especially brutal officer in the

SS. He only escaped the Nuremberg trials because I hid him away. Years of planning have led to this moment of triumph."

Mr. Davalos finally seemed to find his voice. "What are you talking about? This is *my* project. How do you even know about it?"

"I thought I made it clear that I have people in high places, Mr. Davalos, not just here on this base." She tossed off a laugh that chilled Roy's blood. "You thought you were so slick when you stole Andy from me. Little did you realize that you did exactly as I wanted."

Davalos looked more stunned than Roy had ever seen him. "You wanted? We extracted your location from one of your stooges."

Her smile grew larger. "You extracted what I wanted you to extract."

Apparently shocked to his core, Davalos eyed the colonel for help, but the base commander was staring at Ms. G. Roy hoped he was working up some plan to save them all.

"You're telling us that you set all this up." Colonel Walker paused, thinking. "Because you wanted the twins to bring this creature to life."

Even with the cat in her arms, Ms. G managed to put her hands together in mock applause. "Very good, Colonel. Your years in the intelligence division served you well." She eyed Davalos with disgust. "Didn't you ever wonder how Mr. Jäger entered your life at just the moment you needed someone for your experiment?"

From the surprised look on his face, Roy saw that Davalos hadn't thought about that before now.

"Kurt has always been one of my most loyal subjects, beginning when I met him in Germany during the war," she went on, as though reading a bedtime story to a child. "Now, thanks to the superpowered body you've given him, he will be an indestructible soldier for my cause."

Davalos's face fell into open-mouthed astonishment, and he looked at the colonel, who seemed just as shocked. But Dr. Avila, Roy noticed, hovered behind Davalos listening to the exchange looking as though he already knew all this.

"You expect us to believe you were alive during World War II," Colonel Walker said, keeping his voice steady, "when you look like you do now?"

"As Mr. Davalos's men have already learned, Colonel, I'm tough." She eyed Davalos, her blue eyes gleaming with power. "I am sorry about Cole, though. He was a worthy opponent."

She said no more than that, but Roy flinched when he heard Cole's name. That was the cop who'd betrayed them, but then turned out to be a good guy after all. He considered what she was saying now, struggling to remember how far in the past World War II happened. Ms. Ashley had taught them, but he could never remember dates. It was a long time ago; he knew that much. So how could she still be so young?

Alex, who'd been staring at Ms. G, said, "You got some help from them demon things, didn't you, so they can keep you young and stuff?"

Ms. G sneered at him. "You're always so eloquent, Alex. But yes, you are close to the truth."

Roy's face reddened with anger, and he wanted to slap her. He didn't know that word she'd used, but he did know she'd dissed Alex, and he hated her all the more every time she did that.

"Why would you let us destroy your location and capture the boy?" Davalos asked, pointing at Andy.

"We were preparing to abandon that headquarters for a more permanent base," she replied, continuing to stroke the cat, which purred loud enough to be heard over the blowing of the air system. "We thought it best to let you *rescue* Andy and bring him here of your own accord, along with his darling twin, of course."

She cast Alex a nasty smirk, and the hackles rose on Roy's neck. He'd never wanted to punch someone as much as he did her.

"Why do you want this man?" Davalos asked, indicating the reborn Jäger, who was following the conversation with interest now, as though he understood everything.

"A supersoldier with the soul of an SS officer who's loyal to me?" She laughed, sounding like the cackling of a witch. "What's not to like about that plan, Davalos?"

"Just what is your plan?" Colonel Walker made no sudden moves, but Roy could tell he was ready for action.

"You'll know soon enough, Colonel." She turned to face Jäger. "I'm leaving now with the twins. After I do, destroy this lab and everyone in it. Then meet us at the rendezvous point."

Jäger rose to his feet, much more in control of his new body than before. He bowed to her. "Yes, my lady." The voice was different from the old man, and there was no accent. But it sounded breathy, maybe because it hadn't been used much.

Colonel Walker reached for his gun again, aiming it at Jäger. "There's no way you can get off this base," he announced to Ms. G. "I have more men than you do."

"That's quite true," she admitted in that maddeningly calm voice. "Unfortunately, they're all locked in their barracks at the moment."

The colonel flinched, obviously taken by surprise. "Sergeant Stern will—"

"Sergeant Stern," she interrupted, "is locked in the control room where, if he's conscious yet, will have a clear view of us driving out across the desert in our unmarked vehicles. You see, Colonel, I have everything just the way I want it."

Jäger glared down at the colonel, his head almost brushing the ceiling. Then he turned toward Dr. Avila, who cowered and stumbled backward into a table, knocking the glass jars and their colorful contents all over the floor. The glass sprayed tiny pieces up and around his shoes, but he was too focused on the looming figure to pay any attention. Jäger raised a thick arm and made a fist, preparing to smash the whimpering doctor into the floor.

"Stop!" ordered Davalos to the giant. "You are programmed to obey me."

The monstrous Jäger eyed him a long moment as though prepared to stand down. But then he smiled, and the look of evil framing those lips sent a chill through Roy's heart.

"I take orders only from her."

He turned back to the doctor. Colonel Walker made a move to intervene, but the clicking of guns caused him to stop in his tracks. He shot a fierce look at Ms. G. "You can't just murder him in cold blood."

Ms. G. considered his words a moment. "You're right. He might still be useful to us." She waved over one of the airmen and pointed at Avila. "Take him."

The airman, big and beefy, stepped around the supersoldier and grabbed Avila roughly by the upper arm. "Come with me."

Davalos, who'd stood frozen with disbelief, finally came to life, and lunged for the airman. "You can't take him. I order you to stand down."

The airman pointed his gun at Davalos, his face displaying no emotion. "I don't take orders from you anymore, sir."

Jäger swung one arm at Davalos, striking him in the face and sending him flying several inches off the floor to crash into a rolling chair just behind the colonel. He lay on the floor stunned, moaning but unable to get up.

The airman dragged Avila, stumbling, from the lab, while Jäger stood proud and awaited his orders from Ms. G.

Roy knew he should be terrified but, like Alex, he was tired of running from this woman. When she turned to the soldiers, Roy knew they would grab Alex and Andy next, so he acted without thinking.

"No way you're gonna get them, bitch!" He stretched out his hands on both sides. "Quick, guys, circle around Alex." He caught sight of Andy and added, "Andy too!"

"Huh?" Izzy mumbled, gazing in terror at Ms. G.

"Now, Izzy!" yelled Java, who grabbed Roy's hand and then Izzy's.

"Hurry, Jorge," Carlos urged, grabbing Jorge and pulling him closer to the others so he could snatch up Roy's other hand.

With Alex and Andy safe within the circle, Roy urged the others, "Focus on keeping them safe."

Ms. G smirked and shook her head in disgust, mocking them like she'd done so often before. Roy wanted to shove that cat right into her face.

The Colonel stared at the boys, aghast. "What are you boys doing?"

"We can protect Alex and Andy," Roy insisted, resolute and strong. "We're their guardians or something like that. Father Pat told us."

Cackling laughter drew his attention back to Ms. G, whose eyes danced with mirth as she regarded him with contempt. "Perhaps God should've chosen guardians who could count," she sneered. "You have no power over anything if the circle isn't complete."

Roy was about to lash out when he suddenly realized what she meant. How could he be so stupid! All six were needed to complete the circle or it was no good!

And Dane was missing!

CHAPTER TWENTY

GRAB THE TWINS!

THE SECOND DANE SAW WHAT was happening, he knew what he had to do. With him in the circle, they'd have a chance against that bitch. He'd just pulled back his fist to punch out the grill when he heard Shaw in his ear.

"Don't throw your life away, Dane," the man's voice urged him.

"I have to help Alex," Dane hissed.

"If you bust through that grill, she'll just have that monster kill you," said Shaw, his voice strong and steady. "I need you back here. We have guns now, and it's up to us to stop her before she escapes with the boys."

Dane hesitated. He knew Shaw was right. He didn't stand a chance against that creature down there, but he felt weak for not taking action. Still, all that mattered was stopping her from taking Alex, and Shaw seemed to know what he was doing.

"'Kay," he whispered. "I'm leaving the camera in place and heading back now."

"You made the right choice, Dane. Shaw out."

Dane wasn't at all sure he'd made the right choice, but he'd made it, and he was not a guy who second guessed himself. Making sure the camera was lodged firmly within the grill, he backed down the airduct as quietly—but quickly—as he could manage.

***

Allison had been pretending to sleep for some time. Amanda had been sitting in a large stuffed chair beside an end table with a fancy reading lamp illuminating her in a soft pool of light, deeply engrossed in a book. Every time Allison cracked open her eyes, the woman was still there. She had no idea how much time had passed since the colonel left, and she was frantic with worry about what might be happening to her dad. And Alex. She had to get out there and snoop around for herself.

Finally, after an eternity, Amanda stood and stretched. It was late. Allison knew that much at least, and she hoped the woman might go to bed. But the colonel had insisted she be watched, so fat chance of that happening. She clamped her eyes shut and focused on keeping her breathing even as soft footsteps crossed the room and stopped beside the couch. She felt Amanda's eyes on her, searching for assurance that she was asleep. Apparently satisfied, the older woman shuffled quietly out of the room.

Allison opened her eyes and listened for any follow-up noises. She heard a clinking sound and a drawer opening. Easing herself up, she peered over the edge of the couch and saw a shadow moving around through the open door of the kitchen. It sounded like Amanda was making coffee or tea.

This was her chance!

Tossing off the crocheted blanket, Allison slid her legs off the couch until her feet touched the soft carpet. She glanced around and found her dirty sneakers where she'd left them beside the glass coffee table. Standing cautiously in case the couch might creak, she picked up her shoes and clutched them in one hand, facing the entry hall. Beyond, light spilled out of the kitchen, and the sounds of someone moving about were audible.

Tiptoeing with greater care than ever before, Allison eased herself around the couch, out of the living room, and into the entry hall. She hugged the wall in case she needed to hide at a moment's notice, but Amanda didn't appear at the kitchen door. Allison gazed across at the front door. It was maybe fifteen feet away. She could do this!

Stepping away from the wall, she tiptoed in her socks across the tile floor, knowing her sneakers would likely give her away. Her eyes focused on that kitchen door, though she knew if Amanda appeared she'd be caught no matter what. Nearing the front door, she reached for the brass knob and gripped it. Slowly, she turned the knob.

It was unlocked!

Holding her breath, she tugged the door toward her, and it opened without a sound. Once she had it open halfway, she slipped through onto the front porch and eased it closed. Letting out her breath, she turned, suddenly remembering the airmen that were supposed to be guarding the house. There was no one in sight, just a brightly lit, empty tarmac and other officers' homes on either side of the colonel's house.

That's strange, she thought, *the colonel said he would post guards.*

Whatever the reason, the coast was clear, so she slipped on her sneakers and darted off the porch, wondering which way she should go.

***

Alex felt Roy's humiliation and simmering anger. As always, his best friend had only wanted to protect him, and Alex felt deep love and gratitude swell within his heart for this amazing boy.

"It's okay, Roy," he whispered. "You had a good idea."

Roy looked forlorn, like he was the worst failure ever.

Alex sensed this too, and added, "You're never a failure to me."

"Aww, how sweet," Ms. G crooned like some snarky YouTuber mocking viral videos. "Young love."

Alex fumed. "Shut up!"

But Ms. G continued her taunt. "If only you were gay like Roy, then everything would be perfect."

Izzy, who'd been listening for a change, froze, his mouth dropping open. "Huh?" He stared at Roy in horror. "You mean you're a—"

"Don't say it, Izzy," Java snapped. "We all be knowing Roy was gay."

"Yup," Carlos echoed.

Even Jorge nodded.

Now it was Roy who looked stunned. "How...?"

Java shrugged. "We seen how you look at Alex, Roy. It ain't nuthin to me, or these guys. You be our friend no matter what. *Right*, Izzy?" He furrowed his brows and tossed Izzy a fearsome expression.

Izzy, still looking shocked, stared at Java, then Roy, then Carlos and Jorge. "Well, course he's my..." Then he gazed at Alex. "You too, Alex?"

Alex shook his head. "But I love Roy. He's the best friend I'll ever have. I love all you guys. Don't you see what she's doing? She's tryin' to break us up."

"Alex is right," Carlos insisted. "Yeah, I used to mess with him, but

I seen for myself what friendship is, not the street shit the homies talk about, but the real deal. We gotta stick together, Izzy, or she's gonna win."

Izzy's face took on a look of determination and he faced off against Ms. G. "Roy's my friend and you're the enemy bitch we gotta take down, so don't think I'm gonna ditch him."

Ms. G shrugged. "Oh, well, it was worth a shot." She waved over one of the older airmen.

Tall and lean, the man stepped forward, gun aimed at the boys.

"There's one way to stop these so-called guardians from keeping me away from Alex," she explained, still smiling. "Kill one of them."

The boys gasped in unison and Alex's heart lurched with fear.

"Just don't kill the queer one," she went on as though the boys were not even present. "I may need him to control Alex. Otherwise, take your pick."

"No!" shouted Colonel Walker, raising his gun again and aiming at the airman. He glanced at William and nodded.

William started across the room, but the airman had already aimed into the circle of boys, straight at Jorge.

"No!" Carlos jumped in front of the silent boy just as the airman fired his gun.

The bullet struck Carlos point blank in the chest, sending a shower of blood splattering over the others and spinning him backwards into Jorge, who tried to grab him, but they both tumbled to the floor in a tangle of arms and legs.

"No!" Alex cried out in horror, spinning his chair around to face the fallen Carlos, but the boy's wide, staring eyes were clear proof he was already dead. Jorge struggled out from beneath his friend, weeping and grabbing for Carlos's limp hand, pressing it up against his chest as he rocked back and forth.

Everything happened so fast, Alex could barely follow it. Colonel Walker fired his gun at the airman, striking him in the chest and sending him spinning backward, the gun dropping from his hand as he crumpled to the floor.

Furious, Ms. G signaled the other airmen. "Kill him."

The men opened fire on the colonel. He ducked behind a table, but not before a bullet struck him in the upper chest and sent him sprawling onto the floor near the dazed form of Davalos, still moaning and struggling to regain his senses.

The boys released each other's hands and dropped to the ground next to Alex.

William had almost joined them, but now spun around and rushed back to crouch beside the colonel, who lay in a heap about six feet away.

"Colonel, are you all right?" His voice sounded fearful.

Colonel Walker stirred and opened his eyes. From where he sat, Alex saw blood staining the man's uniform a dark shade of blackish red.

"William." He gasped for air, but he wasn't able to lift his head. "Can you defeat Jäger?"

"I don't know, Colonel."

"Come… closer…," the colonel hissed, his breathing ragged.

William leaned down and put his ear close to the colonel's lips. Alex was too far away to make out what he whispered to the younger boy.

William said, "Yes, sir," and rose to his feet, glaring at the airmen and their guns.

Ms. G must've sensed something because she screamed, "Kill that kid. Now!"

William darted across the room as the men fired. The bullets struck him full in the chest, but he didn't even slow down! He grabbed the closest airman before the man could get off another shot and, to Alex's astonishment, hefted the man over his head with ease and threw him at the others, knocking them down like bowling pins, their guns dropping from their hands and skittering along the floor.

Roy and the boys scrambled for cover under anything that was available, while Alex wheeled his chair away from Ms. G, who stood stock still staring in amazement at the young boy who just taken out her men without breaking a sweat.

"Jäger!" she shouted, the smug look finally gone from her evil face as she staggered backward toward the open double doors.

Watching from behind a rolling computer station, Alex was pleased to see that she was afraid.

William's outstretched hands were inches from Ms. G's throat when the hulking Jäger swung out with a fist the size of a cantaloupe, striking the young boy square on the jaw and sending him flying through the air.

He slammed into the metal wall next to the door and collapsed to the floor. But he was on his feet in seconds, unhurt.

Alex exchanged a look of incredulity with Roy, who crouched beside him. Feeling like that time he'd watched *Frankenstein Meets the Wolfman* with Izzy, he stared, open-mouthed, as William wrapped his arms around some kind of power generator that was bigger than he was. He ripped the unit off the floor and hurled it at the massive Jäger like it was a volleyball.

Ms. G leaped aside as the unit flew past her and struck the big man, knocking him off-balance and sending him slamming back against the machine that had created him. William didn't wait for the man to fight back. He leaped forward, jumped onto the machine console, and flipped up and over onto Jäger's back, wrapping his arms around the thick neck and squeezing so hard Alex heard what sounded like cracking bones.

Ms. G scrambled to her feet, assisted by one of the airmen. They had all recovered their fallen weapons.

"Grab the twins," she barked at the men. "And the queer boy. We must get out of here!"

Two of the men, guns pointed, strode to where Alex and Roy huddled together. Alex hadn't seen where Andy went when the fighting began, but now spotted a third man grabbing his brother by the arm and yanking him out from behind a table adorned with laboratory instruments.

"Let me go!" Andy yelled, glaring at Ms. G. "I'll never let you put me in a cage again! Never!"

"We'll see about that," she replied, heading for the open doors, casting a quick look back at the other two. "Take them, and let's go!"

Roy swung a fist at the nearest airman, connecting with his jaw. But the man easily outweighed him. He grabbed Roy's arm, twisting it up behind his back and causing him to cry out in agony.

Roy's cry of pain drew Java out from under the table where he'd hidden. He lunged for the man, but the gun pointed at his chest made him stop his forward movement.

"You wanna die, kid?" The man looked ready to shoot, and Java stopped short, his face conflicted with indecision.

"Java," Alex cried, his wheelchair firmly gripped from behind by the other airman, "don't die for us. They ain't gonna hurt us. Please!"

Java glared daggers as the second airman turned Alex's chair and pushed it toward the double doors. The other man shoved Roy in front of him, arm still twisted painfully behind his back.

Alex had time for one last glance at the flailing Jäger with William wrapped around his neck like a snake, and then he was out into the tunnel. The other airmen followed, leaving the crashing sounds to echo throughout the tunnel as they hustled him after the fleeing Ms. G.

***

Father Pat watched as Martin and the other two men handed guns to Shaw, Nathan, and Dane, his insides twisted with uncertainty. Even after the chaos he'd just witnessed in that lab and the callous murder of young Carlos, he wasn't sure he could shoot another human being, no matter how monstrous that person may be.

Shaw signaled for Martin to speak.

"They have the kids and the doc, so we can't open fire unless there's a clear shot at a soldier or the woman." Martin eyed Dane, Nathan, and especially Father Pat. "We'll try to block their escape route. Mr. Shaw showed you the camera feed of the desert entrance we used. There's a heavy object on top that's preventing the trapdoor being opened from below. Likely, the colonel's men placed it there after they discovered the breach. That means the woman and her party must exit the tunnels into the base itself and go out the front gate. That's the tunnel exit we're headed for. Any questions?"

No one spoke, including Father Pat, who studied the extra gun stuck in Martin's waistband. Should he take it? If nothing else, he might need it for self-defense.

"I'll take a gun."

Shaw studied him a long moment. "You sure, Padre?"

Father Pat nodded. "That evil woman can't get away with the twins. It would be catastrophic."

Shaw nodded and signaled Martin, who slipped the small brown handgun from his waistband and handed it to Father Pat. "It's an M18 semiautomatic. It's very accurate; aim for the chest. There's a twenty-one-round magazine so you're not likely to run out of ammo." He pointed to a small black switch. "That's the safety. Press with your thumb before you fire, or the gun won't work. Shoot only in self-defense, Father."

"Yes, of course." Father Pat took the weapon in his right hand and studied it.

"And don't point it at us," Martin added, noting the muzzle of the gun was aimed right at him.

Father Pat felt himself redden with embarrassment and lowered the gun to his side.

"Let's move out," Shaw ordered.

With Martin in the lead, they filed from the store room into the tunnel. Smashing and fighting sounds echoed from somewhere in the underground complex, but Martin led them away from those sounds, which grew fainter as the team reached a turn and Martin halted them with a raised hand.

Father Pat brought up the rear of the party, along with George, the oldest of Shaw's men. On the journey out to Nevada, Father Pat had learned that George was a veteran of the post-9/11 Afghan war and had been in his midthirties back then. He was a garrulous man who'd told the others detailed stories of battles he'd experienced, and his nonchalance at recounting such atrocities reminded Father Pat how easily what's considered "normal" can shift on a dime.

He glanced at the weapon in his right hand, presently aimed at the floor, and realized that his own "normal" had shifted overnight at that burned-out church.

Martin waved them on, and Father Pat followed Nathan around the corner into an identical tunnel, lit from above, walls covered in metal. Their footfalls barely registered against the concrete floor. Martin jerked to a stop just as they reached an intersection, and then held up a hand. Straight ahead, a metal ladder attached to the concrete wall led upward to what Father Pat presumed was one of the exits. Was that their target?

With everyone stopped, sounds echoed from down the tunnel on their left. Voices and…wheels rolling against concrete. Alex!

"Hurry, you fools, before that monster kid comes after us!" said a woman's voice. She sounded frightened.

"We didn't know anything about the kid, my lady," explained a male voice, slightly winded, as though the man was running. "We thought he was Dr. Shepherd's nephew."

"Well, you were wrong!" snapped the woman.

The wheels of Alex's chair were rolling faster, and the voices drew nearer by the second. Martin gestured for everyone to press up against the wall. Father Pat pushed back against the cold concrete and tried to be as flat as possible. He gripped the gun tightly. At the very least, he didn't want to panic and drop it.

At this point, he didn't know the plan. If that was the exit Alex's kidnappers were heading for, they would turn to the left and perhaps miss Martin and the team altogether, which would allow a rear attack that just might catch them off-guard. Whatever was going to go down, it would happen within seconds.

He held fast to his weapon and steeled himself for the confrontation to come.

***

Colonel Walker knew his wound was serious, mainly because of the heavy blood loss he'd already experienced, but also from the pressure around his lungs and heart. His breathing was uneven. He didn't think any vital organs had been hit, but clearly some large artery had been nicked, at the very least. He struggled to raise himself onto his right elbow. With the bullet in his left side, he feared the pounding of his heart would expel even more blood if he moved too much.

He spotted the three surviving boys huddled near the lab exit. They stared, wide-eyed and frozen, at the sight of William strangling Jäger. He had to get them out.

"Boys, over here!" he called, knowing the flailing Jäger was too distracted to notice.

Led by Java, the three boys circumvented overturned furniture and reached him. Israel, for once, wasn't yammering, for which Walker was grateful. The quiet boy, Jorge, had a look of devastation on his face and kept looking back at the unmoving form of his friend who'd been shot. Java, Walker knew, was the most clear-headed.

"Java, listen to me."

Java dropped to a squat. "What you need me to do, Colonel?"

"Hide and wait for this fight to end."

"I'm not afraid," Java insisted, his chest puffed out in that way teen boys excel at.

If the situation weren't so dire, he might tell stories of his own puffed-up teen years. "Listen, Java. I'm badly wounded, and Davalos is hurt. We'll need your help once Jäger is gone."

Java screwed up his face. "Gone? But William's kicking the guy's ass."

"That's part of the plan. Listen, there's a storage room on the opposite side of this lab. Hide there. When the coast is clear, come back."

Java looked reluctant, glancing at the other boys.

"Please, Java. You're brave, I know, but real bravery often means staying alive to fight when the odds are more in your favor."

Java nodded. "Yes, sir." He offered a respectable salute.

Touched by the gesture, Walker returned it and Java rose to his feet.

"Come on, guys. We got our orders." He grabbed the mewling Israel by the arm and dragged him outside Walker's field of vision.

Jorge stood and gazed down at the colonel, his soft, hairless face a mask of compassion. "Don't die."

"It's all right, Jorge," he assured the boy. "I won't."

He wasn't one hundred percent certain of that, but best to be positive.

Jorge gazed for another long moment, as though he wanted to speak, and then vanished after the others.

William still clung to the neck of Jäger like a tenacious cat, and the big man's face had turned a bluish color beneath the soft overhead lights. The muscular man staggered around, thrashing, knocking over every table and chair in the lab, but was unable to dislodge the determined boy. He flailed with his thick arms, but they were not flexible enough to reach behind and dislodge William, whose face was scrunched up with deep concentration as he applied more pressure.

Pride swelled in Walker at how well William was faring in the fight, his first real test since the debacle of three years ago. The boy was calm and focused and, like a pit bull, determined not to let go.

Jäger staggered back and slammed into a concrete wall. William grunted as he was pressed between the wall and the heavy man. His response seemed to enflame Jäger, who repeatedly swung his torso back against the wall over and over in an attempt to displace the boy. William seemed unfazed by the attack and squeezed even harder, his muscular forearms bulging from the effort, visible through his torn shirtsleeves.

Davalos groaned and rolled toward Walker, who nudged him with one foot.

"Davalos, wake up," he urged. "Davalos!" He gave the man another kick to the hip.

Davalos grunted in pain and opened his eyes, clearly muddled from the blow to his head. His usually perfect hair wildly askew, he focused on Walker, blinking, and shaking his head. That's when he must've noticed the blood.

"Colonel, what…" His voice trailed off a moment. "What happened? You're hurt…"

"Don't worry about that," Walker said, nodding at the struggling duo across the lab. "I have a plan. Play dead."

Davalos furrowed his brows. "Huh?"

"Just play dead!" hissed the colonel, his voice sounding reedy and weak. Playing dead wouldn't be hard for him. "Weapon's about to make his move and I want Jäger to think we're already dead."

Davalos clearly didn't understand, but he nodded and, still weak, lowered himself back to the floor and closed his eyes. He remained on his side, which made his breathing harder to detect.

Good idea, thought Walker. *I'll do the same.*

He glanced once more at the struggling pair. Jäger continued his relentless pounding of William against the concrete wall over and over again, and the boy's grip was loosening. Any second now.

The colonel lay on his right side and focused on keeping his breaths slow and even. If Jäger even suspected they were still alive, he'd kill them for sure. For now, he kept his eyes open to watch the battle.

Jäger whipped his head back and William smashed against the concrete, his head striking the wall like a hammer. His arms slackened around Jäger's neck, and the big man spun to one side, flinging the boy off his back to the floor. Jäger staggered around, gasping for breath, as William rolled around on the floor in an apparent daze.

Walker watched, heart in his throat, as Jäger regained his senses and reached for the stunned boy. Grabbing William in both meaty hands, he raised the writhing boy over his head and flung him with all his strength at the machine that had created him. William struck the machine so hard the plastic casing ruptured, and he vanished inside amidst a shower of exploding sparks, setting off an electrical fire that began licking at the console and spreading fast.

Walker closed his eyes and lay still.

He heard Jäger flinging chairs and debris aside, but there were no further sounds of fight. Just heavy panting as the big man struggled to control his breathing. Heavy footsteps approached and stopped. Walker sensed that he was being stared at by eyes filled with malevolence. The panting was right above him now. A large boot kicked him in the stomach, and it took every ounce of willpower he possessed not to cry out from the pain, or even move in the slightest. He heard a second kick against something he presumed was Davalos and had to give the man credit—he didn't make a sound either.

Apparently satisfied they were dead, Jäger turned away. His weighty footfalls receded quickly as he made for the exit.

Walker opened his eyes.

Jäger was gone.

CHAPTER TWENTY-ONE

DESTROY THEM, JÄGER

DANE PRESSED HIMSELF AGAINST THE concrete wall, fingering the firearm at his side and ignoring the cold seeping through his black hoodie. He was between his dad and Shaw, waiting with anxious anticipation as the rolling of Alex's wheels grew closer. The voices had stopped, but Dane wondered what they'd been talking about. Monster kid? The hell did that mean? She couldn't be talking about one of Alex's friends. That made no sense. But it didn't matter. He needed all his focus to recapture Alex and Roy.

He couldn't quite see around Shaw's wide chest, but he caught a glimpse of a man in uniform pushing a wheelchair at a run and turning left at the intersection toward the ladder that led to the escape hatch. A second soldier raced past forcing ahead of him a tall, brown-haired figure that could only be Roy! Dane's blood boiled.

If you hurt him...

The woman followed, trailed by three other soldiers, one of whom had Andy by the arm. The one with Andy pulled ahead of the woman and ran for the ladder. That's when Martin made his move. He leaped away from the wall, feet planted wide, gun out in front, and yelled, "Nobody move!"

That was the cue for all of them to act. Dane followed Martin's example and did as he had done, poised beside Shaw and Shaw's man named Silvio, a rough-looking guy who'd seen more than his share of battles against terrorists in the Middle East.

The two remaining airmen bringing up the rear of the enemy group spun around, guns raised, but Martin and Silvio were faster. They fired two shots, striking each man solidly in the torso, dropping them to the concrete floor. The shock of what he saw froze Dane in his tracks for a split second before Roy turned to look back at the commotion. Their eyes met for a brief moment, and Roy flashed a smile of relief. But Roy's smile plummeted as the sound of heavy footsteps pelted down the adjoining tunnel.

Dane saw nothing at first, but then the huge man that the twins had brought to life bounded into the intersection and slammed a fist into Martin's chest, sending him sailing back into Silvio. Both men sprawled onto the floor in a heap, their weapons skittering out of their reach.

Alex spun his chair around as the soldier who'd been gripping it let go to draw his weapon. Before the man could get off a shot, Alex pushed him hard, and the bullet went awry, striking the metal wall and ricocheting off to one side.

"No," the woman hissed as the furious airman whirled on Alex. "Use a grenade!"

The airman stepped away from Alex and snatched something off his belt, tossing it to the woman. She, in turn, threw the grenade to the big man, who easily plucked it out of the air.

"Destroy them, Jäger," she shouted, "and follow us up top."

The man grunted and faced Dane and his group. Shaw opened fire. So did Dane, Nathan, and Gus. The bullets struck the huge man full in the chest. Blood dribbled from small wounds as his blue shirt was shredded, but the man didn't even slow down. He reached up with both hands and pulled the pin on the grenade.

"Everybody down!" Shaw shouted and Dane didn't hesitate. He dropped to the hard stone floor and heard the others hitting the deck all around him. He was about to check on his dad when something rolled past him along the floor, brushing against his arm. He swatted it away as hard as he could and then the whole world exploded.

***

Allison crept alongside large, dark aircraft hangars, but after not seeing anyone, she became less cautious. Something was wrong. An Air Force base this size should have people working at all hours, or at least patrolling for security purposes. She knew there were no cameras inside the base because her dad had told her, which meant security had to be maintained the old-fashioned way. And yet, the place seemed like it was abandoned. She avoided the front gate area because she knew there was a guard posted there.

A muffled explosion beneath her feet sent her stumbling sideways. Regaining her balance, she looked around. Was that an earthquake? It felt more like a bomb went off under the ground.

Oh, no! Dad!

About a fifty feet away, she watched as a metal plate lifted upward and flipped over to land on its back with a *clan*g, piercing the eerie silence like a gunshot. A man's head appeared, and Allison darted into a shadowed corner between two buildings. The man, who wore an Air Force uniform, immediately pointed his gun down into the hole he'd just climbed out of. In seconds, another head appeared—Roy's! Allison almost choked trying to stifle a gasp.

Under the bright full moon, his face looked drawn, and his cheeks glistened. Were those tears? What had happened? Roy emerged and stood beside the airman, held at gunpoint. A moment later, Andy appeared and stood as ordered next to Roy.

As Allison watched, a second blond head emerged, and her heart skipped a beat. Alex was at the top, but he couldn't quite pull himself from the hole. The airman waved his gun at Roy and Andy. The two boys squatted on either side of Alex and grabbed his arms, hauling him up and setting him on the tarmac next to the hole. A moment later, Alex's wheelchair emerged, lifted by a second airman, who had it hefted over his head.

The first airman shoved Andy forward and the boy reached for the wheelchair. He set it down and Alex pulled himself up and into the seat. He looked unhurt, at least. A long-haired blonde woman clambered up and out. Allison gasped again. It was the woman from Father Pat's photos, the one who was supposed to be a hundred years old!

Finally, a huge, really buff man squeezed his way out of the opening and stood at attention next to the woman. His clothes were ripped and there was blood staining his uniform, but if he was injured, he didn't show it. Without a word, the group set off in the direction of the front gate. Allison waited until she was sure they wouldn't hear her and then hurried to the opening to the underground. She listened a long moment but heard nothing. Knowing her dad had to be down there, she placed one foot onto the top rung of the ladder and began her descent.

***

The ground trembled beneath Colonel Walker. Had that been an explosion, or had he passed out and dreamed it? He felt pressure on his chest and blinked his eyes to focus. He'd thought they were already open because he'd seen Davalos crawl to him, but maybe he'd passed out again? He'd lost a lot of blood, and that was dangerous. His vision cleared and he saw Davalos, a purplish bruise blooming across his swollen left cheek. He leaned in, pressing something into the colonel's chest wound. Walker realized the man was no longer wearing his suit jacket; he glanced down to see the gray coat completely darkened with his blood as Davalos attempted to staunch the flow.

"Thank you, Mark," he mumbled, struggling to catch his breath. Could there be blood in his lungs?

"It's gone, Colonel," Davalos gasped, sounding weak and guilt-ridden at the same time. "My creation is gone! Where's yours? Where's William?"

"You called me William, Mr. Davalos," came a voice behind Davalos, who spun around in surprise. William stood staring down at the two men. His black shirt was shredded from the fight, revealing small dents in his chest from where the bullets had struck, not to mention some rapidly healing cuts and abrasions from being thrown into the machine, but he was unharmed, as Walker knew he would be.

"Colonel, you're badly hurt!" William dropped to his knees. "Let me, Mr. Davalos. I'm stronger."

Without a trace of his usual haughtiness, Davalos released his hands from the blood-soaked jacket and William took over. He exerted firm, strong pressure on the colonel's upper chest, slowing the bleeding to a trickle.

"We need to clean and cauterize this wound," William told Davalos, who looked stunned. "Yes, Mr. Davalos, I learned first aid. Please find some alcohol and clean cloths. And heat some metal in that fire."

Davalos scrambled to his feet, staggering slightly from the blow he took to the head, and rummaged around while Walker gazed at the destroyed machine now engulfed in flames. Black smoke was beginning to swirl above him. They had to get out soon.

"You were great, William," he said, taking a moment to inhale before continuing. "I'm proud of you. They think you're dead. Now you must track—"

William shook his head. "You first, Colonel. I won't let you die."

Walker sagged back and laid his head on the floor. "Alex is—"

"You, first," the boy insisted. "I'm making a choice, Colonel. I can track Alex. I promise."

Walker heard movement from behind him and William looked over his head at something he couldn't see.

"You guys all right?" William asked.

Then they came into view—Java, Israel, and Jorge.

"Yeah, man," Java answered, his voice tight with worry. "How's the colonel?"

William glanced at Colonel Walker, as though for permission to speak. Walker nodded.

"He's lost a lot of blood. That's not good. I'm going to stop the bleeding. You guys need to help Mr. Davalos get him to the hospital building."

Java gazed down at the colonel. "You got it."

Israel stared straight ahead as though in shock, but Jorge clearly understood what was happening.

Davalos stumbled back through the debris holding a beaker of clear liquid in one hand and the metal arm from a chair in the other. He'd wrapped one end in a thick cloth and the other end glowed with heat. Under one arm, he held clean cloths against his body. William took the beaker and the clean cloths, while Davalos held on to the glowing piece of metal.

William leaned in and tore a hole in Walker's uniform. Blood seeped out in a steady stream. William eyed Walker solemnly. "Ready for the alcohol?"

Walker gritted his teeth and nodded.

William upended the beaker into the bleeding hole, and Walker almost bit his tongue from the searing pain. Without hesitation, William wiped the area with the cloths, which instantly turned red with blood, and then poured the remainder of the alcohol into the wound. Walker grunted but managed to not cry out.

Davalos handed off the covered end of the hot metal bar to William, who took it in his right hand.

"This will hurt much worse than the alcohol, Colonel," William said. "Would you like a gag?"

Walker offered a tight smile. "You didn't miss a trick in your training, did you?"

"No, sir."

"Go ahead, pal. I can take it."

William held out the piece of hot metal.

Walker watched him bring it down with care and press it against his exposed flesh. Pain ripped through his entire body, and he screamed in agony. The last thing he saw before passing out was the astonished face of Davalos, staring at this boy he'd so long disparaged and clearly realizing he'd been dead wrong the entire time.

***

Dust filled the air as Allison made it down the ladder into the tunnels below. She pulled her light jacket up over her mouth to keep from choking, but the particles dug into her eyes and forced her to blink nonstop to clear them. She stared across an intersection to the tunnel straight ahead of her. The walls and ceiling had collapsed in a pile of concrete, sheet metal, and rebar. Terrified for her father, she jogged across the intersection and stared through swirling dust at the rubble.

"Dad! Can you hear me?" She screamed as loud as she could, but there was no response.

She reached for the nearest chunk of concrete. It was jagged and large with two sections of rebar jutting out of both sides. She wrapped her fingers around the rebar and tugged. The chunk didn't budge. She dug in with her heels and pulled with all of her strength. The concrete shifted but didn't come free.

Panting from exertion, she stood back, tears filling her eyes, and stared at the wall of debris with dismay.

Now what do I do?

***

Colonel Walker awakened. He was lying on his back, weak from loss of blood, pain still thrumming through his body, but his wound no longer bled. William gazed at him with a worried expression, and he offered a smile of gratitude to reassure the boy that he would survive. Davalos stood behind William, looking shattered. Then the colonel recalled something. He turned his head and searched the area near the double doors. Two bodies lay on the floor. One was the airman he'd been forced to shoot. The other was…

"Carlos?" he grunted. "Is he dead?"

"Yes, Colonel," William replied. He glanced over where Carlos's legs were visible beneath a table.

Walker squinted up at Jorge, standing over him, tears streaming down his cheeks.

"He was my friend," Jorge said, his voice quiet, almost faint.

Looking awkward, Java wrapped one arm around Jorge's shoulders and one around Israel's. "You still got us, Jorge."

Walker forced himself to focus. "Go, William. Save Alex and the others."

"Is that an order, sir?"

The colonel studied him a moment, trying to discern the meaning of the question. "Does it need to be?"

William shook his head. "No. Alex is my brother. And my friend. But I want my cousins to go with me." He looked at Davalos, who seemed to be staring into space and not listening.

"Davalos," Walker said, his voice sharp, like a rifle shot.

The other man glanced down at him, and the colonel wasn't sure he'd ever forget the expression on his face. This was a man so devastated by his own poor choices that he would never be the same again.

"Davalos, William is going after them. He needs the others to go with him."

"Others?"

William stood and looked into the man's face. "Yes, sir. Wolfboy and the others."

Davalos seemed to register what was being asked of him and said, "But…but they've never been field tested."

"I give emergency authorization," Walker said. "William can control them."

William eyed him a moment. "You can call me by my real name, Colonel. I am on a mission, after all."

"Very well, Weapon." Walker focused on Davalos. "Give him your code so he can unlock the cages, and the device you use to control them."

Davalos looked horrified. "I can't do that."

William reached up and placed a hand on the man's shoulder. There was blood on Davalos's shirt from assisting the colonel, and his swollen face gave him a horror-movie appearance.

"You still don't trust me, Mr. Davalos?"

William's young voice was so earnest that Walker was moved. So, apparently, was Davalos. He rattled off a series of letters and numbers, while William listened. He also explained where to locate the handheld device he used to control the creatures.

"You got all that, Weapon?"

"Yes, sir." He glanced down at the colonel. "I'll take my motorcycle out of the vehicle store." He looked like he didn't want to leave, but finally turned to Davalos and the boys. "Please take care of him. He's my… family."

Choked up at the young boy's concern for him, Walker had to clear his throat. "I'll, uh, be fine, Weapon. Save them. That's your mission."

"It will be done, sir." William saluted the colonel and then ran off to vanish through the double doors into the tunnel beyond.

Walker stared long and hard at Davalos. "We don't know who we can trust anymore. You understand that, don't you?"

The devastated man nodded.

"Right now, you and these boys are the ones I trust." He gazed up at the three boys, who stared at him open-mouthed. "Yes, boys, we will need your help. You up to it?"

Java responded at once with a salute. "Yes, sir!"

Jorge wiped away his tears and also saluted. When Israel just stared, Java kicked him in the ankle.

"Ow!" The blank look cleared from his eyes, and he looked at Java with annoyance. Then he seemed to understand the situation and offered his own lopsided salute.

"Good," said Walker, who fumbled with his small walkie-talkie, grateful that it hadn't been lost in all the confusion. He pressed the "talk" button and the power light went on. "Sergeant Stern, do you read? This is Colonel Walker."

A moment later, a voice came over the walkie. "Uh, Stern here, Colonel." His voice sounded confused. "I… I apologize for how I sound. Someone knocked me out and locked me in the control room. I just came to. Your location, sir?"

"In the underground. Send medics ASAP. Use the old service elevator. I'm wounded and there are others injured. Do you have camera access?"

"Cameras are off, but there's power, near as I can tell. Just need to reboot."

"Do it. Mr. Davalos is with me. I need to have a bullet removed. While I'm in surgery, Davalos will be in command of the base."

Davalos's face scrunched with shock. "But, Colonel—"

Walker held up a hand and focused on the walkie-talkie. "I need to communicate with General Lewis at once. Can you patch him into my walkie?"

There was a momentary pause. "Yes, Colonel, power is back on now. Just give me a moment."

The colonel noted Davalos gazing at him in stunned disbelief.

"You're certain you want me in command?"

"You outrank me at the Pentagon. Lewis trusts you. And right now, trust is a problem."

"I was wrong about you, Colonel," Davalos admitted, sounding like a chastised little boy. "And about Weapon."

The two men locked eyes and he was sure that Davalos was on the level. "And I was wrong about you."

***

Allison struggled with another block of concrete, dragging it away from the pile, when she heard running footsteps coming her way. She let go of the block and spun to find a young blond-haired boy skidding to a halt. He looked only twelve or thirteen, but his black pullover shirt was all ripped up and his bulging chest muscles made him seem older. He had blood on his torso and all over his pants, but he looked unharmed.

"Who are you?" he asked, his boyish voice a weird contrast to the muscularity.

"Please, can you help me? My father and Roy's brother are trapped in there." She pointed to the rubble. "They came to rescue Alex and the others, but…" She trailed off, suddenly feeling overwhelmed with fatigue and emotion. She was about to cry again.

The boy responded at once. "Stand back."

Hearing the resolve in his voice, she stepped back into the intersection, and he strode to the pile of broken concrete. Her mouth dropped open when he gripped the concrete block she'd struggled to move, lifted it over his head, and tossed it down the side tunnel like it was a pebble! And that was only the beginning. He dove into the rubble, yanking blocks and sheets of metal free, even bending rebar like it was licorice and tossing it out of the way.

Little by little, he made progress, clearing the tunnel with ease. He wasn't even sweating or breathing hard. She couldn't believe her eyes. It couldn't have been five minutes before the bulk of the rubble had been tossed away. But then she saw the bodies in the dust-filled tunnel and screamed.

The boy turned to her. "I'll check on them."

As he stepped into the tunnel, she heard, "Weapon!"

She turned and saw the colonel, bloody and clearly wounded, being pushed toward her in a wheelchair by a tall man with a bruised face. Three of Alex's friends trailed behind them.

"My dad," was all she could get out before sobbing into her hands.

The colonel seemed to understand at once and turned to the boy. "Weapon, we'll handle this. Carry out your mission."

The boy glanced at her one last time and Allison saw through her tears how much he wanted to help, but he took off toward the ladder and skittered up it like a monkey. The colonel nodded at the other man.

"Mark, check their status. The medical team is on its way."

The tall man looked at Allison with sympathy before moving down the tunnel to examine the fallen.

"Boys, help move the rest of this rubble aside so the medics can get in," the colonel said to Alex's friends.

"Yes, sir," replied Java. "C'mon, guys."

Jorge eagerly followed and began lifting smaller pieces of concrete away from the tunnel entrance. Java jumped right in and put his muscles to good use, hefting chunks that many grown men wouldn't have been able to handle.

Israel stared a moment at Allison. "You're Shaw's kid, right?"

She nodded, and he offered a tired grin. "You look good with hair."

She eyed his honest expression, the dirt and grime on his face, and nodded. "Thanks."

He clearly didn't know what else to say, and neither did she, so he joined his friends.

The colonel's walkie-talkie crackled. "Stern to Colonel Walker."

"Walker here."

"I have General Lewis on a secure line."

"Patch him through."

A moment passed and then a voice boomed over the walkie. "Lewis here, Colonel. Status report."

The colonel described what had happened, and Allison listened with growing horror. Some of it she didn't understand, but she did get that Alex had been kidnapped by that evil woman, and her fears for him soared. She wanted to enter the tunnel after the other man to find out if her father was… But then, she didn't. She couldn't face it if he… First her mother when she was seven, and now… She could *not* lose her dad. She couldn't!

Then she heard something over the colonel's walkie-talkie that chilled her blood.

"The twins cannot remain with that group, Colonel. I understand your faith in Weapon, but he's untested in a real-world situation. Get a chopper in the air, armed. If the twins cannot be recovered, they must be destroyed. Is that clear?"

The colonel looked even paler than he had before the call. "But General—"

"Is that clear?"

"Yes, sir."

"Keep me updated. Lewis out."

The colonel clicked off the speaker and looked like he might be sick. Allison felt the same way. Kill Alex? They wouldn't really do that, would they?

Dad won't let it happen. Please, Dad, you have to be all right!

CHAPTER TWENTY-TWO

NOW THE FUN REALLY BEGINS

ALEX STARED AT THE TRAUMATIZED Roy and did his best to spin some of the dread from his friend's troubled heart. They had been rushed, pushed, and dragged across the base to the front gate, which the guy in the guard house opened without being told to. He was obviously another one of Ms. G's servants, Alex realized as he was shoved through the gate by the same airman who had grabbed his chair down in the tunnels. To Alex's horror, the supersoldier they'd brought to life had followed them out of the underground. Did that mean William was dead? After all the younger boy had told him, and after what he'd seen with his own eyes, Alex didn't think William would be that easy to kill.

Five identical black vans idled on the dirt road leading away from the base, illuminated by the bright full moon. Four men dressed head-to-toe in black popped open the double back doors of the second van from the right and rushed toward Alex. Gripping his chair, they hefted it with ease and carried him to the back of the van, which was empty, and rolled him into the dark interior. Roy was lifted by two of the same men and tossed inside like he was a sack of dogfood. Alex spotted Andy dragged to another van and thrown inside before the doors of his slammed shut and darkness engulfed them.

He heard someone climb into the front seat next to the driver and close the door. Then he heard Ms. G's voice. "Let's go."

The tires squealed as the van lurched forward and sped off to wherever they were going.

Alex reached out for Roy and found his shoulder, giving it a tiny squeeze. "You okay, man?"

Alex felt Roy move, shifting his position, maybe pulling his legs up under him so he could sit. Then he heard, "Dane. And my dad…"

Alex squeezed the shoulder again. "I'm sure they'll be okay. They's tough, Roy."

Roy hadn't responded, but Alex felt the fear and worry wafting off his friend like plumes of smoke. That's when he went to work, spinning as much anxiety as he could from Roy, while maintaining that hand on his shoulder. In this darkness and after all that had happened, he needed Roy's touch as much as Roy needed his.

Where was Ms. G taking him? And what had happened with Colonel Walker? He knew that if the colonel survived that gunshot wound, he would send soldiers to rescue them. But was it already too late? They would be long gone by the time any rescue team could go out, and might even have arrived at their final destination, depending on what Ms. G was planning.

Settling in for perhaps a long journey, Alex concentrated on helping Roy because, honestly, it helped him too.

***

By the time William had freed his cousins by opening the rear door of each cage, ten minutes had elapsed according to the clock hung high on the wall above the exit. He'd instructed each of the creatures to wait for him outside after making them aware that Alex needed rescue. The creatures seemed excited to be outside and to have something to do at long last.

So was William. This would be his first time off the base since that disastrous time in Los Angeles. He'd learned so much since then and was more than ready for this assignment. He would save Alex and Roy—and Andy too, though he sensed something "off" about that one. Maybe it was the dog DNA that was part of William's makeup, but he'd learned to sense things about people, especially personality traits.

The final cage he opened belonged to Francis, who was still a sad-faced boy with wild curly hair and slightly large ears. He explained about the mission and asked if Francis wanted to come.

"Course, I do," the boy replied with eagerness dripping from every word. "I'm tired of this cage. And I wanna help my big brother."

William nodded, knowing how deeply Francis had attached himself to Roy. "We'll be outside, Francis," he added somberly, "so you'll have to be in your wolf form. Is that okay?"

Francis grimaced with distaste but nodded.

As they stepped outside beneath the bright autumn moon, William watched Francis painfully transform into Wolfboy and then they sprinted to William's motorcycle, which he'd retrieved from the motor pool. William climbed onto the thick leather seat and showed Wolfboy how to sit behind him.

"Hold on tight."

William started the engine and the cycle darted forward, heading toward the front gates. The creatures loped or, in the case of Scorpio, skittered, alongside, easily keeping pace. For his training, he'd learned to drive many types of vehicles, but the motorcycle he'd been given by Colonel Walker was his favorite. It was just the right size for his arms and legs and offered the extreme speed his hybrid body didn't possess.

He knew many in the government didn't consider him truly human because of his origins, but he *felt* human and that's why he'd accepted the name William when it had been given him by the one friend he'd made in Los Angeles. Alex had since assured him he had a soul, which made William feel good about himself. Now Alex was in trouble, and William would save him no matter what.

He slowed at the gates, which hung wide open, to search for the man on duty. Looking into the guard shack, he saw the crumpled figure of a young airman in uniform, either dead or unconscious. He wouldn't be any help. With the creatures alongside, he eased the bike forward and stopped just outside the gates. He spotted five sets of identical tire tracks all heading off in different directions into the desert.

He let the bike idle as he put down the kickstand and clambered off, Wolfboy at his side. They stepped forward, the other creatures just behind. Various sets of footprints in the sand seemed to twist around each other, likely to confuse pursuers. Tracks that could only belong to Alex's wheelchair stopped just outside the gate, most likely to hide which vehicle he'd been put into.

"Sniff around," William instructed them, using Davalos's handheld device to clarify the directive. "Find Alex's scent. Or Roy's." He made several distinct animal sounds that seemed to solidify the command. The creatures spread out and began sniffing, their large noses sliding along the ground like vacuum cleaners. Scorpio wasn't much of a tracker, so it sat and waited.

William dropped to his hands and knees and sniffed the ground near the closest set of tracks. Wolfboy did the same with the next set over, pressing his snub nose to the desert floor and crawling around on all fours.

William knew what the wheelchair smelled like, in addition to Alex. All of them did because they'd been given a highly advanced sense of smell.

Wolfboy jumped up and down and howled at the moon. William crawled over and bent down to the area the young werewolf was indicating. He sniffed around the tracks where the dirt had been stirred up from what looked like spinning tires. Yes! He smelled Roy! There was no doubt.

He glanced over at Wolfboy and grinned. "Good job, Wolfboy." He sniffed around some more and found it. Alex! But then he frowned. There was no indication of Andy's scent. Why not?

He knew none of the others had met Andy, so it was up to him. He crawled along to each set of tracks and sniffed the ground. Finally, he found Andy's scent at the very last set, tracks that went off in a northwest direction from the base.

So the woman had separated the boys. probably so that if one was rescued, she'd still have the other. Clever. But William's job was to save Alex, so it was Alex they would pursue. He stood and dusted off his torn uniform pants, eying his cousins all around him. He could send one after Andy, if he could just make that one understand that Andy looked like Alex but with more hair. He considered which creature to send.

Dog was one of the smartest hybrids Davalos had created, and very eager to please, so William decided on him. He called Dog to him, and the big animal trotted over. Sitting on its haunches, he was almost as tall as William, who barked and growled and used the device to insert into Dog's brain the proper description of Andy. Dog seemed to understand and barked his agreement to head off alone.

"If you find him, Dog, protect him. He's Alex's brother." Dog tilted its head, as though unsure. "Alex," William repeated. Dog barked and then turned to race off along the route Andy's kidnapper had driven, its long, powerful legs propelling it with great speed.

"The rest of you, follow me." He turned to Griffin, who was stretching its wings and clawing at the desert floor with three-inch claws. "Griffin, you fly ahead and let me know what you find." He growled a few times and the massive Griffin—much taller than William when standing on all fours—spread its gigantic condor wings and leaped into the air, that luxurious mane pressing back against its thick neck as the creature sailed into the wind.

The flapping of its wings sent sand flying everywhere and William clamped his eyes shut. The last thing he needed was sand in his contact lenses. Alas, that was his one weakness – aversion to bright light due to the cockroach DNA that made up some of his composition. The contacts protected his delicate pupils from harsh light but did not restrict his flawless night vision. He'd asked Dr, Shepherd why cockroaches and she'd explained that they were perhaps the toughest, most adaptable creatures on earth.

Sprinting back to his idling motorcycle, William kicked back the stand and hopped on. Wolfboy loped forward, leaving paw prints in the sand, and clambered onto the back, once more clutching him around the chest. William gunned the motor and then took off like a bullet across the moonlit desert, his bizarre menagerie of associates close on his tail.

***

Colonel Walker had insisted the medics treat the wounded in the tunnel before transporting him to the hospital wing. The girl, who he now knew was named Allison, was bent over her father, Russell Shaw, the very man who'd installed their security cameras. At least that explained how he'd managed to hack into the system so easily and feed them that looping shot of the empty desert. Empty except for that tiny, unmoving shrew that had given him away.

Shaw now rested up against the wall less than ten feet from Walker. With the help of a medic, the tech mogul been able to walk out of the damaged tunnel under his own power. His hair was speckled with dust and bits of concrete, while numerous cuts and abrasions were visible on his face and hands, but otherwise, he was one of the lucky ones.

Two of his men had died instantly and a third, Martin, was unconscious with a head injury. That left the others in the group—Roy's father and brother, and a Catholic priest. Of those three, the brother was the worst off, run though the torso by flying rebar. He'd already been taken to the base hospital via the service elevator which, thankfully, Davalos had restored when he'd taken over the underground. The other two, still unconscious from the blast, appeared to have suffered no permanent damage and awaited more gurneys to move them.

Java, Israel, and Jorge had worked like dogs to clear the tunnel opening and now sat up against the concrete wall a short distance away, exhausted, and worried about their missing friends. They were good kids, Walker knew, and devoted to each other. Loyalty like that was rare these days.

The base doctor, Mulligan, had insisted the colonel be taken straight to the hospital, but he needed more info from Shaw first. The next gurney would be for him, so he had to finish his questions quickly.

"Mr. Shaw, do you have any intel on this woman and her group that we may lack?"

Shaw eased Allison back so he could make eye contact. "As to where they might take the boys? No." He glanced at Allison, as though weighing whether or not to say something. "If you can't recover the boys, are your orders to terminate them?"

Walker hesitated. That was classified information. But he'd already decided he and this man were on the same side, devoted to saving Alex. "Yes. But I have to give those orders once I get topside and at that point, Dr. Mulligan takes over, so the chopper might not go out for a while."

Shaw's mouth twitched with what could've been a tiny smile. "Alex saved my daughter's life, Colonel."

"And many others you don't know about," Walker replied. "I have one of my men tracking the boys. He'll rescue them long before I send out that chopper."

Shaw raised his eyebrows questioningly but said nothing more.

***

Alex and Roy didn't talk much during the journey. Alex was exhausted and disheartened and sensed that Roy was in the same boat. Would their lives ever belong to them again? Having the Healer's power seemed more a curse than a blessing. Yes, he had helped a lot of people, especially at that bank, but too many others wanted to use him against his will. Andy too.

Were they taking his brother to the same place or somewhere different? And what about Dane and Nathan? He'd been telling Roy they were fine, but he didn't know. They could even be... No! Don't think like that!

They're both okay, and Nathan's gonna adopt you and...and...

If Ms. G had anything to say about it, he'd never see either of them again.

The van bumped again in a deep rut, and Alex's chair bounced up and slid a few inches despite having the brakes firmly in place. Roy looked up, and now that his eyes had adjusted to the darkness, Alex could make out his features.

"Where do you think they're takin' us?"

Alex shrugged, and then realized Roy probably couldn't see such a small movement. So, he answered, "Not the place they kept Andy at 'cause it got blowed up."

"Yeah. But a group that's got spies on army bases gots to have lots of places to hide, don't you think?"

"Yeah." Alex paused a moment. "Got any idea how long we been in this van?"

There was a moment of silence. Then, "I think it's been at least an hour, but I don't know fer sure."

"There ain't been too many big bumps like that last one in a long time. Maybe that means we're out of the desert?"

"Maybe."

They both fell silent, and Alex listened to the van wheels rolling along the ground. He'd used wheels his entire life and he was certain the ground beneath the van was smoother now, maybe not concrete, but definitely a real dirt road. And then the van began to slow. He exchanged a look with Roy as the van made a couple of turns before rolling to a stop.

Heart hammering anew, Alex stared at the inside of the van's double doors, knowing they would open any moment. Then he heard it—the handle being lifted. The doors swung open, and Alex gazed into the leering face of Ms. G, framed by the bright moonlight to look like a terrifying gargoyle.

"Welcome, boys. Now the fun really begins."

***

William found the empty desert comforting as he sped along on his motorcycle, the tires kicking up sand behind him, his perfect night vision easily revealing the tracks of the vehicle that had spirited his big brother away. The full moon added extra light, and the night sky around it looked like a dark blanket scattered with glitter.

He knew, however, that the moon meant torment for Francis, forcing him to maintain his Wolfboy form. But his younger brother didn't complain once. He didn't even howl because William had made him understand that it might alert the enemy to their presence. William had engaged the stealth mode built into his motorcycle, which squelched much of the engine noise. The bike purred, rather than roared.

Griffin hadn't yet returned with a report. With their long legs, Kitty and Scorpio managed to keep pace with the motorcycle, but Bear had fallen behind. William didn't have his motorcycle at full power because he wanted his team with him, despite being able to handle all the kidnappers on his own. He needed his cousins to prove their worth to the Pentagon so they wouldn't have to stay cooped up in those cages all the time.

Studying the stars to gauge direction and tell time had been part of his training these past three years. By his best estimate, he'd been traveling for one hour and ten minutes in a southwesterly direction, but still within the borders of Nevada.

A flapping sound and gust of heavy wind encircled him, and he glanced upward. Griffin's massive lion-bear body glided overhead, pacing him with ease and growling about what he'd found. There were dwellings just ahead, but it was unclear how far. Griffin made other sounds and William understood that it had taken Griffin fifteen flaps of its wings to get from the dwellings to him. With a wingspan of ten feet on each side, one flap would keep Griffin in the air for approximately one minute, so William estimated he'd arrive at those dwellings in fifteen minutes if he maintained a sixty miles per hour speed.

He slowed the bike. In the empty silence of this vast desert landscape, sound traveled far. Now that he was so close, silence was of the essence. He fixed his eyes on the area ahead, seeking his first glimpse of the dwellings Griffin had seen.

There they were!

Appearing small at first, the buildings expanded in his field of vision as he drew nearer. When he felt it unsafe to continue, he slowed the bike to a stop and killed the engine. Letting Wolfboy dismount first, he hopped off and set the kickstand, awaiting the arrival of his team. He studied Wolfboy beneath the light of the moon. The boy's elfin ears were much sharper, his face covered in black fur, with sharp teeth meant for rending flesh projecting upward from his lower jaw.

But his hazel eyes held a hopelessness that was born of self-hatred. The intensity of those emotions made William want to cry, in part because they mirrored his own feelings about himself. Yes, he and Wolfboy understood each other all too well.

Opening a compartment beneath the bike seat. he pulled out a pair of powerful binoculars. Adjusting the focus, he observed what appeared to be a very old town with buildings that looked decrepit and abandoned. He had read about so-called ghost towns, but he'd never seen one except in photos on the internet. What he saw through the binoculars definitely looked like those pictures.

He moved the binoculars to his right toward the largest building, which stood two or maybe three floors high. Even in the darkness, he knew it was made of brick and that it looked in better condition than those along the rest of the dirt street that cut through the middle of the town. Trickles of light spilled out the tall boarded-up windows. Several dark-colored vans were parked at the rear of the building, hidden from aerial reconnaissance by large tent-like tarps.

He lowered the glasses and considered a moment. Why would Alex's captors bring him to a desolate place like this? Was it a permanent head-quarters or just a stop along the way? Whatever the reason, Alex and Roy were inside that building. Andy too, he was sure, and he intended to rescue them all. He preferred not to kill their captors unless it proved necessary. Despite having been created as a soulless killing machine, he'd rebelled against that programming back in Los Angeles and preferred to make choices other than wanton death and destruction. Besides, Colonel Walker would want to question the abductors to learn more about their plans.

Heavy steps slowed to a trot, and William turned as Kitty loped up to him, panting after the long trek through the desert. Its coat of orange and black glistened in the moonlight. From the direction of the buildings came another large shape. Dog! He must've circled around when he followed the other vehicle.

William stroked both of their heads lovingly and then reached back into the compartment to pull out a thick, heavy thermos and several bowls. He set one bowl down before the huge cat and another in front of the massive dog-wolf, poured out some water, and watched them lap it up in seconds.

Griffin settled lightly to the sand with a sweep of its enormous wings and trotted over, so William set a third bowl before the huge lion muzzle and filled it with water. A heavy *slurp, slurp, slurp* sound filled the night as Griffin lapped up the precious liquid.

William took a small swig of the water, but didn't require very much, and wanted his cousins to have their fill. He handed the thermos to Wolf-boy, who gripped it within two thick, hairy paws and upended it into his mouth. After a moment, he handed it back, droplets of water dribbling from his dark muzzle onto the checkered shirt he wore.

Within moments, Scorpio clicked and clattered into view, Bear loping rapidly behind. Even with the dryness of the air, Bear panted as he joined them, but did not seem tired. He *was* thirsty, though, and made that quite clear with a muted growl. William placed another bowl in an open space and filled it. Bear's heavy muzzle dipped in and practically sucked up the contents in a single slurp.

William eyed Scorpio. Being made up of scorpion, cockroach, and beetle, it was created for just this type of terrain and William didn't even offer it water. Scorpio had been well fed earlier that night and had ingested more than enough water through its meal. It twitched its gigantic stinger back and forth as though anxious to plunge it into something. Or someone.

Once all the creatures had finished drinking, William used the handheld device to get their attention and—through various sounds, words, and even thoughts in the case of Scorpio—he explained his plan, solidifying his commands with buttons on the device. The creatures were to surround the largest dwelling in the town while he slipped inside to find the boys. He knew the creatures would likely kill anyone who shot at them, but that couldn't be helped. He would do his best to keep some of the kidnappers inside so they wouldn't run into his team. Feeling certain they understood the basics of what he wanted, he set off on foot toward the large, inhabited building.

I'm coming, Alex...

CHAPTER TWENTY-THREE

ARE YOU READY?

COLONEL WALKER HAD INSISTED THE more grievously wounded Dane be rushed into surgery first, and Amanda reluctantly agreed with him.

"William cauterized my wound like a pro, Amanda," he'd assured her, keeping his voice strong and steady, the way she liked it. "I'm stable."

The base had a top-notch medical unit, but only two surgeons. Both had examined Walker and had, in fact, proclaimed him "stable for the moment." But they insisted that the bullet must be removed without much further delay. Then they'd entered the OR with the wounded Dane while nurses prepped the colonel for his impending surgery. Amanda hovered by his side like a satellite, tense with fear as she held fast to his hand.

He refused to lie down on a gurney until it was necessary, but the medical staff had removed his shirt and cleaned off the blood, impressed by how well the opening had been sealed. They had him hooked up to every machine in the book, monitoring his vitals and assuring Amanda that he was in no danger.

While awaiting his turn under the knife, he made certain Davalos and Stern knew what to do once he entered the OR and command officially transferred to them. The entire base had been secured after his service members and officers were released from their barracks. The gate guard had been found unconscious with the gate wide open and numerous sets of tire tracks leading away from the base. Walker knew William was following the right set of tracks because that boy could track anything. As a test, Walker once hidden a mouse from the lab inside the glove box of a random jeep and it took William a scant ten minutes to find it.

The gate guard had been debriefed by Stern, who reported that, in his opinion, the airman could be trusted. Walker remained unconvinced, but then it was his job to distrust everyone, especially at the present time.

Roy's father, rather tough for a forty-something man, had sustained numerous cuts and abrasions and had been stunned by falling rubble, but now he paced the infirmary like a caged animal, fearful of losing both his sons in one night. Java, Israel, and Jorge hovered around him, almost as though he was *their* dad too. These kids and the tight-knit family they'd created impressed the colonel more and more with each passing moment.

At his urging, Amanda crossed the waiting area to comfort Nathan, sharing with him all that Roy had been doing since his arrival, and assuring him and the others that the missing boys would be found.

Shaw and his daughter sat together in two plastic chairs, arms wrapped around each other. This was a man who was accustomed to getting what he wanted when he wanted it, but at the moment all his millions of dollars couldn't bring Alex back. That realization seemed to deflate him like an old party balloon, but Walker had assured him his "special agent" would save the boy.

While he was aware of William's location, thanks to a microchip transponder that had been inserted into the boy's foot after the Los Angeles incident, he'd neglected to provide William with a means of direct communication. Everything had happened too fast. He knew the boy was approximately eighty miles southwest of the base and seemed to be moving slowly. It was Walker's fervent hope that William had found where the boys were taken and was moving in for the rescue.

Davalos entered the lobby and strode forward, his dress shoes clicking against the linoleum floor like a loud clock. He'd changed out of his bloody shirt and replaced his jacket with another but hadn't bothered to replace the tie. He wore a grim expression.

"Choppers are ready, Colonel," he announced for all to hear, and then lowered his voice to add, "No certainty as to the loyalty of the pilots, however."

Walker nodded. "Understood." He had no intention of following the general's orders, but he did want birds in the air to bring the boys back once William dealt with the kidnappers. "Where is Sergeant Stern?"

"Patrolling the perimeter with men he trusts."

"Good. And that outside entrance into the underground?"

"Being permanently sealed as we speak."

Walker eyed this man who only a few hours before had been an arrogant prick. But now, he was like a spoiled teen who'd grown into a man overnight.

"Thank you, Mark. The base will be in good hands when I'm under."

"Any estimate as to surgery time?"

"Soon as they finish with the kid."

Davalos nodded. "What shall I tell the general when he calls?"

"Tell him the choppers are in the air."

"And if they're not?"

Walker offered a wry smile. "Launch them."

Davalos returned the smile. "Yes, sir." The walkie-talkie attached to his belt beeped and he raised it to his lips. "Davalos here." He listened, frowning.

Walker didn't like that frown. "What?"

Davalos spoke into the walkie. "I'm with the colonel. Hold." He lowered the device and gazed at Walker in confusion. "Someone just took a chopper out of the base."

The colonel flinched. "Not one that we assigned to this mission?"

"No, Colonel. No ID on the pilot either."

"Get ours in the air now. Track the rogue and be prepared to shoot it down on my order. Or yours, if I'm under."

Davalos relayed those instructions into the walkie-talkie and then clipped it back onto his belt. "It must be one of hers."

Walker nodded. "But what for? She already has the boys."

"Maybe for protection. She knows we'll send troops after her."

Walker considered that. "Perhaps."

***

After Alex had been pulled from the back of the van and Roy got dragged out with him, he found himself facing the rear of an old brick building. Beneath the bright moonlight, it looked big—at least two floors from what he could see of the boarded-up windows high over his head. He spotted the supersoldier they'd brought to life towering over the other men, some of whom were airmen from the base and others who were dressed all in black, like Ms. G.

As Alex was pushed toward an old wooden door with peeling paint, he heard her saying, "Secure the perimeter around this building. No one gets through. One of our men is bringing an armed helicopter, but he'll land outside your stations. Jäger, with me."

"Yes, my Lady," replied a deep male voice.

By then, Alex's chair had been pushed roughly over the threshold, causing him to bounce in his seat upon entering the ground floor. A second man had Roy's skinny upper arm in a vise grip, dragging him along. The guy pushing Alex rolled him down a dingy hall painted off-white. The old-fashioned light fixtures attached to the walls contained softly glowing bulbs. An elevator loomed just ahead, and Alex was shoved inside facing the back wall. The man didn't even bother turning him around, so he only heard Roy's grunt of pain as he was shoved in beside him and the doors closed with a brassy *ding* sound.

It seemed to take forever before Alex felt any movement, as if the ancient elevator couldn't make up its mind about taking them. Then with a lurch, the wooden box jolted upward, groaning like an old man struggling to get up some stairs. After what felt like five minutes, the box jerked to a halt only one floor up, and the doors slid open with a second *ding*.

Alex heard the others leave before his chair was grabbed from behind and yanked backward. Whoever these guys were, they sure didn't have orders to be gentle with him. Alex tossed his black-clad captor a look of fury before he was summarily pushed forward toward open double doors at the end of the hallway. The wooden floor creaked beneath his wheels, and Alex hoped it wouldn't collapse. He was shoved into a large meeting room and then released, so he finally had control of his chair, but rather than turn around, he gaped in surprise at what he saw.

"Andy! You okay, bro?"

Andy sat in a straight back wooden chair with another man in black standing guard over him. A large, boarded-up window was directly behind him, but otherwise the room was empty. Andy looked furious, exactly how Alex felt.

"Yeah, Big Brother, except I'm a captive again!" He softened slightly. "You okay? They didn't hurt you?"

Alex shook his head and glanced at Roy, standing beside him while their captors stood guard, arms folded across their chests. He wheeled over to Andy and glared at the man in black, who chuckled and crossed the room to stand with his fellows.

"When they took you in that other van," Alex began, "I was afraid."

A female voice asked, "Afraid of what?"

Alex spun his chair around to confront the smirking Ms. G, who had entered the room flanked by the huge muscular guy he so wished he hadn't brought to life. Her black outfit was slinky and tight-fitting, like she wanted to go clubbing and flirt with all the guys she met.

She ambled casually around Alex and Roy, while the big guy stood at attention near the boarded-up window, thick hands clasped behind his back and a perverse grin on his face. She stopped and looked down at the sullen Andy, who remained seated with his arms folded across his chest. "The prodigal son returns."

Andy didn't even look at her. "I'm not your son."

She laughed. "But you do belong to me, Andy. Never forget that."

Andy grunted with anger but remained stubbornly silent.

She nudged him like an old friend. "I thought you'd love seeing this old ghost town. It's a tourist attraction during the day, one of our more lucrative businesses."

Andy glowered. "Like I care how you make your money? I told you I'd never be put in a cage again and I meant it."

"Tsk, tsk. Such a moody boy. Puberty will do that to you." She turned to Roy and smirked. "Of course, Roy is way past puberty, aren't you? You can barely keep your hands off these boys."

"Leave him alone, you bitch!" spat Alex in fury.

Her eyebrows rose in amusement. "My, my, so angry tonight."

"I don't care what your monster does to me," Roy snarled, trembling with anger, rather than fear as he pointed at Jäger. "I'm not gonna let you hurt Alex."

She leered and sidled over to stand beside him. "Young love is so innocent." She lifted her hand and stroked his cheek with long, slender fingers. "I would so enjoy torturing you just to watch Alex beg me to stop. Mr. Jäger is quite expert at torture, are you not?"

She tossed a grin over her shoulder at the tall man, and he returned it. Alex shuddered at the look of sadistic evil on the man's twisted lips.

Alex was fuming. "Whaddaya want me for this time?"

Ms. G turned to face him, Roy forgotten, which had been Alex's intent. "Why, the same thing as before. We need you to open a gate to let our friends through. And then you'll help us bring this world to its knees."

Alex flinched at the word "gate," his heart pounding and his muscles tightening with dread. The gate had been destroyed, hadn't it, by him and Andy?

"I know what you're thinking," she purred like a cat. "You destroyed the medallion." She tossed back her head and cackled. "That was only a portable gate. The permanent one is what I need you for and it's closer than you think. It has a slight flaw that allows our friends to occasionally seep through. But once it's fully open, they'll flood from their side to ours and the beginning of the end will arrive."

"Why do I have to do it?"

"Because you're the Healer, of course. Only you can open that gate."

Andy stood up now and look annoyed, impatient even. "Can I stop pretending now, Teacher?"

Alex's jaw dropped open and he heard a loud gasp of shock from Roy. But his wide eyes remained riveted on his brother, no longer angry or sullen, but rather…amused.

"Whaa…w-wha…what?" he stammered. "Andy?"

Andy ignored him, stepped to Ms. G's side, and gazed into her delighted face. "Well?"

She raised that delicate-looking hand again and caressed his cheek. "You played your part well. You almost had me fooled when I walked in."

"Part?" Roy gaped at Andy. "You mean…you been playing us this whole time?"

He said what Alex was too afraid to say because he so feared the answer.

Andy eyed Roy with measured contempt. "You. You're the weakest of them all, the way you stare at Alex and dream about me. Pathetic."

Roy blushed red and looked aghast at Alex.

Alex couldn't stop shuddering. This wasn't happening. It couldn't be. "Andy…you…we're brothers! We need each other."

"I don't need you."

Ms. G. placed a hand on his shoulder. "For now you do, little one."

He faced her with an eager expression. "I'm not little, and no, I don't need him. I thought of a way to get rid of Big Brother once and for all."

Her slim eyebrows rose. "Do tell."

Andy smirked, like the cat that finally ate the family parakeet. "I can shift all of his power into me and then keep it. I'll be both Healer and Shifter and have more power than anyone in the world." His face glowed with greed and desire.

Ms. G studied him, her eyes alight with wonder. "Now that's an idea I never thought of. For so many years, I'd assumed the Healer would be only one person. Learning there were two of you has been, well, an adjustment. Are you certain you can pull it off?"

Andy looked more confident than Java in the weight room. "You should know better than to doubt me, Teacher."

"True enough. What will happen to the cripple when you drain him?"

Andy shrugged, like it didn't matter. "Probably die."

"Noooo!" screamed Roy, who lunged at Andy. But Jäger darted forward and grabbed him from behind, wrapping a massive arm around Roy's throat and twisting one of his arms up behind his back. Roy squirmed and struggled, but it was no use against the mountain of a man.

Alex stared at his brother in open-mouthed dismay. He'd been so sure.... Andy had made so much progress, hadn't he?

No, he now knew, his chest heaving with contained sobs of anguish. He hadn't.

It had all been an act.

An act...

Andy stepped over to him, grinning with delight. "Well, Big Brother? Are you ready?"

***

William studied the guards surrounding the old brick building. In addition to the three airmen who'd escaped with the kidnappers, William counted eight men within his field of vision. He guessed that another two or three guarded the front. And then there was Jäger. William had thought about the artificial man on his ride out. There was something he'd sensed when they fought, a weakness or perhaps a genetic flaw.

Whatever the case, William wasn't afraid. The man was bigger and stronger by weight, but William felt his speed and agility would dominate their next encounter, just as it had their last. He'd only "lost" because that was part of the colonel's plan.

Turning to his team of hybrids, he ordered them into position outside the circle of men guarding the large building. The moon's brightness made hiding their movements more difficult, but not impossible. He, himself, would sneak into the building and find the boys. Using the device Davalos had given him, he would signal his team to simultaneously attack the perimeter. He would use the "disarm and disable" setting, but it was possible some of the men would still die, especially if the creatures became angry.

He tapped a button on the device and his team split up, slinking off with extreme stealth to their assigned positions. Lying flat on his stomach, William slipped and slithered along the rough desert floor toward an opening between two of the men. They looked well armed, their military-style rifles most likely automatic to inflict maximum carnage.

The men were patrolling back and forth over a twenty-foot-long section of the dirt parking lot, watching the desert with keen eyes and guns at the ready. William would have to distract them somehow and slip past while they weren't looking. Studying the ground around him, he found several rocks that looked large enough to make some noise. Silent as a scorpion scuttling across the sand, he snaked out his arm and scooped up the largest of them.

As the closest man turned his head to glance behind him, William rose like a shadow and flung the rock hard at the dark vehicles parked beneath the tarp. He dropped flat and heard a satisfying *thunk* as the rock struck one of the vehicles and bounced off.

The two men in that sector whirled around, weapons poised to fire, and then sprinted in the direction of the parked vans. William was up quick as a rabbit and darted into the parking lot, his footfalls soundless against the crunchy ground. He was through the rear door and had eased it shut without even seeing the men emerge from behind the vans. He heard them now, though, as he pressed his ear against the inside of the wooden door.

"Probably just some small animal," one of them said. "Anything bigger and we'd have seen it."

"Yeah."

Their footsteps crunched on the ground outside as they moved back into position. William pulled away from the door and looked down the long hallway. He saw nothing and heard no movement. Hugging one wall, he eased down the hall only a few feet before he spotted an open staircase leading up. He ducked into the shadowy alcove and ascended the steps on soundless tiptoes.

***

Alex stared at his brother as though he'd never seen him before. He was so intuitive about people. That was a word he'd learned from Father Pat because the priest had noticed that he could read people well, and not just their health status. How could he have so misread Andy, especially since their minds were connected?

He glanced at Roy, still struggling against the much taller and stronger Jäger. "Let him go!"

Ms. G slithered over, her tight pants making her hips sway back and forth. "Don't worry, dear Alex. We won't kill him. Where's the fun in that. We'll leave him whatever's left of you when Andy's finished. That sounds fair, doesn't it?"

He stared at her in disbelief. "How can you be so cruel?"

"That's easy. I have no conscience." She nodded at Andy.

Andy reached out a hand to Alex, who gripped his wheel handles with all his might. No way would he let himself be killed without a fight.

Ms. G sighed and waved over one of the men from the door. He was a big guy, small compared to Jäger, but definitely stronger than Alex. Even through the long sleeve black pullover the corded muscles of his forearm bulged as he grabbed Alex by his own forearm and yanked his hand loose from the wheel. Alex struggled, but the goon had such an iron grip on his wrist that he couldn't even make a fist. He watched in horror as the smiling Andy reached out and clasped his extended hand.

The power poured over and through him, slamming him with pure energy. The floodwaters engulfed him as they always did, until he felt frozen in place.

Then Andy began to talk. "Your power, Alex, is my power. You are not the Healer. I am. You are nothing but a weak, crippled little boy who can do nothing to stop me. I am all-powerful, do you hear? Me! Andy is the most powerful person on this planet!"

Alex trembled so hard there might have been an earthquake happening deep inside of him. He felt like his lifeforce, his very essence, was leaving his body. His eyes rolled back into his head and foam dribbled from his mouth. His vision faded, and his conscious awareness grew dimmer by the second. The last thing he heard was Andy's voice shouting, "Healer, to me!"

Pain arced through his soul like electricity, and blackness engulfed him.

CHAPTER TWENTY-FOUR

MY NAME IS WEAPON

WILLIAM SPRINTED UP THE OLD wooden stairs so stealthily that not a creak could be heard. He stopped at a closed door leading out to the upper floor and paused to listen.

A blood-curdling scream of pain echoed from down the hallway.

Alex!

William yanked open the door, pressed the button on the device inside his pocket, and pelted down the hall.

The attack was on!

***

The massive arms released Roy and he staggered forward, gasping for air and gazing in horror at the slumped, unmoving body of the best friend he'd ever have, the boy he'd love forever.

Alex couldn't be dead. He couldn't be!

Roy dropped to his knees beside the wheelchair, easing Alex back to a sitting position. He brushed the thick blond hair off Alex's beautiful face and searched desperately for signs of life.

Andy thrust both arms into the air with triumph, a wild expression of mad power plastered across his face, his flowing hair almost glowing with energy.

"It worked! I'm the Healer now!" He hooted with excitement.

Ms. G burned with glee and wrapped an arm around his shoulders like a loving parent. "And now it can finally begin."

Roy's heart thundered in his chest as he continued gulping air to compensate for his near strangulation, but Alex was all he cared about. He was about to press his ear to Alex's chest when the double doors ex-

ploded inward so hard that both guards, struck from behind by the shattered wood, were lifted off their feet and thrown across the room. One of
them just missed slamming into Andy, while the other struck Jäger hard
in the chest and sent him reeling.

Roy looked over his shoulder and gasped. William stood within the
shattered remnants of the doorway, a look of fury on his young face; lips
twisted, eyes narrowed, a low rumble emanated from deep within him.
His eyes seemed to take in everything at once, widening when he spotted
the slumped, unmoving form of Alex.

Ms. G dragged Andy behind Jäger in obvious fear. "You said you
killed him!"

The big man's face remained expressionless, like he hadn't yet figured
out how to use his facial muscles. "I thought I had, my lady."

Like a cornered cat, Ms. G hissed, "Then finish him now, you fool!"

Jäger stepped forward, but William was already on the move. Faster
than Roy would've thought possible, the boy ran at the man and slammed
into his midsection with his head. The blow sent Jäger pinwheeling back,
and Ms. G was barely able to jump away in time to avoid his heavy fist
smashing her head as he staggered backward.

William righted himself at once and came at the man again, landing another bull-ramming smash to the midsection. Jäger grunted and
stumbled once more, unable to recapture his footing. A third time, like
a vicious rhino, William slammed his body into the taller man, wrapping
his arms around Jäger's midsection, forcing him back toward the boarded-
up window. Jäger grabbed William in a bearhug, and they collided with
the boards, shattering them with a loud *crack* and sending both boy and
man tumbling out the window.

"Come, Andy!" Ms. G grabbed the energized boy by the arm and
dragged him past Roy through the shattered remnants of the door.

Roy's mind reeled because everything had happened so quickly, but
his main concern was Alex. He pressed his ear against Alex's chest and
listened for a heartbeat. His own heart was so damned loud he couldn't
tell! Staggering to his feet, his grabbed Alex's chair to steady himself as his
head swam with momentary dizziness.

He had to get help!

Gripping the back of the wheelchair, he held Alex back, so his head lolled behind and to the right, and then he pushed the chair forward. He kicked aside broken chunks of the splintered doors to allow the chair to roll through and in seconds they were into the hall, Roy pushing and stumbling his way toward the elevator. There was no sign of Ms. G or the traitorous Andy and that was for the better. Furious, Roy slammed a fist against the down button so hard he almost broke it.

How could Andy do this to his only brother?

The elevator doors creaked open so slowly Roy wanted to scream, but finally they were inside, and he pounded the first-floor button. As the doors rumbled closed, Roy wondered what had happened to William.

***

William hadn't planned to go through the window with Jäger, but once he did, he vowed to make the best of it. The heavier weight of the big man played out in his favor as Jäger failed in his attempt to spin in midair so William would hit the ground first. As they dropped, William kept a firm grip on the man's muscular torso while pressing back against the snake-like arms wrapped around his body. They hit the ground with a massive thud and an explosive grunt of pain from Jäger. The impact caused him to loosen his grip, and William wriggled free, rolling off the man's chest and leaping to his feet, not the least bit disoriented. He heard the screams and shouts of the other men engaged in battle with his team, punctuated by roars and growls and the *rat tat tat* of repeated gunfire, but his focus was the supersoldier before him.

Jäger reeled as he tried to regain his footing, which allowed William to run hard and kick him in the face, sending him sprawling once more.

More gunshots and animal snarls caught William's attention. He turned his head quickly, catching in an instant the mayhem wreaked on their opponents. Screams of pain filled the night air as needle-sharp teeth tore at human flesh. Scorpio plunged its stinger into one of the men and plucked it out. The man staggered, gun clattering to the ground, as white foam bubbled forth from his mouth.

William spun around as Jäger came at him like a rampaging elephant, growling with rage. He had to end this now and return to Alex. He leapt aside and, using his smaller size to advantage, kicked Jäger's ankle, making him stumble. As Jäger crumpled to his knees, William jumped onto his back and wrapped his arms of steel around the man's neck. This time he wouldn't let go until the monster was dead! He gripped with all his might, and Jäger flailed about, his breaths bursting from his constricted windpipe in short, staccato gasps. William squeezed harder, the veins in his arms and forehead bulging. The man's struggles grew weaker. It would be over in a matter of seconds.

Movement from the building caught his eye and William turned his head to see the woman and Alex's brother hurry out the front door and dart around the side of the building like frightened rabbits. She raised some kind of walkie-talkie and shouted into it, "Destroy everything and everyone!" Then they were gone out of sight toward the rear.

Should he stop them? Jäger was just a monster bodyguard. The woman was the real prize. If he could stop her, he might stop it all. His cousins had already disabled or killed her soldiers and now prowled among the bodies to make certain no one was still able to fight.

Then William spotted something in the air that stopped his breath cold. A helicopter, one of the gigantic Pave Hawks from the base, bore down on them from out of the desert. And it was one of the armed models.

Destroy everything and everyone!

That's what she'd said. The pilot must be one of her minions. William knew those choppers. Colonel Walker had taught him how to fly them—and how to deploy the missiles they contained. He knew that one Pave Hawk could lay waste to this entire town. He and his cousins could withstand the blasts, but…Alex and Roy!

He released Jäger's thick neck and dropped off the man's sagging back. Pelting toward the old building like a track star, he spotted Wolfboy loping toward him and called out, "Wolfboy, with me!"

Wolfboy increased his pace. A black van careened around the building from the rear, swerving toward the gagging, gasping form of Jäger. William and Wolfboy took the front steps three a time and plowed into the heavy wooden doors like a double battering ram.

***

Roy hit the ground floor and thought the elevator doors would never open!

Come on!

Finally, they slid open, and he lurched forward, shoving the wheelchair into the hallway, flicking his gaze side to side. Which way? Momentarily confused, he spun to the left toward the back door through which he'd entered. He yanked the chair to a halt, snagging Alex's limp form to prevent him toppling out of the wheelchair onto the floor. With his free hand, he grabbed the knob.

It was locked!

Frantic, he yanked the knob so hard that sharp pain shot up his wrist and forearm. Cursing under his breath, he slammed one shoulder against the door like he'd seen the hero do in every movie ever made. The door held fast, while sharp, stabbing pain made him wince.

Now what?

He spun and scanned the hallway behind him. It must lead to the front door, he guessed, so he whipped the wheelchair around and sprinted down the hall past several closed wooden doors. When he reached the end he swerved to the right, grabbing at the slumping Alex with one hand to steady him, and continued along another darkened corridor. The wheels echoed all around him and then he was out into a cavernous lobby with a tile floor, huge walls, and high ceilings. A massive, elegant staircase rose from the center of the tiled floor up to the second floor and split off in both directions.

The way out, where is it?

He spun in the other direction and spotted double doors large enough to drive a truck through. He'd just started in that direction when the doors blew open from the outside, slamming back against the wall and revealing two small silhouettes standing on the front steps.

William and Wolfboy!

As they stepped inside, Wolfboy twitched and spasmed, almost toppling as the wolf-part vanished and he became…Francis again!

Before Roy could react, William dashed forward and snatched Alex from his chair like he was a baby.

"Hurry! Francis, grab Roy!"

He turned and sprinted madly back toward the open doors, Alex's limp body flopping up and down like a fish. Before Roy could do anything, the smaller form of Francis was at his side.

"Don't worry, Big Brother, I'll save you!"

The boy swept him off his feet into his arms and sprinted after William. Roy bounced up and down, but the young boy gripped him like steel and Roy felt the rock-hard muscles in his small arms.

Just as Francis got him to the front steps outside, Roy saw William leap high into the air with Alex, landing at the bottom of a long flight of concrete steps. Roy heard the *whup, whup, whup* of a helicopter somewhere behind him. What did it mean?

"Hang on, Big Brother!"

Francis jumped, just as William had, and Roy's heart flew into his throat. The free-fall sensation was worse than any ride at Six Flags as Francis sailed through the air and dropped like a rock, just clearing the stone steps and landing in the dirt of the street. To Roy's astonishment, the young boy not only kept a solid hold on him, but also landed on his feet like guys in the Olympics and then sprinted after the retreating William toward one of the abandoned buildings.

The sound of the helicopter was deafening.

Just before Francis followed William into what looked like an abandoned store, Roy risked a glance back and saw the copter high in the sky behind the brick building. Moonlight reflected off its windshield and gray metallic frame. Something flew from beneath the copter, something sleek and fast. It left a plume of smoke in its wake. Roy just realized what it was when William shouted, "Down, Francis."

Francis dropped to his knees, letting go of Roy and then jumping on top of him as a shield. Roy felt the air pushed from his lungs, and he'd barely clamped both hands over his head when the world exploded in a fierce blast of fiery light.

He felt, more than heard, the building across the street come apart at its core, blown to bits of shrapnel by the missile that struck it. Chunks of brick and masonry blasted their way through the old, decrepit wood of the building surrounding Roy, but Francis did his best to protect him, despite being so much smaller. Something must've struck Francis in the back because he grunted in pain. Then another and another. Roy heard each thud, but he dared not raise his head as the bricks fell like hail all around them and clouds of dust obscured his vision. Within moments, there was silence.

Hearing nothing more dropping out of the sky, Roy removed his hands and lifted his head as he felt Francis clamber off his back. The roof above was shattered where bricks and chunks of debris had smashed through and the area around the front door had been nearly destroyed, and yet the doorframe itself stood intact.

"Are you hurt, Big Brother?" Francis's boyish voice sounded odd after so much destruction. Because he wasn't in the direct moonlight, he hadn't changed back, and his handsome face was etched with concern.

"I think so," Roy muttered, raising himself to his knees and studying the younger boy. Francis's mop of bushy hair was covered in dust and bits of masonry and his shirt had been torn in several places, revealing more muscles than Roy would have thought possible on a twelve-year-old.

Alex!

Roy glanced around in fear. Just ahead, William was getting to his feet, revealing the prone, unmoving form of Alex. Roy pushed himself upright. Pain shot through him from more places that he could count. His pants were ripped and shredded, blood seeping from numerous cuts and scrapes. But all that mattered was Alex.

As he staggered forward, Francis trotted after him. William's clothes were even more ripped and torn, revealing his own set of defined muscles, but like Francis, he didn't look injured at all.

Alex lay on the wooden floor, face up, unmoving.

William said, "Francis, protect them. I have to stop that helicopter."

Roy turned to look at him, confused. "How can you—"

But William was already gone, dashing through the doorframe and out into the unpaved street. Roy stepped forward to gaze out a shattered window at the destruction and saw…were those dead bodies? And the creatures! The ones from the base! William bolted for the gigantic lion-thing, the one with the wings. He leapt onto its back, and it took off into the air, massive condor wings banking a turn and heading for the helicopter that was circling around for another attack.

Roy ran back to Alex and knelt beside him and Francis. Moments later, the gigantic dog-wolf stuck its hairy snout through the doorframe. Roy shrank back, but Francis placed a calming hand on his shoulder.

"Do not be afeared, Big Brother," he said, his boyish voice soothing. "My cousins want to pay respect to Alex. They won't not harm you."

Roy glanced at Francis's open expression and wide hazel eyes, and then faced the door again. The dog-wolf had entered and was padding in his direction, tail down, looking sad. Behind it, the huge tiger-thing stuffed itself through the opening. Both crept up to Roy on bloodied paws that were big enough to lop his head off with one swipe.

Blood stained the fur around the giant cat's mouth, and Roy shuddered with disgust until a slippery red tongue slid from between the jaws and slurped it away. Roy was still filled with revulsion, but when the big cat gently rubbed its head against Alex's face and the dog licked his hands, Roy glanced at Francis in amazement.

"See, Big Brother? They love him. So does Bear." He pointed at the doorframe where the monstrous bear had its head poking inside; its body was far too large to squeeze through, however. It let out a low growl that touched Roy's heart because it sounded so sad. The dog-wolf lifted its head after slobbering all over Alex's hand and barked twice. As though Bear understood, it lay down and planted its massive bulk just outside the door, watching the others.

Roy turned to Francis. "What did Dog say to him?"

"He told him Alex was alive."

Roy's heart soared, but then sank almost as fast. "Then why doesn't he wake up?"

Francis frowned, for he obviously didn't know.

***

William whispered into Griffin's large, tawny ear and the creature flapped its colossal wings in sweeping strokes as it picked up speed and sought to intercept the chopper before it completed its turn for another run at the town. Another direct hit would surely kill Roy and Alex.

The copter was almost in position, the whirling blades deafening as Griffin brought William in on an intercept trajectory from below. The pilot's face was obscured by his helmet, so William couldn't tell whether it was a male or female. He'd know soon enough. The churning air from the rotors fought against Griffin's rise, but the creature's powerful wings beat furiously against the downdraft, bringing William to within jumping distance of the open bay door.

The pilot had spotted him and swerved to one side, but the Pave

Hawk was bulky and not nearly so agile as the lithe Griffin, who darted upward and closed the gap. William rose to a squat on the creature's back, maintaining his balance against the wind. Griffin gave a massive sweep of its wings, jolting its body higher and William jumped. The combined momentum of the Griffin's push and his own powerful legs sent William soaring up and into the open bay door just as the copter banked back toward the town.

William rolled, and almost tumbled out when the pilot tilted the Hawk in the direction of the open bay door. Grabbing for one of the dangling seatbelts, William held on until the Hawk righted itself and then he muscled his way up and pulled himself all the way in. Leaping to his feet, he clambered forward into the two-seat cockpit where a single pilot sat on the left side, his right hand gripping the throttle. The dashboard was shaped like a *T*, running beneath the curved windshield and then down between the two pilot seats. There were so many gauges, buttons, and switches that it had taken William eight weeks before he'd had everything memorized. At the moment, his only interest was the launch switch that he needed to disengage. The light indicating an armed missile glowed brightly and the pilot had his left hand poised to fire.

William stood behind him in the tight confines of the cockpit, feet planted against any potential rolls, arms flexed for action. "Stand down."

The pilot, whom William did recognize but didn't know well, glanced back at him, and then focused on flying. "You're that woman doctor's nephew."

"No, I'm not, Airman. My name is Weapon and that is what I am. I won't let you kill my friends. I'm giving you a choice to stand down or die."

The pilot glanced back, a sneer visible to William through the visor. "You're just a kid. 'Sides, if I die, so do you."

"No, just you. I know how to fly this bird. Will you stand down or not?"

The pilot looked afraid for the first time. "I can't. She'll kill me."

William saw through the windshield that the town was right beneath them. He easily spotted the building which housed Alex and Roy because Bear's enormous bulk stuck out of the shattered doorway into the street.

The pilot reached for the firing switch. William whipped his arms up and around behind the pilot, grabbing his head in a tight told and snapping the pilot's neck in an instant.

The pilot slumped, his fingers brushing the switch as he did, but not hard enough to activate the missile. Without hesitation, William crawled over and planted himself in the other seat and took over the throttle from the dead man. He'd never officially flown one of these, only taken it up and then landed it inside the base, so he would not make the foolish choice to try anything fancy. He would land the chopper outside the ghost town and call Colonel Walker on the radio.

William banked a lazy turn to bring the Hawk away from town and that's when he spotted them—more choppers headed right for him. An unarmed Pave Hawk and two well-armed Black Hawks. Could she have control of that many base personnel? He couldn't imagine, but then this woman seemed to possess supernatural powers that even he, with his own unnatural origins, didn't understand.

He snatched up the headset and clamped it over his ears, blocking out much of the roaring rotor noise that filled the cockpit. He heard one of the incoming Hawks hailing him. Flicking on the headset, he glanced around the cockpit for a moment. He didn't know which Hawk this was so he couldn't use the correct call sign.

"This is Special Agent Weapon controlling the Pave Hawk in front of you. The pilot who stole it is dead. Identify yourself."

The voice crackled through his headset, muffled slightly by external noise, but clear enough to calm William's beating heart. "Agent Weapon, Colonel Walker sent us to escort you back to base. Over."

Relieved, William urged them to hurry. "We have wounded who need transport. And my cousins too."

"Cousins? Over."

"You'll see when you land. Over."

Weapon focused on landing the Hawk in one piece. The Pentagon already considered him a mistake. They'd be doubly furious if he damaged a multimillion-dollar piece of hardware.

CHAPTER TWENTY-FIVE

WHAT DOES THAT MEAN?

R OY SAT BESIDE ALEX'S BED in the base hospital, tears in his eyes, gazing with deep longing at his comatose friend. They'd been flown back in the first helicopter to land at the ghost town, and all the base doctors had examined Alex, including Dr. Shepherd.

A coma. That's all they could determine. His heartbeat was low, almost nonexistent, like all the energy had been drained from his body.

Of course, Roy knew that it had, in fact, been drained away, and he shared with them what Andy had done. Unfortunately, none of them, including Shepherd, who'd spent the most time with the boys, understood their power enough to formulate a treatment plan. It had been hours and, if anything, Alex had grown weaker. A machine monitored his heart rate and Roy eyed it again. Each blip on the scope seemed to be farther and farther apart, and yet he looked so peaceful, like he was enjoying a wonderful dream.

Java, Jorge, and Israel hovered around the bed, refusing to leave. Amanda brought them all some food, but Roy refused it. His stomach roiled with anxiety. He couldn't lose Alex. Life would have no longer have any meaning for him.

The door opened and William stepped inside, Francis at his heels. Both boys had changed out of their shredded clothes, now sporting nearly identical plain black t-shirts and sweatpants which made them look like regular kids. Roy acknowledged them with a tiny smile and William placed a hand on his shoulder.

"Any change?"

Roy shook his head, studying these boys who'd done so many impossible things to save his and Alex's lives, and he understood now what William had explained back in that lab with the creepy fish tanks.

"I have a surprise for you, Roy," William said, offering him a warm smile.

He pulled open the door and Nathan entered, pushing a wheelchair into the room. Dane sat in the chair, white as the gown he wore, but alive and healthy. Father Pat, looking like he'd been in a bar fight, entered after them. Alex's room was filling fast.

"Hello, Little Brother," Dane said, offering that rakish grin that said more about his health status than all the words in the world.

Roy sighed with relief and bent to wrap his brother in a gentle hug.

"Uh, not too hard," Dane cautioned with a slight grunt of pain.

"Sorry, Dane," Roy muttered, leaning back, and wiping tears from his eyes. "You're gonna be okay now?"

Dane's eyes twinkled with mischief. "Well, I won't be body-slamming your ass for a while, but yeah, I'm good."

That got a laugh out of Java and Izzy.

Roy grinned, studying his dad. "You okay too, Dad?"

"Tough as nails," Nathan replied, looking strong, despite all the cuts and abrasions he'd sustained. "This head of mine must be made of rocks to survive all the pounding it's gotten lately." He fixed his compassionate gaze on Alex. "Dr. Shepherd is doing her best for him, son."

Roy nodded, filled with so many emotions he didn't know which to focus on first. His dad and Dane were gonna be okay. Java, Izzy, and Jorge were fine. But Carlos... He'd been so worried about Alex that he hadn't given the murdered boy much thought.

Does that make me a terrible person?

Carlos had been new to their group and, yeah, he'd been a punk before Alex helped him against Jane, but…he really *had* come around and been a solid member of their team, a true friend.

Roy eyed Jorge standing on the other side of the bed. "I'm sorry about Carlos, you guys. He saved your life, Jorge."

Jorge's face reddened and his eyes began to water. He'd been crying off and on since Roy returned. "He was good."

Roy nodded, his breath hitching in his throat. "Yeah, he was."

There was a moment of heavy silence in which they all stared at Alex while the breathing machine filled the room with its whooshing sounds.

"We could try that power thing on Alex," Java finally broke the silence, "you know, when we hold hands and think real hard."

"We don't got Carlos no more," Izzy mumbled, looking sadder than Roy had ever seen him. "Gotta be six of us, like the preacher said."

"Oh, yeah," Java muttered, visibly deflating now that his idea had been shot down.

Father Pat eased his way to the foot of Alex's bed. He had a thick bandage around his head, and one arm was in a sling, but his face had taken on an energetic expression that Roy couldn't help but notice.

"You might not need Carlos," the priest murmured, rubbing his good hand along the stubble adorning his chin.

"What do you mean, Father?" Nathan asked, head tilted quizzically.

The priest was silent for a moment longer, but Roy could tell he was deep in thought, or maybe prayer. Both looked the same to him.

"I told Alex that God would not give him this power and then abandon him," he said, almost to himself. "It's true that the Healer must always have six protectors to keep him safe, but who's to say it must be the same six every time?"

Roy saw that everyone looked as confused as he did. "What does that mean?"

"To be a protector, one must care deeply for Alex, even love him," Father Pat continued, his voice rising with excitement. "Is there someone on this base who fits that description, other than you boys?"

Roy swung around to William, standing beside Francis in one corner and listening to the discussion. "You really like Alex, don't you?"

William nodded. "He is my big brother. He understands and accepts me."

Father Pat's eyes went wide with joy. "Then you can take Carlos's place."

William stepped up to the excited priest, his face filled with resolve. "Tell me what I must do."

"Can you move Alex's bed more to the center of the room? I understand you're, well, quite strong for a boy."

Roy shook his head. "Superboy is more like it."

William smiled and squeezed between the wall and the back of Alex's hospital bed. With ease, he rolled it outward so there was room for him to stand at its head.

"Good," affirmed the priest. "Now everyone join hands."

"Hell yeah," declared Java, who stretched out his hands to Izzy and Jorge on either side of him.

Knowing what they had to do, both boys gripped his hands and extended their own.

Father Pat eyed Dane in his wheelchair. "Can you stand, Dane?"

"Alex is my little brother too." He pressed both hands against the arms of the wheelchair and pushed upward. He winced from the pain, but slowly rose to his feet.

Nathan rolled the chair away and then moved into position behind Dane, hands on his upper shoulders for support. "I got you, son."

Dane extended his hands. Izzy took one and Roy took the other. That left only William. Roy extended his free hand and William took it at once. Roy almost flinched, fearing the boy's hand would feel unnatural, but it was soft and warm, just like any other kid.

"Once you complete the circle, focus on how much you care about Alex, how much you want him to heal, how much he means to you. Concentrate with all of your energy and don't let anything distract you. You'll probably feel warm, like you did the other time. Send that energy into Alex. You understand?"

Each of them nodded.

William stretched out his other arm and Jorge grasped his hand with a determined look on his soft face.

Roy felt a jolt run through him. The others did too. He saw it written across their faces like a group tattoo. His body thrummed with power, just as it had when they'd freed Alex from those demon things back at the old church. Roy fixed his gaze on Alex, his best friend, the boy he would always love in ways that Alex couldn't return, the boy who would help anyone at the risk of his own life.

Please, Alex, he begged in his mind, *come back to us. Come back to me. I know the world needs you, but I need you more. Please, feel our power and come back!*

He focused every ounce of his will toward sending their combined energy into his immobile friend on the bed.

Please, God, don't let him die. He's the best thing you ever made and we need him!

From the corners of his eyes, he noted beads of sweat breaking out on the brows of his friends, including William, who seemed astonished by what they were doing. Roy's body temperature rose. Sweat broke out all over his body. The room was cold, and he shivered. The tremors throughout his body grew stronger, more potent. He noticed Izzy swaying and Java flexing his huge arm muscles, as though bench pressing his power into Alex.

A groan caught his ear. He glanced down and his heart froze in midbeat. Alex was stirring, twisting his torso, and moving his head back and forth. He concentrated more, willed every ounce of himself into his friend.

Please, God, if you need somebody to die, take me, but let him live!

The biggest jolt yet twanged through him. He felt light-headed and faint.

Then Alex opened his eyes.

"It worked!" cried Father Pat jubilantly.

Alex looked lost, like in a dream, unable to fathom what was happening. His eyes took in the group surrounding him, all except for William who stood behind him, and then settled on Roy's grinning face. Roy couldn't help himself. Despite all the tragedy and betrayal, his heart soared with elation.

Alex was alive!

Roy broke the link first, releasing his hold on Dane and William, staggering slightly. William grabbed his arm in a steel grip and kept him upright.

Nathan eased Dane back into his wheelchair, while Izzy offered a loopy grin, and Java wiped the sweat off his brow, studying Alex with great care.

"You good now, bro?"

Alex smiled, the most beautiful smile in the world as far as Roy was concerned. "You guys… saved me… again." Alex's voice sounded dry and far away. Then he frowned, taking on a look of deep sadness. "But Carlos, he… how did you do this?"

Roy beamed, pulling William around so Alex could see him. The two boys who looked so much like siblings locked eyes, and Alex smiled. "Thanks, Little Brother."

William grinned, looking happier than Roy had ever seen him.

The door opened, and in strode Davalos and Amanda, followed by Shaw and Allison. Dr. Shepherd came last, pushing another wheelchair. In it sat Colonel Walker, wearing a hospital gown covered by a robe. He spotted Alex and pushed his chair as close to the bed as he could get.

"Alex, my boy, you're back. How?"

Roy heard such joy in the man's voice that he felt moved again to tears.

Alex lifted one arm and waved it at the boys. "With a lotta help from my friends."

The colonel swept his gaze around the room and settled on William. "You too?"

William nodded, and the colonel smiled, his body sagging with relief. "I expect a full report on my desk ASAP. Got that, Java?"

Java saluted. "Yes, sir!"

That brought a laugh from everyone.

Allison beamed at seeing Alex, and the look Alex returned bothered Roy, but he forced down his jealousy because he felt good for the first time in ages.

Then darkness swept over him again. "What about Andy?"

He'd already detailed Andy's betrayal to Colonel Walker and to his friends, and now the boys grumbled about what they would do to Andy when they caught him.

The colonel cleared his throat, and everyone felt silent. "I apologize for being out of uniform for a war council, but these are extreme circumstances."

"War council?" repeated Father Pat, sounding worried.

"I'm afraid so."

Alex pushed himself toward his pillow. "Roy, Java, help me up, please."

Amanda rushed forward. "Are you sure, dear? You need your rest."

Alex nodded. "I'm good now, Amanda, just a little weak. If we's gonna talk, I wanna be able to see you all."

Roy got on one side and Java on the other and gripped Alex under his arms. Pulling gently, they eased him up to a sitting position while Amanda fluffed his pillow and stuffed it behind him. Just sitting up seemed to put more color in his face, Roy noted, and his fears that he might lose Alex receded.

"I know it's crowded, but this is a safe place to talk." The colonel looked over the faces surrounding him. "You here are the only people I can fully trust."

Dane gasped. "The hell?"

The colonel nodded. "The Pentagon has been briefed and all agencies are on the lookout for that woman."

"And that little bitch, Andy," spat Izzy in anger.

"Please, Israel, let me finish."

Izzy looked abashed, his face reddening. "Sorry, Colonel."

"Based on their infiltration of this base, we must assume that she has followers at all levels of government. We cannot be too careful. As far as I'm concerned, even the White House might be compromised. Mr. Shaw has agreed to use his vast resources to help our tracking efforts, especially since it doesn't look like she will come for Alex again. Mr. Davalos has also agreed to use his contacts to locate this shadow group, and Father Pat will work with his Vatican connections. From what Roy and William told me, they now consider Alex expendable. I'll let them fill you in on what happened."

Davalos cleared his throat. "If I may say something, Colonel?"

"By all means, Mark."

Davalos looked around at all the faces and, to Roy, he looked different from before. The arrogance was gone, that look in his eyes that Roy had seen in way too many bullies over the years, the look that says without words, "I'm better than you," that was gone too.

"First of all, I want to thank Colonel Walker for putting his trust in me when I have never given him any reason to do so." Then he worked his way through the crowded room to stop before William. "I owe you a major apology, William, for the many times I've disrespected you. I was wrong, and my behavior was childish. You have made better choices these past few days than I have in all my years at this base. Please accept my apology and my thanks for what you did tonight."

He extended a hand. William, always impassive at the best of times, looked touched by the man's words and shook his hand with great gusto, causing Davalos to wince. "Uh, not quite so hard, my boy."

William looked sheepish and a ripple of laughter filtered through the room as he released the man's hand. But then all fell silent again as Davalos stood before Francis, gazing with acute sorrow etched on his tired features at this young boy he helped create in a laboratory.

"Francis, I owe you the biggest apology of all. I made you into something horrifying and forced you to suffer in ways I can't even imagine, all because of my hubris and twisted sense of humor. I did this to you simply because I could, without ever considering the ramifications. I'm so sorry."

As though not expecting a response from Francis, he turned toward the bed, but the boy said, "Mr. Davalos?"

The shamed man turned back to face him, eyebrows raised, face slumped with remorse.

Francis didn't look angry or even sad, as he had when Roy had first met him. He looked… content. "I don't want to become Wolfboy when the moon is full. It hurts real bad, and it's embar—" He turned to William. "What's that word?"

"Embarrassing," William whispered.

"Yes, that's it, embarrassing. But if you didn't make me, I wouldn't have William and I wouldn't not have met Roy, who is now my Big Brother because he wants to be." He offered Roy a shy smile, and Roy placed a hand on his solid shoulder. "If you and those doctors didn't make me, I wouldn't be able to help good people like Alex. So, I'm glad I'm alive."

William nudged him and pantomimed a hand shake. Turning red in the face, Francis stuck out a hand to Davalos.

The man looked more stunned by this gesture than anything else that Roy had witnessed. Speechless, he shook Francis's hand. Then he turned to Alex, sitting up in his bed.

"Alex, I saw you and your brother as tools, a way to assure national security and maybe to even end war itself. I forgot that you have lives of your own, and I fear I might have encouraged Andy's ambitious nature. I promise to do all that I can to help bring down this group that's made your life a living hell, and maybe I can earn your trust as well."

Alex nodded, looking amazed by all that the man had said, glancing at Roy as if to say, "Can you believe this is the same guy?"

Roy nodded his agreement.

Davalos faced the colonel once more. "Thank you, Colonel, for allowing me that time."

"It was time well spent," the colonel replied with a nod. Then he turned to Roy. "Roy, please tell us what happened."

Nervous to be speaking in front of so many, Roy—with help from Alex—shared their kidnap story up to the point where Andy had nearly killed his brother. Then William took over, describing the attempt to blow them all up, including Alex. He casually described his own actions, not even aware that everyone had their mouths open in amazement by what he and Francis had accomplished.

When they finished, a heavy silence settled over the room, leaving only the whooshing of the oxygen machine. A clearing throat directed Roy's attention toward Dr. Shepherd.

"Did you see any sign of Dr. Avila, Roy?" she asked, looking concerned. "Or you, William?"

Roy shook his head and William said, "No, Doctor. I don't think he was there."

She faced the colonel. "Where did they take him, do you suppose?"

"Most likely to one of their other headquarters," he replied, looking thoughtful.

She furrowed her brows. "Do you think…he was one of them?"

The colonel paused to think. No one spoke, awaiting his answer. He turned to Davalos. "Other than the Joint Chiefs and Avila, who else knew about your supersoldier program?"

Davalos looked thoughtful as he rubbed his beard stubble once again. "Some of the other bioengineers, like Dr. Shepherd, were aware of the project's existence, but not its ultimate outcome." He stopped, his face becoming a frozen mask of understanding. "Of course!"

"What?" The colonel leaned forward in his wheelchair, but Amanda quickly eased him back.

Davalos ran a hand through his hair, once more looking guilt-ridden. "It was Avila who suggested we use Jäger for the life force. He said he'd known the man for years and that Jäger would be an eager candidate. I'm sorry, Colonel. I trusted Avila."

"He fooled all of us, as did my men under her control," said the colonel, his voice sounding weary. Then he gazed at Alex. "Can you still heal people, Alex, after what Andy did?"

Alex bit his lower lip. "I know you all hate him for what he done, but I don't."

The boys exploded with indignation and even Allison reminded Alex that what his brother did was evil.

"He could of killed me. I felt it." Alex paused a moment, choosing his words. "I guess maybe spinning people *is* me, what I am, cause I felt me, whatever makes up me, leaving my body with his shifting. All he had to do was go a little longer and I would've died. But he stopped." He paused. "I can't spin no more, least not yet. But I don't think Andy's evil."

"Yeah, well I do," Java spat, making a fist and thumping it into the palm of his hand. "When I get that little punk, I'm gonna pound his face to mush."

"Calm down, Java," Father Pat said, his tone calm and reassuring. "Alex knows his brother better than anyone. They're twins. They share a connection none of the rest of us have."

"You're correct, Father Pat," agreed the colonel soberly, "but as of now, Andy must be considered an enemy."

Heads nodded and even Alex didn't argue the point.

William stood tall and expectant. "What is our plan, Colonel?"

"We stick together," the colonel asserted, his voice filled with conviction. "We're a small team against a big enemy who now possesses the power of life and death. What I need from you all right now is a promise that whatever happens, we remain a team."

Alex looked around at them all. "Not a team, Colonel. A family."

He stuck out his fist. Java immediately reached out to place the flat of his hand atop it, followed by Jorge, Izzy, and Roy adding theirs. William joined into their ritual at once, drawing a smile from Alex, who swept his gaze over the others. Catching on, they crowded around, and each placed one flat hand atop the pile until only the colonel remained. He gazed at them with gratitude flickering across his lined face. Then he rose out of his wheelchair and extended his arm, completing the ritual by tapping the pile with the flat of his hand.

Roy exchanged a quick glance with Alex, who offered him a little smile to warm his heart. He knew the worst was still ahead. But this group was tough. They'd already survived a lot and could handle whatever came next. They had each other, and in the end, their bond, born of love and commitment, would triumph over anything.

EPILOGUE

AGE 12

ANDY SAT IN THE COMFY chair in his glass cage waiting for them to punish him. It had been over a week since he'd shifted Death into Teacher and still they had done nothing. He'd not even been taken to Doctor. One of the clipboard people brought his meals, but only left the food and exited the outer chamber. He knew the cameras still watched him, their tiny red eyes glowing nonstop, but he didn't know what they would do to punish him.

Then one day the door opened and someone new entered the chamber. This one looked different from all the others and Andy didn't understand how or why. This person had hair almost as long as his and almost the same color except his was more white, the other's yellow. The body looked different too, the shape of the torso and even the legs. It was mystifying and provoked his curiosity,

He rose from the chair and approached the glass barrier. "Who are you?"

The newcomer flicked the switch outside and said, "I'm your new Teacher."

Now Andy understood. They'd decided to give him a new teacher. Well, he wouldn't cooperate with this one either. "I see. You look different from my other teacher."

Teacher smiled, but Andy thought the smile looked crooked somehow. "Care to tell me what you did to your previous teacher?"

Andy remained calm, as always. He would never tell because he wanted to do it again. He'd never felt more powerful than at the moment Teacher realized what he'd done, just before Death took Teacher away for good.

"I see," the new Teacher said when Andy refused to answer. "Very well. Tell me, Andy, are you loyal to our cause?"

Of course, Andy had memorized their loyalty oath. He'd had no choice. But ever since he'd shifted Death and realized the extent of his power, he'd decided to negotiate with these people.

"You want my power."

Those slender eyebrows rose higher. "What power is that?"

"You know I shifted Death into Teacher, but you don't know how I did it."

"Are you going to tell me?"

Here was the most important moment. "Are you going to let me out of this cage?"

Teacher paused to think, brushing some of that long yellow hair back over one shoulder with fingers painted red at the nails. "Would that buy your unwavering loyalty?"

Andy considered a moment. His loyalty lay in never being locked in a cage again and he would do whatever it took to make certain that's what would happen. He still wasn't sure about the existence of love, but he knew hate was real because he hated this enclosure. He hated everyone who'd kept him prisoner and tortured him. He would gain control of his destiny.

Somehow.

"Yes, Teacher, that will assure my loyalty." He smiled.

Teacher returned it.

THE HEALER CHRONICLES CONCLUDE IN BOOK 3

SPOILER

ABOUT THE AUTHOR

Michael J. Bowler is an award-winning author of the five-book urban fantasy series *The Lance Chronicles*, the mystery-thriller *The Film Milieu Series*, the supernatural-sci-fi *The Healer Chronicles*, and several standalone books. He also writes screenplays. His horror screenplay, "Healer," was a Semi-Finalist, and his urban fantasy script, "Like A Hero," was a Finalist in the Shriekfest Film Festival and Screenplay Competition, and his sci-fi screenplay, "The God Machine," was the 2017 Scriptapalozza First Place Winner.

He worked as producer, writer, and/or director on several ultra-low-budget horror films, including "Fatal Images," "Hell Spa," "Club Dead," and "Things II."

He taught high school in Hawthorne, California, both in general education and to students with learning disabilities, in subjects ranging from English and Strength Training to Algebra, Biology, and Yearbook.

He has also been a volunteer Big Brother to eight different boys with the Catholic Big Brothers Big Sisters program and a long-time volunteer within the juvenile justice system in Los Angeles.

He has been honored as Probation Volunteer of the Year, YMCA Volunteer of the Year, California Big Brother of the Year, and 2000 National Big Brother of the Year. The "National" honor allowed him and three of his Little Brothers to visit the White House and meet the president in the Oval Office.

His goal as an author is for teens to experience empowerment and hope; to see themselves in his diverse characters; to read about kids who face real-life challenges; and to see how kids like them can remain decent people in an indecent world. The most prevalent theme in his writing and his work with youth is this: as both a society, and as individuals, we're better off when we do what's right, rather than what's easy.

CONNECT WITH MICHAEL

Website:
http://michaeljbowler.com/

FB:
https://www.facebook.com/michaeljbowlerauthor/

Twitter:
https://twitter.com/MichaelJBowler

Instagram:
https://www.instagram.com/michaeljbowler/

tumblr:
http://michaeljbowler.tumblr.com/

Pinterest:
https://www.pinterest.com/michaelbowler/

Goodreads:
https://www.goodreads.com/author/
show/6938109.Michael_J_Bowler

YouTube:
https://www.youtube.com/channel/UC2NXCPry4DDgJZOVDUx-
VtMw

HERE IS A PREVIEW OF THE
HEALER CHRONICLES BOOK 3

SPOILER

CHAPTER ONE

YOU SUMMONED ME, TEACHER?

IT HAD BEEN THREE DAYS since his brother tried to kill him and Alex shuddered each time he replayed the incident in his mind. In addition, it seemed like everyone had descended on the Air Force base where he currently lived, all for the purpose of tracking down and killing his twin before Andy could... what? He wasn't completely sure, though that general guy seemed to think his brother had already caused large-scale riots in several cities since he went over to the other side.

Alex had sat in on more meetings with adults than ever before in his life and, frustrated, he'd finally wheeled himself out of the hangar that housed Operation Kalandrian (supposedly the name of the group that Andy had joined.) Crossing the tarmac beneath a warm October sun, he trundled up the makeshift wheelchair ramp the Colonel had installed and entered the base commander's house, which was blessedly empty. Rolling down the long, carpeted hall to the back bedroom, he entered and closed the door, sitting beside his bed so he could think about, well, everything.

He glanced down at the brand-new wheelchair Mr. Shaw had had flown in for him yesterday. It replaced his old one that got blown to pieces when Ms. G had one of her soldiers destroy the ghost town where

Andy tried to kill him. Alex missed his old chair, despite the fact he'd been outgrowing it anyway. It had been a prized possession and great for doing stunts— especially landing flips at the skate park. This new one was a bright, shiny blue that moved well, from what he could tell so far, and, knowing Mr. Shaw, probably cost a lot more than his old one. Even with this generous gift, the man had told him yesterday, "I've ordered you a custom chair, Alex, top of the line and almost indestructible, with extra bells and whistles. Given all that's happened to you of late, it could come in handy." He'd offered a wry smile and Alex, already overwhelmed by the gift of this new one, returned it.

"Thanks, Mr. Shaw, but what about this one? It seems perfect."

"That'll be your backup chair."

Alex had thanked him again and then the man excused himself to continue setting up the hangar where he would be working.

As Alex sat rubbing his fingers along the pristine surface of his wheel handles, he considered all that had happened to him since being brought to this base less than two weeks before. He still didn't understand everything, but what he did know, and what hurt the most, was that his only brother, his identical twin, the sibling he'd only just been reunited with, had turned on him like a rabid dog.

Alex still refused to believe his twin intended to *really* kill him because his innate connection to Andy encouraged him to think it wasn't so, but Andy *had* stolen his healing power, which made Alex feel… what did he feel? Useless? That wasn't quite the right word. Worthless came closer, but the emptiness inside his very soul went deeper. He felt like he'd lost the essence of who he was as a person—maybe his only reason to live. On second thought, maybe Andy *had* killed him after all.

Andy already belongs to me.

Those were Ms. G's words in that dream he had last week. Were they true? Had he completely misread the affection he'd felt from his twin? He didn't want to believe it, but… He desperately wanted to find Andy and talk with him alone, without Ms. G present. He was certain he could discern the truth—that Andy would not be able to hide it from him.

But you don't have your power no more.

That was the big problem. Without his power, maybe their psychic bond no longer existed. It was all so maddening! Especially since that old guy, the hard-ass General Lewis from the Joint Chiefs, announced at the first meeting a few days back that Andy would be shot on sight. They already knew that Ms. G couldn't be killed, so they figured taking his brother out of the picture would solve many of their problems.

Alex understood the reasons for that decision. He hated it, of course, but it made a kind of sense to him. But had Andy fully turned against him? Maybe Alex wanted it to not be true, but since he no longer felt a link to his twin, he couldn't be sure. His only hope was that Andy could've killed him back in that ghost town but chose not to. Yes, that was the image he would cling to until he knew for sure.

He didn't know how long he'd been sitting in that room, staring at Andy's unslept-in bed, and brooding about what the future held, when there came a knock on the door. It cracked open and he heard Colonel Walker's voice. "May I come in, Alex?"

Alex turned his wheelchair to face the door. He'd known someone would come looking for him. Better the colonel than anyone else. "Yes."

The door swung open, and Colonel Walker sat just outside in his own wheelchair, a regular medical chair on account of having been shot by Ms. G's followers. Amanda stood behind him smiling at Alex in that motherly way he'd come to love. She pushed the chair into the room so the colonel could be face-to-face with him.

"I'll be in the kitchen, Bryan, when you finish," Amanda said. "Anything I can get for you, Alex?"

She looked pretty in a flowered dress with her curly hair framing her face, but tired, too, probably from all the drama that'd been going on the past week.

"No thanks, Amanda," he replied. "Not hungry."

She seemed to understand at once and just placed a comforting hand on his shoulder. "If you change your mind, let me know." She paused a moment. "I agree with you, Alex, that the jury is still out on Andy."

He pulled a face, never having heard that expression.

"It means we don't know for sure that he's turned against us," she explained, her voice soft and soothing. "The affection I felt from that boy when he was helping me cook and clean was very real. There's hope." Then, with another warm smile, she stepped from the room and closed the door.

Alex gazed at Colonel Walker. The man looked older than when they'd first met, but that could've been his imagination. But he looked healthier than he had the day before, with more color in his complexion.

"I told Amanda I could walk over here, but she insisted on the chair," the colonel said with a shrug. "I'm pretty independent, as you've probably noticed."

"Does it make you feel weak, Colonel, the wheelchair?"

Colonel Walker looked surprised by the question but didn't hesitate in his answer. "Before I met you, it would have. But you're the strongest person I know, and I mean here." He tapped his chest. The large white bandage was visible beneath his open blue Air Force jacket. "You've never let that chair stop you from doing whatever you wanted, and neither will I." He offered a crooked smile. "I just wish I could control mine as well as you do yours."

That made Alex smile. "It takes practice."

There passed a moment of camaraderie between them. Alex had liked this man from the moment they'd met and considered him a friend.

"I understand, Alex, why you got frustrated and left the meeting. All those adults pressing you with questions, laying out plans, plotting how best to…"

Now he trailed off, but Alex knew what he'd intended to say. "To kill my brother?"

Colonel Walker nodded, his craggy face filled with deep sadness. "I know how much you love him, Alex, and I thought I saw love from him toward you. Maybe you and Amanda are right about him, but we can't take any chances. I'm sorry."

No, I did feel it, Alex thought, but didn't say that. Could Andy be that good of an actor to fool even him?

"So, what's happening now?"

"We don't think Ms. G, as you know her, got out of the country, which means Andy is still here, too. Every road and airport have been under surveillance. Private planes have been checked, as well. Shaw is coordinating with General Lewis on using technology to locate them, devices such as traffic cameras installed all around the country. Father Pat's friend from the Vatican arrives today, that Cardinal Leone. Says he has some ideas where the group might be holed up, but he needs to talk with you in person."

"What's the Vatican and why does this guy wanna see me?"

"The Vatican is the headquarters of the Catholic Church, the capital, you might say," the colonel explained with the kind of patience Alex had seldom seen from teachers back home. "He wants to speak with you because of what happened at that old church when those, whatever they were, possessed you."

Alex's eyebrows flew up in surprise.

"Father Pat and Shaw shared with me happened back there, so we'd have a fuller picture of what we're dealing with," Colonel Walker explained, and Alex relaxed. It made sense to know everything if they were going to defeat Ms. G.

Just the thought of her made Alex cringe with hatred, especially after turning his brother against him. He'd never forgive her for that!

The colonel studied him a long moment. "Still no return of your power? Can you sense my health status as I speak to you?"

Alex focused on the man before him, feeling deep within his soul for… anything. Despair welled up in him once more and he shook his head, looking down at his knees, feeling hollow.

"It's all right, Alex," the colonel assured him in a voice that pretended everything was fine.

"No, it's not!" He looked up into the colonel's compassionate brown eyes. "That was all I could do, Colonel. If I can't heal no one, I'm… worthless."

Colonel Walker's face flashed anger at him for the first time. "Never say that, Alex. Didn't you hear what I said about that wheelchair? You're a born leader, whether you like it or not. Those other kids need you. William needs you. Sure, he can flip over a jeep, but inside he's a thirteen-year-old boy who looks up to you more than to anyone he's ever met. That's who you are, Alex."

Alex choked up with emotion and couldn't respond. He saw in his mind's eye his friends from school rallying around him when he'd first joined their special ed class. They didn't know about his power back then. And William? What had he said, something about Alex having a kind face and that's why he wanted to meet him? William hadn't known what Alex could do, either, not at first.

"Thank you, Colonel," he mumbled, feeling stupid for being sorry for himself. His friends needed him, and he needed them. "Where are the other kids?"

"Having lunch in the DFAC."

"I think I'll head over there."

"They'll be happy to see you."

Alex nodded and wheeled easily around the colonel's much bulkier chair, feeling the man's eyes on him the whole time. Stopping at the door, he spun around and pointed at the other wheelchair.

"If you need tips on doing any stunts, Colonel, I'm your man."

Colonel Walker laughed.

Grinning, Alex wheeled himself from the room.

www.ingramcontent.com/pod-product-compliance
Lightning Source LLC
Chambersburg PA
CBHW031630200726
48288CB00019B/558